BALLAD of SWORD & WINE

QIANG JIN JIU

WRITTEN BY
Tang Jiu Qing

ILLUSTRATED BY
St

TRANSLATED BY
XiA, Jia, amixy

Seven Seas Entertainment

Ballad of Sword and Wine: Qiang Jin Jiu (Novel) Vol. 2

Published originally under the title of《将进酒》(Qiang Jin Jiu)
Author©唐酒卿(Tang Jiu Qing)
English edition rights under license granted by 北京晋江原创网络科技有限公司
(Beijing Jinjiang Original Network Technology Co., Ltd.)

Cover & Interior Illustrations: St

TRANSLATION: XiA, Jia, amixy
ADAPTATION: Dara
COVER & MAP DESIGN: M. A. Lewife
INTERIOR DESIGN: Clay Gardner
INTERIOR LAYOUT: Karis Page
COPY EDITOR: Jehanne Bell
PROOFREADER: Kate Kishi, Hnä
EDITOR: Kelly Quinn Chiu
PREPRESS TECHNICIAN: Melanie Ujimori, Jules Valera
MANAGING EDITOR: Alyssa Scavetta
EDITOR-IN-CHIEF: Julie Davis
PUBLISHER: Lianne Sentar
VICE PRESIDENT: Adam Arnold
PRESIDENT: Jason DeAngelis

ISBN: 979-8-88843-310-2
Printed in Canada
First Printing: September 2024
10 9 8 7 6 5 4 3 2 1

BALLAD of SWORD & WINE

QIANG JIN JIU

Luoxia
Pass
Glacial River
Huaizhou
Northeast Provisions Trail
Quancheng
Chuncheng
Dancheng
Cizhou
Qudu
Cuocheng
Mount
Feng
Nanlin
Hunting
Grounds
Wucheng
Jincheng
Chazhou
Dicheng
Chuancheng
Kailing River
Sea
Hezhou
Juexi
Port of
Yongyi
Qinzhou

Hongyan Mountains
Libei
Hongjiang River
Chashi Sinkhole
Duanzhou
Dunzhou
Zhongbo
Fanzhou
Dengzhou
Chashi River
Tianfei Watchtower
Cangjun
Bianjun
Qidong
Chijun
Suotian Pass

TABLE OF CONTENTS

41

LANZHOU (PART 2)

XIAO CHIYE slept.

All his fury and ferocity had settled into his features, giving him an expression of determined frustration. He held tight to one of Shen Zechuan's wrists, forcing the semblance of intimacy on this winter night long after they had transformed merciless kisses into scalding passion.

Outside, all night, snow drifted like catkins, the air still and silent. Just before daybreak, Shen Zechuan extracted his wrist from Xiao Chiye's grip. Xiao Chiye's fingers chased after his warmth, stirring beneath the covers.

Chen Yang was waiting outside the door when Shen Zechuan stepped out of the room.

"Drill grounds," Shen Zechuan said shortly.

Chen Yang nodded. As he shifted aside, he caught a glimpse of the cut on Shen Zechuan's lip and hesitated, as if to speak.

Shen Zechuan saw through him at a glance. "The redeployment order for the Embroidered Uniform Guard should be issued very soon. Thank you for your generous accommodation all this time."

Chen Yang began, "What happened a few days ago—"

"What's done is done; there's no need to speak of it." Shen Zechuan was frostier than usual today. "We're sure to run into each other now and again while patrolling the city. I shall be prudent in my actions, and I advise my brothers from the Imperial Army to do the same."

Chen Yang pressed his lips shut.

Shen Zechuan smiled. "It hasn't been easy for the Imperial Army to reach their current heights, but times change, and every dog has its day. Who can say for sure what the future holds?" Without waiting for Chen Yang to respond, he swept the hem of his robe aside and walked off.

Ding Tao dusted snow from his shoulders and flipped over to hang upside down from the roof. Swinging gently in midair, brush in his mouth, he watched Shen Zechuan's receding back with a frown.

"What?" Chen Yang asked, noticing his look.

"Don't you think he seems a little sad today?" Ding Tao said around the brush.

Chen Yang turned his head, glimpsing the last corner of Shen Zechuan's robe as it disappeared from sight. "Is that so? He seemed fine to me; he even smiled."

Still upside down, Ding Tao fished his book from his lapels and wrote a few words. "Maybe it's because he and Er-gongzi fought last night. I heard quite the racket."

Embarrassed, Chen Yang raised his eyes to the roof. "Gu Jin, didn't you teach him about the birds and bees? The boy's sixteen already. In Libei, that's old enough to take a wife."

There was no reply.

"Did you hear me?" Chen Yang repeated.

"He stuffed his ears!" Ding Tao slid the notebook into his robes and flipped back up to pluck the cotton from one of Gu Jin's ears. "Jin-ge!" he yelled. "Chen Yang is calling you!"

Gu Jin gave a start and nearly slipped off the roof. He shoved Ding Tao's face aside and frowned as he poked his head out. "What?"

Chen Yang pointed at Ding Tao. "Get rid of him. Sell him and add the balance to your wine money this month."

Gu Jin grasped Ding Tao by the neck. "Won't get much for this one even if they're going by weight."

There was movement inside the room; all three fell silent. After a moment, Xiao Chiye stepped out. As he stood at the threshold, donning another layer, he swept a glance around, settling his gaze on Ding Tao.

"Dage will be in the capital in a few days." Xiao Chiye's lips felt slightly raw as he spoke. He pressed his tongue against them but gave up quickly. "No need to report any of these trivial matters to him."

Ding Tao nodded as vigorously as a chick pecking at grains.

After a moment's pause, Xiao Chiye asked, "Why are you still here?"

Ding Tao scratched the back of his head and looked from Chen Yang to Gu Jin, then finally back at Xiao Chiye. "I'm on duty today, Young Master."

"And where's the man I told you to keep an eye on?"

"H-he's already left..." Ding Tao said, confused.

Xiao Chiye said nothing as Chen Yang led the horse over. He swung into the saddle and pointed at Ding Tao. "Throw this away."

Before Ding Tao, who had yet to climb atop his own horse, could react, Chen Yang and Gu Jin had already hoisted him up. Color drained from his face as he clutched his lapels where his little notebook was stowed. "Please don't. Young Master, Young Master! I haven't done anything wrong yet—"

Too late.

After disposing of him in the snow, Chen Yang stepped forward. "Master, Shifu should be arriving today."

The instant he heard those words, Xiao Chiye dug his heels into the horse's flanks and sped out of the city at a gallop.

Shen Zechuan did not go to the military drill grounds at Mount Feng; instead, he braved the snow and returned to the Temple of Guilt.

Ji Gang hadn't seen him for several days. After letting him in, he rushed off for a roast chicken. Grand Mentor Qi had likewise missed him; he was sweeping a calligraphy brush across paper, squinting down at his work, but as soon as he saw Shen Zechuan enter, he dropped his brush and called, "Lanzhou!"

Lifting the hem of his robe, Shen Zechuan took his seat across from Grand Mentor Qi.

"The Embroidered Uniform Guard's deployment order will be issued any day," Grand Mentor Qi said. "Where do you want to go?"

"The Carriage Office," Shen Zechuan replied. "It's close to the throne."

Grand Mentor Qi nodded, then turned his attention to the wound on Shen Zechuan's lip. "Did something happen out there?"

After a lapse of silence, Shen Zechuan answered, "Now that His Majesty has Hai Liangyi at his side, even a rotten plank of wood can pose as a pillar of the state. I saved Xiao Er that day because His Majesty's ascension to the throne was a foregone conclusion. Letting him die would have disrupted the entire gameboard."

"A disrupted board is nothing. One must be wary of a disrupted mind," Grand Mentor Qi noted, looking at him. "Have you gained any insights during the days you've spent at Second Young Master Xiao's side?"

Shen Zechuan wiped at the ink staining his fingertips and considered for a long moment before answering. "It's truly a pity he was born after Xiao Jiming. Perhaps he can be contained, but if not..." He glanced at Grand Mentor Qi and fell quiet.

"Lanzhou, you still don't understand."

Shen Zechuan waited.

Grand Mentor Qi stood and paced a tight circle. Gazing out at the snow in the courtyard, he heaved a sigh. "You killed Ji Lei."

Shen Zechuan's hand holding the handkerchief stilled.

"Lanzhou, we're trapped here. We subsist on hatred, but we mustn't let it poison us," Grand Mentor Qi said in a raw show of emotion. "Five years ago, you couldn't have performed such a ruthless deed. Now, you're able to stand alone and do it without hesitation. I have been your scroll and taught you all I know; I don't want to you twisted by hatred. Killing rarely leads to a righteous end; those who walk too far down that road may never turn back. You must exorcise your inner demons, or you'll forever be trapped in nightmares. Yes, Ji Lei deserved to die—but a clean slash of the blade would still have been death. Remember your days in Duanzhou. I have no wish to see you walk down a cold-hearted path that rejects all sentiment. You've said it's a pity Xiao Chiye was born after Xiao Jiming. But let me tell you, it is the exact opposite.

"Imagine for a moment that Ji Mu is the Heir of Libei. Mightn't there be a reason for him to leave you in Qudu other than resignation to fate? A fine blade develops its edge by careful honing. Xiao Chiye is a blade. He has yet to notice it himself, but his elder brother has for many years pinned high hopes on him, and Libei has never been stingy when it comes to the praise he deserves. Had he been an expendable son, they could've indulged him and let him live a life of pleasure. Yet Xiao Jiming not only took him into battle, he gave the young Xiao Chiye a free hand in leading the troops. Even if Libei was backed into a corner with no room to retreat, do you really think the heir handed over his younger brother just to make him miserable?

"The Xiao Chiye who came here from Libei five years ago knew not the meaning of restraint, yet now he's learned to keep a rein on his arrogance and willfulness. What is taught in words can easily slip away; only painful experience confers real wisdom. Xiao Jiming is a good elder brother. The least pitiful thing about Xiao Chiye is to be born after him. Lanzhou, their brotherly bond should've been one you understand best, yet somehow it has become the one you understand least."

After a long, gloomy pause, Grand Mentor Qi looked over and knelt to pat Shen Zechuan on the head with his wizened palm.

"I have taught you and given you the name *Lanzhou*: Serene is the orchid that grows on palace steps; boundless the horizon of the boat that crosses the sea of misery.[1] Wide is the heart that accommodates a hundred rivers, broad the vision that encompasses a thousand lakes. You're a good child. A death is merely a death. It may be hard to step away from hatred, but your heart must remain the same. Lanzhou, oh Lanzhou—don't you still have your shifu and xiansheng? Why must you force yourself to these ends? Perhaps we should talk about the unhappiness you've felt over these five years."

Shen Zechuan stared wide-eyed at Grand Mentor Qi.

"Twenty-five years ago, His Royal Highness the crown prince passed away. I regret every day, and resent every night, that I was unable to take that blow for him or kill his enemies with my own two hands. I stewed in resentment until I became what I am now. I became your xiansheng, but I—" Grand Mentor Qi seemed to choke on his words. "I want you to be my sword, but I can't let you

---

1 兰 (lan): lily magnolia or orchid, one of the Four Gentlemen among plants in Chinese art; 舟 (zhou): boat. Lanzhou (兰舟) as a whole has a specific connotation in poetry: a boat of lily magnolia wood.

become a blade who has forgotten what you are. You are human, Lanzhou. Don't forget your carefree days in Duanzhou. Ji Mu died, but it wasn't your fault; it was heaven's decree, and we cannot change the past. You didn't survive the Chashi Sinkhole only to live crushed under the burden of guilt. No—you live on behalf of him, on behalf of those thirty thousand soldiers! Silly child. Ji Gang has been so careful; how did you still lead yourself so astray that you've blamed the wrong person?"

Shen Zechuan closed his eyes.

He heard Ji Mu's cries, and he thought of the way Xiao Chiye smelled. All at once, he understood why he was so infatuated with that scent. It was the brilliance of the scorching sun—the light that allowed him to escape the darkness of the Chashi Sinkhole. For a fleeting moment, he could forget the tides of blood and the rush of arrows, the bitter cold and the stiff corpses beneath him. He could no longer remember those days in Duanzhou. They were too far away, as distant as memories of a past life. He couldn't even recall Ji Mu's face as he laughed. He had tumbled into a nightmare, tormenting himself every second of every day.

Ji Mu was dead. Why hadn't *he* died instead?

That his shifu didn't blame him was the greatest reproach of all; a lifetime of guilt from which he would never be freed. He couldn't be honest with Grand Mentor Qi—after living like this day after day, he had finally killed himself.

Xiao Chiye was the bright reflection who possessed everything Shen Zechuan did not. He had observed Xiao Chiye, had tried clumsily to imitate him to give himself the semblance of a person. He couldn't tell anyone that the Shen Zechuan living in this body was repulsive, a killer with a grotesque mask for a face.

He was already standing at the edge of the abyss.

Shen Zechuan sat with lashes lowered under Grand Mentor Qi's palm, a child respectfully accepting the lessons of an elder. He was devout and obedient, yet it was in this moment he realized he could no longer shed tears.

His throat bobbed. Eventually he murmured, contrite, "It's...just as Xiansheng says."

Three days later, the Embroidered Uniform Guard's deployment order arrived. Han Cheng, formerly the assistant commander of the Eight Great Battalions, was transferred to the Embroidered Uniform Guard as chief commander, while staff from the Twelve Offices were all reassigned. Shen Zechuan was transferred from the Elephant-Training Office to the Carriage Office, and Ge Qingqing received a promotion from company commander to judge.

Shen Zechuan's new authority token was inscribed with the words *Emperor's Entourage*. The Carriage Office was a plum position; working so close to the throne would give him many more opportunities to get in the emperor's good graces.

Xiao Chiye, already supreme commander of the Imperial Army, also took over the Eight Great Battalions as their new Military Commissioner, officially granting him oversight of all patrols in the capital. Since the morning he had parted with Shen Zechuan, he had welcomed Zuo Qianqiu's arrival and remained with him at the drill grounds at Mount Feng; he hadn't seen Shen Zechuan again over the rest of his stay at the Imperial Army compound.

"Master," Chen Yang said quietly from beside Xiao Chiye. "The original arrangement was the Horse-Training Office. Somehow when it was issued, the order changed to the Carriage Office."

Xiao Chiye's fingers stilled on the nine-rings puzzle he was solving. "Perhaps he didn't care for it."

"But isn't it a greater risk to his life to work beside the emperor? Secretariat Elder Hai was the one who urged the late emperor to kill him."

"Living on the edge—it was never his intention to be a law-abiding citizen." Xiao Chiye tossed the rings down. "Ji Lei is dead, and Han Cheng is a stand-in from the Battalions. The Guard is unclaimed land. What do you suppose he intends by stepping up now?"

Chen Yang pondered. "If he succeeds..."

Xiao Chiye looked out over the drill grounds. "If he succeeds, he'll be armed with claws and fangs."

Chen Yang said no more.

"The Ji Clan dominates the Embroidered Uniform Guard," Xiao Chiye continued. "With Ji Gang as his shield and old sentiment as his blade, climbing the ranks will be effortless. But even if we can't get our own men in, we can still restrict his opportunities. Promotions and monetary rewards must be justified. As long as nothing unexpected happens before the throne, we can prevent him from making any moves. The Imperial Army is responsible for patrolling now; why trouble the Embroidered Uniform Guard?"

"Understood."

Xiao Chiye took a sip of water and pondered a moment. "Pick a secluded spot and lay out a feast. He and I—we can pick our fights and still feed ourselves." He pursed his lips where he'd been bitten. "After all, we're both disciples of the same martial line."

RED PLUM BLOSSOMS

XIAO CHIYE SCHEDULED their private dinner before the date of the Court Officials' Feast. When Chen Yang delivered the invitation, Ge Qingqing was the only one present to greet him.

"Lanzhou hasn't been able to step away from his post, so I hope you don't mind if I receive this on his behalf." Ge Qingqing served tea and exchanged some pleasantries with Chen Yang before venturing, "With all the glory and honor bestowed upon the Imperial Army these days, I suppose Deputy General Chen is quite busy as well?"

"Our supreme commander is swamped with paperwork every day. For the men who follow and serve him, busy is a given." Chen Yang sipped his tea. "But it seems Ge-xiong's recent misfortune has become a blessing with your promotion to judge. To have such a bright future ahead of you is true glory."

Conflicts had recently arisen between the Embroidered Uniform Guard and Imperial Army, resulting in a simmering discord. The mere sight of one another was abhorrent. Nevertheless, the two men put on a cordial performance.

After his second cup of tea, Chen Yang finally rose to take his leave. The moment Ge Qingqing had seen him out, Shen Zechuan emerged from behind the curtain to the inner room.

"What bad timing." Ge Qingqing handed him the invitation. "Are you really going to go?"

"Why wouldn't I?" Shen Zechuan opened the carefully folded invitation and caught sight of the wild, bold strokes of Xiao Chiye's calligraphy.

"Xiao Er has been hard at work keeping the Embroidered Uniform Guard down; our duties have been overtaken by the Imperial Army one by one. Worse, he has the trust and favor of the emperor. If he were to pull something now..." Ge Qingqing didn't finish the thought.

"His intentions couldn't be more obvious." Shen Zechuan closed the flaps of the invitation. "He wants to suppress the Guard and gain a monopoly over the military powers in Qudu so the emperor will have only his Imperial Army to rely on. I'd guess he still has a few more tricks up his sleeve."

"That's exactly why it's too risky to take Uncle Ji along to a feast right now," Ge Qingqing said.

Shen Zechuan tossed the invitation onto the table. "This involves Zuo Qianqiu; he won't lay a trap with him there."

Still, Ge Qingqing worried.

Shen Zechuan pressed his lips together; the wound there had healed. "I'm going out," he said, draping his coat over his shoulders and bracing himself to face the snow.

The flurries weren't heavy today, but the wind was strong. Shen Zechuan made his way to Donglong Street and entered Ouhua Pavilion, a pleasure house that sat on the corner opposite Xiangyun Villa.

Xi Hongxuan had taken up composing verses lately, which he had set to music and directed the courtesans on Donglong Street to perform; the production had become massively popular. Even better, he had secretly hollowed out the stage at Ouhua Pavilion and filled it with wide-mouthed copper vats before replacing the wooden planks. He had extensively trained the new batch of young dancing girls bought from Juexi; when they were ready, he tied tiny bells to their ankles so that when they danced onstage their wooden clogs kept the beat and the tinkling bells echoed within the copper vats, producing an ethereal music.

At present, the women onstage were still warbling his verses. Folding fan in hand, Xi Hongxuan reclined against a rattan chair on the third-floor mezzanine and listened with closed eyes. A maidservant soundlessly stepped across the woolen rug in her socks, knelt outside the bead curtain, and murmured, "Second Master, your guest has arrived."

Xi Hongxuan flicked his fan shut without opening his eyes. The maidservant rose and lifted the curtain.

When Shen Zechuan entered, another girl was already kneeling at Xi Hongxuan's feet, massaging his legs.

"See Young Master Shen to his seat." Xi Hongxuan kept time with gentle taps of his fingers, absorbed in the song.

The kneeling girl shuffled over and attempted to help Shen Zechuan out of his shoes. He raised a hand to forestall her and took a seat.

When the final notes faded, Xi Hongxuan straightened up in his chair. He sipped his tea and pointed his fan at the girl by his feet. "This one's new. Untainted."

Shen Zechuan didn't look at her.

This made Xi Hongxuan laugh, but still he watched Shen Zechuan carefully as he said, "Don't tell me you've really gotten into bed with Xiao Er? What, are you keeping yourself chaste for him?"

The locks of hair framing Shen Zechuan's face looked as if they'd been dipped in ink; in this warm room, his features had a cool, otherworldly air. "Get to the point."

Xi Hongxuan flicked open his fan; it filled his hand as broadly as his body filled the rattan chair. "We're buddies. I called you here for a good time, since Xiao Er's been giving you a hard one these days. When it comes to misfortunes, you, Shen Lanzhou, win hands down. That kick from Xiao Er all those years ago left you with an illness that plagues you every day, and now you have to play nice with him at night. He really is your nemesis."

"Yeah." Shen Zechuan answered candidly, as if resigned to the fact. "A jerk."

"It seems he doesn't plan to go easy on the Embroidered Uniform Guard," Xi Hongxuan said. "Your pillow talk needs work, Lanzhou."

Shen Zechuan wiped his hands with the hot towel the girl presented to him. When he looked over with a smile, the coolness he had carried inside vanished without a trace, melting into his usual unassuming mask. "You're a besotted man so infatuated with your dear sister-in-law that the passing years mean nothing to you. One night together and you became enamored. Xiao Er and I have a mere physical connection; he would hardly listen to me."

Xi Hongxuan picked up his chopsticks. "So you're saying...it was just a bit of fun?"

"There's a method to such fun," Shen Zechuan said. "A tumble in the sheets satisfies one's needs, that's all. Once you've enjoyed yourself, it's over and done with. If you obsess over it, it loses its simplicity, don't you think?"

Xi Hongxuan clapped his hands and laughed. "Well, well! What a fine Lanzhou. I was afraid he might have you by the balls, and you'd forget *we're* brothers on the same side. Come, try this dish.

These are foraged greens delivered straight from Qinzhou. It's good stuff, not seen even in the imperial kitchen."

As they sampled the dishes, Xi Hongxuan continued, "Xiao Er is truly ruthless. No one paid him any heed until he showed his edge during the Autumn Hunt. He can't hide anymore, so he faces everything head-on. He took over command of the Eight Great Battalions, then handed all the key positions to his own trusted aides. At this point, none of the Eight Great Clans wield any real power. But on the surface, he's kept the peace so flawlessly that no one can scrape up any leverage against him. Both annoying and despicable."

Shen Zechuan spotted a plate of shredded cucumber on the table, but his chopsticks made no move toward it. "Xiao Er put all his chips on the table at the Nanlin Hunting Grounds in the hope that His Majesty would consider their friendship and let him go home. But his efforts were like drawing water through a sieve, and after all that, he now finds himself under the close watch of the Six Ministries. He can't turn back time, so all he can do is gather the military power in Qudu into his own hands. Comparing the Imperial Army to the Eight Great Battalions is like comparing a firefly to the moon—the former is useful, but not *that* useful. Now that he holds this hard-won prize, he will naturally not pass up any opportunity."

"In the past, we still had Pan Rugui in the Twenty-Four Yamen; at the very least, the Eastern Depot could knock him down a peg. Now that Pan Rugui is dead, the Eastern Depot is weak. Very well; there really is no one in the whole capital who can take down this Xiao Ce'an!" Xi Hongxuan took a bite. "I've fallen out of His Majesty's favor these days; Hai Liangyi has his ear. Now that he's made up his mind to become the wise monarch of a golden age, he's much less willing to play with me."

Shen Zechuan had finished eating. "A man who has lived over twenty years has formed a fixed character," he said steadily. "If a handful of words was all it took for His Majesty to mend his ways, nothing in this world would be difficult."

Xi Hongxuan's hand paused. "You mean..."

"Hai Liangyi is a gentleman among gentlemen." Shen Zechuan set aside his chopsticks. "He is water so clear one can see right to the bottom. But his encounter with the current emperor is water meeting hot oil. Sooner or later, there will be an explosion. Xue Xiuzhuo has already reached a position of high honor; can't he climb even higher? The Grand Secretariat is his for the taking, is it not? It's not as if he's unqualified, and the central administration needs talents like him."

Xi Hongxuan mulled it over in silence.

"With enemies on our doorstep," Shen Zechuan continued, "how can the Eight Clans expect to gain any ground if they stand divided? You've finally become the head of the Xi Clan; as they say, fortunes rise and fall. Now that the opportunity is within reach, are you going to let it go?"

Xi Hongxuan laid down his chopsticks as well. He mopped his brow with a handkerchief and looked at Shen Zechuan. "You want me to unite the Eight Great Clans against Xiao Er?"

"Xiao Er is only one factor. At the moment, civil officials have the emperor's favor, and the Imperial College is on the rise. In a few years, when these sons of common families enter the official ranks one by one, what will happen to all the precious children of the Eight Great Clans who are used to loafing around? If the common-born scholars gain power, a new nobility will be born; then the Eight Great Clans will no longer be *the* Eight Great Clans."

"Even so," Xi Hongxuan said after a pause, "this is too thorny an issue. All else aside, Yao Wenyu would never agree. He's Hai Liangyi's student, personally instructed by the man himself. He's spent years traveling the four corners of the land, learning from countless scholars and sages. There's no way he'll allow the Yao Clan to ally with us against his teacher."

"The Eight Great Clans need only be eight in number," Shen Zechuan answered with a smile. "There's no reason they must stay *these* eight clans. If the Yao Clan is unwilling, simply pick another."

Xi Hongxuan pushed aside his chair and paced around the room. After some time, he looked at Shen Zechuan.

"But do you have any way to pin Xiao Er down? He wants to protect the emperor; he won't sit idle while we make our move. Him we can deal with, but the Libei Armored Cavalry stands behind him. As long as Xiao Jiming's around, Xiao Ce'an is untouchable. What a headache!"

"Xiao Jiming is formidable, but his power and prestige lie on the border." Shen Zechuan leaned a cheek on his hand, eyes hidden in shadows. He gave Xi Hongxuan a final push: "Qudu belongs to all of *you*. As the saying goes, even a dragon can't defeat a snake in its own garden. There are plenty of ways to keep Xiao Er so up to his neck in his own affairs he can't interfere in yours."

Deep in thought, Xi Hongxuan entirely missed that Shen Zechuan had said *you* and not *us*. "What ways?" he asked.

Shen Zechuan let out a soundless laugh. "Xiao Er's influence hinges entirely on His Majesty's trust. They're friends with many merry years of drinking behind them, not to mention Xiao Er just saved his life. Certainly there's nothing to be done about that at the moment. But here's the thing about sentiment—it's no more solid than autumn dew on the branch; it will evaporate as soon as the sun comes out."

Suddenly Xi Hongxuan was reminded of Ji Lei's fate on that rainy night. Those rare delicacies churned in his stomach. He strove to keep the discomfort from showing, forcing a smile. "Well, since you've got it all worked out, you might as well tell me."

After Shen Zechuan left, Xi Hongxuan had the servants remove the table and lay back on his rattan chair, letting the maidservants help him get comfortable, then sent a servant to open a window and air out the inexplicably stuffy room.

When Xue Xiuzhuo stepped out from behind the room's partition, Xi Hongxuan exclaimed, "You heard him, right? Thank heavens he was born Shen Wei's son. If he ever got his hands on real power, he'd be an even greater headache than Xiao Er."

"To use someone, you merely need to find the right method," Xue Xiuzhuo said as he poured tea. "No one in this world is without desires. Shen Lanzhou has his weaknesses. As long as we can grasp them, even the most ferocious dog is nothing to fear."

"The problem is that we can't find any." Xi Hongxuan tapped the center of his forehead with his fan. "Look how callous he is toward Xiao Er. It's obvious he turned his back on him the moment he got out of bed. Neither humiliation nor flattery works on a monster like that; you can't even threaten him."

Xue Xiuzhuo smiled and gulped down his tea. Every inch the gentleman, he asked, "What's the hurry? Just do as he says. Whether it works or not, it spells disaster for Xiao Er. By the time he's taken care of, Shen Zechuan's true motive will come to light."

Shen Zechuan had drifted downstairs, but he didn't rush to leave.

The madam knew him only as Xi Hongxuan's honored guest, so as soon as she saw him, she started fawning. "Does Master see a girl he likes? Looking cannot compare to trying for yourself."

He sized up the lavishly dressed women and asked, "Do you have male courtesans?"

The madam turned at once to the servant behind her. "Lead this master upstairs and find a few clean, tender-faced boys to serve him."

Shen Zechuan had hardly settled himself in the private room when three male courtesans entered. He swept a glance over them; all were neatly made up.

The madam was astute, with a good eye for picking people. She knew she couldn't find anyone more striking than Shen Zechuan in the whole building, so she had thought outside the box and sent him several fresh-faced and delicate-looking young men.

One of the boys stepped forward to remove Shen Zechuan's shoes, but Shen Zechuan shifted his feet slightly away. They all knelt before him and dared not move again.

Shen Zechuan gazed out the window. Eventually, he said, "Strip."

The three obediently shed their clothes. Shen Zechuan looked over all those fair and sloping shoulders, but from start to finish, his heart remained as calm as still water. He looked to their hands; their slender fingers looked like they belonged to young maidens, pampered to softness all their lives.

There were no calluses or thumb rings on those hands.

Shen Zechuan breathed a slow sigh and rose to his feet. Without a word to anyone, he pushed the door open and departed, leaving the three male courtesans to look at each other in confusion.

Ding Tao had been tailing Shen Zechuan from the rooftops. Upon seeing him finally walk out of Ouhua Pavilion, he jotted down a meticulous note in his wrinkly little book. When he looked up again, Shen Zechuan had disappeared into the crowd. Ding Tao didn't dare be negligent; he chased after him.

Shen Zechuan hadn't been walking fast, yet in a blink of an eye, he had vanished.

Ding Tao exclaimed and hurried forward, only to find his path blocked by a tall, sturdy man in a bamboo hat. The moment he drew near, he could tell this man was well-versed in martial arts. There were people all around them. Ding Tao didn't wish to involve innocents; rather than risk drawing notice, he let Shen Zechuan slip away, shaking his fist in frustration.

Yet as he made his way back, the thought struck him—there was something familiar about that man.

The sky darkened, and the snow grew heavier.

The stranger walked for some distance, bamboo hat pulled low over his face. At his next turn, he realized he'd entered a blind alley.

Shen Zechuan stood behind him.

"You've been following me for half a month. What do you want?"

The man chuckled, pressing the brim of his hat lower. "How perceptive. When did you notice?"

"You're very good at concealing your breathing," Shen Zechuan said. "Didn't you show me some of your tricks when you disappeared the moment you were released from prison, leading your pursuers on a wild goose chase out of Qudu? You've certainly gone to great pains."

Finally, the man tilted the brim of his hat to reveal a stubbled face. Qiao Tianya blew a wisp of hair off his forehead and said, "You could've lured me into a wine shop. Do we have to talk standing out in the cold?"

"Rabbits are hard to snare." Shen Zechuan studied him. "Should I call you Qiao Tianya, or Songyue?"

"As you please," Qiao Tianya said. "Call me Qiao Tianya, and we're on friendly terms. Call me Songyue, and you'd be my master."

"The judge of the Embroidered Uniform Guard is a capable man. Why take orders from my teacher?"

"It can't be helped." Qiao Tianya barked out a self-mocking laugh. "I owe Grand Mentor Qi a debt that can only be repaid with a lifetime of servitude."

"So the reason everything went so smoothly at the Autumn Hunt," Shen Zechuan replied, "was due to you."

"As your subordinate, I follow your cues," Qiao Tianya said. "You set out to kill Prince Chu that night; you just didn't expect Xiao Er was brazen enough to stick him right in the midst of the Embroidered Uniform Guard and take them all for a ride. But you're quick-witted—you seized the opportunity to make sure Xiao Er owed you a favor."

"That's all I can do," Shen Zechuan said.

Qiao Tianya brushed snow off his shoulder. "From now on, I'll follow you, Master. If there's meat in the future, just don't forget to spare me a bowl of broth; I'm much easier to provide for than those personal guards Xiao Er keeps."

"Ding Tao is young." Shen Zechuan tossed him a money pouch. "But Chen Yang and Gu Jin are tough nuts."

Qiao Tianya caught the pouch neatly. "You've dug up all there is about Xiao Er, yet he still remembers the kindness you did him in saving his life."

Shen Zechuan smiled. "Sounds like you want to work for *him*."

Qiao Tianya raised his hands innocently. "My loyalty is unwavering toward my master. If Xiao Er is willing to buy me for a thousand gold, of course I'll be willing to go through hell for him instead."

"A pity there's already such a crowd around him," Shen Zechuan observed. "It seems there's no space for you."

"My young lord"—Qiao Tianya cocked his head and squinted—"has a truly vicious mouth."

Shen Zechuan's expression all but said *you flatter me*.

Qiao Tianya gave him a smile that was all teeth. "Then again, what you said applies to us both."

Eight days later, Shen Zechuan and Ji Gang arrived at the dinner as promised.

Ding Tao had clearly lodged a complaint. Gu Jin, who hadn't touched a drop all day, stood outside the door of the manor with him. He spotted Qiao Tianya walking behind Shen Zechuan from a distance away.

Ding Tao immediately went up on his toes and whispered in Gu Jin's ear, "Jin-ge, that's him. He's the one!"

When Chen Yang led Shen Zechuan and Ji Gang through the door, it should have been obvious Qiao Tianya ought to remain outside. But he didn't seem to notice; just as his foot was about to cross the threshold, Gu Jin stopped him.

"I heard you stood in this brat's path a few days ago." Gu Jin swept his sharp eyes over the bamboo hat. "What kind of hero are you, bullying a child?"

Ding Tao harrumphed with righteous indignation and parroted, "Yeah, what kind of hero?!"

Qiao Tianya burst out laughing. He pulled off his hat and said with an impish grin, "I thought we were here to eat. Do we have to fight too? This is my first time meeting your little buddy. Perhaps you got the wrong person?"

"Hey! How can you say that?" Ding Tao fumed. "There's no way I got the wrong person!"

Gu Jin pulled Ding Tao back and faced Qiao Tianya straight on.

The two men were of similar height; as they squared off, they came so close to each other they were almost bumping chests.

"This isn't the time," Gu Jin said. "We'll settle this later."

"I'm busy." Qiao Tianya tugged at the lock of hair on his forehead and threw Gu Jin a provocative grin. "After all, my master only has me. I don't have the leisure to raise a little brother for fun."

Gu Jin spat coldly, "Let's have your name. There will be plenty of occasions for us to meet in the future."

"This humble servant is Qiao Yueyue." Turning to Ding Tao, Qiao Tianya tapped his temple with two fingers and continued, "Also known as Xiao-Songsong."

Chen Yang led Shen Zechuan and Ji Gang deeper into the sprawling estate. They strode down a covered walkway and stepped through a moon gate into an elegant courtyard abloom with red plum blossoms. Xiao Chiye was waiting under a tree when Shen Zechuan arrived. Their eyes met for a flashing instant; before any subtle feeling could be conveyed, both men averted their gazes.

Xiao Chiye turned to Ji Gang with a smile. "Please excuse me for not going out to greet Shishu when you braved the snow to come here. The table is set, and Shifu is waiting inside."

Ji Gang held out a hand to stop Xiao Chiye from bowing. "Your shifu broke away from the Ji Clan more than twenty years ago, and your martial arts now has a distinctive style all its own. We aren't of the same martial clan; there's no need to be so polite."

"We come from the same martial line, so we're of the same martial clan," Xiao Chiye said. "It's all thanks to learning Ji-Style Boxing that I could master the blend of martial arts from various clans. I've long admired Shishu's reputation. This respect is only what's owed."

After making his bow, Xiao Chiye led Ji Gang inside, though he didn't forget to turn to Shen Zechuan and say, "It's also been a while since Lanzhou and I saw each other."

Shen Zechuan smiled as he strode across the threshold. "You've such power and influence now; Shixiong must be busy these days."

"We're brothers of the same martial lineage," Xiao Chiye said calmly. "No matter how busy I am, I'll always make time for you."

"It wouldn't do for you to neglect official business on my behalf," Shen Zechuan answered. "My duties have been much lighter in my new post; it seems Shixiong's already been looking out for me."

"It's been my pleasure." Xiao Chiye lifted the curtain. "If you want to be busy, just come to me. I'll make the bed in welcome and have it ready for you any time."

The phrase was a politeness you would offer any guest, but the back of Shen Zechuan's neck ached as soon as he heard the word *bed*. A phantom heat lingered where those teeth had pierced skin, so searing his smile faded.

Zuo Qianqiu was attired in a wide-sleeved robe with slanting collars, his white hair pulled into a neat topknot. He looked like neither a refined scholar nor an awe-inspiring general. Although he had a few years on Ji Gang, he seemed younger. The only way to describe his aura now was otherworldly—it would appear the rumors that he'd forsaken his mortal identity and become a monk were not totally groundless.

He turned and saw Ji Gang, dressed in a short, rough-spun tunic with a thick jacket. Ji Gang, with his disfigured face, looked back at Zuo Qianqiu. In an instant, the past surged up—the cheers and laughter of youth rang in their ears—but the man before him was already old and white-haired.

Xiao Chiye broke the silence. "Both shifu shall have their meals here. Lanzhou and I will wait outside."

"Chuan-er, fasten your overcoat properly." Ji Gang looked rather forlorn as he half-turned and urged Shen Zechuan, "Come in if you feel cold."

Shen Zechuan nodded.

"A-Ye, take care of your shidi,"[2] Zuo Qianqiu said.

Xiao Chiye smiled in acknowledgment, and both men retreated.

The air was cold outside, yet it was a rare clear night. Shen Zechuan descended the steps. Looking out at the groves of red plum blossoms crossed here and there with a slim, arching bridge, it occurred to him that this place had an elegance incongruous with Xiao Chiye's style.

Xiao Chiye seemed to sense his thoughts. "I bought this place from the Yao Clan." Standing behind Shen Zechuan, he raised a hand and brushed aside a branch of red plum blossoms to reveal a clear stream winding through the courtyard. "Pretty. Expensive, too."

"Yet you willingly parted with the money." Shen Zechuan did not look back.

Xiao Chiye swayed so close his chest brushed Shen Zechuan's back, raising a hand to shield the top of Shen Zechuan's head from falling petals. He leaned in close to Shen Zechuan's ear and said lightly, "Snow envelops the red plums; fragrance envelops Lanzhou. For his smile, I'd pay a thousand gold."

A smile slowly spread across Shen Zechuan's face. "When you already had to sell the clothes off your back for this house?"

"I spent a sum, yes. But Yao Wenyu was selling it at a low price." Xiao Chiye paused. "You certainly ran fast. You've spared no effort avoiding me."

---

2 *Younger martial brother, used to refer to younger disciples of the same generation.*

"It's not that I'm avoiding you." Shen Zechuan lifted a finger to push away Xiao Chiye's hand. "But really, what important matters do we have that must be discussed face-to-face?"

Xiao Chiye smiled and said ruthlessly, "Shouldn't you show your Er-gongzi a little tenderness after bedding him?"

Shen Zechuan took a few steps forward, widening the distance between them. Turning, he scrutinized Xiao Chiye in silence.

Under that starry sky adorned with plum blossoms, both men, in retrospect, came to understand something.

Xiao Chiye realized what he'd grabbed that night was water. Once it flowed through his fingers, it was gone. Shen Zechuan had not been even remotely reluctant to leave. After the frenzy of biting and tearing, the scalding heat of their tryst was buried in the inky night. When Shen Zechuan had arched his neck in searing ecstasy, he had not burned Xiao Ce'an into his memories at all.

Once again, Xiao Chiye was forced to face facts: he was the only one defeated by lust that night.

"I advised you already." Shen Zechuan raised his hand to pull down a branch and said to Xiao Chiye, his tone almost bewitching, "It would be best not to bite this neck."

"The pleasures of the bedroom," Xiao Chiye challenged with a frivolous smile, "are not something I can take sole credit for."

"The greatest difference between you and me is desire. You are filled with it, and trying desperately to hide your wild ambitions. The nape of a neck is a single minor adversity. You've clung to me, wanting to resist it, wanting to defeat it; in the end, you've lost. You see, Ce'an," here Shen Zechuan plucked a plum blossom, tore the petals, and put one in his mouth, "I am not at the mercy of lust. So how do you plan to win against me?"

Xiao Chiye stepped closer and grabbed Shen Zechuan's hand that held the flower. He leaned in, his features indifferent. "What is but one time? If you found it lacking, we should go a few more rounds. You had no use for the girls in Ouhua Pavilion, and you didn't dare to touch the boys either. You pretend to be a sage, celibate and aloof, but I'm not the one who moaned and panted so delicately that night."

Xiao Chiye pulled Shen Zechuan's knuckles to his lips, pressed against them dangerously, and snickered. "I've lost to lust, that's true. But if you're really so steadfast, then why did you feel the need to take that tumble in the sheets with me? Shen Lanzhou, I think you're much more terrified of succumbing to desire than I am."

CARTOGRAPHS

After three rounds of drinks between Ji Gang and Zuo Qianqiu, much of the awkwardness of estrangement had bled away. Though the atmosphere still wasn't warm, it felt like more than enough for them to have a chat over wine.

Between sips, Ji Gang removed the muffler around his neck. When Zuo Qianqiu saw that the burn marks covered his neck as well, he couldn't help asking, "When the Biansha Horsemen invaded Duanzhou, how...how did you end up like this?"

Ji Gang turned his wine cup in his hands and chuckled. "Shen Wei beat such a quick retreat that Duanzhou fell in less than a day. The Biansha horses were swift, and my legs aren't what they used to be; what chance did I have? Back then, I was ready to fight to the death." Thinking of Hua Pingting, he choked with emotion. He turned aside and rubbed his face, letting the words die.

Zuo Qianqiu downed his wine. "Shen Wei deserved a thousand deaths!"

"Not just him," Ji Gang said bitterly. "The fall of Zhongbo was suspicious in more ways than one. They pushed the blame onto Shen Wei because they were certain he wouldn't survive."

"You've been away from Qudu so long. How can you be sure Shen Wei was a scapegoat?"

"Five years ago, when Chuan-er was brought to the capital, someone tried to kill him in the prison," said Ji Gang. "Shen Wei was dead and gone, yet someone wanted to ensure no member of the family survived. Why, if not to tie off loose ends?"

Zuo Qianqiu drank his wine in silence. After a moment, he mused, "Now that they're all dead, it won't be easy to conduct a thorough investigation into the fall of Zhongbo. Does your disciple seek revenge for Shen Wei?"

Ji Gang had abstained from drinking the past five years but had broken his sobriety for Zuo Qianqiu tonight; the wine had already gone to his head. "Revenge?" he sneered, clutching the table edge for support. "Why would Chuan-er seek revenge for Shen Wei? Zuo Qianqiu, how can you be as closed-minded as them?! Is everyone in the world with the surname Shen guilty? Chuan-er has grown up; he has the sense to know better, and he can tell right from wrong. He happens to be Shen Wei's son, but other than that accident of birth, they have no connection. Why do you all push him into a corner? Shen Wei is dead! Shouldn't you look to the Biansha Horsemen to avenge this so-called blood debt of Zhongbo?!"

He smashed his wine cup on the ground, chest heaving. "A thorough investigation of the Zhongbo defeat isn't for any revenge, but to discover the reason behind his suffering! You were a general, too; has it not occurred to you? If they could raze Zhongbo five years ago, then they can do the same somewhere else five years later. Back then, the Biansha Horsemen kept such a close pursuit. How could they have done it unless they had a map and some help from within?!"

Zuo Qianqiu sighed. "Gang-di,[3] don't be angry. When Jiming arrived in Zhongbo, the first thing he did was cut off the route between Zhongbo and Dancheng, specifically for the sake of investigating

---

3 *Di, a term of address for one's younger brother.*

the source of Biansha's intelligence. But the situation was critical then. Do you know how difficult it was? All evidence pointed to Shen Wei, yet he self-immolated, leaving only a single disfavored son of common birth. How could this survivor not arouse suspicion?"

After a moment of silence, Ji Gang said, "That kick from your disciple nearly killed him."

Zuo Qianqiu drank deep again. "I won't defend him, but please understand, Gang-di. We each have our own experiences and act in pursuit of our own goals."

"Sure," Ji Gang sneered. "Just pay lip service and consider it a closed case."

Zuo Qianqiu set another empty cup on the table and shouted, "A-Ye!"

The door opened at once. Zuo Qianqiu poured wine into the cup with one hand and tossed the cup toward Xiao Chiye with the other. "Apologize to your shishu and shidi."

Ji Gang reached out and intercepted it, balancing the cup on one end of his chopsticks. "We were the ones whose skills left much to be desired back then. Chuan-er, why don't you come and make the toast?" As the words left his mouth, he sent the cup spinning toward Shen Zechuan.

Xiao Chiye intercepted it midair. "Lanzhou, it's my responsibility. Don't fight Shixiong on this, all right?"

Shen Zechuan lifted a leg and tapped Xiao Chiye's arm with his toe, knocking it aside. "Shifu's orders must be followed. Shixiong, please allow me." The wine cup pitched and fell from Xiao Chiye's hand. Their palms brushed past each other. Xiao Chiye drew back and shoved Shen Zechuan's arm away, but just as the cup was about to crash to the ground, Shen Zechuan caught it with the top of his foot and flung it back into the air.

Their exchange stirred up an audible breeze. The wine cup had fallen and flown between them, but not a single drop had spilled. Ji Gang, who had been holding his chopsticks the whole time, now applied them to some of the cold dishes. "These moves were not passed down by the Ji Clan."

Zuo Qianqiu watched them fighting. "Those are the Xiao Clan's moves. They resemble a fierce raptor grabbing its prey; once caught, it's hard to break free. Lanzhou, focus your attacks on his legs—disrupt his balance."

Shen Zechuan immediately retracted his hand and, taking a short step back, launched a kick. Xiao Chiye dodged. There were things he wanted to say to Shen Zechuan, but before both shifu, he kept silent. He parried the kick, grabbing Shen Zechuan's ankle. Using his own body to block Shen Zechuan from the elders' view, he ran his hand along the curve of Shen Zechuan's calf before gently tugging him closer.

"How terrifying," said Xiao Chiye calmly. "I'm powerless against your kick."

Xiao Chiye's touch almost sent Shen Zechuan rocking off balance, but he still had to reach out to grab the cup as it fell. Xiao Chiye patiently waited for him to catch it before throwing a punch straight at Shen Zechuan's face.

"Ji-Style Boxing!" Ji Gang's chopsticks paused. He held back judgment for a moment as he watched, then conceded, "No wonder Chuan-er spoke highly of him."

Xiao Chiye's physique was perfectly suited for it. This punch was so well executed not even Ji Gang could find fault.

Cup in one hand, Shen Zechuan dared not take the punch straight on; he leaned backward; the gust of wind from Xiao Chiye's fist brushed the hair at his temple. Before he could straighten,

Xiao Chiye pressed in. Following the momentum of his punch, his hand darted into Shen Zechuan's collar, picking out the remnants of the plum blossom Shen Zechuan had bitten.

"You've fallen into my trap." Xiao Chiye's eyes glinted with mischief as he slid the rest of the plum blossom onto his tongue. Shen Zechuan struggled to rise, still holding the cup, but Xiao Chiye thwarted his attempt. He suddenly looked up and cried, "The wine is spilled!"

Stunned, Shen Zechuan lifted his head to see; Xiao Chiye seized the chance to grab his wrist. Pressing his thumb up along Shen Zechuan's pulse, he tilted Shen Zechuan's palm toward him and downed the wine in one draft.

"Thank you for the wine, Shidi," Xiao Chiye said, backing away and assuming the posture of a gentleman. "The taste of it leaves a lingering aroma in my mouth."

Shen Zechuan rose to his feet and returned the bow with a sweep of his sleeves before setting the empty cup back on the table. His wrist burned from Xiao Chiye's touch.

Oblivious to the surging undercurrents between them, Ji Gang said, "The difficulty in weaving the threads of a hundred schools of martial arts together lies in creating a seamless whole. You taught him well."

"He has a long way to go," Zuo Qianqiu demurred. "I can see Lanzhou specializes in Ji Clan mental cultivation techniques. His focus is truly impressive."

As the two elders refilled their cups, Xiao Chiye and Shen Zechuan retreated for the second time. The instant the door shut behind them, Xiao Chiye grabbed hold of Shen Zechuan. "They're likely to drink into the night. It's cold out. Let's sit inside."

The north end of the corridor led to the Yao Clan's old study. To keep the room dry and protect the books, a heating system had been installed beneath the floor. The books had yet to be removed, and all four shelves of the open bookcase were filled with antique ornaments, calligraphy, and paintings.

Xiao Chiye shed his heavy overcoat and sat behind the desk with a foot propped on his knee as he flipped through a book. "This estate was built by the old master of the Yao Clan. Plenty of good stuff is hidden here. Yao Wenyu doesn't like to play, so they've been left here all this time, untouched."

Shen Zechuan wiped his hands clean before reaching for the books on the shelf. The Yao Clan loved books. The old master of the house had arranged them neatly by subject, and though a long time had presumably passed, the pages showed not a speck of dust. Xiao Chiye must have given orders to take good care of them.

Each took a side of the room and kept to themselves.

Shen Zechuan, with his discerning eyes, spied a bound book of illustrations of the Hongyan Mountains among the travelogues. He opened it and, sure enough, found cartographs of the northern mountain range.

The Hongyan Mountains were divided into two ranges, east and west. The western range extended down to Luoxia Pass and wrapped around Quancheng, separating it from Huaizhou in the west. It was the frontier of the Zhou empire until Xiao Fangxu expanded the territory and pushed the border all the way to the eastern side of the mountain range, thus carving out present-day Libei.

Shen Zechuan flipped to a detailed description of the Northeast Provisions Trail.

Qudu controlled and coordinated the logistics of all the granaries in the land, and mostly transferred its army provisions from Juexi's Qinzhou region to its troops in the north and east. These two major regions could not be accessed via waterways, so Qudu had constructed highways specifically for the transport of provisions. The situation in Qidong had always been more complicated, but Libei's Northeast Provisions Trail was clear-cut. Grains were transported from Qinzhou to the Port of Yongyi, traveled from the Port of Yongyi to Qudu, then from Qudu to Quancheng. From Quancheng onward, they proceed straight along the Northeast Provisions Trail to reach Libei.

The Northeast Provisions Trail was an important transport route for Libei's military supplies, guarded at multiple points along the way by the Libei Armored Cavalry. Even if the emperor himself stepped onto this road, he couldn't pass through without Xiao Jiming's commander's tally for authorization of passage. The defense of the Northeast Provisions Trail had ever been unassailable, no matter how brutal the battles at the borders became. Not once did the Biansha Horsemen manage to even get within sight of it.

Five years ago, Xiao Jiming was able to deploy troops to the south so swiftly precisely because the Northeast Provisions Trail happened to pass near the northwestern side of Cizhou. The security of this supply line gave him the confidence to dispatch his troops without delay.

"The Northeast Provisions Trail." Xiao Chiye had drawn close up behind him at some point, looking at the pages in Shen Zechuan's hands. "Are you interested in military strategy?"

"Nope," Shen Zechuan replied without thinking.

"That's all right. Er-gongzi will teach you." Xiao Chiye took Shen Zechuan gently by the wrist and guided his finger, sliding it toward the Chashi River at the eastern edge. "You recognize this place, right? The Chashi River of Zhongbo is our Great Zhou's easternmost line of defense. Ford its waters, and you'll find yourself in the Great Desert of Biansha. It's actually pretty interesting. Until that battle, the Biansha tribes of the south only ever dared attack the Bianjun Commandery."

Shen Zechuan looked where his fingertip rested at the southeast corner of Tianfei Watchtower. There, abutting the desert, was the Bianjun Commandery: the only break in the fortress of the Zhou empire.

"It's because of the location of Bianjun Commandery. To its north is Tianfei Watchtower, to its south is the Suotian Pass. Bianjun sits at that crucial weak point in our southeast corner with no geographical defensive advantage." Xiao Chiye leaned in closer, his focus on the map. "The Lu Clan guards this land. Do you know Lu Guangbai's nickname? They call him Beacon-Smoke and Rising Sand because the Lu Clan defends tens of thousands of li of smoke beacon towers in that desert. The Biansha Horsemen are crafty and favor night assaults. Every time they clashed, Lu Guangbai would light up the smoke beacons. The Bianjun Commandery Garrison Troops are the best infantry in the empire for night strikes. They're experts at laying ambushes."

Getting a little excited, Xiao Chiye slid Shen Zechuan's finger across the map to the Bianjun Commandery. "Of the Four Great Generals, Shifu is most skilled in defense. Because of the terrain around Tianfei Watchtower, there's no need to initiate attacks or dispatch troops. Don't be fooled by how unremarkable the Bianjun Commandery looks. In fact, Lu Guangbai is the best in the country at attrition warfare. Neither my eldest brother nor Marshal Qi is as formidable as he."

"The Bianjun Commandery has no cavalry." Shen Zechuan turned his head slightly and cast Xiao Chiye a glance.

Xiao Chiye smiled. He seemed particularly relaxed at this moment. "Lu Guangbai doesn't need them. His soldiers are the bane of cavalries.

The Lu Clan has stood guard in the desert for generations. The climate is harsh, and the barren land can't be cultivated at all; they are truly so broke they can't afford to raise horses. But with or without them, battles need to be fought. Working around these constraints, the Lu Clan managed to develop battle formations for the express purpose of holding off mounted attackers."

Shen Zechuan looked back at the map. "When you say 'pretty interesting,' you're referring to how unusual it was for the Biansha Horsemen to deviate from their usual pattern to ford the Chashi River five years ago?"

"That's right." When Xiao Chiye was deep in thought, he had a habit of spinning his thumb ring; now, with his hand covering Shen Zechuan's, he squeezed Shen Zechuan's finger absentmindedly. "There's one thing you should know first: the Twelve Tribes of Biansha is a collective moniker. At the start, there were more than twelve tribes in the desert. The Huiyan tribe, which now has dealings with Libei's trade market, is a small tribe that was driven out of the richest grassland by the others. They had to throw in their lot with our Great Zhou to survive. Of the current Twelve Tribes of Biansha, some are stronger than others. They've never been unified under one ruler, so they've never been able to come to an agreement with us and could only fight us and each other. But each battle fought takes a heavy toll on Biansha. Their strongest tribe, the Hanma tribe, lies to their north, and clashes primarily with the Armored Cavalry of Libei. Meanwhile their swiftest Goushe tribe lies to the south and engages the garrison troops of the Bianjun Commandery. These were predictable patterns formed over long periods of conflict. But five years ago, without warning, the Hanma and Goushe joined forces and met in the middle to deliver a severe blow to the Chashi River border." Xiao Chiye paused. "There is only one possibility for such a change in tactics."

"They had absolute confidence in their plan," Shen Zechuan said. "They were sure Zhongbo couldn't stop them, and that Libei and the Bianjun Commandery would not come to the rescue in time."

"And that was how the rumor started that Shen Wei colluded with the enemy," Xiao Chiye said. "Cutting through the center of Zhongbo was risky. In a strange environment, it was a dangerous gamble to rely solely on the spoils of war to feed their army. These warriors are used to galloping across the desert. To them, combat on city streets is like fighting with hands and feet bound. Besides, the closer they got to Qudu, the more obvious their true goal became."

"A direct attack on Qudu was not at all a good choice," Shen Zechuan replied. "Qudu is the heart of Great Zhou. If they remained here too long, they would end up besieged on three sides by the Libei Armored Cavalry, garrison troops from all five of Qidong's commanderies, and the Eight Great Battalions." He lowered his eyes. "I never believed the Biansha Horsemen meant to take Qudu."

"Clever," Xiao Chiye praised. He slid Shen Zechuan's finger back across the entire breadth of the map and pointed at Juexi on the westernmost edge. "I think they were heading here. Juexi faces the sea. It boasts two major ports and three major grain reserves. All the military provisions for Libei, Qudu, and Qidong come from this region. Once they entered Juexi, they wouldn't even need to attack the cities; they would already have all three forces by the throat."

"Without help from the inside, this would all be a flight of fancy," Shen Zechuan mused.

"From Zhongbo to Juexi, it's a straight line east to west. The shortest path there is through Zhongbo. Shen Wei opened the gates and gave them the courage and provisions to push farther in. If it wasn't for the Northeast Provisions Trail, Dage couldn't have sent troops for at least seven more days. In those seven days, if the Eight

Great Battalions failed to stop them, the Biansha Horsemen would have arrived at the Port of Yongyi," Xiao Chiye said. "This is the real reason for Libei's wrath. In war, nothing is too trivial for scrutiny. We could forgive Shen Wei a defeat; we can never forgive him a stab in the back."

Shen Zechuan suddenly turned and looked up from their hands on the map; Xiao Chiye's eyes were mere inches from his.

"What's the matter?" Xiao Chiye had no intention of letting go.

"Shen Wei colluded with the enemy." Shen Zechuan's mouth quirked in a peculiar smile. "Shen Wei colluded with the enemy; the Twelve Tribes of Biansha wanted to take Juexi. But how did Shen Wei get his hands on a strategic map of Juexi?"

"The Ministry of War has one," answered Xiao Chiye. "Even ghosts will do your bidding for enough money. It can be obtained with a hefty bribe."

"In that case," said Shen Zechuan, "it's not just Shen Wei. Anyone could have done it."

NIGHT CHAT

"THAT MAY BE SO." Xiao Chiye looked down. "But Shen Wei was the one who determined success or failure on the front line." His features held an uncharacteristic tenderness with his lashes lowered like this. The brilliant interest from earlier had yet to dissipate; it shimmered in his eyes like fireflies in the night.

Shen Zechuan watched him for a moment. "The Ministry of War has had no significant personnel changes in the last five years."

"You can investigate if you want," Xiao Chiye said. "I won't stop you."

"Of course you won't." Shen Zechuan shifted his gaze back to the book. "Because you want to look into this too. The Hua Clan should be the most likely suspect, but there are a thousand simpler ways to dispose of a tainted blade like Shen Wei. Involving too many people would only leave a more damning trail."

"Well, you killed Ji Lei." Xiao Chiye smiled. "I imagine he gave you plenty of information. Hiding it away is no fun; lay it out on the table so we can speculate together."

"Oh? But I already knew everything you said, and you know nothing of what I might say." Shen Zechuan extracted his hand inch by inch out from under Xiao Chiye's. "That doesn't sound like a fair exchange."

Xiao Chiye thought about it. "How about this? We'll do a one-for-one trade."

"Sure," Shen Zechuan replied. "But first, get out of my way."

Making full use of his towering stature, Xiao Chiye had barricaded Shen Zechuan next to the bookshelf. He flipped through the pages lazily. "Don't you know the rules? Secrets ought to be whispered."

Shen Zechuan leaned forward to move away from him. "Whispered doesn't mean we have to be stuck together."

"The walls have ears." Xiao Chiye replaced the book, leaned an arm against the shelf, and smiled down at him. "After all, I've only just bought this estate, and haven't acquainted myself with its secrets yet. It's better to be cautious."

"Xiao Er." Shen Zechuan dropped his eyes to the book. "You really are an asshole."

"Sure," Xiao Chiye said. "But what can you do? All right, I'll go first."

Shen Zechuan waited, eyes downcast. When he heard no sound, he turned back and realized Xiao Chiye was still looking at him. It was only when their breaths tangled between them that Xiao Chiye began.

"Shen Wei didn't set himself on fire. The fire at the Prince of Jianxing's manor was set by the Embroidered Uniform Guard, and Ji Lei had orders to go there. But you know that already, don't you."

"Yes," Shen Zechuan said calmly. "It's no secret."

"Then, do you know the real reason behind the fall of Duanzhou?" Xiao Chiye asked.

Shen Zechuan couldn't look away—he couldn't even take a moment to think. The instant he failed to keep pace with Xiao Chiye's train of thought, he would fall into his trap. "During the attack at Chashi River, Shen Wei ordered the Duanzhou Garrison Troops to withdraw, leaving behind his heir, Shen Zhouji, to cover their retreat," Shen Zechuan said. "Shen Zhouji was cut from the same cloth as his old man. Faced with a hopeless battle, he abandoned his troops at Chashi River and fled with his personal guards. The Biansha Horsemen dragged him down the public road to his death the same day. With Shen Zhouji dead, morale at Chashi River plummeted. After the massacre, there were no more soldiers on the front line in Duanzhou."

"Correct," Xiao Chiye confirmed. "But there's something you don't know. Before Shen Zhouji died, he and Shen Wei strangled the commander of the Duanzhou Garrison Troops, Tantai Long, to death."

Tantai Long... Tantai Hu!

No wonder Tantai Hu said his own brother had been at the Chashi Sinkhole.

Shen Zechuan frowned. "Strangled to death?"

"Tantai Long insisted on deploying troops to meet the enemy head-on. He repeatedly contradicted Shen Wei in public. When Shen Wei issued his withdrawal order, Tantai Long refused to obey. Shen Wei pretended to make amends over drinks, then—together with Shen Zhouji—strangled Tantai Long in his room." Xiao Chiye paused. "Lao-Hu doesn't know this; he thinks Tantai Long was killed in battle. This is the first matter I'm confiding to you. Your turn."

Hastily, Shen Zechuan gathered his thoughts. "Shen Wei was party to the struggle for the throne during the reign of the Guangcheng Emperor and carried out assassinations for the empress dowager, who then put him under close watch. When he realized the danger, he bribed Pan Rugui and fled to Zhongbo."

"One oughtn't be too quick to dispose of one's watchdog," Xiao Chiye said. "Under normal circumstances, the Hua Clan wouldn't have made such a risky move to dispose of Shen Wei. There was no benefit to the empress dowager, who already controlled most of the government's levers of power. The costs of the battle far exceeded the funds in the empire's treasury, and the empress dowager was yet looking forward to holding court as the emperor emeritus behind the screen. Having Shen Wei killed would have been detrimental to her own plans. His death wasn't worth the price."

Shen Zechuan nodded slightly. "So what Ji Lei said might not be the entire truth; he was just a pawn. To investigate properly, one must start at the Ministry of War. From there, you can follow the trail up or down."

"I'll go up, and you can go down," said Xiao Chiye.

"Top and bottom are linked; they are inseparable." It was only after he spoke that Shen Zechuan realized Xiao Chiye was making a pass at him. He flipped through the book and feigned obliviousness.

With a hint of a smile, Xiao Chiye stepped aside. "Have a seat."

The study was awfully hot. Xiao Chiye was dressed in a scarlet court robe, the lion of his military rank roaring on his mandarin square. He was now a real second-rank supreme commander of two armies in Qudu. Presumably, he had come straight from the palace and hadn't had a chance to change. His features were all the more striking against the vivid color of his outfit, lending him an air of upright handsomeness that replaced his usual frivolous manner.

The two men faced each other across the table. Xiao Chiye fixed his gaze on Shen Zechuan, who kept his eyes on his book. He didn't bother to hide his interest now; his examination idled around Shen Zechuan's neck and settled on his hands. He was no longer relegated to considering one spot; he wanted to behold every inch of Shen Zechuan. He watched Shen Zechuan's fingers curl as he reached out to flip a page, and thought of those same fingers, damp with sweat, and how they had curled just like this as he gripped the sheets, rocking like surging waves.

Shen Zechuan felt Xiao Chiye's gaze on him as a physical touch, as though he was still holding Shen Zechuan's finger in his hand. A strange restlessness came over him. He closed the book and looked squarely at Xiao Chiye.

"Hm?" said Xiao Chiye.

Shen Zechuan laced his fingers together, curling his lips in the ghost of a smile. "The Imperial Army is so busy these days. I'm afraid you'll have no time to investigate these extraneous matters."

Xiao Chiye twirled his ring around his thumb. "It's temporary. If the Embroidered Uniform Guard has time to spare, they can share the Imperial Army's burdens."

"I'm a humble soldier with neither an official post nor the favor of the emperor. How could I have any say in what the Embroidered Uniform Guard does or does not do?" Shen Zechuan leaned back in his chair. "The Imperial Army has to manage capital patrols as well as private cases of the imperial court. The supreme commander must go to great pains to exercise prudence in all matters. It must be exhausting."

Ever since he'd sidelined the Embroidered Uniform Guard, Xiao Chiye truly had been busy. He could hear the condemnation in Shen Zechuan's words, so he also folded his hands, set them on the table, and said with certainty, "You want to make trouble for me."

"Tit for tat," Shen Zechuan replied pleasantly. "You interfered with my rotational duties, which has granted me free time. Naturally I must thank you properly."

"There are so many ways to express gratitude. Why not choose one that would please everyone involved?" asked Xiao Chiye. "It seems you indeed have friends in the Six Ministries."

"Money at home cannot compare to friends at court. A friend told me something. I have a feeling you'd be interested too."

Xiao Chiye looked at him steadily. "I'm all ears."

Shen Zechuan surveyed the study. "Come to think of it, it's a pity I've yet to meet this 'Unpolished Jade' Yao Wenyu. I imagine you're on good terms with him?"

"A passing acquaintance," Xiao Chiye said. "Nothing compared to you."

"The Yao Clan is on the decline, yet they still stand among the Eight Great Clans. Some people may find that unacceptable," Shen Zechuan noted. "Yao Wenyu is Secretariat Elder Hai's official pupil, yet he keeps his distance from the imperial court—such a stance is as good as throwing away his weapon and offering himself up for slaughter."

"The Yao Clan may be on the decline, but the echoes of power and prestige accumulated over three reigns remain," Xiao Chiye said. "Yao Wenyu is a virtuous gentleman scholar, but he is by no means a fool. Who would want to cross the Yao Clan?"

Shen Zechuan affected a contemplative expression. "How should I know?"

Xiao Chiye fell silent, but a moment later he was forced to admit, "You aren't so generous, Lanzhou. In pretending to make me your confidant, you've only made me uneasy."

"If we're going to investigate together, I'll gladly help within my capability," Shen Zechuan said. "It only occurred to me today since you're on such good terms with the Yao Clan. The Eight Great Clans have stood tall for such a long time. Look how important you've become; isn't it to be expected that they would scheme against you? And if the Yao Clan isn't willing to play along, it will inevitably become the target of the other clans' ire."

By taking command of the Eight Great Battalions—the Eight Great Clans' most important asset in Qudu—Xiao Chiye had broken their hold on military power. Losing a position in court was nothing; younger generations at home could replace them. But losing the Eight Great Battalions meant they were truly under someone else's boot. It was one thing for the eight clans to counterbalance and plot against each other, and quite another to be under the control of Xiao Chiye. As the adage went, what was long divided would surely unite, and what was long united would surely divide.[4] Now, the Eight Great Clans had a reason to unite: their common enemy, Xiao Chiye.

Shen Zechuan was right, but Xiao Chiye still smelled something fishy in this seemingly candid answer. Without batting an eyelid, he said, "I don't pose that great of a threat to them yet."

"The key to long-term success is to nip threats in the bud," Shen Zechuan replied. "You showed your edge once already, at the Autumn Hunt. Pretending now that nothing happened is like covering your ears while stealing a bell."

"Who's your friend?" Xiao Chiye asked abruptly.

Shen Zechuan smiled. "Even if I told the truth, would you believe it?"

Xiao Chiye stared restlessly at Shen Zechuan.

He wouldn't.

This man was as sly as a fox. Every word he said sober was an alloy of truths and lies. He was far too difficult to deal with like this—Xiao Chiye had found him much easier to talk to in bed.

"I'll find him." Xiao Chiye leaned in, closing the distance between them. "As long as you leave the slightest trail, you won't be able to escape my eyes."

---

4 *Opening line of* Romance of the Three Kingdoms, *attributed to Luo Guanzhong, a historical war epic considered one of China's four great classic novels.*

"You're going to be scrambling just to keep your head above water," Shen Zechuan said cheerfully. "Better think of a way to safely ride out this storm first."

"To think your heart doesn't ache for me at all." Xiao Chiye lightened his solemn expression. "One night spent as husband and wife, affection for a hundred days of your life. Lanzhou, you're too callous."

Shen Zechuan parroted his words from earlier: "That's right. But what can you do?"

Xiao Chiye sat down and, leaning back, propped his leg on his knee. He considered a moment. "This matter can be easily resolved; it's a minor concern. But I'll have to thank you properly for this reminder tonight."

"That's much too kind of you," Shen Zechuan said. "One hundred taels will do nicely."

"I'm broke." Xiao Chiye drawled his words. "My annual salary as a second rank official is only one hundred and fifty taels. But I have other things I can offer in exchange—Er-gongzi can warm your bed."

"Forget it, then." Shen Zechuan smiled politely. "I'm used to sleeping alone. I don't need a bed warmer."

"Habits can change." Xiao Chiye lifted his knuckles to his nose to smell Shen Zechuan on his skin. Casting a sly glance at Shen Zechuan, he said, "Have you gotten used to sniffing my handkerchief?"

Caught off guard, Shen Zechuan clenched his hands, leaving red marks on his fingertips.

Xiao Chiye studied the face of this beauty under the lamp light: the calm facade he clung to, the reddened fingertips he tried to hide. Finally, he pointed to his own ear and declared wickedly, "Lanzhou, you're blushing."

NEW BLADE

WAVES CRASHED through the still waters of Shen Zechuan's heart. Lying in the pocket of his sleeve, that handkerchief seemed to have caught fire; the flames burned right up to his ears. Shen Zechuan knew even the hint of a flush against the snowy backdrop of his skin was eye-catching. Any denial would be unconvincing.

Xiao Chiye had led him right into this predicament. There was nowhere to hide—bright mirrors seemed to surround them on all sides. He looked as if he was waiting for Shen Zechuan to cast aside his protective shell and reveal his true colors.

Shen Zechuan licked his lips to chase away the dry heat in his throat. Curling his fingers, he ignored the provocation; he refused to give Xiao Chiye a chance to pry further. "It's getting late," Shen Zechuan declared. "Let's go get them."

Xiao Chiye watched him. Shen Zechuan's unspoken *I'm ignoring you* itched at him; it stirred up his desire to chase his momentum to victory. Haste, however, was no path to success, and impulsiveness would only lead to pitfalls. He had to let this one go.

"Our shifu have their own arrangements; there's no need to worry about them. If you want to sleep, take your time here; the east wing has been vacated."

Shen Zechuan stood at once.

Ji Gang and Zuo Qianqiu had shared so many rounds they would be drunk well into tomorrow. Shen Zechuan helped Ji Gang up into the carriage to head back.

Xiao Chiye watched them go. When they were alone, he said to Chen Yang, "Keep a close eye on the Eight Great Clans for the next few days; see who's on the move."

Chen Yang nodded his acknowledgment.

Carriage swaying around him, Shen Zechuan closed his eyes to rest. They made a detour to change to their own smaller, nondescript carriage before finally arriving at the Temple of Guilt.

Qiao Tianya carried Ji Gang on his back into the courtyard. Ge Qingqing had been waiting half the night; when he saw them, he started forward.

"It's all right," Shen Zechuan assured him. "Shifu is just drunk."

Standing under the eaves, Grand Mentor Qi called, "Qingqing, help Ji Gang inside and let him sleep it off."

Ge Qingqing took Ji Gang from Qiao Tianya and carried him into the house. Freed of his burden, Qiao Tianya fell to his knees in the snow. "Has Grand Mentor been well?"

"All is well upon seeing you." Grand Mentor Qi lifted a hand. "Now that you've changed your name to Qiao Tianya, that indenture is no longer of any use. Yet for that bit of sentiment, you stayed. I should thank you."

"To Grand Mentor Qi, those past events were the effortless lift of a finger, but to me, it was the kindness that saved my life." All signs of frivolity had vanished from Qiao Tianya's face. "That year, when the Guangcheng Emperor sentenced corrupt officials to death and my father and brother were framed, if it hadn't been for the grand mentor's integrity and willingness to help us, all twenty members of the Qiao Clan would have met an unjust death before the Meridian Gate."

"Your father and brother were both upright and loyal subjects. The false charges against them wouldn't have stuck. Even without me, they would've been safe and sound."

Qiao Tianya paused for a long moment before he countered respectfully, "The Qiao Clan cannot thank Grand Mentor enough for his kindness."

During the years of Yongyi, when Qiao Tianya's father still served as an official in the Ministry of War, the Guangcheng Emperor dealt harshly with any whiff of corruption. The Chief Surveillance Bureau had received reports that Qiao Tianya's father was in possession of properties and lands of unidentified origin. His father was helpless against the accusations until Qi Huilian had the case reinvestigated and cleared the names of the senior Qiao and a few others from the Ministry of War. Afterward, Qi Huilian betrothed his daughter to the eldest son of the Qiao family.

Yet this was not the end of the matter. A few years later, the Eastern Palace was itself falsely accused, and Qi Huilian was demoted from grand mentor to a commoner; when he retreated into the Temple of Guilt with the crown prince, the senior Qiao defected to the empress dowager.

The Eastern Palace fell, and Empress Dowager Hua leveraged Pan Rugui's authority to order its remaining followers investigated in the name of the Guangcheng Emperor. Despite throwing in with the empress dowager's faction, Qiao Tianya's father was imprisoned again. This time, there was no Grand Mentor Qi to plead his case; both he and his eldest son were beheaded and the rest of the Qiao family banished to Suotian Pass. Qi Huilian's daughter—Qiao Tianya's eldest sister-in-law—perished on the journey.

"Let's not talk of the past." Grand Mentor Qi tugged at his snow-white hair. "It can't have been easy for you to break free of your low caste, so now you must think this through. Once you decide to serve Lanzhou, it will be a lifelong commitment—your life and death will no longer be your own."

A gust of wind ruffled Qiao Tianya's hair and he grinned, wide and unrestrained. "Grand Mentor, I have no home to return to. In this lifetime, I've received too many favors from both you and my sister-in-law, sinful debts I had no way of repaying. Now I can be of use, and I shall dedicate my life to my master. Qiao Songyue died alongside his sister-in-law in the Cangjun Commandery. Today's Qiao Tianya is merely a blade. A blade knows not life or death, let alone freedom. These are dark times, and trouble looms like clouds shadowing our road. I urge you to wield this blade as you please."

Grand Mentor Qi took a slow step out from under the eaves. One hand on the pillar for support, he looked toward Shen Zechuan. "Lanzhou, this year is almost over. Xiansheng has yet to give you a gift to celebrate your coming-of-age."

Shen Zechuan's sleeves billowed in the wind. He seemed to know what came next.

Grand Mentor Qi continued, "You can stand on your own now, but this road will be long. Killing your sworn enemies, dismantling the Eight Great Clans, overturning wrongful judgments, bringing peace to Zhongbo—none of it will be easy. Ji Gang means to give you a blade, and so do I. Receive it well."

Fine snow fell over the courtyard. Shen Zechuan looked down and let Grand Mentor Qi lay cold fingers atop his head.

Ji Gang didn't wake up until dinner. After some congee, he called Shen Zechuan into the house.

"Do you remember the blade I mentioned last time? I hadn't forgotten it. It was delivered last night." Ji Gang shifted aside a shelf to reveal a saber rack.

Shen Zechuan's heart stirred. He found he could no longer move his eyes away from this saber.

Ji Gang wiped a clean cloth along the blade's edge. "Ji Lei couldn't use it, but this blade suits you very well. I had someone re-forge the sheath. Its old name is no longer appropriate; you should give it another."

Shen Zechuan studied the lustrous blade with fascination. It was a straight blade that spanned almost four chi[5]—unsheathing it would have to be quick work, though its width of only two fingers meant it would be especially maneuverable for swift attacks. The sandalwood hilt was newly constructed. It was bare of any carvings; its only embellishment was the gold plate at the top of the hilt and a single pearl embedded in the center.

It was an excellent saber, expertly forged and thoroughly tempered. Even left to gather dust for so long, its naked blade radiated a grim, imposing presence. It was as if it were immersed in a clear stream on an autumn day: pristine, untainted, and haughty, as though it knew it was without peer.

"Something's bothered me recently, but I only put my finger on it when I saw Xiao Er last night. I've been too inflexible in my teachings, and so you've become overly cautious and hesitant." Ji Gang laid down the cloth. "With this blade, not even Xiao Er's Wolfsfang will be a match for your draw speed. The sandalwood hilt is lighter than steel; it will allow you to be more agile. When it comes to martial arts, nothing can beat speed. This was my father's beloved blade. Nowadays, we say the Ji Clan's martial arts should

---

5 尺, *chi, an ancient measure of length. One chi is approximately 13 inches.*

be ferocious, but those mental cultivation techniques were my father's own creation. If he could do it, so can you—you, too, can carve your own path."

Grasping the hilt of the blade, Shen Zechuan lifted it before him.

Ji Gang took a few steps back. "Give it a name."

"Shifu would give me a blade of this caliber?" His hands on the blade were reverent.

Ji Gang laughed heartily. "Shifu would rather use his fists; I don't like blades. It would be wasted on me."

Shen Zechuan thought for a moment. "Then I shall name it Avalanche."

That night, Grand Mentor Qi sat on his heels atop the table, writing the surnames of the Eight Great Clans on a piece of paper.

"The Court Officials' Feast is fast approaching. The Four Great Generals will be reunited, and the regional officials will return to the capital as well." Grand Mentor Qi continued as he waited for the ink to dry, "With the coronation of the new emperor, there will surely be a formal review of his officials. This matter is of utmost importance and will determine political stability over the next year. Everyone will use the days around the Officials' Feast as an opportunity to reassess the situation in court. If the empress dowager wishes to stage a comeback, this is her chance."

"After Hua Siqian's death, the empress dowager was confined to the palace and hasn't shown her face since." Shen Zechuan furrowed his brow. "The younger members of the Hua Clan have all been demoted and banished. If she intends to make a move, she will have to find external allies. But the example of Xi Gu'an is fresh in everyone's mind; who would dare side with the empress dowager now?"

"Cowardly vermin will not achieve greatness. All alliances are motivated by mutual benefits. As long as the empress dowager still holds bargaining chips, why would she worry about finding new allies?" Grand Mentor Qi put down a few strokes on the paper under *Hua*. "Moreover, the men of her clan were never dependable to begin with. You've forgotten; the one the empress dowager has been personally mentoring is a girl."

"The third lady," Shen Zechuan said. "Xiansheng refers to Hua Xiangyi."

"Given the height of her favor during the Xiande Emperor's reign, many thought Third Lady Hua would be conferred the title of imperial princess," continued Grand Mentor Qi. "But it didn't happen—not because the Xiande Emperor was stingy, but because the empress dowager wouldn't allow it."

Shen Zechuan took a mouthful of tea, contemplated for a moment, then swallowed it. "I understand."

"Then let's hear it."

Shen Zechuan propped an arm on his knee. "If Hua Xiangyi had become a princess of Great Zhou, her marriage would be out of the empress dowager's hands. The marriage of a princess is a state affair, subject to the discretion of the emperor and his court officials. But if she remains Third Lady Hua, the empress dowager alone decides whom she will marry. Xiansheng suggests that the empress dowager plans to marry her off."

"If the mountain does not come to me, then I will go to the mountain," Grand Mentor Qi said, dipping his brush in ink. "The empress dowager has sacrificed a pawn to save a rook. With Xi Gu'an's loss, she's given up military hold of Qudu—but if Hua Xiangyi marries Xiao Chiye, the loss is easily resolved."

Shen Zechuan tapped lightly on his teacup and lowered his lashes. "This endeavor is harder than ascending to heaven. Xiao Er will never hand over power to someone else."

"I've heard Hua Xiangyi is lovely enough to bring whole cities to ruin," Grand Mentor Qi pointed out. "There's no guarantee Xiao Er won't change his mind once he sees her."

Shen Zechuan sipped his tea and kept very quiet.

"But it is indeed no easy feat," Grand Mentor Qi conceded. "Even if Xiao Er were to well and truly fall for her, Xiao Jiming won't sit idly by. Xiao and Hua are as incompatible as fire and water; there's no reason for the Xiao Clan to bury the hatchet when they hold the advantage."

Shen Zechuan thought it over. "It might be worth it to the empress dowager to sacrifice military power to gain more control of the central administration. But there are very few exceptional up-and-coming officials, and Hai Liangyi still heads the Grand Secretariat. The empress dowager can't be expected to lower Hua Xiangyi's status by making her someone's concubine. It really does seem that in all of Qudu, there is no other fitting candidate for a groom."

"If not in Qudu, she can look elsewhere." Grand Mentor Qi wrote the word *Qidong*. "If Libei won't do, there's still opportunity on the other frontier."

"Marshal Qi and Lu Guangbai are both unmarried," Shen Zechuan agreed. "In that case, it can only be Lu Guangbai. However, the Lu and Xiao Clans share a friendship that goes back decades; it's not the kind of relationship that can be picked apart with one move."

"Why have you dismissed the Qi Clan?" Grand Mentor Qi grumbled. "There are others there besides Qi Zhuyin."

Shen Zechuan's mouth dropped open in astonishment. "It can't be..."

A few days later, Xiao Chiye accompanied Li Jianheng out of the city to welcome the two generals from Qidong. Lu Guangbai rode at Xiao Chiye's side on the way back. Removing his helmet, he said, "I heard some news on the way here. Do you know anything about it?"

Xiao Chiye spurred his horse forward. "What?"

Before Lu Guangbai could speak, Qi Zhuyin galloped up behind them and slapped him on the back.

"Marshal!" Lu Guangbai yelped in pain.

A rare scowl creased her brow. Resting a hand on her blade, she leaned toward Xiao Chiye. "When did these rumors start in Qudu?"

Xiao Chiye blinked back at her, increasingly baffled.

Qi Zhuyin clenched her jaw and fumed, "Someone's going to be my stepmother."

Stunned, Xiao Chiye blurted, "Old Marshal Qi is taking a new concubine?"

"Concubine, ha!" Qi Zhuyin sneered. "They're saying he's going to remarry! Third Lady Hua will be my stepmother. Isn't she younger than I am?"

BANQUET

HUA XIANGYI was indeed younger than Qi Zhuyin—by two years. Her recent days residing deep in the inner palace had thinned her considerably. When she saw Qi Shiyu's portrait on the empress dowager's desk, realization finally dawned on her.

The empress dowager took her hand and held it for several moments before saying, "It's a spring-and-winter marriage, but Qi Shiyu is doting."

Hua Xiangyi settled her lilac palace robe and laid her head on the empress dowager's knee. A hand came down to stroke her long hair. "No need to be sad," the empress dowager continued. "This is how all the Hua Clan's daughters marry. Marry him now and in a few years, you will become the true mistress of Qidong and its five commanderies."

Aunt Liuxiang finished lighting the incense in the hall and silently motioned for the maids and eunuchs to vacate the room.

"I just can't bear to leave you, Auntie." Hua Xiangyi smiled. "Cangjun Commandery is so far away; I'll have to wait a year whenever I wish to see you again."

"Auntie can't bear for you to leave either." The empress dowager wrapped gentle arms around her. Hua Xiangyi nuzzled against her as she had when she was a little girl, listening dutifully as the empress dowager said, "When I left Dicheng and married the Guangcheng Emperor, I was but fifteen. I couldn't bear parting with the swing in our manor. I loved being on it; with each rise and fall, I could feel the wind and hear the clamor beyond those high walls. My mother promised me that when I came to the imperial palace of Qudu, if I wished, the emperor would build me one just like it."

Hua Xiangyi stayed perfectly still.

The empress dowager had been most favored by the Guangcheng Emperor, yet what he'd given was not what she'd wanted. The moment she'd set foot in Qudu, she realized her husband's doting affection was as fleeting as clouds in the sky. She had been left to vie with countless women in the imperial harem for a single moment of happiness.

In Qudu, love was the most worthless thing of all.

The empress dowager patted Hua Xiangyi's head. "It's already been thirty-seven years since I came to Qudu—it's passed in the blink of an eye. Now my baby niece is to wed; I've truly grown old. Here, I learned that men are powerful in this world because they can take the imperial exams and rise above their station; they can wield spears and ride horses into battle. Meanwhile, we women are kept in lady's chambers and taught virtues and precepts. No matter how talented you are, how keen your intelligence or thirst for knowledge, there will come a time when you eventually must marry."

The empress dowager's eyes were calm. "My father taught me that in this world, he and the emperor were the sky above my head. How ridiculous. Becoming empress means the empire is shared equally between the emperor and me. Who could be the sky above my head? No one! My brothers are useless; not one good head on all their shoulders. For generations, the Hua Clan relied on marrying daughters out to keep up the appearance of an affluent clan, yet we aren't permitted to make a single complaint. What kind of kinship is that?

Well if the world determines success purely by strength, then I, too, can emerge victorious."

She stroked Hua Xiangyi's temples. "Remember: it is not Qi Shiyu who chose you, but you who chose him. I may yet be defeated in days to come, but it certainly won't be now. My precious niece is not fleeing desperately to Qidong; you go there now to bide your time and ready yourself for action. Whatever happens in the future, you may sigh, but you mustn't wallow in resentment and self-pity. This is a game with the world at stake; once you make a move on the board, there's no going back. Wolves surround us at every turn, but we shall fight them to the bitter end."

The bamboo chimes in the hall swayed in the breeze. Hua Xiangyi squeezed the empress dowager's hand. "I will not forget Auntie's teachings."

The Court Officials' Feast was held on Yuanchun, the first night of the year. Local officials flooded into the capital in a steady stream. All were aware Hai Liangyi was keeping close watch on them this year, and there were thus far fewer family feasts and informal banquets—any sort of gathering could become evidence of clique-forming.

Li Jianheng had ascended the throne mere months ago; for many, the Court Officials' Feast was their first opportunity to observe their new master. Everyone spoke and acted with caution, unsure which way the wind was blowing in Qudu. Only the rumor of Third Lady Hua's betrothal spread like wildfire—leaving Qi Zhuyin with nowhere to vent her displeasure.

This matter also piqued the interest of Xiao Chiye, who had been looking into the Eight Great Clans in secret. When Xiao Jiming arrived in the capital, the brothers sat together in the manor for a leisurely chat.

"The Hua Clan is obviously trying to rise from the ashes. No matter how much of a lecher old Commander Qi is, there's no way he'll agree to this marriage," Xiao Chiye mused, looking over the Libei Armored Cavalry's expenditure accounts for the year.

Xiao Jiming sat at the desk, going through military papers. "It's hard to say."

Xiao Chiye raised his eyes. "How would this benefit Qidong?"

"You've been in Qudu this long and have taken command of the Eight Great Battalions." Xiao Jiming didn't look up from signing documents. "Haven't you reviewed the Eight Great Battalions' accounts?"

"The Court of Judicial Review showed them to me during their cleanup. All the surplus money and provisions from the Eight Great Battalions were supplied to the Imperial Army this year to make up our shortfall. Why do you ask?"

Xiao Jiming pondered the document in front of him. "When Hua Siqian was still alive, the annual salary and provisions budget for the Eight Great Battalions was several times that of the Bianjun Commandery. That money Xi Gu'an couldn't account for—where's it gone? Hua Siqian kept two account books; couldn't the empress dowager have done the same? Money flows in and out, but the audit remains a constant. As long as Hua Siqian instated his own man as the auditing official reviewing the ledgers of the Eight Great Battalions, they'd have been able to write anything they wanted in the annual accounts. The properties under the Hua Clan might be searched and their possessions confiscated, but who dares touch the empress dowager's private coffers? That money is Hua Xiangyi's dowry. Whether for official or personal reasons, Qi Shiyu ought to be tempted."

"Qi Zhuyin is the current grand marshal of Qidong's five commanderies," said Xiao Chiye, displeased. "She will never agree to it."

Finally, Xiao Jiming looked at Xiao Chiye. "Even if she disagrees, she can't stop it."

Xiao Chiye lay back and thought for a spell. "We've been on good terms with the Qi Clan for years now. If Qi Shiyu really marries the third lady, Qidong will no longer consider Libei a brother in arms."

"That's of little importance. Once the Biansha tribes attack, everyone will still have to fight side by side. And with Third Lady Hua on their side, the Qidong Garrison Troops won't lack for money."

"Then tell them to pay for Libei's horses in the future." A cold glint shone in Xiao Chiye's eyes. "How long can the empress dowager's private coffer last them? Providing for two hundred thousand soldiers isn't like raising a dozen lap dogs. The military expenditure will shock her; a single person can't possibly sustain it."

"With the Qi Clan backing her, the empress dowager has the means to break the stalemate in Qudu. Once power returns to her hands, she'll easily recoup the money."

Xiao Chiye sat up. "This union must not be."

"There are ways, of course."

Xiao Chiye looked at him. "The easiest is to kill Third Lady Hua."

Xiao Jiming glanced up at him in surprise. "You are also a thorn in others' flesh; the Eight Great Clans would be all too happy for you to give them an excuse."

"The rumors are everywhere. If we try to stop it after the new year, it'll be too late."

Xiao Jiming pondered in silence. Finally he said, "If the empress dowager wants this union, she must make an appearance, and the Court Officials' Feast is her only opportunity. Given what's at stake, Hai Liangyi may not be willing to let it happen. When the time comes, there will be a war of words."

"Some of the last three generations of Hua daughters were married out to Qidong. If we delve deep enough in the records of the Ministry of Rites, Third Lady Hua may turn out to be Qi Shiyu's distant blood relative." Suddenly, Xiao Chiye set aside the ledger and laughed. "Yes, I *want* Third Lady Hua to become a distant blood relative of Qi Shiyu. This marriage must not come to pass."

Xiao Chiye got up and opened the door to summon Zhao Hui.

"It's the Spring Festival," Xiao Chiye said. "You haven't gone to see your younger sister yet."

Zhao Hui turned to Xiao Jiming, who smiled. He understood. "I'll pay her a visit tomorrow morning."

Han Cheng, third son of lawful birth from the Han Clan of the Eight Great Clans and erstwhile assistant commander of the Eight Great Battalions, had only recently taken up his position as the new chief commander of the Embroidered Uniform Guard. He had happened to be off duty during the Autumn Hunt, so he did not follow Xi Gu'an, nor did he heed the empress dowager's commands. Rumor had it that he was still asleep when the Imperial Army knocked on his door. By sheer dumb luck, he had escaped the autumn wind that swept the Hua faction clean.

Shen Zechuan, however, knew this man was Xue Xiuzhuo's plant.

On the eve of the Court Officials' Feast, the Embroidered Uniform Guard sorted out their patrol schedule. Shen Zechuan had planned ahead to stay close to the throne, so it came as no surprise when he received the authority token.

Han Cheng personally delivered it to Shen Zechuan in the Embroidered Uniform Guard's office. "The candles stand ready; they lack only the match. I'll be on duty at the banquet too. No matter what, His Majesty mustn't come to harm."

"Of course." Shen Zechuan affixed his authority token to his waist and said with a smile, "We're depending on you, Your Excellency."

Even if Han Cheng was apprehensive, he couldn't show it. He simply repeated, "If anything goes awry tonight, it's a death sentence for us both. But if we succeed, the Embroidered Uniform Guard can swipe some of our own back from the hands of the Imperial Army. Everyone will live well after that, and good days will be upon us."

"Please rest assured, Your Excellency," Shen Zechuan said, solemn. "We brothers here are of one mind. Nothing will go wrong."

Seeing how composed and confident he was, Han Cheng breathed a sigh of relief.

The snow fell fast and thick outside; it was still falling when dawn broke on the day of the feast.

Before the Court Officials' Feast began, the emperor performed the sacrificial ceremony to the gods and ancestors. The Imperial Army stood at the ready; they had been on full alert since early morning. Dressed neatly in his court attire, Xiao Chiye came face to face with Han Cheng as he stepped through the palace gates. As they exchanged greetings and small talk, Xiao Chiye spotted Shen Zechuan behind him.

"The Left Guard stands before the throne," Xiao Chiye said to Han Cheng, eyeing Shen Zechuan as if he were a stranger. "Why has the position been assigned to an Embroidered Uniform Guard below the rank of company commander?"

"The Embroidered Uniform Guard has been reorganized; many positions are vacant," Han Cheng said, following the line of Xiao Chiye's gaze. "Everyone on duty today is a first-rate expert. They may appear junior in rank, but many of them are only being kept back to await the right time for promotion."

Xiao Chiye was wary the instant he laid eyes on Shen Zechuan, but his authority over the Embroidered Uniform Guard didn't extend to commanding a change in post; no matter how many pegs the Embroidered Uniform Guard had been knocked down, they and the Eastern Depot served directly at the emperor's pleasure. Unless Li Jianheng said something, anyone who gave summary orders would be overstepping their authority.

As if sensing his thoughts, Shen Zechuan glanced over at him, eyes heavy with some meaning Xiao Chiye couldn't read.

Ahead of them, the Elephant-Training Office had already herded the animals out. Li Jianheng was about to step out of the hall. Unable to linger, Xiao Chiye marched away.

Today was the first time Li Jianheng had held the ceremonial greatsword; it was so heavy he could barely lift it. He hadn't even stepped out the doors of the palace hall, yet he could already feel his neck aching from the weight of the crown atop his head. The coronation robe, with its sun and moon on either shoulder and stars heavy across his back,[6] had finally smothered his usual carefree attitude and given him a trace of sober, imposing bearing.

Palms sweating, Li Jianheng adjusted his hold on the greatsword before stepping over the threshold.

The court elephants, draped with red velvet and gold saddles, flanked the path. Hundreds of officials in the courtyard kowtowed and chanted wishes of longevity. Li Jianheng stood atop the steps, taking in the panorama of thick clouds in the east, the sky and earth cloaked in a blanket of boundless snow. From where he looked down

---

6 Part of the Twelve Symbols of Sovereignty on the emperor's ceremonial robe. In addition to the sun, moon, and three stars, others include a dragon, a pheasant, a mountain, a pair of goblets, seaweed, an axe head, and a traditional fu symbol.

high above them, he seemed to float among the clouds. The deafening chants of "Long live Your Majesty!" reverberated in his ears. Li Jianheng's heartbeat quickened, and a surprised pleasure gradually crept over his face. His eyes moved from Hai Liangyi down to Xiao Jiming, to all the living creatures of the world kneeling before him, the one and only supreme ruler.

So this is how it feels to be emperor.

He couldn't help but grasp the greatsword tighter. Standing on the receiving end of this grand show of obeisance, he felt as if he really had obtained the strength and courage to contend with the heavens. It was entirely unlike the feeling of sitting in the Imperial Court; it was the same thrill he had felt as everyone dropped to their knees before him for the first time at the Autumn Hunt.

Li Jianheng made his way slowly up the long staircase toward the ceremonial terrace, reveling in every step of this journey covered in glory.

Of the tens of thousands at his feet, only Shen Zechuan slowly raised his head. He looked past Li Jianheng and saw not only the tall stairs but also the dark, threatening sky lurking behind the dancing snow.

As the feast began, the Court of Imperial Entertainments brought out dish after dish, while the Winery kept the cups filled to the brim. Li Jianheng was fond of sweets, so the Imperial Bakery had produced quite a number of silk-nested tiger's eye candies.

Li Jianheng sat on the dragon throne. The empress dowager and Hua Xiangyi sat beside him, followed by Mu Ru, who had just been conferred the title of imperial concubine. Shen Zechuan and Han Cheng stood at the bottom of the steps, facing the Imperial Army. A eunuch from the Imperial Food Service knelt behind

Shen Zechuan's right shoulder; every dish on Li Jianheng's table had to be tasted before he could eat.

The emperor was in high spirits. The wine had gone to his head, and he repeatedly urged all in attendance to drink up. Looking down from the high dais, he said, "Ever since we ascended the throne, we've been fortunate to be assisted by wise and capable hands. With a clear mirror like Secretariat Elder Hai by our side, we daren't forget to self-reflect for even a day."

He had a habit of shooting his mouth off as soon as he drank too much, and today was no exception. "We are incredibly grateful to Secretariat Elder Hai and wish to regard Secretariat Elder Hai as the Second Father of the court. Such an honor has never been accorded to other secretariat elders in the past, but today, we shall—"

Second Father!

How could he say such a thing?! The color drained from Hai Liangyi's face. Before Li Jianheng finished, he had already risen to his feet in astonishment, about to kneel in protest.

Li Jianheng let out a drunken belch, waving his hand unsteadily. "There's no need for that, Secretariat Elder. It's no more than what we should do..."

"I think it is improper." The empress dowager peered down at Hai Liangyi and paused a moment, taking in Hai Liangyi's shock. Turning to Li Jianheng, she murmured, "Secretariat Elder Hai is a leader revered by scholars across the land. His character is solemn and dignified. Since entering the court to serve as an official, he has conducted himself with virtue, always candid and resolute in his speech. Bestowing an address of *Second Father* on this kind of trusted aide may demonstrate Your Majesty's favor, but it would negate the secretariat elder's impartiality in his critiques."

Encouraged by her mild demeanor, Li Jianheng laughed. "The legendary King Xiang[7] valued loyalty and honored his advisor Fan Zeng as his second father. Today, we likewise wish to express our gratitude for the secretariat elder's wise counsel and address him as Second Father. It's meant to bring us closer, and the title itself would be an ever-present reminder for our own self-reflection! Come, Secretariat Elder, what say you?"

Head already sunk low in a kowtow, Hai Liangyi resolutely called out, "Absolutely not!"

Li Jianheng felt as if he had been doused with cold water. Such a sternly uttered refusal drowned his warm enthusiasm, turning it instantly to displeasure. His expression underwent several changes before he eventually bent his mouth in a smile. "It's only meant to signify how close we feel to the secretariat elder. What does it matter?"

"Your Majesty is the highest sovereign of the land, poles apart from King Xiang, a warlord of the past presiding over a narrow corner," Hai Liangyi said. "This old subject was born in the mountain ridges of Hezhou; I am but an uncouth, lowly servant of the throne. How could I share the address of *father* with the divine and sagely Guangcheng Emperor?!"

Li Jianheng's original intent was to curry favor with Hai Liangyi, and thus all the scholars in the land. He wished to demonstrate that he was not an idiot who disrespected the pursuit of knowledge. But clearly he had been limited in his readings; how could he have known a mere address would elicit such a vehement objection? All at once he was astride a tiger with no way to safely dismount;

---

7 *Xiang Yu was a powerful warlord instrumental to dismantling the Qin Dynasty. He was eventually defeated by Liu Bang, whom he attempted to assassinate at the famous Hongmen Banquet. Fan Zeng was Xiang Yu's closest advisor.*

the sheer awkwardness sobered him up several degrees. Awash in embarrassment, Li Jianheng attempted to gloss over the whole thing. "If the secretariat elder is unwilling, then forget it..."

"It is this old subject's opinion that those at the bottom will imitate the propensities of those at the top," Hai Liangyi continued. "If His Majesty establishes this precedent tonight, others will follow suit in the future. When that happens, cliques and factions will form, impede the court, and jeopardize the state. It has been merely a month since the dust from the Hua Faction case has settled. Past experiences must serve as a guide for the future, not be forgotten after a moment's peace. Truly, Your Majesty should've drunk more moderately tonight!"

Li Jianheng clenched the wine cup and surveyed the crowd below. It was only when he saw the officials hanging their heads and not daring to look directly at him that his fury eased. He couldn't vent his temper on Hai Liangyi, but neither did he want to acknowledge his fault. He shifted restlessly on the dragon throne. After tasting the sweetness of submission from all under the sun, how could he willingly accept such censure?

He was the emperor!

In the end, Li Jianheng swallowed the last mouthful of wine in his cup and said with reddened eyes, "Forget it. Help Secretariat Elder Hai back to his seat."

Hai Liangyi was well aware that this was not the right moment to admonish him, but it was hard to change his frank and outspoken nature. "This aged subject still has something to say."

Li Jianheng pressed his lips into a tight line and said nothing.

Silence reigned in the banquet hall. Hai Liangyi knelt where he was, awaiting the emperor's response. They were frozen in a deadlock. No one touched their chopsticks; even the reed pipes had stopped playing.

Suddenly, a sharp *clack* echoed through the hall.

Xiao Chiye had laid down his chopsticks on the table before him; now he barked out a boisterous laugh. "It delights me to no end to see such a close relationship between Your Majesty and the secretariat elder. A prime example of a sagely ruler and virtuous subject, their interplay as harmonious as that referenced in ancient writings. To be graced with such a wise ruler and upstanding official in our Great Zhou is an indication that a new age of prosperity is upon us."

"His Majesty's generous acceptance of open speech and criticism is a blessing to all his officials." Xue Xiuzhuo raised his cup. "On this New Year's night, why not raise a toast to this estimable scene?"

The officials lifted their cups and chorused their well wishes.

Li Jianheng was mollified somewhat by the sounds of the toast. When he saw that Hai Liangyi was still on his knees, he heaved a sigh. "Secretariat Elder, please rise."

The crisis had been smoothly averted. Eyes on Xiao Chiye, the empress dowager was quiet a moment before raising her voice in the hall: "That's right, our supreme commander is here. It's said that a man's ultimate destiny is in starting a family and establishing one's career. Does Ce'an have any young lady in mind?"

Shen Zechuan, too, glanced toward Xiao Chiye.

"Your Majesty." Xiao Chiye grinned without the slightest scruple. "Look at me! Which of the esteemed ladies in Qudu would be willing to lower themselves to marry me? Besides, I do not aspire to start a family or establish a career."

"The supreme commander is too modest," said the empress dowager. "Noble sons with your prospects are few and far between in the capital. And with that face, there are no shortage of beauties beckoning when you cross the bridge on the east street. Heir Xiao, if you leave him be, it may be too late."

Xiao Jiming was all politeness. "Our father thinks his temperament is too volatile yet. He fears A-Ye will hold a nice girl back."

The empress dowager turned to Li Jianheng with a smile. "See how none of them are in a hurry. Why, when the Prince of Libei was his age, he was already a few years into his marriage."

Li Jianheng had yet to recover from his previous setback and was still feeling low. Not daring to leave the empress dowager hanging, he glanced at Xiao Chiye and said, "Imperial Mother may not be aware, but Ce'an is reckless. Not just any noble lady from Qudu would be able to handle him."

"That's no way to look at things; you can't delay his marriage without good reason," the empress dowager chided. "It doesn't have to be a noble lady from Qudu. The Helian Marquis's daughter, Commandery Princess Zhaoyue, is around Ce'an's age; they'd make an excellent match."

The Helian Marquis was the Marquis of Chuancheng and a member of the Fei Clan, one of the Eight Great Clans. This seemingly casual suggestion from the empress dowager was indeed well-matched with Xiao Chiye in status.

Fei Kun, the Helian Marquis, promptly lifted his cup in a toast and glanced in Xiao Jiming's direction.

Xiao Chiye had expected the empress dowager to discuss Hua Xiangyi's marriage at the banquet, not his own. Outright rejection was not an option, but neither did he plan to go along with this haphazard arrangement.

"We—Princess Zhaoyue..." Caught off guard, Li Jianheng stuttered as he looked at Xiao Chiye in a daze. An idea struck him. "The nation is still in mourning. We're afraid it's not appropriate to confer a marriage at this time."

"It's one thing to confer a marriage and another to complete it.

There are no auspicious days coming up, anyway. We could establish the engagement first and wait for summertime to seek an auspicious day for the wedding." The empress dowager added affectionately, "Zhaoyue and Xiangyi are bosom friends from childhood. It would be a blessing for them to be married at the same time."

In saying nothing about whom Hua Xiangyi was marrying and pushing Princess Zhaoyue to Xiao Chiye, the empress dowager sent a clear message: Xiao Chiye's marriage was a state affair, while Hua Xiangyi's was a private matter.

Qi Zhuyin's expression was solemn, but she remained surprisingly quiet. As soon as Lu Guangbai saw this, he knew it didn't bode well. Qi Shiyu must've already given his approval for the betrothal and instructed Qi Zhuyin to say nothing. But this matter of marrying Princess Zhaoyue was completely out of the question. If this engagement was settled, the empress dowager could use the occasion of her marriage to elevate Zhaoyue's status from a commandery to a true imperial princess, a status equal to the emperor's sister or daughter. An imperial princess's husband had no power in the Zhou empire, only a title in name—Xiao Chiye would be stripped of the military power he had only just grasped.

The wine in Xiao Chiye's throat burned like fire. He had risen to his feet when the empress dowager spoke again. "Heir Xiao married the daughter of the Earl of Biansha from the Bianjun Commandery. Your son must be around four or five years old now, is that right?"

"He is four years old," Xiao Jiming replied.

"The son of the heir is already four years old, yet his uncle General Lu remains unwed." The empress dowager looked toward Lu Guangbai and added, "Bianjun is a desert land; standing guard there must take a great toll on the general. Surely seeing you properly wed would put the Earl of Biansha's mind at ease. General Lu is similar in age to Heir Xiao. Is it also not the general's aspiration to start a family?"

Lu Guangbai was momentarily lost for words. "Your Majesty—"

"Zhaoyue is a girl with a lively and playful disposition," the empress dowager continued. "It's true that Ce'an is quite reckless. The general seems much more reliable. But Ce'an, what do you think?"

If Xiao Chiye wouldn't marry Princess Zhaoyue, Lu Guangbai would have to. This trap laid over the banquet was designed to pin him down.

Xiao Chiye had sent Zhao Hui to bribe someone from the Ministry of Rites days ago. He'd only been waiting for Her Majesty to open her mouth tonight so he could testify to the fact that Hua Xiangyi was a distant blood relative of Qi Shiyu. With the laws of propriety and a generational gap blocking the way, the union would have fallen apart. But the empress dowager hadn't given him any chance to counter. Who would have guessed it would be *his* future at stake this evening?

As this dilemma pressed down on him, Xiao Chiye's gaze met Shen Zechuan's for the briefest flicker through the crowd—just long enough for him to catch the look in Shen Zechuan's eyes.

A eunuch from the Imperial Food Service was delivering new dishes on behalf of the Bakery, meekly dividing out the portion to be tasted for poison. He picked up the chopsticks and looked at Li Jianheng, an arm's length away from him.

Xiao Chiye took a step forward. "Your Majesty—"

Li Jianheng was frowning, listening to this confrontation play out. Suddenly he sensed the stillness of the eunuch beside him and glanced over. "What are you standing—"

In a blink, the eunuch clenched the gilded chopsticks in his fist and jabbed them toward Li Jianheng's neck.

Li Jianheng had no time to react. All he could do was watch as the sharp tip of those chopsticks came at him. His body stiffened and his eyes went wide; he couldn't move even a finger. In that fraction of a second as the color drained from everyone's faces, Avalanche sprang from its sheath, its straight blade glinting coldly. Li Jianheng's throat tightened around a scream; before the sound left his throat, hot blood spattered onto the front of his robe. Li Jianheng's shout burst from his lips:

"Guards—!"

The eunuch's head toppled from his shoulders and fell into Li Jianheng's lap. Gripping the arms of his throne for support, Li Jianheng breathed the stench of blood as hands grabbed the headless body about to pitch forward onto him. Shen Zechuan tossed the corpse aside, then turned and commanded coldly, "Protect His Majesty!"

Ge Qingqing drew his saber. A row of snow-white glints cut the air as the Embroidered Uniform Guard stepped between the throne and the Imperial Army, a solid and impregnable fortress shielding Li Jianheng.

Xiao Chiye could do nothing but look up the steps at Shen Zechuan over the heads of the Guard. The precarious balance they had maintained until this moment finally shattered. Shen Zechuan looked down from above with a meaningful smile, the look in his eyes heavy enough to trample Xiao Chiye's chest.

POWER STRUGGLE

LI JIANHENG, horrified, kicked the head away with shaking legs. He wanted nothing more than to cast aside appearances and curl up like a child on the dragon throne. Blood roared in his ears as he watched the scarlet stain soak through his robe. For a long time he couldn't utter a word, as if a hand grasped his throat.

Dropping to one knee, Shen Zechuan said solemnly, "Fear not, Your Majesty. The assassin has been slain. This humble subject was late to your rescue and should be severely punished!"

Li Jianheng's limbs were paralyzed; he struggled to hold onto the armrests. He looked away from the fallen corpse toward Shen Zechuan, half-choking with sobs as he grasped feebly at his savior's sleeve. "No...not late at all! You...Lanzhou, you've done well! We—we almost..."

"Summon the imperial physician!" The empress dowager hurried over, ignoring the corpse entirely. She held Li Jianheng's hand in her own and called out softly to him, "Your Majesty, Your Majesty..."

Still gripped by panic, Li Jianheng gulped through a dry throat and jerked his hand out from under the empress dowager's to grasp Shen Zechuan's sleeve more tightly. "Stay here," he pleaded. "Stay here with the Embroidered Uniform Guard to protect me!"

"The Embroidered Uniform Guard are the emperor's own guards," Shen Zechuan said without blinking. "For Your Majesty, the Embroidered Uniform Guard will willingly brave fire and flood. Allow this humble subject to escort Your Majesty back to Mingli Hall."

Everyone in the banquet hall was badly shaken. Xue Xiuzhuo stepped forward and barked, "Arrest and detain everyone from the Food Service, Court of Entertainments, Bakery, and Winery. To think there was an assassin hiding among the Son of Heaven's personal attendants—all those involved in arranging the inner palace eunuchs and guard detail will be held accountable!"

"Who was in charge of patrols tonight?" the empress dowager asked.

The banquet hall fell silent.

Xiao Chiye bowed. "Your Majesty, it was this subject."

The empress dowager did not pursue the matter further. Instead, she looked at Li Jianheng. The other officials all stared at him too.

For a eunuch to join the Imperial Food Service, he had to have a clean family background and personal history. His actions and demerits since the first day he'd entered the palace, where he'd worked in the Twenty-Four Yamen, and even which inner-palace eunuchs he'd been friendly with—all must be investigated. On top of that, everyone he came in contact with had to be checked and noted in the official record. Xiao Chiye was responsible for overseeing the security. He ought to have vetted everyone here before the Court Officials' Feast. The assassin had walked in through *his* layers of defenses; there was no way he could escape responsibility.

Pale and drenched in cold sweat, Li Jianheng said, "Take the eunuchs of the various offices into custody first. We..."

Before he could finish, he fainted dead away.

It was a sleepless night. Li Jianheng lay insensible in the inner chamber, imperial physicians hovering at his bedside, while the empress dowager once more listened to a diagnosis behind the hanging curtain. Hai Liangyi waited just outside the curtain with her permission.

Han Cheng led the Embroidered Uniform Guard to stand guard under the eaves, sabers in hand, while the court officials knelt outside. The first night of the year was bitterly cold. Many elderly officials were already shivering, propped up only by sheer force of will. An eerie silence filled the palace, adding another layer of cold to the night's chill.

Xiao Chiye was not among those shivering officials. He was needed by the Ministry of Justice and the Chief Surveillance Bureau to carry out arrests of the implicated palace eunuchs. The Imperial Army was likewise detained, and its assistant commander, responsible for screening those on duty tonight, had already had his authority token revoked and now sat in jail beside the eunuchs.

Inside the hall, no brazier was lit; the only light came from the lanterns.

Xiao Chiye sat to the right of Kong Qiu, the Minister of Justice. Cen Yu, the Chief Surveillance Bureau's Left Censor-in-Chief, and Fu Linye, the Right Censor-in-Chief, sat in the more prestigious position on Kong Qiu's left. Under normal circumstances, Xiao Chiye and the Minister of Justice would have conducted the trial together, with equal authority. Due to the conflict of interest this time, he had no choice but to accept this seating arrangement and hand supervisory power over to the two head officials from the Chief Surveillance Bureau.

This year had truly been a time of troubles, each fresh wave of problems arising before those that came before had subsided. The Three Judicial Offices had never presided over back-to-back cases like this before, especially major ones that concerned an emperor's life.

Kong Qiu finished his long-cold tea in silence as they waited for the next prisoner to be summoned. From the moment they sat down, they wore solemn expressions. No one made any small talk; everyone knew it was not the time to make light of things.

Xiao Chiye turned his thumb ring in contemplation. This was a premeditated act, just as Xiaofuzi's death had been. It had upended everything the moment it happened, but that instant was a careful facade—the work of countless strings pulled behind the scenes concealing an even deeper motive.

The inner palace eunuchs from the Imperial Food Service were charged with tasting dishes for the Son of Heaven. Each one, top to bottom, had been thoroughly vetted going back three generations. Turning such a person into an assassin would be terribly difficult—yet also very simple. Whoever incited them must be someone who came into contact with inner-palace eunuchs, or a eunuch who was working for powers on the outside. No one else could coerce or entice a eunuch into murdering the emperor.

Xiao Chiye suddenly recalled something. His fingers paused on his thumb ring just as the summoned prisoner was brought up: the assistant commander of the Imperial Army.

Kong Qiu wasted no words. "As the Imperial Army's assistant commander, you are responsible for evaluating the armed personnel of the Imperial Army who stood before the throne tonight, as well as the food-tasting eunuchs arranged by the Food Service. What do you know about this eunuch?"

The assistant commander was Meng Rui, a man from a military household whom Xiao Chiye had promoted in the sixth year of Xiande. He was a prudent man who had originally served as the office manager in the Imperial Army. He answered steadily, his gaze unwavering. "The eunuch assassin went by the name Guisheng.

He was twenty-six and came from the city of Chuncheng; his father was registered in a civilian household residing on Baishui Street and passed from illness in the sixth year of Xiande. Guisheng was his only child; he entered the palace during the Yongyi era and worked there for twelve years. He joined the Food Service in the first year of Xiande and started tasting dishes for the late emperor three years later. He had no unusual hobbies and associated with very few people."

Kong Qiu thought for a moment. "Who arranged for him to taste the dishes tonight?"

"A female attendant from the Food Service—Fuling."

First Kong Qiu looked at the men from the Chief Surveillance Bureau, then at Xiao Chiye. He nodded. "The weapon he used was the same gilded chopsticks reserved for imperial use. A body search by the Imperial Army would have found nothing. How about this: Assistant Commander Meng, please wait here. Summon Fuling from the Food Service."

Meng Rui stepped aside. Throughout, he never made eye contact with Xiao Chiye.

Anyone who had expected Xiao Chiye to be nervous would have been disappointed. He knew full well this assassination could not strip him of military power. Perhaps he would be punished with a salary cut, but that was far from a disaster. At the crucial moment, he had been too far away—there was no way he could have beaten Shen Zechuan to it and saved the emperor—so he was not derelict in his duty. The seating was arranged according to the demands of etiquette, so no one could fault him for his distance either. And there was one thing more: the speed at which Shen Zechuan had drawn his blade was much too fast. His saber had returned to its sheath before the assassin's head rolled. It was entirely beyond the speed he had exhibited that rainy night on the hunting grounds. Even if Xiao Chiye had been standing right beside him, he might not have beat him to the draw.

Thus the trial itself didn't worry him—what worried Xiao Chiye was what awaited after. His mind was already working to keep this fire from spreading to him.

He thought again of that look in Shen Zechuan's eyes.

The Embroidered Uniform Guard's usual practice was to have a period of promotion once every eight years. Members were assigned to one of the Twelve Offices according to the classification of their household register when they entered the Guard, then promoted according to performance; exceptions were rare. Shen Zechuan's family background was unusual to say the least. Although he was officially absolved of guilt, he didn't technically qualify for military status. If he wanted to command the Embroidered Uniform Guard, he had to find another avenue to promotion.

Xiao Chiye had been knocking the Embroidered Uniform Guard down for the past few months to consolidate the Imperial Army's monopoly over military power—but equally to guard against Shen Zechuan's advancement through the ranks. The political landscape in Qudu was chaotic, yet the divisions between factions were clear as night and day. Everyone was familiar with one another, and whether they collaborated or fought, it was all out of self-interest. Shen Zechuan was the sole unknown. Xiao Chiye had tried every possible method to sound him out, yet he still couldn't pin down Shen Zechuan's true goal.

Until he could work out Shen Zechuan's motives, any cooperation between them would be without trust. He had hoped Shen Zechuan would stay quietly at the bottom of the ladder; this assassination was his answer.

Impossible.

Shen Zechuan was his own blade; he would carve his own bloody path. He was not content to remain at the beck and call of others. He wanted to tear others apart, not obey.

What could one night of pleasure change? That was merely a howl of resentment vented in the pitch-dark night, an animal panting born of entangled desire. The rough union of their bodies had felt like the shared suffering of wounded creatures, but sentiment was not enough to turn either of them from their path.

Xiao Chiye would never give up the power he held; this was the blade on which his own survival depended. If he could not return to Libei, he must grasp this blade and never let go. Likewise, Shen Zechuan would never allow himself to kneel while others decided his fate. He wanted to rise through the ranks. He *had* to.

His fingers curled into a fist.

Shen Zechuan was at the heart of this plot. Who were his accomplices?

Leaving Li Jianheng under his physicians' care, Shen Zechuan hung up his token to get a little rest. As he wiped his hands in the duty office, he heard the creak of the door behind him.

"I thought we agreed Han Cheng should be the one who saved the emperor tonight." Xue Xiuzhuo rolled up his sleeves and slipped his hands into the cold-water basin in the room. He smiled. "We brothers have been played for fools by Lord Shen."

"The situation was critical." Shen Zechuan didn't look behind him. "If Han Cheng was capable, then of course he should have done the saving. But he was slow. What could I do?"

"This incident won't take Xiao Er down. At most, he'll be impeached for negligence in supervision. You, however, have shown your claws in front of him. Even if you move up the ladder now, he's bound to make things hard for you in the future."

"We're passengers in the same boat, Your Excellency. If he gives me a hard time," said Shen Zechuan, glancing back with a smile, "do you think you'll have an easy one?"

"I've heard there's a breed of mad dog ruthless enough to attack its brothers." Xue Xiuzhuo looked at Shen Zechuan. "It's being in the same boat as someone who will use one of his own without a second thought that keeps me from resting easy."

"What are you saying?" Shen Zechuan asked. "My brothers are precisely the ones who benefited from our actions tonight. As for me, am I not the painted target pushed before Xiao Er? From now on, I'm the thorn in Xiao Er's side. He ought to hate me to death."

"The friendship between His Majesty and Xiao Er runs deep. His rescue of His Majesty at the Nanlin Hunting Grounds is impossible to forget. You stood out tonight, but you can hardly replace Xiao Er."

"The first step is the hardest." Shen Zechuan smiled. "If His Majesty was truly so grateful to Xiao Er for saving his life, he wouldn't keep him trapped in Qudu. This thing we call gratitude is only worth so much."

Xue Xiuzhuo wiped his hands and laughed. "Despite the slight departure in execution, our plan was still a success. Please look out for me in the future, Lord Judge."

The judge of the Embroidered Uniform Guard was a fifth-rank official post; Xue Xiuzhuo was pointing out how high Shen Zechuan could rise once the emperor began conferring awards for this night.

Shen Zechuan's expression didn't change. "The eunuchs from the Food Service will have to stand trial. The Minister of Justice, Kong Qiu, is a principled man and impartial judge. Your people had better not buckle under his interrogation."

"Since we dared to do it, surely we don't fear an investigation." Xue Xiuzhuo rearranged his sleeves and offered courteously, "I hope we can continue to work together in the new year. May we soon achieve our hearts' desires."

Meeting his eyes, Shen Zechuan said genially, "I'm indebted to Your Excellency for your care. Have no doubt—I will fulfill my long-cherished wish."

48 MIND GAMES

THAT EVENING, Li Jianheng had a nightmare.

He dreamed of that rainy night at the Nanlin Hunting Grounds. Branches whipped harshly against his face as he frantically covered his head. The horse he rode galloped wildly onward. Li Jianheng was afraid; he wanted to hang on to the reins, but Xiao Chiye suddenly turned, grabbed him by the collar, and tossed him off the horse.

"Ce'an, save me!" Down in the mud, Li Jianheng pleaded on his knees. "Ce'an, Ce'an! We're brothers! Don't leave me here!"

Amid the flash of lightning and clap of thunder, Xiao Chiye's expression was as dark as the storm. Staring him down, he said coldly, "Knock him out; get him out of here!"

Li Jianheng watched through snot and tears as Chen Yang approached. He reared back, waving his arms as he shrieked, "I—I'm the emperor! How can you treat me this way?" His back bumped into something behind him. Whipping his head around, he saw the Xiande Emperor stooping to take his wrist. "Imperial Brother! Imperial Brother, save me!"

The Xiande Emperor tightened his grip, fingers digging into Li Jianheng's skin. Coughing blood, he spoke with an icy chill: "He who saves you today can kill you tomorrow! Do you understand?"

Pain shot through Li Jianheng's arm, but no matter what he did, he couldn't free his wrist from that grip. The rain turned thicker, sticky. Li Jianheng reached out; his palm came away scarlet with blood. He looked up and saw a head tumbling down from the darkness, landing in the dirt with a *thud*. With a sudden burst of strength, Li Jianheng tore himself free. He scrambled up from the mud, gasping and trembling, and kicked the human head aside. "I am the emperor," he shouted tearfully into the black shadows around him. "I—we are the Son of Heaven! Who wants to kill me? Huh?!"

"Your Majesty," a voice called softly. "Your Majesty."

Li Jianheng opened his eyes. He stared blankly at the golden ceiling above him, murmuring, "Who wants to kill me...who wants to kill me..."

The empress dowager was dabbing his sweat with a handkerchief. She leaned in to say, "Jianheng, Imperial Mother is here!"

Jianheng!

Sorrow washed over Li Jianheng. His mother had died early, and the Guangcheng Emperor had never once looked upon him seriously. He had indulged in play and pleasure all these years, but no one had ever addressed him so intimately.

"Imperial Mother." Li Jianheng's voice was thick with sobs. "Mother!"

The empress dowager turned her head slightly, as though to wipe away tears. "You were unconscious all night. I was truly afraid. If anything hurts, you must tell me."

Li Jianheng saw she was still wearing her formal robe from the banquet—she must have been at his side the entire night. As he levered himself up to sitting, he could see the gray hair at her temples and the redness at the rims of her eyes; she looked exhausted. Warmth bloomed in his chest. Li Jianheng wiped his eyes and clutched the empress dowager's arm. "I'm sorry to have worried Mother. I'm fine now."

Hai Liangyi had also been keeping watch all night, kneeling outside the curtain. When he heard Li Jianheng's voice, he sagged with relief.

Moments later, the palace maids entered to help Li Jianheng wash and dress. The empress dowager took the bowl of medicine from them and tasted it herself before feeding it, spoon by spoon, to Li Jianheng.

After finishing the bowl, his complexion, though still wan, had improved considerably. He slipped into his boots and walked out to where Hai Liangyi knelt. Touched, he stepped forward to help him up. "Secretariat Elder, we are well!"

Hai Liangyi almost couldn't stand after so long on his knees; Li Jianheng sent him to rest and dismissed the other officials kneeling outside as well. He kept only Kong Qiu, Cen Yu, and Fu Linye, who had investigated through the night.

"What have you found?" Li Jianheng asked, impatient. "Hurry and tell us, Minister Kong."

Kong Qiu kowtowed. "The Ministry of Justice has learned that the assassin was a eunuch named Guisheng. He was assigned to taste the dishes at the feast by Fuling, a female palace attendant of the Food Service."

"Female palace attendant?" Li Jianheng asked in astonishment. "Why would this female palace attendant want to harm us?"

"Her motive remains unknown," Kong Qiu replied.

"You found nothing more after investigating all night?" Li Jianheng probed anxiously.

Kong Qiu exchanged glances with the two men beside him. Finally he said, "Your Majesty, Fuling knew she couldn't escape the reach of this investigation; she ingested poison and destroyed her voice while waiting to accept her punishment."

"Why would she do such a thing?" Understanding suddenly dawned on Li Jianheng. "She's afraid of letting something slip under interrogation, so she rendered herself mute! There must be someone behind her!"

"Your Majesty is wise," Kong Qiu replied. "My two colleagues from the Chief Surveillance Bureau and I had the same thought. When we dug into her background, we discovered she has an elderly mother who resides in a corner alley off Donglong Street. Her dwelling is small, but it's still not something a mere palace attendant could afford. After some digging, this humble subject discovered Fuling did not buy the house herself; her mother is living there on credit from a broker on Donglong Street."

Li Jianheng was intimately acquainted with Donglong Street, and Kong Qiu's words immediately roused his suspicion. "If only she and her widowed mother are left, she can't have had anything of value to put up as collateral for a house."

"Exactly," Kong Qiu agreed. "This subject found many points of suspicion, so I summoned the staff from the brokerage for questioning and learned it was out of respect for the Imperial Army that the broker made this deal with her."

Li Jianheng's heart stuttered. He was on pins and needles; finally he asked, "What does this have to do with the Imperial Army?"

"One Yuan Liu, a sixth-rank judicial administrator of the Imperial Army's Judicial Office, is the one who made contact with the broker," Kong Qiu said. "Although Yuan Liu and Fuling weren't formally betrothed, there are long-standing rumors of an affair between them."

Li Jianheng suddenly stood. "Does Supreme Commander Xiao know?"

Kong Qiu knew the emperor was on good terms with Xiao Chiye. He couldn't tell if Li Jianheng intended to defend or condemn the man, so he answered truthfully. "The supreme commander claimed to be unaware of this matter."

Li Jianheng remained rooted to the spot. His face cycled through a number of expressions until at last he declared, "The Imperial Army is large. It stands to reason that he wasn't aware. Keep this matter quiet for now. You may go. Summon Han Cheng and Shen Zechuan. We'd like to reward them."

After trudging through a yard of hardened snow, Xiao Chiye kicked open the door to the prison. The guard inside had been warned of his arrival and hurriedly led Xiao Chiye inside.

The young woman Fuling, only twenty-three, was locked within. She had endured a grueling physical interrogation and now sat motionless on the hay, her bun disheveled.

Chen Yang took Xiao Chiye's cloak as he stepped into the cell. He cut an imposing figure at the best of times; now, the very sight of him in the doorway made Fuling tremble.

Xiao Chiye had a strikingly handsome face, and his complicated aura blended frivolity and ferocity. As a result, he could either present as a carefree young master or a chilling lord of the Asura. He switched masks freely, and once he did, even his smallest mannerisms would change to fit the role.

Right now, he was a rich young master passing by.

Xiao Chiye sized up the cell, bending slightly to peer through the narrow window. When he saw the only view it offered was the high walls of the prison, he immediately lost interest. He straightened to his full height, then turned and looked down at Fuling on the ground.

Fuling shrank back against the wall; even she could see this man's eyes were filled with an innate contempt.

"Female palace attendant of the Food Service," Xiao Chiye stated.

Fuling didn't raise her eyes from his boots.

Chen Yang brought a chair for Xiao Chiye. He sat, propping an elbow on one knee and gazing down at the top of Fuling's head. "Yuan Liu has a wife and a concubine, yet he still risked his job to arrange a residence for you. What kind of extraordinary beauty could you be to coax him into abandoning his whole life? Raise your head. Let me see."

Fuling huddled into herself and didn't respond.

Xiao Chiye leaned back. "He's old enough to be your father, and you're all right with that? A palace attendant is unlike a palace maid. When you'd served out your contract and it came time to leave, you could've married a proper man from a good background. Yuan Liu is an inconsequential sixth-rank official, and a military thug to boot. He has neither affluence nor influence. Are you blind or just infatuated to have chosen him?"

The cell was quiet.

"Let's set Yuan Liu aside. What could you possibly have used to convince Guisheng to commit a regicide? You have no money to bribe him with; someone else must have been the instigator. Your voice is gone now. You're a scapegoat whose fate was decided long ago. Your master is a brilliant manipulator, to use you as much as he can and kick you aside after. Whether you die is no concern of mine, but since you dragged me, Xiao Ce'an, into this mess, do you think I'll let you die easily?" Xiao Chiye chuckled. "I don't think so, little miss."

Chen Yang turned and nodded to the prison guard behind him. Shackles clanked as Yuan Liu, covered in filth, was dragged into view.

Yuan Liu scrambled toward Fuling. "You bitch! How could you smear me like this?!"

She trembled and tried to crawl away, pressed tight to the wall. Yuan Liu grabbed her ankle. "What am I to you? I treated you so well, and this is how you repay me!"

Fuling's tears fell without cease as she was dragged away from the wall. She kicked out at Yuan Liu and opened her mouth in a quiet, raspy scream. Yuan Liu held her fast. "When your mother was ill, I carried her to the physician on my back! I denied you nothing. You deceived me, and now you're trying to kill my whole family! Despicable woman!"

The shackles clanged again as Chen Yang pulled the raving Yuan Liu back. Arms still outstretched, he snarled, "You won't get away with this! Even when I'm dead I'll haunt you!"

Xiao Chiye, indifferent to the domestic drama playing out before him, peeked again through the small window and realized he could see a square inch of sky outside. There was no snow today; pale clouds piled up against the blue.

Yuan Liu knelt, bawling inconsolably. He crawled through the filth toward Xiao Chiye and kowtowed. "Supreme Commander, Supreme Commander! Forgive me this once! I'm begging you. I was bewitched and blinded by lust! I'll do anything to repay this mercy!"

Xiao Chiye looked down at him. "I'm not the one who holds your life in my hands. Spare me your begging and go beg her instead. Kowtow to her for the sake of the young and old in your family. Consider it a repayment of the debt you owe your wife and son for chasing your own pleasure behind their backs."

Yuan Liu turned to Fuling, sobbing and kowtowing. "Have mercy! Have mercy on me, please! I have nothing to do with this!

I'm begging you! I'm begging you! There are eight people in my family—I don't want them all to die here!"

Fuling wept, but she didn't look at him.

Tears streamed down Yuan Liu's dirty cheeks. Consumed by fear, he knocked his forehead against the ground until it bled. "Fuling—one night as husband and wife is worth a hundred days of affection! Even if we couldn't marry, the sentiments of these years remain! I'm begging you, please don't pin this on me! I'll be your son, your grandson in my next life! Have mercy! I gave that house to your elderly mother as a show of filial respect. How could you—" He was sobbing so hard he almost choked. "How could you use it to... to threaten my family's lives? Have you no heart?!"

Fuling, looking pained, spoke hoarsely; she turned and kowtowed to Yuan Liu too. Her mouth opened and shut, shaping a silent apology. Yuan Liu shuffled forward on his knees and grasped Fuling by the arms. Blood streamed down his forehead as he cried in despair, "I don't want your kowtows! I want you to explain! I don't want to die—Fuling! Don't ruin me!"

Xiao Chiye, judging this had gone on long enough, chimed in. "Plotting an assassination will not just land *you* a sentence of decapitation. If you want to die, it's your business, but it will be a pity for your elderly mother to endure the torture of interrogation at her age. Surely you know what kind of place the Imperial Prison is? If she falls into the hands of the Embroidered Uniform Guard, stripping her skin and pulling out her tendons are not out of the question."

Fuling threw her head back and wept.

"Did your master not tell you?" Xiao Chiye continued. "I'll make sure this case drags on without closing. Every day's delay is another day of punishment for you, for him, and for your mother. We won't say our goodbyes until I'm satisfied."

The girl sobbed hatefully at him. Xiao Chiye remained still and merely looked at her. "Isn't it said that before kicking a dog, you should look at his owner? Now that you've taken a bite of Xiao Ce'an, we shall all suffer together. I'll whip you until your skin flays open, until you'd rather die than live. Let's see who's more stubborn. Chen Yang, bring her mother in."

Chen Yang bowed his way out of the cell.

Fuling screamed. The poison had damaged her voice; the sound was the cry of a beast on the brink of despair. She charged toward Xiao Chiye, dropping to the ground and wildly scrawling out words with her fingers.

Xiao Chiye leaned over and watched for a while before saying, "Give her paper and a brush. I want this in black and white."

In the end, Chen Yang took Fuling away to sign her confession, leaving only Xiao Chiye and Yuan Liu in the cell. As Xiao Chiye was about to leave, Yuan Liu grabbed at the corner of his robe.

"S-Supreme Commander! Now that it's over with—does that mean I can..."

Settling his cloak over his shoulders, Xiao Chiye turned. "When did you take up the post of judicial administrator?"

"The third year after the supreme commander was appointed," Yuan Liu rushed to answer.

"I see. So you've been following me," Xiao Chiye said.

Yuan Liu nodded in a panic. "I'm the supreme commander's man!"

Xiao Chiye was tired and irritable after staying up all night. Hand on the hilt of his blade, he pushed away Yuan Liu's hand with the sheath. "My men don't have enough clout to keep a tab with brokers on Donglong Street. And in the Imperial Army, all newly bought estates have to be reported, but you didn't. Apart from that residence, you own farmlands outside the city. You're faring pretty well for a sixth-rank official. Are you really ignorant of who's feeding you?"

Tears and snot covered Yuan Liu's face as he wept. "I was deceived. I shouldn't have coveted those things, Supreme Commander! But I never betrayed the Imperial Army."

Xiao Chiye tilted his chin and stretched his neck, which was becoming sore. He didn't spare Yuan Liu another look. "How old is your son?"

"Four...four years old."

"I'll raise him for you," Xiao Chiye said expressionlessly. "When this case ends, you can end yourself too."

Yuan Liu collapsed limply to the ground as the cell door slammed shut.

Xiao Chiye strode through the dark, damp hallway of the prison, listening to the wails behind him as he took Fuling's confession from Chen Yang. He had just stepped out of the prison's main gate when he saw Gu Jin hurrying up.

"Gongzi," reported Gu Jin. "Fuling's mother is dead."

Chen Yang furrowed his brow. "It's fortunate Master came straight here instead of entering the palace this morning. If word had gotten out, Fuling would have no regrets, and we wouldn't have obtained this confession."

"It's only a stack of paper." Xiao Chiye flipped through the statement under the sunlight. "Fuling didn't even see the other person's face. We can't snare anyone with this alone."

"At least the Imperial Army is in the clear," Chen Yang said. "Master, will you present this to His Majesty?"

Xiao Chiye glanced at him. "Why must the Imperial Army be in the clear?"

Chen Yang and Gu Jin were dumbfounded.

"If I'm to be a caged beast, I should act the part." Xiao Chiye sneered. "They're in such a hurry to sling mud, but it's still not enough. I'll not only take this mud right in the face, I'll roll in it. The filthier, the better. Let them vilify me with their newly united front and think themselves accomplished schemers whose hand can cover all the eyes of the world. If they trample the supreme commander of the Imperial Army underfoot so easily, once His Majesty has a moment to think about it, he will be rightly suspicious and afraid. It's not even been half a year since the Hua Clan fell. Whoever seeks to form a new faction now is seeking their death."

COLD GLINT

By the time Xiao Chiye entered the palace that morning, Shen Zechuan had already had an audience with Li Jianheng in Mingli Hall, where he was conferred the title of fifth-rank judge of the Embroidered Uniform Guard. His wooden authority token was replaced with gold-plated bronze embossed with the image of a mythical one-horned xiezhi[8] amidst clouds; one side read *Guard*, while the other read *Emperor's Entourage*.

Han Cheng, who had received only monetary rewards, was deeply unhappy. He knew Shen Zechuan had used him as a stepping stone, but this same Shen Zechuan was now in the emperor's good graces; he couldn't afford to let ill will fester between them.

Back at the office hall, the other guards came forward one after another to congratulate him. Shen Zechuan thanked them all. When the men dispersed, Han Cheng said, "It's your first time carrying a gold token. There must be some matters you're unsure of."

Shen Zechuan assumed a mask of humility. "I'd be very grateful for Your Excellency's guidance."

Mollified by the flattery, Han Cheng went on, "This gold token for guards must be worn at the waist when you're on duty and should be

---

8 A legendary creature shaped like a goat or ox with one horn, known for its ability to tell right from wrong, or the guilty from the innocent, and for its habit of charging at and devouring corrupt officials.

tucked away when you're off the clock. It's customary for those who are part of the emperor's entourage to retain a post in the Twelve Offices. You can't behave like you used to; you have to be more prudent. You've carried out assignments in the past, but it's different now. If it's an arrest warrant, don't rush out to make the arrest; you must first head to the Office of Scrutiny for Justice and let the supervising secretary affix his signature. If it's an order that requires you to leave Qudu to investigate the case, before you leave, you must go to the Ministry of Justice and Chief Surveillance Bureau and get their signatures."

Shen Zechuan listened humbly.

When Han Cheng saw he was just as respectful as before his promotion, he couldn't help his urge to mentor this young talent. He continued, "In the past, the Eastern Depot lorded over us. Whenever we saw those eunuchs, we had to bow and pay our respects. But the Twenty-Four Yamen is vacant and unattended, and the Eastern Depot is an empty shell of its former self. They should bow to *us* now. You needn't play nice with the eunuchs. But there is one thing you must remember: although the Embroidered Uniform Guard takes orders from the emperor, we still have dealings with the Three Judicial Offices. Most of the time, when we travel to outside towns and cities for fieldwork, we go with a censor from the Chief Surveillance Bureau. Everyone's functions and authority may seem separate, but in fact, we all rely on one another. You must maintain a friendly relationship with the Three Judicial Offices on your assignments. Never lose your temper at them. If you get careless and cross them, you'll have a hard time with future cases."

Shen Zechuan already knew all these truths by heart, but he listened as intently as if this was his first time hearing them. Finally, Han Cheng decided to do him a favor and said, "If you need to build your team, just go to the duty office and choose from the register."

After thanking him, Shen Zechuan strolled along the veranda on his way out. He was in no rush to head to the duty office to choose his men. When he exited the palace gates, Xiao Chiye was in a carriage, waiting for him.

Shen Zechuan stopped in his tracks and made to turn around.

Lifting the curtain halfway, Xiao Chiye said casually, "Now that you've gotten a promotion and a raise, you're not too stingy to treat me to a drink, are you?"

Ding Tao and Gu Jin stood on either side of Xiao Chiye, eyes fixed on him like tigers watching their prey. Shen Zechuan scoffed a breath of cold air and replied calmly, "I'm not. In fact, I was just looking for you."

The two went back to the manor where Xiao Chiye had invited their shifu for a meal. The inside of the house had been cleared of tables and chairs. Small screens carved with ornate reliefs had been set up to partition the room into a square, and a low table with curved edges stood in the middle. It was simple yet elegant—a perfect place for a drink and a chat.

Both men eased off their coats in the warmth of the room. Xiao Chiye dropped cross-legged into his seat, casual and at ease, while Shen Zechuan sat on his heels, upright and proper. Xiao Chiye laughed. "You look more like a noble gentleman than I do. Do we have Ji Gang-shifu to thank for this too?"

It had all been beaten into him by Grand Mentor Qi's ruler. In lieu of answering, Shen Zechuan asked, "So why were you waiting for me by the gates today?"

Xiao Chiye looked on as a maidservant set out a hospitable meal, including a pot of bubbling stew. He waited until she shut the door behind her before saying, "Didn't you say you were looking for me? You first."

"You didn't come into the palace to see His Majesty today. If you were working all night, I assume you spent it in the prison." Shen Zechuan took a few sips of tea to warm himself. "Fuling was easy to crack, wasn't she?"

"Indeed." Xiao Chiye poured wine for himself. "So easy she doesn't seem like the kind of person you would use."

"An elderly mother and a soft heart—with so many points of leverage, someone like her is the easiest to control, but also the easiest to turn." Shen Zechuan smiled. "You're right. If it were me, I'd never use someone like her."

"Well, Shen Lanzhou." Xiao Chiye watched him as he drank, taking a moment to moisten his throat. "Rest easy; I wouldn't be surprised no matter *whom* you used."

"I'm human too." Shen Zechuan took the wine carafe from Xiao Chiye. "I still have some feelings."

"But you've reserved none of them for me," Xiao Chiye lamented.

Shen Zechuan slowly poured wine into his own cup. "The same goes for you."

"I've extended a hand to you repeatedly," Xiao Chiye said, genial, "but you turn a blind eye to my efforts. Are you so set on fighting me?"

Shen Zechuan put down the carafe and looked at him. "If you extend a hand only to offer me useless intelligence, it's a bit of a cheap alliance, no?"

"So you turned around and got into bed with Xi Hongxuan," Xiao Chiye scoffed. "What's so good about him? Is he better than your Er-gongzi?"

"Er-gongzi was more impressive when tyrannizing me," Shen Zechuan said. "But you can't blame a capable man for taking the top position."

"How could I bear to blame you?" Xiao Chiye asked through the steam from the pot between them. "You must be awfully put out that you didn't get to step on my throat last night."

"Not at all," Shen Zechuan answered with a smile.

"Sometimes, your eyes are so very ruthless." Before he could reply, Xiao Chiye continued, "But of course, a little ruthlessness lends flavor."

Shen Zechuan restrained himself a moment before retorting, "Then you certainly have peculiar tastes."

"Yours aren't bad either." Xiao Chiye's tone was heavy with suggestion. "This is the first time I've met someone who enjoys getting bitten."

"Let's stay focused," Shen Zechuan replied. "What did you want?"

"To have a drink," Xiao Chiye drained the wine in his cup, "and a little chat. Someone's behind that broker on Donglong Street. Whoever it is, they've minded their own business in the past, and everyone lived in harmony. But now they've a mind to pin this on me; of course I'll have to investigate them."

Shen Zechuan fished some greens from the pot.

"How strange that my investigation only led me to Xi Hongxuan," Xiao Chiye continued. "Last time we were here, you went out of your way to warn me that the Eight Great Clans would join forces against me, but then you turned right around and joined them in knocking me down. I thought and thought, yet I still couldn't figure out your motives—but as soon as I reversed the order of events, I understood."

Shen Zechuan ate fish as a cat would—neatly and prettily. Without raising his head, he murmured, "Mm-hmm," to indicate he was listening.

Xiao Chiye spun the wine cup round on the table. "The alliance of the Eight Great Clans wasn't the first step in your scheme to knock me down—knocking me down was the first step in your scheme for the alliance. That way, everything made sense. I was never your target. You urged Xi Hongxuan to ally with the other clans, but you also leaked that news to me. You wanted me to react and use my control over the Battalions as bait to convince the other clans against working with Xi Hongxuan. A classic strategy: divide and conquer. It's a trivial matter, using words to sow discord and sabotage a potential alliance of the Eight Great Clans. The grudges left behind from that fallout are the real prelude to your great undertaking."

Shen Zechuan glanced at him. "You came up with all this just because you found out Xi Hongxuan has ties to the Donglong Street broker?"

"Traces, like cobwebs, can never be wiped entirely clean," Xiao Chiye said. "When Xi Gu'an was in prison, Xi Hongxuan sold his brother in exchange for an official position. Now that I think about it, that must've been your suggestion too. Otherwise, Xi Hongxuan wouldn't heed your advice so readily."

Wiping his fingers with a handkerchief, Shen Zechuan thought for a moment. "The one he most readily listens to isn't me."

"At first I thought you were in a hurry to rise so it would be easier for you to investigate what happened in Zhongbo." Xiao Chiye poured more wine into his cup. "Who knew you'd have such a voracious appetite? How does dividing the Eight Great Clans benefit you? Qudu is surrounded by the eight cities; their existence predates the Li emperors. Take Hua Siqian's attempted coup at the hunting grounds: high treason, yet the empress dowager managed to emerge unscathed. Are you so deluded you imagine one man's schemes can break them up and oust them from power? Part the mists of Qudu and take a good look beneath. They've stood tall for several hundred years; their tangled roots snake deep into the ground."

Shen Zechuan's chopsticks stilled. He straightened his spine as though readying himself for a scholarly debate. He was not angry. In fact, he was very composed. "I'll ask you one thing."

A pause. "Go ahead."

"All along, the Xiao Clan and Hua Clan have counterbalanced each other. The Hua clan diminished following the events at the Nanlin Hunting Grounds, while the Xiao Clan's fortunes rose. But have you won?"

Xiao Chiye tightened his grip on the cup.

Night had descended outside, but the lamps in the room had yet to be lit. In the faint light from the window, Shen Zechuan's shadow was thin. "You're coming to realize it's not just the Hua Clan you're up against. Perhaps in the beginning, you could console yourself with the thought that the clans only wanted the Battalions. But you have only to look at Zhongbo to understand they want much more."

"There's no conclusive ruling on the defeat of Zhongbo." Concealed in the shadows, Xiao Chiye was briefly silent. "How can you be certain they were behind it?"

"A conclusive ruling—that's an exercise in futility," Shen Zechuan said. "We've all been through the case a million times trying to pin down the person at fault, but this was never something a single person could control. Besides, there's something about Zhongbo no one has puzzled out, even to this day."

"Why." It was a statement, not a question.

"Yes, why? Biansha stormed our border and entered our territory in a blow designed to destroy morale. The tens of thousands of lives lost in Zhongbo were only the first problem. More problems followed. Losing tax revenue from the six prefectures of Zhongbo in the years after the invasion, resettling the displaced populace, redistributing farmland, rebuilding the ruined cities and towns—this was a burden the state treasury couldn't bear, and thus Zhongbo became a gaping hole in the middle of the empire. The greatest difficulty lies in putting together another garrison to replace the troops lost. But without sufficient fighting power, Zhongbo will be defeated again. How long can the reinforcements from Libei and Qidong last? This directly concerns the safety of the capital. Did these questions not occur to anyone before Zhongbo's defeat, or is this exactly what the culprits had in mind? Perhaps the Eight Great Clans were not the direct instigators, but Zhongbo's fall couldn't have been accomplished without their power and influence."

He continued, "These clans have been involved in every spark of unrest since the formation of the empire. The Hua Clan's rise to power began twenty-five years ago, while the Guangcheng Emperor sat on the throne—the year the empress dowager murdered the crown prince, a virtuous and benevolent successor, to fortify her own power. But eighty years ago, during the Yong'an Emperor's rule, it was the Yao Clan who held sway over the imperial court. They were a prestigious clan that produced so many capable talents that the Grand Secretariat was known as the Hall of Yao. Then a hundred years ago, there was the Xi Clan, who became the master of our Great Zhou's granaries when Juexi opened the Port of Yongyi. They capitalized on the opportunity to claim the salterns along the coast of the Sea of Xuhai to the west and became the greatest business magnates in the land. Even the Li Clan had to borrow from them to pay for weddings and ceremonies of state. These periods of influence never came out of personal feuds. Rather, the clans took their turns at the top while emperors came and went. Since the beginning, none of these clans have truly been on the decline—they have only been dormant."

Shen Zechuan smiled wryly now. "Common households cannot produce noble sons. Very few officials capable of shaping Great Zhou are born from humble families. How many years did it take for someone like Qi Huilian to appear? Or Hai Liangyi? They're a happy accident, a sloppy stroke of a brush that, despite having made it this far, is easily overlooked in the grand scheme of things. If there's one person able to stand tall amid the steel web woven by the Eight Great Clans, it's a man you're most familiar with."

He leveled Xiao Chiye with an unwavering gaze, each word slow and clear. "The Prince of Libei had a humble beginning at the foot of the Hongyan Mountains. At fifteen, he was drafted as a soldier at Luoxia Pass, and he was promoted to the garrison by twenty. When he was twenty-three, the garrison troops were defeated at the foot of the Hongyan Mountains. He went on to establish the stables there at twenty-six and the cavalry by twenty-eight. When he was thirty, he once more fought the Hanma tribe. He traversed the Hongyan Mountains when he was thirty-two and had trekked all over the eastern range by thirty-five. From then on, the Luoxia Cavalry became the Libei Armored Cavalry. He split from the Luoxia Pass Garrison and was thrice conferred titles until he became the Prince of Libei of Great Zhou, despite having no connection to the imperial family. The size of Libei's Great Commandery was determined, and Great Zhou thus occupied the entire Hongyan mountain range.

"The war between the Xiao family and the Eight Great Clans isn't merely an internal power struggle; it is a battle between the nobility and the common people. That man who smashed through every barrier and climbed the peak was Xiao Fangxu. Between you and the Eight Great Clans, there was never any chance of reconciliation."

Shen Zechuan lowered his eyes and arranged his bowl and chopsticks at neat angles. "If you wish to ally with me, at the very least you must show a sincerity that matches this, not a few words about the Imperial Army's accounts. Those are worthless to me."

The small screens muffled the sound of wind. In the gloom, the two men faced each other across the table. The weak glow off the snow outside threw hazy light on their profiles through the window, a bright contrast against the ink-black night. Wolfsfang and Avalanche were sheathed beside their masters, yet the room flashed with cold glints from their sharp edges.

IN THE SAME BOAT

"BEFORE WE WERE merely testing the waters." Xiao Chiye's eyes were cold. "Sincerity is a process of undressing. Only by peeling off layer after layer can we have this heart-to-heart today. You're right. After the incident at the Nanlin Hunting Grounds, I expected Hai Liangyi to enact changes to the Grand Secretariat. Yet he continued to put his support behind Xue Xiuzhuo of the Eight Great Clans and placed him in an important post in the Court of Judicial Review. Even in such a high position, the secretariat elder must still bow to the noble clans' power and influence. In these circumstances, the Xiao Clan cannot manage alone, much like one log cannot support a whole building."

"How should one describe these clans?" Shen Zechuan pondered a little. "When there is no common enemy, they fight amongst themselves. Preventing the bowl of water from overbalancing from too much force on any one side is vastly more difficult than dealing with a single foe. Before the emergence of the Xiao family, the Eight Great Clans merely traded power internally; the rise of one clan led to the fall of another. But after the Xiao appeared, the clans began to separate the wheat from the chaff. The Hua Clan is only temporarily defeated. The new emperor purged the Hua remnants from court, but no one, not even Hai Liangyi, suggested holding the empress dowager accountable. This marriage alliance between Hua and Qi is a prime example of why they've kept the Hua around—to chip away at the Xiao Clan's external supports. Some things, when seen on their own, hardly merit notice; only when one joins the pieces will they see the full and terrifying picture."

"You mean the fall of Zhongbo and the Hua-Qi union?" Xiao Chiye asked.

"It's a well-known strategy: make a distant friend while attacking a nearby enemy." Shen Zechuan extended a finger and sketched a circle on the table. "After the fall of Zhongbo, a defensive void opened to Libei's southwest. Cizhou, one of Zhongbo's six prefectures, is right next to the Northeast Provisions Trail—the lifeblood of Libei. With no one guarding Zhongbo, oversight has fallen into the hands of the Eight Great Clans. Once the Hua Clan seals a marriage alliance with the Qi Clan of Qidong, Libei will be left high and dry with the Hongyan Mountains at its back, the Biansha tribes to its east, and double the enemies to its south."

"There's a five-year gap between the fall of Zhongbo and this betrothal. Who could have predicted with certainty that Hua Siqian would revolt? And who could have known I'd successfully come to the emperor's rescue?" Xiao Chiye's brow furrowed in thought.

"There must be a larger purpose behind Zhongbo," Shen Zechuan said after a moment of silence. "It's not hard to control a situation in the moment. The difficulty lies in controlling the direction in which it develops. Unless I've missed my guess, someone hidden among the Eight Great Clans has just such an ability."

"If such a person exists," said Xiao Chiye, "then everyone is a pawn, and every step is anticipated. That's not just some genius but a near-god who has all of Great Zhou in the palm of his hand. How do you plan to oppose him? Driving a wedge between the Eight Great Clans today can't sever connections forged through decades of intermarriage. In the face of a mutual enemy, they're inseparable."

"The turbulence of a tempest is better than a tranquil sea. When the water is muddied, it's difficult to distinguish between friend and foe. Besides, they've never been an impregnable fortress." Shen Zechuan lifted his finger from the circle he'd made. "How was Xiao Fangxu able to break through the noble clans' defenses? If this web was so tightly woven, how did Qi Huilian and Hai Liangyi rise to such eminent positions despite their common birth?"

Shen Zechuan continued, "Your father managed to establish the Libei Armored Cavalry's predecessor, the Luoxia Cavalry, because the officials at the time, with the then-crown prince at the helm, implemented the Yellow Register to record civil and military households. The borderlands recruited soldiers with the incentive of giving those who joined military status that could be passed down through the generations. This also put those households under jurisdiction of the commandery city's military and isolated them from the rule of local administrators, who were largely made up of scions of Qudu's noble clans appointed to posts outside the capital. Thus the Prince of Libei was able to consolidate military power and escape the control and surveillance of the local civil officials. Not only that, today's thriving cavalry in Libei also has Great Zhou's implementation of the supply-farm system to thank. You know better than I how important the military fields are."

Why did Lu Guangbai struggle so much more than Xiao Jiming? Because the Bianjun Commandery had no way of implementing military farms. The barren desert produced no food, so Lu Guangbai relied completely on Qudu's military funds and provisions. Allocating two-thirds of its soldiers to farming and one-third to military duty might not allow the frontier troops to be fully self-sufficient, but it greatly reduced Libei's reliance on military provisions. This made all the difference for the troops stationed at the border.

Grand Mentor Qi would feign madness if it allowed him to live, however demeaning that life might be. He was sustained by his unquenchable hatred, but he was also loath to abandon the crack they'd made in the armor of the institution. In his day, the Eastern Palace had dozens of subordinates, all officials from common households handpicked by the crown prince himself. Qi Huilian had taken all the accumulated learning of his lifetime and invested it in this imperial son. Five years ago, when he had shouted "The die is cast!" with his arms raised to the heavens, those words had been tears of blood, his refusal to resign himself to fate.

"You encroach into my territory one step at a time and indulge me again and again as I test your limits, all for tonight—to persuade me to climb into the same boat with you." Xiao Chiye leaned forward slowly, no trace of warmth in his eyes. "But had I not followed the trail to Xi Hongxuan and guessed your intent, would you have merely kicked me to the ground and used me as a stepping stone?"

"You're a wolf with a keen nose," Shen Zechuan said. "Why do you pretend to be so pitiful? If it were anyone else, you wouldn't have given them the chance to encroach; you wouldn't even be having this conversation. You and I are the same. Instead of questioning me, why don't you ask yourself?"

"*You're* the real asshole," Xiao Chiye said.

"It's not easy to find like-minded assholes."

Xiao Chiye stopped bickering and cut to the point. "So you want to borrow my power. But what's in it for me? One needs some guarantee before a treaty is established."

"We share weal and woe. Your Yao Clan is about to be shoved off the gameboard. Does that not make you anxious, Er-gongzi?"

"Yao Wenyu isn't someone I can use," Xiao Chiye said. "There's something you don't understand. The reason the Yao Clan is friendly with me isn't some strategic power grab, it's only because Yao Wenyu is—well, if you meet him, you'll understand. He didn't become an official, not because Hai Liangyi couldn't bear to let him, but because he didn't want to. The Yao Clan has produced a number of notable ministers in the past; it was only during his father's time that they fell into decline. His grandfather's prestige remains. They're a prominent family, highly respected among the literati, and their reputation among civil officials can't be compared to the likes of Hua Siqian. If Yao Wenyu wanted to, it would be easy enough to stage a comeback, but he would rather be free as a wild crane and leisurely as the drifting clouds. If Xi Hongxuan truly succeeds in kicking the Yao Clan out of the game, Yao Wenyu will be only more carefree and unfettered by worldly concerns."

"The Yao Clan is connected to the Fei Clan through marriage. Isn't he Princess Zhaoyue's elder cousin?" Shen Zechuan asked suddenly.

"He is." Xiao Chiye picked up his chopsticks. "Zhaoyue most likely wants to marry him, but the Helian Marquis is cowardly; he dances to the empress dowager's tune."

"Then perhaps you will become relatives."

"The betrothal fell through, didn't it?" said Xiao Chiye. "You sabotaged my marriage and cost me a beauty. Shouldn't you compensate me?"

Shen Zechuan arched a brow.

Xiao Chiye rinsed his chopsticks in the cold tea and lifted his eyes to Shen Zechuan. "Did you know there's only a two-word difference between 'sharing a boat on the same river' and 'sharing a pillow on the same bed'? If you ask me, there's no harm in mixing up the words or even actions in the future."

The heat in the room was stifling; Shen Zechuan felt slightly dizzy. Without replying, he turned to open the window.

Xiao Chiye didn't touch any of the dishes. "I brought you here, let you eat my food, drink my wine, and you aren't even a little suspicious?"

Shen Zechuan studied Xiao Chiye. The caress of the cool wind stirred something parched and hot in him. A thin layer of sweat coated his skin; he had hidden his fair neck within a tightly fastened collar, and the red plum blossoms leaning down from the window complemented his inky hair so that he looked all the more breathtaking.

Snow like fine salt fell outside. A scattering drifted in through the window and landed on the back of Shen Zechuan's hand, where it quickly melted. This drop of coolness only heightened the heat gathering in his body. As his attention wandered, certain thoughts started to creep in. He suddenly wanted to undo his clasps.

"This clause is not part of the treaty," Shen Zechuan said. "And I have no need of anyone to warm my bed."

Xiao Chiye crossed his long legs. "Right now, you don't look like the kind of person who has no need. Work and play are separate matters. Now that we're done talking business, we can linger over personal affairs. Were the boys in Ouhua Pavilion last time sent by Xi Hongxuan? I heard he only likes girls. Have his tastes changed?"

"Trysts between men have long ceased to be a novelty," Shen Zechuan retorted. "I don't know if his tastes have changed. Have Er-gongzi's?"

"My tastes aren't fixed." Xiao Chiye picked up a lock of Shen Zechuan's hair where it fell to his waist. "It depends on my mood."

Shen Zechuan lifted a finger and extricated the stolen lock. His back was clammy with sweat. "Some people talk big—they make themselves out to be romantic and charming, calm and composed. But the truth is they only know how to gorge themselves ravenously. Perhaps they're out of practice."

Xiao Chiye pushed aside the small table between them and grasped the wrist Shen Zechuan was about to retract. "And some people look so pitiful drenched in sweat."

The fire in Shen Zechuan burned hotter where Xiao Chiye held him. Propping an arm on his knee, Shen Zechuan demanded, "What did you put in the food?"

"Guess." Xiao Chiye pulled Shen Zechuan closer by the wrist. Changing the subject, he said, "Ji Gang can't be teaching you all this, so who is your shifu—or should I say, your xiansheng?"

The corners of Shen Zechuan's eyes reddened as he replied softly, "Not telling."

Xiao Chiye inhaled from where he sat and blurted, "You smell so good."

Shen Zechuan's breathing quickened. "Are you so desperate you need to lay a honey trap?"

"I'm no honey. What? Is our little chat making you anxious?"

Sweat soaked through Shen Zechuan's inner garment. The heat he felt, caught in this sudden ambiguous tension, turned sticky and damp. He wanted to wipe his brow. Frowning, he asked, "What exactly did you put in it?"

"I'm messing with you." Xiao Chiye laughed aloud and said shamelessly, "It's just medicinal wine—to warm you up."

Shen Zechuan saw danger in his gaze. He closed his eyes and forced himself to composure.

Xiao Chiye raised his cup and tipped back the rest of the cooled wine.

"Xiao Er—"

At the sound of his name, he leaned down and captured Shen Zechuan's lips, pressing him back against the window; the plum blossom branch shook as they knocked against it. Shen Zechuan leaned away, feeling his back was going to break under Xiao Chiye's tight grip. Snow fell on the back of Xiao Chiye's neck, but he ignored it as he pressed desperately down on the man below him. His fingers pushed their way between Shen Zechuan's, lacing their hands together.

Ever since that look at the Court Officials' Feast, Xiao Chiye had wanted to kiss him. That flicker of desire grew into a fire over the course of their conversation; he had been restraining himself all night. He saw how ruthless Shen Zechuan was, how he retreated and advanced as he pleased, but among all these myriad impressions, Xiao Chiye couldn't put a finger on exactly how he felt about the man. All he wanted was to pin Shen Zechuan down and kiss him until he was flushed all over, that elusive desire brimming in his eyes.

Shen Zechuan's chest heaved. The wind had cooled the sweat on his body, chilling him so he shuddered. His teeth were no barrier to the wine Xiao Chiye was passing into his mouth. He choked as it slid down his throat, but Xiao Chiye bit the tip of his tongue, preventing him from coughing. Shen Zechuan's eyes watered. Even if the sky were to fall at this moment, Xiao Chiye would not release him.

A sudden *thud* sounded above them, followed immediately by someone tumbling off the roof. Ding Tao plunged headlong into a snowdrift, then abruptly popped his head out. He rubbed his arms to chase away the cold. Just as he was about to loose a string of curses, he looked up and came face-to-face with the window; his jaw dropped, and his eyes went so wide it looked as if his soul had left his body.

Shen Zechuan kicked Xiao Chiye away and started coughing, gripping the windowsill for support. His ears were scarlet, while his mouth was filled with the fragrant taste of wine.

Xiao Chiye was slightly breathless as he looked darkly out the window.

Ding Tao's teeth chattered. Trembling, he stretched his forefinger and pointed upward as he whispered, "Sor-sor-sorry, Gongzi..."

Above him, Qiao Tianya and Gu Jin held their breath, looking on with rapt attention as they wisely pretended not to exist. Before Xiao Chiye could say a word, Ding Tao fled. Shimmying swiftly up a tree, he made his way back onto the roof and vanished, leaving the two of them alone together.

MARSHAL

IN THE DIMNESS, Xiao Chiye swiped his thumb across the corner of his mouth where drops of wine lingered. "One kick for one kiss. A fair exchange."

Shen Zechuan looked back at him.

Xiao Chiye laughed. "Let's not conflate the issues. Aren't you still going to ride roughshod over me in public in the future? Go ahead and step on me, Lanzhou. I'll demand each debt paid in full with interest."

Running his tongue over the spot where he'd been bitten, Shen Zechuan said, "You won't have a chance like this every time."

Xiao Chiye took a step closer, shrouding Shen Zechuan in his own shadow. "And you won't be able to run every time."

He extended his hand to pluck a red plum blossom from the branch nearest Shen Zechuan. He crushed it between his fingers and slid the bright red petals into his mouth. Shen Zechuan, under his gaze, had the uncanny sensation that he was that plum blossom. In his mental evaluation of Xiao Chiye, he quietly added *tenacious* below *keen sense of smell*.

Shen Zechuan had once thought desire would overpower Xiao Chiye and send him back in defeat. This behavior was beyond his expectations. Xiao Chiye's arrogance meant that he only ever charged forward, never back. Every retreat or concession was merely a smokescreen while he considered his next plan of attack.

He was a profoundly dangerous threat, a force of nature.

Above him, Xiao Chiye turned his head to call out, "Light the lamps."

Within moments, maidservants entered; silently, they moved the small screens out, cleared away the dishes, spread a mat over the rug, and swapped the narrow dining table for a large, square tea table. When they had finished, Chen Yang removed his shoes and entered. He placed the Imperial Army's records of military affairs and register of names on the table, then took the pot from the maidservant and knelt off to the side to brew the tea.

Thus observed, by the time both men took their seats again, they had resumed the roles of upright gentlemen.

Shen Zechuan had sobered somewhat; the chill wind had shaken him free of his tipsiness. Only a light wash of pink clung to his cheeks, warm in the dim lamplight. Not even Chen Yang dared look at him straight on, as if afraid his gaze would be an affront to both of them.

Chen Yang busied himself with the tea. *No wonder Tantai Hu was worried,* he thought. *Shen Lanzhou is clearly a ruinous beauty capable of bringing a nation to its knees and raining doom upon the people. What's more, his face comes with a fiery temperament. Anyone familiar with Master, even a little, would be afraid.*

What was Xiao Chiye most fond of?

Why, horse taming and falconry of course!

While conditioning a falcon, Xiao Chiye wouldn't sleep when the falcon was awake. The harder an animal was to tame, the more he focused, and the more he favored it. When they had fought the Biansha Horsemen back then, Xiao Chiye had been able to lie in wait so long precisely because he adored this process of taming and torment. He had inherited from Xiao Fangxu that rare and all-consuming desire to subjugate, to conquer—this was the biggest difference between him and Xiao Jiming.

Chen Yang presented the tea with a slight bow. "If my lord has any instructions, please call for me."

With that, he rose and retreated, slipping back into his boots to stand guard outside the door.

Gu Jin stuck his head down over the eaves and tossed a wineskin to Chen Yang, then shot him an inquiring glance.

Chen Yang exhaled a slow breath. "It's fine. Master knows what he's doing."

Up on the roof, Ding Tao was still clutching his head and muttering, "Am I going to die, going to die, going to die..."

"Doesn't look good." Qiao Tianya brushed away enough snow to pull out his pipe and laughed. "On this day next year, Gege will remember to burn paper offerings for you."

Ding Tao was on the verge of tears. Grabbing his hair, he glared at them and snapped, "It's all your fault! If it wasn't for the two of you fighting, I wouldn't have tried to break up the fight, and I wouldn't have fallen off. If I hadn't fallen off, then I wouldn't be doomed to die! I hate you both!"

Qiao Tianya became totally absorbed in his flint and tinder, while Gu Jin sat with arms folded and dozed off.

Ding Tao fished out his book and wrote furiously, cursing them both as the world's greatest bastards. He paused only to wipe the tears at the corners of his eyes, before continuing to scratch down his vengeful thoughts as they gushed forth like spring water.

The two in the room were left with their fresh pot of tea.

"Back to business," Xiao Chiye said. "You suspect there's someone in Qudu capable of manipulating all of the Eight Great Clans. Now that I think about it; I don't believe it's possible."

The heat from the medicinal wine had burned Shen Zechuan's throat to smoking. Now, after several cups of tea, it was less difficult to speak. "You don't believe it's possible because the execution of such a plan would be too difficult."

"Exactly," Xiao Chiye replied. "Setting aside everyone else, the empress dowager would never deign to subjugate herself to another's plans."

"What if she wasn't aware of it herself?" Shen Zechuan asked. "Sometimes, you don't need to give orders to manipulate the situation. A single piece, the single push of a finger, can set the whole board in motion; from there, one can change many things."

"You have to first prove the existence of this mastermind." Xiao Chiye eyed him. "You look like you're quite warm."

Shen Zechuan lifted a hand to unfasten the clasp at his throat. His collar fell away to reveal his smooth neck in the gaps between his fingers, stopping at the top of his collarbone. Tiny beads of sweat slid along the contours of his neck into that depression, dampening his fingertips.

"Xi Hongxuan's hand in this case is conspicuous, but he still has an important role to play. Without him, there's no way to confirm this person exists; you can't take him off the board just yet." Shen Zechuan paused. "You couldn't take him down with what you have, anyway. He never once showed himself during this whole assassination case. Fuling's confession only proves she was coerced. The most likely suspect right now is you."

"Pinning it on me was your idea." Xiao Chiye watched a bead of sweat slip down Shen Zechuan's collarbone and disappear.

"You are an official in the emperor's inner circle, deeply favored by His Majesty. If this incident can remove you from your post and see you cast aside, Xi Hongxuan won't pass up the opportunity;

he'll take this opening and seize control of the Eight Great Battalions. Only by luring them out of their lairs can we get a clear look at our adversaries. Besides, His Majesty trusts you. Even if he demotes you, he won't so easily put his trust in another. After a while, he'll see the warning smoke of the Eight Great Clans rising and realize he's been played for a fool. He'll be overcome with guilt toward the innocents who were implicated in the process and try to make it up to you." Shen Zechuan's throat bobbed as he sipped his tea. "I'd wager you already thought of a solution before coming to me."

"Sure, let's play." Xiao Chiye refilled Shen Zechuan's cup. "I'll go along with your moves and let you guys walk all over me."

"That would be far wiser than fighting back. The more anxious you are to clear your name right now, the more suspicious His Majesty will become."

"I know His Majesty. He is credulous and susceptible to persuasion. He can't stand being provoked, but he can't abide being humiliated either. I'm his drinking buddy, and the first person he promoted to his side after he ascended, a symbol of the way he faces his court officials. Trapped on all sides, I've become livestock in his hands—and he keeps me penned up. In his eyes, I have no one to rely on and secured this position solely with his support. If someone were to knock me down, it would be a blow to him too. The Hua faction is a sore spot and a source of great anxiety. The reason he allows Hai Liangyi and no other to make decisions regarding government affairs is because he knows Hai Liangyi won't form cliques and factions."

"We can't afford to let this opportunity slip." Teacup in hand, Shen Zechuan considered a moment. "This time, we must force Xi Hongxuan to take action."

"I'll remind you of one thing." Xiao Chiye put an elbow on the table and beckoned Shen Zechuan closer.

Shen Zechuan set down his cup and leaned in.

"If you can't hold your liquor, don't go drinking with others," Xiao Chiye whispered. "Not every asshole has Er-gongzi's level of willpower and can remain an honorable, well-behaved gentleman before you."

Shen Zechuan looked askance at him and said deliberately, "But this honorable gentleman has had a number of dishonorable thoughts, has he not?"

Xiao Chiye stared back. "Once we step out this door tomorrow morning, you and I will be mortal enemies. Enemies know best the regard their adversary is due; is it not fitting for me to think of you?"

"I don't think of you," Shen Zechuan said.

"Every plan you make these days involves me," Xiao Chiye said. "I'm afraid it's not that you don't think of me, but that you think of me all day long, and then all night."

Shen Zechuan raised his hand to block Xiao Chiye as he pressed in. "I should have stepped on you harder during the Court Officials' Feast. It might've sobered Er-gongzi up."

The tip of Xiao Chiye's nose was against Shen Zechuan's palm. He stared at Shen Zechuan over the line of his fingers and said wickedly, "How callous, Lanzhou. You tease me every possible way before bedding me. Yet now that you've had me, you set up every possible wall. Heartless cad. Fickle man."

Under his gaze, Shen Zechuan averted his eyes. "Xiao Er, you've had too much to drink tonight, hm?"

Xiao Chiye suddenly drew back. "During morning court tomorrow, some will undoubtedly raise questions and attempt to assign blame. Kong Qiu will present Fuling's confession statement, such as it is. The Chief Surveillance Bureau will have no choice but to hold me accountable for negligence in supervision."

Shen Zechuan's palm was empty now. "You need to back down, but you can't make it too obvious."

"Once I'm enduring the siege of verbal and written condemnations, it'll fall to His Majesty to decide my punishment."

"At best, your salary will be suspended for a few months. At worst, your authority token will be revoked while you reflect on your mistake. The Heir of Libei is still in Qudu. Everyone has to show him respect; they can't deal too harshly with you."

"Dage's time in Qudu is brief." Xiao Chiye paused. "Once I'm in disgrace, there'll be no one to stop the marriage between Hua Xiangyi and Qi Shiyu."

"That union will take time." Shen Zechuan thought a moment. "Qi Zhuyin is grand marshal of Qidong's five commanderies. Perhaps we can start with her."

Xiao Chiye remembered something. "I have an idea."

"What?"

"The Ministry of Rites holds past marriage records of the Hua Clan. I'll get someone to polish them up a little, then give Qi Zhuyin a copy. She won't accept Hua Xiangyi easily after that."

"It's not taboo for distant relatives to marry in Great Zhou; even marriage between cousins is acceptable," said Shen Zechuan. "Would Marshal Qi be so bothered by this?"

"She would," Xiao Chiye answered firmly. "Qi Shiyu is a lecher. He's taken many beautiful women from all over the five commanderies into his manor, one of them his very own niece. A few years back, this woman gave birth to a child who was abnormally sick and weak. The babe lived only a few days. From then on, any time Qi Shiyu took a concubine, Qi Zhuyin would do her due diligence. If she had even the slightest blood connection, even a distant relative, Qi Zhuyin forbade the union."

"But Hua Xiangyi's marriage to Qi Shiyu was specifically bestowed by the empress dowager," Shen Zechuan said. "I doubt the grand marshal can stop it even if she wants to."

"There's no way she can stop it; she can only step back and let Third Lady Hua marry her father." Xiao Chiye's eyes were cold. "But she'll never allow her to birth a child. Hua Xiangyi is marrying Qi Shiyu as his second wife, not a concubine—she'll be the rightful mistress of Qidong. Any child would be of lawful birth, with the same claim as Qi Zhuyin. It hasn't been easy for her to subdue and command the military forces of the five commanderies all these years as a woman. She's a great general who has shed hot blood on the field. But who can guarantee others won't have their own ambitions? If Hua Xiangyi birthed a son, Qi Zhuyin would face an internal struggle for military control. We need to give her a legitimate reason to keep Hua Xiangyi down."

"I've heard the Qi Clan has sons, but Qi Shiyu was hell-bent on giving Qi Zhuyin the position of grand marshal," Shen Zechuan said. "Was this not out of an appreciation for her talent?"

"Sure was," said Xiao Chiye. "Qi Zhuyin is the daughter of his first wife, and a talented military commander he personally brought up. When he had no sons, he treated and raised Qi Zhuyin as one. Later on, when he did, none of the boys could compare to her. Qidong was at war with Biansha at the time. There was an occasion when Qi Shiyu was seriously injured; his forces were trapped on the east side of some linked Biansha camps, and none of the Qi Clan sons had the balls to step up. It was Qi Zhuyin with a blade on her back who rode through the night, drumming up reinforcements from the Chijun and Bianjun Commanderies as well as the Suotian Pass Garrison Troops and convincing them to follow her into battle. Then, with the wind at her flank, she set fire to the Biansha camps and burned them to the ground. This battle made her famous. She's called Windstorm through the Scorching Plains precisely because of how she rode ahead of her soldiers in that battle, drew her sword, braved the fire, and carried Qi Shiyu out on her back. Qi Shiyu had hesitated before, but after that incident, he handed over the commander's seal and granted all the military troops of the five commanderies to Qi Zhuyin."

"The conferment of the rank of grand marshal requires approval of the capital," Shen Zechuan said. "It's no easy feat."

Xiao Chiye smiled, touching the ring on his thumb. "Yet the Guangcheng Emperor was not the one who conferred the title on her."

Shen Zechuan cocked his head—a question.

"Back then, when news of Qi Shiyu's plans spread back to Qudu, they were roundly denounced on all sides. Because Qi Zhuyin is a woman, the Ministry of War questioned whether her military exploits were fabricated. They submitted a petition to the Grand Secretariat, requesting that it dispatch the Chief Surveillance Bureau censors and Embroidered Uniform Guard to Qidong to carry out a thorough investigation. When he saw the furor it caused, the Guangcheng Emperor denied Qidong's request until her meritorious military service could be verified. When it was, the Ministry of Rites submitted a memorial permitting her conferment but insisted she not be allowed to climb the Jade Dragon Terrace, the traditional honor afforded military officers and generals, to receive her accolades. She could only kneel and kowtow before the stairs of Mingli Hall."

Xiao Chiye paused. "It was the empress dowager who stood against the objections of the masses and allowed her to step onto Jade Dragon Terrace so she could be conferred, openly and officially, the title of grand marshal of the Qidong Garrison Troops."

DENOUNCEMENT

WHITE SNOW fell in flurries; the night was coming to an end.

Shen Zechuan couldn't stay. As he rose to leave, Xiao Chiye stood as well, retrieving his overcoat from the rack and handing it to him.

"This blade of yours is unfamiliar." Xiao Chiye bent to pick up Avalanche. It was light in his hands. "New?"

Shen Zechuan nodded and turned away from him to put on the overcoat.

Xiao Chiye thumbed the blade slightly out of its sheath and revealed a cold glint. "An excellent saber. Does it have a name?"

"Avalanche," Shen Zechuan answered.

"From one breath of its spout falls three mountains' worth of snow; it once opens its mouth and devours a hundred rivers."[9] Xiao Chiye returned the blade to its sheath and stepped forward, pressing himself against Shen Zechuan's back. With practiced fingers, he replaced Avalanche on Shen Zechuan's waist. Xiao Chiye lowered his lips to his ear. "It's not just pretty; it even has a pretty name."

---

9 *From "Gufeng: Thirty-Three" by Li Bai, a poem about the kun peng ("a massive fish in the North Sea; body as long as a thousand li"), a mythological creature that could appear as a fish (kun) or a bird (peng). The poem and its ambitious subtext is the source of inspiration for the name of Shen Zechuan's blade, Avalanche.*

Shen Zechuan whipped his head around, but Xiao Chiye beat him to it; he grabbed him by the waist to take him into his arms.

"How are you going to look at me after leaving here today?"

"However I ought to look at you." Shen Zechuan hastily turned aside; in this position, it looked like he was intimately nuzzling their faces together.

"If it becomes too much, you can always ask your Er-gongzi for help." Xiao Chiye's fingers roughly spanned Shen Zechuan's waist.

"Er-gongzi can barely fend for himself. Seems you're more likely to ask me."

Xiao Chiye released him. "You're much thinner than last time. I'd bet you're still taking some decoction that conceals your physique."

Shen Zechuan fastened his overcoat and said no more.

"A word of advice," Xiao Chiye said. "That medicine damages the body more the longer you take it. In a few years, you'll have wrecked your health for nothing."

Shen Zechuan sighed softly as he stopped by the door. "Your shifu has sharp eyes. One meeting and he could tell."

"You're willing to go so far for this?" asked Xiao Chiye.

"My life and death hang on the whims of so many; naturally, I must exercise caution in everything I do and diligence everywhere I go." Shen Zechuan's hands were ice-cold. "I've practiced Ji-Style Boxing for a long time. If I hadn't gone to such lengths, I would never have deceived Ji Lei."

"Ji Lei is dead," Xiao Chiye said.

The faint scent of wine lingered on Shen Zechuan's body. "I've stopped the medicine."

After seeing Shen Zechuan off, Xiao Chiye stood in the blizzard, recalling Zuo Qianqiu's words.

"This type of medicine comes from the east; it allows a person to fake illness and pull the wool over the eyes of others. Taking it once or twice is harmless, but long-term consumption comes with serious consequences. It's both medicine and poison; the effect is negligible in the short term, but eventually you pay the price."

"The price?"

Zuo Qianqiu had fixed his gaze on the teacup in his hand. "Accumulated poison will become a lasting injury. If he's not careful, he'll damage his health irrevocably."

In the snowstorm, Xiao Chiye raised his hand and let the wind scour away the lingering warmth in his palm. He recalled that freezing night when he thought he'd melted Shen Zechuan with his caresses; now it seemed the warmth he'd given Shen Zechuan was all too fleeting.

A beauty always gave the impression of fragility.

Qiao Tianya, bamboo hat on his head, drove the horse carriage toward Shen Zechuan's dwelling on Donglong Street. Inside, Shen Zechuan leaned against the wall and closed his eyes for a nap. It wasn't long before they arrived; Qiao Tianya reined the horses to a halt and lifted the curtain for Shen Zechuan to step out. He wasted no time retiring inside to take a bath and change his clothes.

According to the official court memorial, Shen Zechuan had enjoyed a meteoric rise, going from a common guardsman to a fifth-rank judge of the Embroidered Uniform Guard in a single bound. This position, however, was split into two—north and south. The northern judge oversaw the Imperial Prison, while the southern judge oversaw the Embroidered Uniform Guard's military craftsmen. Li Jianheng had uplifted him to the important position of northern judge with the intent to make full use of his talents, but the civil officials of the Grand Secretariat had their own misgivings. Due to Shen Zechuan's background, they were unwilling to cede him control of the Imperial Prison. Thus, after some deliberation, Shen Zechuan's appointment as northern judge was rejected and changed to southern judge.

Li Jianheng was by no means happy to be gainsaid in this matter. To appease him, the Grand Secretariat raised Shen Zechuan's military appointment to fifth-rank Embroidered Uniform Guard battalion commander, overseeing a thousand men. This was a great honor, especially when coupled with the additional python-embroidered robe—a sign of the emperor's special favor—and phoenix-tail belt that Li Jianheng personally bestowed upon him.

Shen Zechuan had long anticipated the Grand Secretariat's revenge. This time, he had made his way up using Han Cheng as a stepping stone. Xue Xiuzhuo allowed him his promotion yet gave him a kick down to the southern judge at the crucial moment. The message was clear: even with his new-gained glory, he was far from capable of crossing swords with these noble sons.

When Shen Zechuan emerged, neatly dressed, Qiao Tianya was holding an umbrella. "This house was shabby to begin with. Now that my lord's been promoted, there will be visitors coming and going; it won't be suitable to accommodate them."

"There's no hurry." Shen Zechuan lifted the hem of his robe to step into the carriage. He took hold of the curtain and said, "We can always move after I'm promoted to chief commander."

With that, the curtain dropped, and he sat back in repose.

The storm showed no sign of stopping; the officials waiting outside the palace all had snow on their shoulders. Etiquette kept them frozen in place—they couldn't walk around as they pleased, make a racket, or even cough.

Shen Zechuan followed Han Cheng, standing at attention with his blade at his side. His skin, set against his crimson python robe, was white as snow. This man was breathtakingly gorgeous when a smile curved the corners of his eyes, yet behind that affability was a hostile note of danger.

Xiao Chiye had on a red robe too. The second-rank lion on his mandarin square set him apart from the crowd, a crane among a flock of geese. He seemed in low spirits, and merely glanced sidelong at Shen Zechuan.

Though the two stood many lengths apart, onlookers felt a palpable tension. Even Hai Liangyi turned to glance at them.

The civil officials exchanged looks, coming to a tacit understanding.

"Let's go," Han Cheng said in a hushed tone.

When the palace doors opened, eunuchs from the Directorate of Ceremonial Affairs and major ministers of the Grand Secretariat should have been first to enter. But now, the Directorate of Ceremonial Affairs, previously the domain of Pan Rugui, had been purged; only the important ministers of the Grand Secretariat, led by Hai Liangyi, stepped forward. Han Cheng followed next, leading Shen Zechuan up the stairs to take his position at the lower left side of the throne.

Li Jianheng planted his hands on his knees. "It has been two nights since the assassination incident. Does the Ministry of Justice have any progress to report?"

The Minister of Justice, Kong Qiu, stepped forward with a bow. "Your Majesty, the evidence that Fuling, the female palace attendant of the Food Service, instigated Guisheng to carry out the assassination is conclusive. This subject plans to hand her over to the Court of Judicial Review today for a second trial."

For some reason, Li Jianheng darted a glance at Xiao Chiye before turning back to ask, "Why did she do it? Have you gotten to the bottom of this?"

"Our inquiries found that Fuling once broke a plate from the Court of Imperial Entertainments," said Kong Qiu. "This left a demerit in her file, and the term of her service was extended. She often told those around her that her mother was advanced in age, and that she wanted to leave the palace to care for her. But owing to palace rules, she was unable to do so. She repeatedly bribed the former Director of the Directorate of Ceremonial Affairs, but he did nothing, and she was cheated out of her entire life savings. She harbored a bitter resentment, from which grew the brazenness to exact revenge."

The Vice Minister of the Court of Judicial Review, Wei Huaixing, stood next. He was the second son of lawful birth of the Eight Great Clans' Wei Clan, as well as the elder brother of the Xiande Emperor's ill-fated Imperial Concubine Wei. He stepped forward with a bow. "This subject has a memorial to present."

"Vice Minister Wei, please speak," Li Jianheng said.

"This subject has ascertained that the palace attendant of the Food Service, Fuling, had a sexual relationship with Yuan Liu from the Judicial Office of the Imperial Army. It was Yuan Liu who negotiated the credit for the house where her mother lived." Looking straight ahead, Wei Huaixing continued, "This case is presided over by the Ministry of Justice, and this matter concerns Your Majesty's safety; it is of utmost importance. Yet Minister Kong chose not to mention this part of the confession before Your Majesty. Is it that there's something that can't be said, or someone who can't be mentioned?"

Kong Qiu turned to look at him. "I mention this matter in my memorial; what deception is there to speak of?"

"The morning court is vital for the discussion of governmental affairs. His Majesty asked if you have gotten to the bottom of it, yet you told only half the truth, focusing on the favorable while avoiding the damning evidence." Wei Huaixing raised his head. "Officials, on entering service, should diligently and earnestly serve with utmost loyalty. The court hall is no place for gathering filth and hiding sins. What are you afraid of? If you daren't say it in this man's presence, I will. Your Majesty, this matter concerns not only the Twenty-Four Yamen in the palace, but more importantly, the Imperial Army!"

Xiao Chiye wore a look of displeasure, almost a sneer.

Li Jianheng had initially meant to keep this matter quiet, but now that it was exposed, it wouldn't do to play dumb. After a long moment of hesitation, he said, "Ce'an, what do you say to this?"

"The Imperial Army has twenty thousand men on its payroll," Xiao Chiye answered. "This subject can check their household registers one at a time but cannot reasonably dig into all of their personal affairs. Even so, I was negligent in the supervision of my men. Your Majesty, please punish me as you deem fit."

Before Li Jianheng could speak, Wei Huaixing dropped to the ground in a kowtow before the throne. "Supreme Commander Xiao, why do you not speak the truth before His Majesty? Perhaps it's not easy to probe the common affairs of all twenty thousand men in the Imperial Army, but Yuan Liu shares an uncommon relationship with you. How can you feign ignorance?!"

Shen Zechuan's eyes found Xiao Chiye in the crowd.

"There are too many people with whom I share an uncommon relationship." Xiao Chiye swept his eyes over Shen Zechuan and smiled carelessly. "But with a beauty in my arms, I'd be blind to bed Yuan Liu, a fellow old enough to be your father. Your Excellency Wei, it's understandable if you have no evidence, but why go so far as to bring false charges against me?"

Hai Liangyi cleared his throat. "Please watch your language in the Imperial Court, Supreme Commander."

"His Majesty is only too aware what kind of bastard I am. I've no need to pretend otherwise." Xiao Chiye was a tyrant when he played the scoundrel; even Hai Liangyi received no respect. "If you want to investigate the Imperial Army, be my guest. If you're worried about a conflict of interest, I'll hand over my authority token today and let my esteemed colleagues investigate. But if you want to pin this groundless, trumped-up charge on me, don't expect me to lie down and take it."

"Such vulgar language. Such impetuousness before the throne. The Xiao Clan has certainly produced a praiseworthy son!" Wei Huaixing pulled a memorial from his sleeve. "The supreme commander claims I have no evidence—I remind you I am an official of the Court of Judicial Review. Would I dare speak unless I did?"

Xiao Jiming, who had stood listening all this while, raised his head slightly to look at Wei Huaixing.

"Yuan Liu was originally a squad leader in the Imperial Army," Wei Huaixing said. "It was the supreme commander who personally promoted him to the position of vice judicial administrator. Not two years later, the supreme commander promoted him again, this time to main judicial administrator. I'd like to ask His Excellency: Until recently, the Imperial Army has had no important duties. On what grounds was Yuan Liu promoted again and again?"

Xiao Chiye scoffed. "He was a senior officer. Although he had no merits to speak of, he had also made no errors. The Imperial Army has recruited many new men in recent years. I'm a sentimental man; Yuan Liu isn't the only old-timer I've promoted. Would Your

Excellency Wei like to list them all out as well and count them among my personal affairs?"

"Is it not true that in recent years the supreme commander's word is law in the Imperial Army?" Wei Huaixing said deliberately. "I suspect each of these veterans pledged allegiance to the Xiao Clan, not His Majesty."

His words were laced with insidious meaning—though directed at Xiao Chiye, they were designed to implicate Xiao Jiming.

As expected, Xiao Chiye lost his temper. "Keep to the topic at hand; stop fucking bringing in the Xiao Clan every other sentence! I, Xiao Ce'an, followed His Majesty to where I am now. I'm not like Lord Wei, born to a noble family with a silver spoon in my mouth and the path to court smoothly paved for me."

Wei Huaixing had been waiting for Xiao Chiye to blow up before opening the memorial. "The supreme commander went drinking with his men before the new year. During the feast, Yuan Liu gifted you a large sum of money. Does the supreme commander admit to this?"

Even Li Jianheng was stunned to hear it. He clenched his fist and said nothing.

"I have never gone drinking with Yuan Liu," said Xiao Chiye.

"The courtesans of Xiangyun Villa on Donglong Street will attest to it. That night, Yuan Liu spent a large sum on the feast to entertain the supreme commander. The supreme commander had much to drink, and Yuan Liu gifted you a basket of solid gold peaches," Wei Huaixing said. "Does the supreme commander still deny it?"

"Let me ask you," Xiao Chiye replied, "as a puny sixth-rank official, where on earth would he even get *solid gold peaches* to gift me?"

"That's something to ask the supreme commander." Wei Huaixing went in for the killing blow: "When Yuan Liu obtained the house on credit for Fuling, he also purchased three houses facing Donglong Street. I have ascertained that he acted on the supreme commander's written instructions to do so! In the past five years, the Imperial Army first carried out repairs on its barracks, then expanded the drill grounds at Mount Feng. Where did the money come from? Isn't it true that the supreme commander used his position to extort these funds from the broker? Yuan Liu was the one who handled this matter for you. And now that Yuan Liu is found to have instigated Fuling in the assassination of His Majesty, you dare say it has nothing to do with you?"

Xiao Chiye didn't answer.

Fu Linye, the Right Censor-in-Chief of the Chief Surveillance Bureau, stepped forward. "This subject, too, has a memorial to submit."

Li Jianheng's fingertips were trembling violently. "Speak!"

"This subject also brings charges against the supreme commander of the Imperial Army," Fu Linye said. "According to law, before the Joint Trial by the Three Judicial Offices concludes, no unauthorized person is allowed to visit major criminals without His Majesty's imperial edict. Yet the supreme commander acted on his own initiative and went to the prison yesterday but made no report of it afterward."

Xiao Chiye's expression grew colder still.

"The moment the supreme commander left the prison, Fuling's mother died." Fu Linye kowtowed. "As for what happened in between, I'd like to ask the supreme commander for a clear account in His Majesty's presence."

"You two are quite in sync," Xiao Chiye remarked. "What a stunning coincidence."

"Don't dodge the question, Supreme Commander," said Wei Huaixing coldly. "I'd advise you to explain yourself!"

"He who wants to incriminate a man will always find some charge to throw at him." Xiao Chiye appeared to be cornered. He was silent a moment, then said to Li Jianheng, "I've never done any of the things they're accusing me of. I will leave the judgment to Your Majesty."

In such a tense, anxious atmosphere, Li Jianheng's fingers clenched his knees until they were soaked with sweat. He looked back at Xiao Chiye, then blurted out, "How do you explain these written instructions?"

Xiao Chiye lowered his eyes to the floor and said with what might have been a smile, "This subject has never written such a thing."

Li Jianheng shot up. He took a few agitated steps forward and demanded, "Let us see it!"

Wei Huaixing handed over the papers. Li Jianheng flipped through them for a moment and suddenly began to tremble. His lips quivered. "Is this not your handwriting...? Ce...Ce'an!"

Xiao Chiye reasserted, resolute, "This subject has never written such a thing."

Li Jianheng clutched the paper in horror, then threw it away as if burned. On the edge of losing control, he cried out, "Then, that Yuan Liu—is he your man or not?!"

Xiao Chiye raised his eyes to look at him.

Li Jianheng clutched the armrests; fear rose in him. He recalled the coldness and indifference with which Xiao Chiye had abandoned him at the hunting grounds and a pit of disgust opened within him. As if warding off some terrifying beast, he raised his hand and cried with all his might, "Strip him of his authority token!"

Xiao Chiye began, "This subject—"

"If he dares disobey, we can detain him right here according to the law!" Wei Huaixing barked.

Xiao Chiye whipped around and stared at Wei Huaixing before turning back to Li Jianheng. He said coolly, "I, Xiao Ce'an, may be detained, but not without a credible allegation."

Li Jianheng felt he had misplaced his trust. Caught in the crossfire, he was already inclined to believe the others. Now, Xiao Chiye's insolent manner fanned the flames of his fury sky-high. He snapped, "Kneel! We *will* revoke your authority token today!"

Xiao Chiye made no move. Li Jianheng could no longer contain his rage. "We said, *kneel!*"

SEARCH

SO SILENT was the imperial court one could hear the drop of a pin. Xiao Chiye's eyes dimmed as he removed his authority token.

Chest heaving, Li Jianheng announced, "The supreme commander of the Imperial Army, Xiao Chiye, is henceforth suspended from duty and confined to his residence to await investigation! The internal and perimeter patrols of Qudu are to be taken over by the Embroidered Uniform Guard and the Eight Great Battalions."

Standing among the crowd of officials, Xi Hongxuan looked past the sea of black gauze hats at Xiao Jiming, who had yet to speak. He remained perfectly still, unperturbed by what was unfolding before them.

He's too damn steady. Xi Hongxuan cursed inwardly.

As expected, Xiao Jiming was a tough nut to crack. Even with Xiao Chiye in such a predicament, he displayed not the slightest agitation. He watched and uttered not a single word.

After morning court concluded, two men met in Ouhua Pavilion on Donglong Street.

Shen Zechuan, having removed his gold token and changed into an elegant moon-white embroidered robe with wide sleeves, allowed a courtesan to lead him upstairs. Xi Hongxuan was lying on the settee watching as the tea was brewed. He laughed out loud when he saw him.

"Lanzhou, how satisfying was that! Ever since the hunting grounds, Xiao Er has been one-upping us again and again. Payback feels so good!"

Shen Zechuan took his seat. "Using Fu Linye was a smart move. I didn't think you'd recruit him into your camp as well."

"Do you know the Fus' background? In the old days, they collected cow dung outside Chuncheng's city gates. If not for our Old Master Xi's appreciation of talent and his help breaking them free of their low status, their little Fu Clan would still be herding cattle today." Xi Hongxuan accepted the tea from a maidservant and sampled a few mouthfuls before continuing, "But what a waste of the trap set by Elder Wei—Xiao Jiming didn't take the bait."

"Taking down Xiao Er was no easy feat." Shen Zechuan sipped his tea as well. "I'm afraid the losses will far outweigh the gains if you provoke Xiao Jiming now."

"Striking while the iron is hot is the best strategy. If not now, then when?" Xi Hongxuan dismissed the maidservant with a wave and straightened in his seat. "Even if Xiao Jiming suffers only a small loss over this, it's still a chink in their armor."

"I thought you had your sights set on Qudu. How can you pick a fight with the frontier before your foundation is stable?" Shen Zechuan asked. "You've yet to secure your hold on the Eight Great Battalions. If you back off Xiao Er now, you'll trip over him in the future."

Xi Hongxuan set his tea down. "Then, in your opinion, what should we do?"

"You said it earlier." Shen Zechuan smiled. "Strike while the iron is hot."

Xi Hongxuan pondered. "Our move today has lost Xiao Er the emperor's trust; he has no authority token and is trapped in place until spring at least. But he's been friends with the emperor for years. One setback won't take him off the board."

"As long as Xiao Er remains supreme commander of the Imperial Army, the defense of Qudu will fall back into his hands eventually. Did we all go through so much trouble just to play with the Eight Great Battalions for a month or two before returning them to him, whole and untouched?" Shen Zechuan asked. "You dealt Xiao Er a blow this time. But come spring, when he's rested and recovered, will you be ready for his counterattack?"

Xi Hongxuan spread his folding fan and cooled himself with it. "What else can we do? There's no way to get rid of him for good."

"You can't get rid of him, but you can wear him down." Shen Zechuan wasn't fond of strong tea; after the first sip, he left his cup untouched. "His Majesty already suspects him, and in the days to come, his suspicion will grow. Now is the time to make your move."

"I have neither prodigious military talent nor a record of meritorious service," Xi Hongxuan laughed. "How can I compete with him?"

"No need to be modest." Shen Zechuan tapped the tabletop with a finger. "The tunes in this Ouhua Pavilion are lively and original. Even His Majesty, once a frequent visitor of pleasure houses, would find them a breath of fresh air. Second Young Master Xi, do you really feel you can't compete with Xiao Er when it comes to fun?"

"Leaving aside Secretariat Elder Hai's disapproval of such stuff—even as a companion in fun, there's no way I can rival Xiao Er," Xi Hongxuan said. "You must have another trick up your sleeve."

"Since Xue Xiuzhuo entered the Court of Judicial Review, he's handled major cases one after another. But he is, after all, only one man. And when it comes to talent and scholarly reputation, he is also outdone by Yao Wenyu, who roams unfettered over the land. If Xue Xiuzhuo wishes to advance his career into the Grand Secretariat, he needs someone to lionize him." Shen Zechuan's fingertip inscribed a small circle on the tabletop. "You made a good impression before the students of the Imperial College last time; they can be leveraged to do Xue Xiuzhuo a favor. Secretariat Elder Hai has lately been thinking of expanding the Imperial College. When that happens, Xue Xiuzhuo will naturally be able to handpick his own cohort from the ranks of rising scholars."

"Raise the tide of opinion through sheer numbers." Xi Hongxuan turned it over in his mind. "But Yanqing has his own people. Why must he go to the Imperial College for them?"

"To oppose Xiao Er effectively, all eight clans must make peace and join hands against the enemy—but the Yao Clan is unwilling. Think about it. In the hearts of the literati, the Yao Clan is as lofty and immovable as a rocky spire. Never mind if they're unwilling to work with you; the real threat is that they'll turn around and ally with Xiao Er. If that's the case, why not kick the Yao Clan out now and clear a space for someone up to the task?"

He didn't expect Xi Hongxuan to laugh. "You were born in Zhongbo, so you don't understand the history of the Eight Great Clans," Xi Hongxuan said. "Even if the Yao Clan isn't willing to join hands, we can't kick them out. It's *impossible* to kick them out."

"Think back to the imperial court during the peak of the Yao Clan's glory. There was no place for the Xi Clan then." Shen Zechuan fished out his handkerchief to wipe some water droplets off the table. "I know the noble clans have a long history. I'm simply asking you to push aside the Yao Clan for now. The situation is delicate; we can no longer tolerate unpredictable actions from a third party. Second Young Master, he who hesitates has lost."

Xi Hongxuan didn't dare make such a decision unilaterally. "We'll discuss this again. Let me think about it."

Xiao Chiye was sharpening his blade. He wiped down Wolfsfang carefully, leaving not a speck of dust.

Zhao Hui handed Lu Guangbai a cup of tea. "Er-gongzi has been wiping that blade for ages. Is he planning to hack someone with it?"

Lu Guangbai laughed into his tea. "After today, even venturing outdoors with his blade is going to be tough. Jiming, did you get a good look? I thought this brat was going to cry when he removed his token earlier."

"It was a rare sight." Xiao Jiming smiled too. "To think there'd come a day when the little jerk can't vent his anger."

"Whom are you slandering?" Xiao Chiye folded his handkerchief rather petulantly.

"We're praising you," Lu Guangbai sighed. "All these years in Qudu weren't for naught. What an act—I almost believed it."

"What else is there to learn here?" Xiao Chiye sheathed his blade, then took his seat and crossed one leg over the other. "Old Wei certainly put the effort in; I should give him more credit. He's one thing, but why are my gege," he said, casting a look that implicated each of the older men, "so delighted to see me pinned down and beaten black and blue?"

"It's not every day you see such a thing," Zhao Hui marveled.

"I was worried you'd be upset," said Lu Guangbai. "You can be buddies with anyone, just not the Son of Heaven."

"His Majesty ascended to the throne abruptly and has had his life threatened time and again. He's not a brave man to begin with; it's only to be expected that he would be afraid now," Xiao Chiye said. "I just never anticipated Fu Linye throwing in with them."

"Fu Linye has connections with the Xi Clan, but he's not the type to bend over as the noble clans' lackey," Xiao Jiming said. "He's most likely hoping to win His Majesty and Wei Huaixing's favor by impeaching you."

"You pushed Wei Huaixing pretty hard, too, to make him lay down his trump card," said Lu Guangbai. "Now that he's shown it, we can fight back."

"Wei Huaixing has served so long, yet he has never been promoted to the Grand Secretariat. It has everything to do with his temperament." Xiao Chiye thought a moment. "Although Hua Siqian used him when he was alive, he did so with great disdain. Now that Secretariat Elder Hai is fearful of the noble clans taking over the Grand Secretariat, he's also holding him back from promotion. Wei Huaixing bears a grudge. If he wants to challenge Secretariat Elder Hai, he has to join forces with Xi Hongxuan and be the vanguard that charges into enemy lines. All this so he can step over the threshold that's been too high for him for more than ten years. I only needed to flinch back, and he couldn't wait to give chase and present that final memorial."

"A great deal hinges on this—even if the instructions were forged, it's an excellent forgery," Xiao Jiming warned him. "He began by calling into question the Imperial Army's accounts, knowing Hai Liangyi is nervous about the disbursement of military funds after the Hua faction embezzled them. He cannot tolerate any numbers being unaccounted for. The Chief Surveillance Bureau will be investigating you in the next few days. We can't let Fu Linye take the case alone. We need to ensure someone conducts the investigation with him—someone fair and impartial from of the Chief Surveillance Bureau or the officials authorized to perform audits."

"Fu Linye will most likely be working with someone from the Embroidered Uniform Guard." Zhao Hui paused. "This is an assassination case, after all."

"Embroidered Uniform Guard." Lu Guangbai looked at Xiao Chiye. "We're without a single ally there; on the contrary, it's full of adversaries. A-Ye, you're going to take a beating this time."

Xiao Chiye grinned wickedly. "Embroidered Uniform Guard, huh. I happen to know someone."

A few days later, the Chief Surveillance Bureau began their investigation into the Imperial Army's accounts. Before Fu Linye set off, he met with Shen Zechuan, who had been tapped to help him with the audit. Knowing this man was a new favorite of the throne, Fu Linye didn't dare slight him; he instructed someone to serve their guest the quality tea.

Shen Zechuan took a few sips and said cordially, "It's my first time on the job, so I'll be troubling Your Excellency for guidance."

Fu Linye regarded Shen Zechuan as someone, like himself, who was in the noble clans' camp, yet he still had some fear of him. Thus he merely replied, "I'm afraid I'm not worthy to be your guide. I'll have to trouble the lord judge to split the work with me. The Imperial Army is as impenetrable as a metal bucket. I'm afraid they're keeping two sets of account books, so I'll be relying on the lord judge to do a thorough search."

Regarding whom and where to search, Fu Linye spoke not a word. He was reluctant to commit himself to the noble clans and offend Hai Liangyi, but he also had no wish to join Hai Liangyi in stepping on the noble clans' toes. The man was a skilled fence-sitter who leaned whichever way the wind blew. This time, he had severely offended

Xiao Chiye, and the supreme commander's people were bound to make things difficult when he went to check the accounts. Xiao Er was a notorious asshole; searching his residence was asking for trouble. In this matter, Fu Linye was unwilling to stick his neck out. He planned to push Shen Zechuan to the fore and let him conduct the search—he could be the pawn who drew Xiao Chiye's ire.

To his surprise, Shen Zechuan readily accepted the role.

Fu Linye's wariness of him receded; he looked at Shen Zechuan now and saw a greenhorn.

The two split up, and each went on their way: Fu Linye headed for the Imperial Army's office, while Shen Zechuan made for the manor of the Prince of Libei in the company of a censor from the Chief Surveillance Bureau and a contingent of men from the Embroidered Uniform Guard.

They were still a ways off when Ding Tao, sprawled on the rooftop, spotted Shen Zechuan and sighed. "How could he do this?"

"How could he do what?" Gu Jin asked.

Ding Tao hemmed and hawed.

"You mean how he's chummy with Er-gongzi but still helps others investigate him—that?" Gu Jin asked.

"They're more than *chummy*!"

"That's men for you." Gu Jin twisted his wineskin open. "You'll understand when you're older. Everyone is like this. An embrace behind closed doors is a private matter; what happens once you put on clothes and step outside are public affairs. You can't talk about them in the same breath... You don't need to write this down!"

At the door of the manor, Shen Zechuan's party was greeted by Zhao Hui and Chen Yang. Since Zhao Hui held an official military appointment, Shen Zechuan was the one who had to bow.

"The heir's courtyard is on the north side of the estate," Zhao Hui told Shen Zechuan. "It mostly houses records of Libei's military affairs."

"The purpose of this humble servant's trip here today is to investigate the second young master," Shen Zechuan replied tactfully. "It has nothing to do with Libei."

Satisfied that Shen Zechuan hadn't come to make trouble, Zhao Hui nodded and shot a glance at Chen Yang, who stepped forward to lead the way. "The second young master's courtyard is on the east side," he explained as they walked. "Lord Judge and the other Embroidered Uniform Guard brothers, please follow me."

Shen Zechuan bowed again to Zhao Hui and followed Chen Yang.

Xiao Chiye's courtyard was spacious. Strictly speaking, its scale surpassed that of the heir, but Xiao Fangxu had been too lazy to change it, and the brothers themselves paid no mind to such things. Xiao Chiye had lived here all this time, though after he took up his post as the Imperial Army's supreme commander, he rarely spent his nights here. Most of the time, he rested in a smaller house near the Imperial Army's office.

When Shen Zechuan caught sight of him, he was fishing by a tree-lined pond, draped in a fisherman's cloak of woven straw.

"Your Excellency is here so early," Xiao Chiye remarked. "Have you had breakfast?"

"I ate at the Chief Surveillance Bureau," Shen Zechuan said, "I see the supreme commander has refined taste in leisure."

"I'm just an idler on suspension. How can I compare to Your Excellency?" Xiao Chiye shook the fishing rod as if to prove his idleness. "Though if you're here to search my courtyard, you must first show me the warrant."

"We're all old hands here," Shen Zechuan said placidly. "Isn't it rather silly for the supreme commander to obstruct me so stubbornly for just a few moments' delay?"

"I only recognize official warrants." Xiao Chiye stood and tossed away the cloak and rod. "If you want to enter my courtyard, show me the warrant."

The censor from the Chief Surveillance Bureau who had been tagging along stepped forward at once to mediate. "Gentlemen, easy now, let's be civil. Supreme Commander, please wait a moment. Lord Judge, please don't get angry."

"The Embroidered Uniform Guard knows better than anyone the importance of doing things by the book." Xiao Chiye stepped closer, his tone chilly. "Have you not learned even this much since you left the Temple of Guilt?"

Shen Zechuan looked back at him steadily. "A tiger stranded on the flatlands will be insulted even by wild dogs. Whether a dog like me shows you the search warrant or not, you'll have to welcome me with a smile."

Wiping sweat from his brow, the censor squeezed his way between them and cupped his hands politely as he pleaded, "Let's just talk this over. It's all—"

"That's quite the mouth you have." Xiao Chiye nudged the censor aside without so much as a look and stepped closer. "I wonder if you'd dare say it again with your fists?"

"No fists! You mustn't fight!" the censor strained forward and shouted. "We do have a search warrant—please take a look, Supreme Commander—and we do have to search the compound too—Judge, please wait—let's just talk this over—Whoa there! Y'all don't need to be hollerin' like this—why y'all getting' so bowed up?!"

In his moment of anxiety, he had lapsed back into his local dialect.

ON THE OFFENSIVE

THE ACCOMPANYING CENSOR was Yu Xiaozai, an investigating censor of the seventh rank. It was a position similar to the Chief Supervising Secretary of the various offices: a low-ranking post, but with great authority to inspect and supervise. There was no more appropriate person to step forward and play mediator.

It was the dead of winter, but Yu Xiaozai was sweating buckets. Though he often went out on assignments, traveling out of the capital for various inspections, he'd never been placed in such a difficult position where he couldn't afford to offend either side. After his outburst, both men, previously engrossed in their own heated exchange, were now looking at him.

Frantic, Yu Xiaozai tried to persuade them. "It's mighty early for two men like y'all to be fightin' like this—I'll hand over the search warrant in just a tick, Supreme Commander." As he spoke, he took the document from his lapels and handed it to Xiao Chiye.

Xiao Chiye gave it a cursory flip-through and looked toward Chen Yang, who immediately said, "Right this way, Lord Judge."

Yu Xiaozai clasped his hands together and exclaimed with relief, "That's just how it oughta be done, by the book. All of us are here t'do official business for His Majesty. Ain't no need for y'all to get your ox in a ditch."

"It's cold outside. Gu Jin, please invite this…" Xiao Chiye paused.

Yu Xiaozai cleared his throat and gathered himself; when he spoke again, it was in the official dialect: "This humble servant's surname is Yu—Yu Xiaozai. Please call me Youjing. I thank the supreme commander in advance for your kindness, but I'll pass on the tea. There's official business to be done, so this humble official must accompany the judge."

Xiao Chiye nodded once. Gu Jin stepped forward and bowed to Yu Xiaozai before leading him into the courtyard.

Shen Zechuan ascended the stone steps, where the doors to a neat room already stood open. Attendants, heads bowed, stood on either side.

"This is the supreme commander's study," said Chen Yang. "Your Excellency, please go ahead."

Shen Zechuan raised his hand, and Ge Qingqing turned to nod to the rest of the Embroidered Uniform Guard behind him. The group dispersed and began to look through the books on the open shelves.

Chen Yang motioned for Ding Tao to keep an eye on things here and led Shen Zechuan alone farther along the veranda. After turning a corner and passing through a gate, they arrived at Xiao Chiye's bedchamber.

"This is the supreme commander's bedroom," Chen Yang explained. "Within are many fragile, precious objects bestowed by the emperor. I'd appreciate if Your Excellency took personal charge of examining them."

After thanking him politely for the trouble, Shen Zechuan ventured in.

Xiao Chiye's room was large but simply furnished and surprisingly tidy. Behind the silk entrance screen sat a long table with feet carved like horse hooves, upon which a few books on military strategy were stacked. There were no floral arrangements or antique calligraphy, only a large landscape painting of the mountains and rivers of the Zhou empire hanging across one wall.

Shen Zechuan picked up a book and flipped through. The pages were pristine, as if no one had ever read it. A few seconds later, he heard the door close on the other side of the screen.

Shen Zechuan's eyes never left the book. "Lord Yu, the accompanying censor, will be here once he's finished checking the study."

"The study will keep him occupied until after noon." Xiao Chiye shrugged out of his overcoat. "Fu Linye must think he's been clever. To keep out of my sight, he shoved you here instead."

Shen Zechuan flipped a page with careful fingers. "He just wants to wrap up the investigation and close the case without offending anyone."

Xiao Chiye cocked his head, considering Shen Zechuan's silhouette through the screen. "Why are you hiding in there?"

"Checking the accounts," came the reply.

"You won't find what you're looking for."

Shen Zechuan closed the book and placed it back on the tabletop. "I won't know until I've checked."

Xiao Chiye raised a finger to tap the screen separating them. "Why does it sound like you want to check something else?"

"Treasonous texts, bribery ledgers, military correspondence—I have to check for them all."

"Didn't you miss something?" Xiao Chiye asked. "Aren't you going to check for lewd poems, forbidden plays, and erotic art?"

"I'm here on *official* business," Shen Zechuan said quietly. "Besides, it's broad daylight. I wouldn't dare be so impetuous."

The silk panels of the screen were translucent, the figures of both men faintly visible to one another. Xiao Chiye's fingers slid along the screen until they touched the dark silhouette of Shen Zechuan's neck. Even from the other side, it ignited a warmth in Shen Zechuan, as if that hand caressed his skin.

"Xi Hongxuan invited you for drinks," Xiao Chiye stated with certainty.

"Mm-hmm," Shen Zechuan hummed, distracted.

Xiao Chiye's finger slid down to the shadow of Shen Zechuan's collar. "Did you have fun drinking with the courtesans?"

"Yes." The reply was calm.

"Did you feel overheated from the wine?"

"I did."

Xiao Chiye felt hot too. Three of his fingers slid down, as though along Shen Zechuan's neck, prying apart the collar of his robe before slipping further down. Instead of retreating, Shen Zechuan stepped forward and let Xiao Chiye's fingers slide across his chest through the hazy screen, tracing the ink paintings.

"Do you wear earrings?" Xiao Chiye suddenly asked.

"Nope." Shen Zechuan tilted his head to expose his ear. "Do you want me to?"

"Er-gongzi will get you a little jade pendant earring," Xiao Chiye said.

"Just one?"

"One." His eyes followed the smudged contours of Shen Zechuan's jaw as he said, "Wear it on your right ear."

Xiao Chiye was used to pulling him closer with his right hand. He only had to bend his neck slightly when he turned Shen Zechuan over,

and he could take his earlobe into his mouth. Jade set against satiny white. His dazed and satiated expression as his sweat-soaked hair was brushed aside to show that gleam of green would surely be a sight to behold.

Shen Zechuan didn't answer but flashed an evocative smile through the screen. Xiao Chiye couldn't see his eyes clearly, but the curled corners of his lips seemed to exude that same subtle invitation.

Hold me. Touch me.

Xiao Chiye closed his eyes; he felt Shen Zechuan left the door open for more every time. Such unvoiced lines sent waves of desire crashing over him more violently than ever. He swore he hadn't always been a man this easily aroused. The totality of his desire used to lie in the blue expanse and grassy wilderness.

Shen Zechuan was unaware of the implications of his silence. "The wine at Ouhua Pavilion is delicious, as is the wine at Xiangyun Villa. You've been visiting Xiangyun Villa for years; I suppose you didn't expect the courtesans to throw themselves into another man's arms."

"There are new lovers, and then there are old flames," Xiao Chiye remarked. "It's only natural they'd be jealous now that I'm drunk on you."

"I didn't know Xi Hongxuan had gotten his hands on Xiangyun Villa either," said Shen Zechuan. "Now that they're claiming you accepted bribes, what are you going to do? Will you melt them with tenderness and convince these old flames to amend their testimonies?"

Xiao Chiye retracted his hand. "The owner of Xiangyun Villa isn't Xi Hongxuan. At least not while I was hanging around there. Courtesan Xiangyun of Xiangyun Villa is well-read and resourceful. Among the civil officials and even the students of the

Imperial College, she enjoys a glowing reputation. Xi Hongxuan is no man of letters; she wouldn't be intimidated by him."

"What do you mean?"

"There are only two possibilities regarding Xiangyun's false testimony. One is that she's fallen in love with some noble young master and happily sold me out for the sake of the other man. The second is that her cooperation was coerced," Xiao Chiye said. "If it's the latter, we'll need to find out by whom."

Shen Zechuan smiled. "Seems like your old flame still has some place in your heart."

"Xiangyun was always the one who leaked news of the Chief Surveillance Bureau's movements in Qudu to us," Xiao Chiye explained. "Even if she's really switched allegiances... I can't bear to see her suffer."

"What a considerate man," Shen Zechuan replied. "The period after the new year is crucial. Whether or not you can turn the tables in the spring depends on how you take the beating now. Don't lose your head and misstep for the sake of a beauty."

"I'm idling away at home at present. I can't go out, so I'll have to ask you to investigate on my behalf. Please pass a message to Xiangyun: tell her Er-gongzi is still thinking of rekindling old flames with her."

Shen Zechuan gently pushed the screen aside. "I'm busy with work these days; I'm afraid I haven't the time. Why don't you ask Ding Tao or Gu Jin to pay a visit?"

Finally getting a clear look at him, Xiao Chiye asked, "Why? Don't you live on Donglong Street?"

Shen Zechuan had parted his lips to answer when he heard footsteps outside. Before he could move, Xiao Chiye bent down and hoisted him over his shoulder. In a few long strides, he leapt over the table and whisked Shen Zechuan into the inner chamber.

Outside, Yu Xiaozai ascended the steps, lifting the hem of his robe. He knocked and called out, "Lord Judge?"

The lord judge was pressed tight to the wall behind the clothing racks and couldn't answer. His day robe was plastered against his body. Shen Zechuan reached up and jammed his palm against Xiao Chiye's chest. He turned his head to call out, but Xiao Chiye suddenly lifted him up, knocking him into the clothing rack. As the rack teetered, Shen Zechuan raised his leg to arrest its fall—Xiao Chiye seized the chance and lifted Shen Zechuan's other leg up next to his hip, trapping Shen Zechuan against him.

"He has the authority to present a memorial directly to the emperor," Xiao Chiye drawled. "If he catches us together, we'll never explain our way out of this."

Yu Xiaozai rapped on the door again. "Is the lord judge in here?"

Shen Zechuan held Xiao Chiye's hand in place and hissed, "Taking advantage of someone's predicament isn't what a gentleman should do."

"Me? Take advantage?" One hand firmly under Shen Zechuan's rear end, Xiao Chiye brushed his nose against Shen Zechuan's and smiled. "That's right. I'm taking advantage of your predicament."

Shen Zechuan locked eyes with him, chest heaving.

Having received no response, Yu Xiaozai pushed the door open. He stepped in, search warrant tucked under his arm, and began to survey the room.

Shen Zechuan slowly hooked his long leg back to set the clothing rack upright. His hips shifted against Xiao Chiye's palm as he stretched. By the time he managed to set the rack back in place, he was covered in a thin layer of sweat.

Once the clothing rack was stabilized, Xiao Chiye pressed in against his ear and murmured ever so softly, "It wasn't actually going to fall."

Shen Zechuan looked at him out of the corner of his eye and mouthed with a smile: *You—son—of—a—bitch.*

Xiao Chiye cheerfully accepted the label and whispered, "Wear an earring, Lanzhou."

Yu Xiaozai was mumbling to himself. After peering around the antechamber, he turned toward the inner chamber.

Shen Zechuan flinched, but Xiao Chiye pressed against him insistently, as if he had no intention of stepping aside.

"Wear it." Xiao Chiye's voice was sultry in Shen Zechuan's ear. That heat pierced him, and that breath sent Shen Zechuan's spine tingling. Xiao Chiye murmured with a smile, "Wear it for my eyes."

Wear it for my eyes.

What an arrogant and presumptuous request. Xiao Chiye no longer hid his wolfish nature. He pushed all his ardent desire toward Shen Zechuan, urging him to feel its scalding heat.

When they had plunged into the abyss that night, their entanglement was one of desperation and despair, two blood-soaked chests pressing desperately together, their vulnerabilities exposed to each other's eyes. Xiao Chiye had no intention of reliving it alone after daybreak. He would grab Shen Zechuan by the ankle and drag him back, inch by inch, drowning him in a sea of desire where only the two of them rode the waves.

Yu Xiaozai had already walked up to the curtain that separated the inner chamber from the outer room. Shen Zechuan clutched at the material on Xiao Chiye's chest, no room for daylight between them anymore, and, in this moment of crisis, stared into his eyes.

Yu Xiaozai lifted the curtain but saw no one. The clothing rack in the corner was cluttered with casual day robes. Rummaging through them would be inappropriate, so he only peered carefully around the area.

Trapped under the bed, Shen Zechuan was struggling to breathe. There wasn't nearly enough space for two people to lie on top of each other; the weight of Xiao Chiye pressing down on him left him gasping for air. That strong and well-built body was far too heavy.

Xiao Chiye looked down into his eyes.

Shen Zechuan immediately caught his intent. *No way,* he mouthed. *Nope. No—*

Xiao Chiye kissed him, robbing him of any chance to gasp for breath. Shen Zechuan tightened his grip, digging his fingers into Xiao Chiye's back hard enough to bruise, but still Xiao Chiye kissed him with suffocating force. Shen Zechuan was on the verge of fainting; he could do nothing to ward off Xiao Chiye's offensive. He felt he was drowning in deep waters and Xiao Chiye was the only thing he could grasp onto, but this driftwood was as forceful and possessive as the raging waves that battered him. As if he wanted Shen Zechuan to feel all his ruthlessness, and to remember the panic of gradually succumbing.

ACCOUNT LEDGERS

XIAO CHIYE KISSED Shen Zechuan mercilessly, with tongue and teeth, throwing Shen Zechuan's mind into chaos as his lungs cried for air. As time ticked by, his tightly clenched fingers slowly lost their strength; he was so short of breath he was dizzy. In this murky, narrow space, he seemed to sink deeper into the drowning waters under Xiao Chiye's weight as the sensation of suffocating intensified. Xiao Chiye kept him captive in his arms, caging Shen Zechuan's struggling body until he was the only thing Shen Zechuan could rely on.

Yu Xiaozai approached the bed, his shoes shuffling beside their ears.

A rustle of footsteps sounded outside.

"So this is where the lord censor has gone!" Chen Yang said. "Please come with this humble servant. There are some documents in the study awaiting Your Excellency's personal review."

Yu Xiaozai followed him out with the warrant still under his arm. "And where is the lord judge?"

Chen Yang didn't dare look around the room. Leading Yu Xiaozai out and shutting the door behind him, he answered, "The lord judge was drinking tea in the den earlier. He should be on his way here as we speak."

"Didn't he come this way a few moments ago?" Yu Xiaozai asked.

"It's freezing out," Chen Yang replied. "A warm cup of tea is a must to feel refreshed and energized..."

Their voices faded as they walked away. Only then did Xiao Chiye release Shen Zechuan's lips.

Lying beneath him, Shen Zechuan panted for breath. He lowered his eyes and swallowed, throat bobbing in tandem with the rise and fall of his chest. His lips had gone crimson, glossy from the kisses that had nearly ended his life.

Xiao Chiye was gasping for breath too.

Shen Zechuan reached a hand out from under the bed to crawl out. "You—"

Xiao Chiye grabbed his outstretched wrist, pressed the tip of his nose against Shen Zechuan's, and kissed him once more.

When Shen Zechuan said Xiao Chiye was *ravenously gorging himself* last time, he had obviously borne a grudge over it. This time, Xiao Chiye savored and teased as he devoured, stopping Shen Zechuan's soft moans from escaping and swallowing any words between them.

It was a little less than an hour later when Yu Xiaozai saw Shen Zechuan again. As he stepped forward to bow, his face paled with alarm. "Your Excellency, what—"

"The tea was too hot," Shen Zechuan replied expressionlessly.

The Embroidered Uniform Guard were still flipping through books in the extensive library. Ge Qingqing trotted over and shook his head at Shen Zechuan. They were only here to go through the motions in the first place. Seeing they would get no further, Shen Zechuan said to Yu Xiaozai, "We're almost done here. Why don't you and I head back to the bureau office first to report to Censor Fu?"

Yu Xiaozai concurred and scanned the room once more. "The supreme commander is still sitting outside to avoid any conflict of interest. We should notify him before leaving."

In silence, Shen Zechuan pressed his tongue to the corner of his mouth and nodded in agreement.

Sure enough, Xiao Chiye was still sitting by the side of the pond fishing with the same woven straw cloak draped over him, as if he hadn't moved all day.

"It's late. Why don't Your Excellencies eat before you leave?" Xiao Chiye held the fishing rod with his foot propped on his knee. Had he caught even one fish?

Yu Xiaozai tactfully declined. "I'm afraid we've imposed on Your Excellency the entire day; I wouldn't dare tarry longer. Next time, I'll invite the two lords to wine."

"Sounds good." Xiao Chiye shook his rod and pulled a small silver carp out of the water. He laughed out loud as he unhooked the fish into the basket and carried it over. Ducking a little as he emerged from the grove around the pond, he tossed the basket to Yu Xiaozai. "I'm indebted to Lord Yu for the consideration you've shown me today. Consider these fish a small token of my appreciation."

A light snow was falling. Yu Xiaozai looked down into the basket, oblivious to what was going on between the two men beside him.

Shen Zechuan glanced at Xiao Chiye, who casually rubbed his right ear with a thumb. Shen Zechuan promptly averted his eyes.

Overwhelmed by the gift, Yu Xiaozai said, "Oh, goodness no, how could I..."

"What?" Xiao Chiye patted Yu Xiaozai on the shoulder. "Don't tell me the Chief Surveillance Bureau would consider a couple of fish a bribe?"

Yu Xiaozai hastily said, "It's not that—"

"Don't be a stranger." Xiao Chiye moved aside to make way. "Chen Yang, see the gentlemen out."

Yu Xiaozai, having been thanked out of nowhere, was baffled all the way out the door.

Shen Zechuan was stepping into the carriage when he suddenly brought his fingers to his right earlobe. He felt as though the spot had been rubbed raw by that jerk; the searing heat vexed him to no end.

Fu Linye was in the courtyard of the Imperial Army's office, waiting with one leg crossed casually over the other. Assistant Commander Meng Rui stood politely at his side. Seeing him drink cup after cup of their best tea without shifting from his place, Meng Rui knew he wouldn't leave today unless he pried something useful out of them.

In truth, Meng Rui was fed up, but he didn't dare show it. He served more tea and said with a smile, "Your Excellency has looked through all the Imperial Army account books. The gentlemen from the Ministry of Revenue have checked the calculations as well. If Your Excellency would like to see anything else, please don't hesitate to tell this humble subordinate."

"Things like account books must be carefully audited again and again," Fu Linye said, unperturbed. "There may well be an omission or mistake somewhere. It can't be rushed. We're still looking."

Wei Huaixing had claimed Xiao Chiye's repairs of the Imperial Army office and expansion of the military drill grounds couldn't be accounted for, but in fact, every cent of it was detailed in the Imperial Army's books. Fu Linye knew Xiao Chiye wouldn't have made this easy, but he still needed to churn some dirt out of this clear water. Otherwise, he'd have nothing to report back to Wei Huaixing.

Moreover, Li Jianheng had always shielded the Imperial Army in the past; most had decided it was simpler to let Xiao Chiye be than submit memorials to condemn him. But this time, Li Jianheng had obviously grown tired of the man. Everyone could see which way the wind was blowing—it was time to make Xiao Chiye suffer a little.

The other officials he'd brought from the Ministry of Revenue clacked noisily away on their abacuses in the lit hall, determined to leave no stone unturned.

When Shen Zechuan arrived, he said nothing to Tantai Hu, who was standing in the corridor; Qiao Tianya, in disguise and dressed as an Embroidered Uniform Guard, followed him through the door.

The clacking of abacus beads echoed throughout the hall. Fu Linye set his teacup aside and rose to greet Shen Zechuan. Shen Zechuan bowed, and the two took their seats.

"Did the search of the manor go smoothly?"

"Xiao Er delayed us for quite some time," Shen Zechuan replied.

I knew it, Fu Linye thought. Outwardly, he asked with concern, "Did he get physical? That man is a thug. It must have been hard on the lord judge."

He did get physical, but it has nothing to do with you. He smiled. "It's all right. What's a little hardship for His Majesty's sake? Xiao Er tried to block me from searching his courtyard. Fortunately, Lord Yu was there and successfully persuaded him."

Fu Linye scoffed, as if venting on Shen Zechuan's behalf. "We act on His Majesty's orders. By obstructing our work at his own whim, Second Young Master Xiao not only disrespects us, but His Majesty as well."

Shen Zechuan looked into the hall. "Your Excellency, is the investigation here not done yet?"

"It's done," Fu Linye replied. "But one can't have too many reviews. As you know, account books are easy to fake."

Shen Zechuan caught the meaning behind those words as surely as if he'd said it aloud. After a moment's pause, he answered, "Your Excellency is the chief official in charge of this search; I will follow your lead."

Fu Linye smiled and said nothing. He drank tea with Shen Zechuan until midnight, when the newly audited account books were presented.

Fu Linye flipped through, then suddenly asked Meng Rui, "At the start of spring last year, a temple was constructed in the palace by imperial decree. The Ministry of Works entrusted the important task of transportation of materials to the Imperial Army, but construction of the temple was abandoned. The supreme commander leaned hard on the Ministry of Works to demand payment for labor, is that right?"

"That's right," Meng Rui replied. "Payment was delayed by several months. It was all the Imperial Army's hard-earned money. The supreme commander was anxious, so he personally went to ask for it."

Fu Linye closed the account books and smirked. "Back then, the state treasury's annual expenditure hadn't been fully accounted for, and they couldn't disburse the funds. The Directorate of Ceremonial Affairs wouldn't have dared arbitrarily approve it either. How did the supreme commander get his money?"

"He didn't," Meng Rui clarified. "It was the Secretary for the Ministry of Revenue, Wang Xian, who made the decision to pay the debt with a batch of silk from Quancheng, which the Imperial Army traded for silver. This was also recorded in the ledgers, and the transaction clearly marked down."

Fu Linye smacked the tabletop with such force it rattled the teapot; if Qiao Tianya's swift reflexes hadn't caught it, the tea would've spilled over Shen Zechuan's lap. Shen Zechuan remained smiling in his seat, waiting for Fu Linye to continue.

This transaction had occurred at the start of spring. At that time, Shen Zechuan was still in the Temple of Guilt, but he had heard of the exchange. He knew that in reality, the debt was eventually settled not because of Wang Xian, but Xue Xiuzhuo—then the Chief Supervising Secretary of the Ministry of Revenue—who had stepped forward to mediate and settle the debt by offering Xiao Chiye the silk from Quancheng.

Shen Zechuan tapped his fingers on his knee.

This transaction is a weak spot.

Sure enough, Fu Linye puffed out his chest. "This account book indicates that a total of six hundred and sixty bolts of silk were allocated to the Imperial Army, which you recorded as low-grade silk from Quancheng. But the Qudu treasury records state that they were *top*-grade silk from Quancheng! A difference of one word, but the discrepancy amounts to four thousand taels! I'm asking you, where did these four thousand taels go?"

"The bolts allocated to us were indeed of a low grade," Meng Rui answered evenly. "The silk was dispatched by the Ministry of Revenue itself, and the written transfer order indicated them to be low-grade silk from Quancheng."

Fu Linye flung down the account book. "Of course. Wang Xian, right? He's long been colluding with you people. He wrote low-grade silk from Quancheng on the handwritten transfer order, but the treasury records clearly state that it was top-grade silk from Quancheng that had been taken out. What did Xiao Chiye promise Wang Xian to get him to falsify the order?!"

"These are baseless accusations!" Meng Rui blurted in shock. "Censor Fu, you—"

"The way I see it, the Imperial Army is a front for laundering ill-gotten gains. Xiao Chiye has been making a fortune through you people. Anyone with eyes could see he was fooling around on Donglong Street all these years, eating, drinking, and making merry! First Wang Xian is in cahoots with him, and now he has Yuan Liu offering him golden peaches. Xiao Chiye enjoys the honor of His Majesty's favor, yet all he does is line his own pockets!" Fu Linye snickered. "Lord Judge, do you see this? Qudu's foremost rising star is also its foremost thieving traitor! Tonight, you and I shall examine these books once again. We're sure to find more rotten accounts!"

Shen Zechuan fixed his gaze on Fu Linye until apprehension started to creep over the censor. "This matter does not concern the assassination case, so it's outside the scope of my duties at this time," Shen Zechuan said. "Your Excellency, it's your decision."

Fu Linye had intended to make an accomplice of Shen Zechuan, but now he wavered—Shen Zechuan wasn't falling for it. Still, this could be big news if he reported it up the chain. He wasn't willing to lose his claim on this discovery; he steeled himself and slapped the table. "Keep going! Tonight, check all the Imperial Army's account books over the years a thousand times!"

Shen Zechuan smiled and lowered his lashes as he sipped his tea. But his heart sank. If it weren't for Xue Xiuzhuo's involvement in that transaction, he might have overlooked it himself. Xiao Chiye had most likely forgotten about it too. *Was Xue Xiuzhuo already wary of the Imperial Army back then?*

Shen Zechuan blew at his tea foam in silence.

FANNING THE FLAMES

THE CANDLES in the Imperial Army's office burned until dawn. The men from the Ministry of Revenue plucked at their abacuses until their heads spun; at long last, they sorted the problematic accounts into one booklet and placed it in Fu Linye's hands. Shen Zechuan reviewed them all.

Fu Linye attached the memorial and submitted the booklet, along with their progress on the assassination case, to Li Jianheng's desk. In short order, the Grand Secretariat met to discuss this matter before the throne.

"Your Majesty," Fu Linye began, "one can know the flavor of the entire pot from a single bite. Xiao Chiye has been taking bribes for a long time. He's kept a tight grip on the Imperial Army for the past few years; I'm afraid there may be many more falsified accounts like this one. The state treasury is impoverished, and the tax arrears have been piling up one after another. Retaining a man like him is like setting a torch under a bed of kindling—he's a danger that will jeopardize the whole state."

Kong Qiu had looked through the booklet too. "The assassination case is not yet concluded. We shouldn't complicate matters at this time. In this subject's opinion, the investigation of the bribery case can be postponed—at present, we must focus on the assassination."

"How strange." Wei Huaixing scoffed. "Both implicate Xiao Chiye. Why should we investigate the cases separately? We may as well pull out the mud along with the radish and use the opportunity to make a clean break!"

Kong Qiu was steadfast. "This case has already deviated from its course. The way I see it, you gentlemen aren't trying to expose the mastermind behind the assassination but root out those who disagree with you!"

"The bribery case is the melon we found at the end of the long vine," Fu Linye retorted. "Why is it that when Minister Kong investigates, he is pursuing the case, but when we do it, we are slinging personal attacks? The Chief Surveillance Bureau is duty-bound to surveil and supervise. Was it wrong of me to indict him for taking bribes?!"

"Wang Xian has not yet stood trial," Kong Qiu explained. "If we passed judgment on the bribery case based on your words alone, what need is there for the joint trial by the Three Judicial Offices? Perhaps we should let Censor Fu make the rulings alone! The Ministry of Justice should be verifying the statements presented by Vice Minister Wei. It's been only one night; I've yet to even examine the witness testimony, yet all of you are so anxious to convict him. If he's truly guilty, why the hurry? Any ruling and sentencing must follow the proper procedures! Otherwise, why have laws?!"

The three quarreled before the throne, leaving Li Jianheng unable to get a word in edgewise. He turned to Hai Liangyi, who sat listening with his head lowered. When he'd heard what everyone had to say, he gave a slight nod.

"What does the Secretariat Elder think?" Li Jianheng hurried to ask.

"What did the Secretariat Elder think?" Shen Zechuan fiddled with a copper coin in his hand. "Naturally, he dismissed the memorial for the bribery case. Hai Liangyi is rigid in his ways; everyone regards him as an upright lone minister who shuns cliques, yet he led the way in bringing down Hua Siqian and propping up Li Jianheng. It'd be stranger if he *couldn't* tell what was going on. Xi Hongxuan and the others want to use him as a shield to make their move. Little did they know the Secretariat Elder is one who can bide his time while keeping an eye on the brewing storm."

"You've done well." Grand Mentor Qi sat on the other side of the small table. "Instead of stopping Fu Linye, you let him make the call. The credit belongs to him alone. He's too anxious and impatient to wait for a more suitable opportunity. He wanted to present the memorial immediately and seek praise. Hai Liangyi had only to watch that round of mudslinging before the throne to get an inkling of what's happening behind the scenes. By now, he's surely guessed who wants to take down Xiao Chiye."

"We're fanning the flames in the direction of the wind, but the fire still isn't raging hard enough," Shen Zechuan said. "It can't scorch Xiao Chiye, let alone Xiao Jiming. Anyone who looks into the Quancheng silk case will see it's nonsensical. The important thing now is not to get it to make sense, but to guide His Majesty's biases."

"Just so. A reproach and suspension may seem serious, but it's a slap on the wrist. His Majesty has no desire to strip away Xiao Chiye's military power just yet." Holding a weiqi piece, Grand Mentor Qi hummed to himself. He deliberated and said, "We need to keep it that way. Don't let the emperor entertain the notion of taking down Xiao Er for good. Otherwise, this minor victory will sow the seeds of great disaster."

Shen Zechuan toppled the copper coins he'd arranged and began to stack them up again, one at a time, never tiring. "Hai Liangyi controls the Grand Secretariat. Although he's placed men of noble birth like Xue Xiuzhuo in important posts, he has also established the Imperial College and elevates minor officials from common households. Xiansheng, he wants to take one step at a time, and slowly confront the noble clans. He cannot let Xiao Er fall."

"Indeed. The Xiao Clan is sanguine now precisely because they understand this. Xiao Jiming stands calmly aside because he wants to contain this battlefield to Qudu and ensure it doesn't come anywhere near Libei. If it stays in Qudu, it's easier to resolve, and Xiao Er will have fewer issues from home to worry about." Grand Mentor Qi set the piece down. "Everyone is frantically kicking the man while he's down; His Majesty is still angry and thinks of Xiao Er as a disloyal, unfilial, and unrighteous person. But once the wave swells high enough, it breaks on the shore. When the time comes, His Majesty will surely turn around and start pitying his good friend who has been abandoned by all."

Li Jianheng hadn't seen Mu Ru for several days. After the attempted assassination, he could only sleep with his surroundings brightly lit. No eunuch was allowed to set foot in his bedchamber; those attending him had all been replaced with palace maidservants.

It was snowing heavily again today. Hai Liangyi was sick, so he could not go near the emperor. Li Jianheng ordered the Court of Imperial Physicians to Hai Liangyi's residence to take a look at him, then bestowed a great deal of precious tonics. He assured Hai Liangyi repeatedly that he would be diligent in his readings and keep up with his studies.

Thus Mingli Hall was quiet. Li Jianheng flipped through only a few pages of his books before he felt his back aching. He rose to look out the window and saw the snow drifting across the sky like puffs of cotton. Struck by the sudden urge for a stroll, he summoned the palace maidservants to dress him in warm clothes and a cloak so he could go out.

Li Jianheng roamed the snowy garden with his entourage. When he saw the lake frozen over, he recalled the sleigh he used to play with in the palace.

"When the lake freezes solid, it's the perfect time to play," Li Jianheng said to his attendants. "Why didn't anyone remind us this year?"

The moment the words left his mouth, he remembered. The Xiande Emperor had just passed, and it wouldn't do for him to frolic during a time of national mourning; he would undoubtedly receive a lecture from the Chief Surveillance Bureau. His mood soured again. Having had his fill of the snow, he returned to the hall and sent someone to summon Mu Ru.

The young woman arrived in a hooded cloak, her graceful figure supported by a maidservant's proffered arm. As soon as he spied her through the window, Li Jianheng stepped out the door to greet her.

"Darling," Li Jianheng gushed, "the view of you walking in the snow is truly magnificent! We must get someone to put it in ink so we can hang it in the palace to look upon it every day."

"That wouldn't do." Mu Ru lifted the hood of her cloak and smiled, taking a wooden food box from the maidservant's hands. "It's so cold out. I've made soup for Liu-lang."[10]

Li Jianheng's spirits soared when he heard that intimate moniker. He led her inside by the hand and dismissed the attendants, then took his seat on the throne where he handled governmental affairs.

---

10 *Lang, young man; a term of address often used by a woman toward her lover. The address of Liu (six) suggests that he's the sixth prince.*

Mu Ru ladled soup for Li Jianheng as he groused. "The assassination attempt by that castrated traitor frightened us to death. We can hardly sleep these days."

"We?" Mu Ru said playfully. "Only the two of us are here now. Is Liu-lang here, or is the emperor here, to be using such a formal term?"

Li Jianheng gave himself a light slap on his own mouth. "My fault, your husband wasn't thinking!"

Mu Ru cupped his face in her hands and scrutinized him for a moment. "You do look a little careworn. Would you like me to keep you company tonight?"

"You're the only one in the entire world who dotes on me... I treated Ce'an as a brother. Who'd've expected him to be part of this assassination business?" Li Jianheng heaved a sigh. "Just stay with me."

"Her Majesty is very concerned for Liu-lang too. She's been chanting sutras and abstaining from meat for the past few days, all to pray for a peaceful new year for Liu-lang."

Li Jianheng caressed Mu Ru's hand. "I wasn't close with Imperial Mother in the past. I saw her as the villain. I never expected her to treat me so kindly. I—I... It's all the fault of that old dog, Hua Siqian!"

"Who said it wasn't?" Mu Ru gazed at him with fond eyes. "Liu-lang has suffered so much because of the trouble stirred up by that Hua Siqian. Back then, Her Majesty tried to talk sense into him every way she could...but she is, after all, a woman; her words hold no weight against a man's. He brushed off her advice and laid all the blame on her anyway."

"They say words are just rumors; only seeing is believing," Li Jianheng sighed regretfully. "If I could have reconciled with Imperial Mother earlier, there wouldn't be so many misunderstandings between us."

"There was an opportunity in the past." Mu Ru seemed to hesitate. "I heard many years ago, when Liu-lang was still an infant and Her Majesty was raising the former crown prince, she saw that Liu-lang had no one to rely on and mentioned taking Liu-lang into her care. The Guangcheng Emperor agreed as well."

Li Jianheng had never heard such a thing. He couldn't help but ask, "And then what happened? Why didn't she take me?"

Mu Ru laid a soothing hand on him before replying. "Later, the Prince of Libei, Xiao Fangxu, submitted a memorial saying Her Majesty already had the heavy responsibility of nurturing the heir apparent to the Eastern Palace. The crown prince wasn't a child anymore, and raising another prince in her palace might invite internal strife."

"Li... It was the Prince of Libei!"

The seeds of discord had been sown between him and Xiao Chiye. Now, hearing this long-buried secret—one Xiao Chiye had never once mentioned to him—a roil of emotions welled up in him. Xiao Chiye, he thought, had hidden his true feelings far too well. He had never genuinely opened his heart to him as a friend.

"So," Li Jianheng said bitterly, "when all's said and done, he's no different from everyone else who treats me as a stepping stone. How pitiable am I. Born the most elite of nobles, yet without even a brother to rely on!"

Mu Ru took him into her arms. "But he was no blood of yours, after all. Who can compare to the late emperor when it comes to treating Liu-lang well?"

"A pity...a pity the imperial heirs of our Li Clan are few and far between. I'm the only one left now." Li Jianheng suddenly turned to Mu Ru. "Your younger brother has been hiding in Xue Xiuzhuo's residence since Pan Rugui was beheaded. Is he doing well?"

"Yes..." Mu Ru turned and covered her face to sob.

"My dear, what's wrong? Why are you crying all of a sudden?" Li Jianheng hurriedly asked.

Mu Ru wiped her eyes with a handkerchief, looking at him tearfully. "He's doing fine, but he's not by my side, and I can only see him once every few months. My brother—he can neither marry nor make great contributions to the nation. All he can do now is... serve others."

Li Jianheng never could bear to see her cry. "You should've said something earlier. We are husband and wife; we must be of the same mind! Only say the word and I will do it. Of course it's natural to miss your brother. Don't be sad, please, my heart's going to shatter from your tears. My dear Mu Ru, I'll have Xue Xiuzhuo bring him back tomorrow and put him to work at my side, all right?"

"How could you do that?" Mu Ru protested, tears in her lashes. "How could you justify it to the secretariat elder? The others won't agree either. I can't bear to put you in such a difficult spot."

Li Jianheng held her in his arms. "I'm the emperor. I have final say when it comes to affairs in the palace. Besides, if we change his name, will anyone really insist on digging up his past? Pan Rugui is already dead!"

Mu Ru let him cajole her for a few more moments before breaking into a smile. "Fengquan would want to kowtow in thanks to you too."

"We are family," Li Jianheng said generously. "Whether from sentiment or reason, I'm only doing what I ought."

Days passed, and the assassination case was in full swing. Yuan Liu contradicted himself repeatedly under torture, yet with each statement, he insisted he had never given any golden peaches to

Xiao Chiye and knew nothing of the shady deal with the Donglong broker. Several times he considered giving the interrogators what they wanted so it could end, but each time, he remembered his family's lives were in Xiao Chiye's hands. Yuan Liu had been with the Imperial Army a long time; he knew as well as anybody that Xiao Chiye was a different man when it came to how he treated outsiders versus insiders. If the second young master had promised to look after his son in his stead, he would do it—but if Yuan Liu said so much as one wrong word, his son would suffer as well.

Yuan Liu was caught in the middle of this power struggle, unfit to seek life and unable to pursue death. He could only hope for the case to conclude quickly so he could receive a swift end.

The opportunity came soon enough.

The conflicts at court grew more intense by the day. Memorials indicting Xiao Chiye arrived in an endless stream, citing all sorts of bizarre crimes. After Li Jianheng personally took up his brush to give Xiao Chiye a dressing-down, the Secretary for the Ministry of Justice submitted a report before the throne, revealing that their investigation had turned up a new lead—a person.

This person's name was Yinzhu, a eunuch from the Imperial Bakery. According to his verbal testimony, he had been distributing fortune candies to the imperial concubines four hours before the start of the Court Officials' Feast when he saw someone berating Fuling outside Caiwei Palace. Caiwei Palace—where Mu Ru lived.

CASE CLOSED

"IT WAS A COLD DAY. The sky was overcast with dark clouds and the wind was strong. This servant was distributing fortune candies to the various palace ladies. As I left Caiwei Palace, Concubine Mu was just setting out, so I withdrew into a corner to clear the path. That's when I heard a voice reprimanding someone. I poked my head out and saw the chief eunuch of Caiwei Palace arguing with Aunt Fuling."

"Why did you keep silent on this matter during the first trial?"

It was quiet in the hall aside from the swish of the scribe's brush. A handful of lamps lent their glow to the room. Kong Qiu, who had been working through the night, had already emptied many pots of strong tea. At this moment, he had his hands clasped before him as he questioned Yinzhu, who knelt in the hall.

Yinzhu's lips moved. "Your Excellency, this servant thought this was a trivial matter. And because of the strong wind that day, I couldn't quite hear what they were arguing about. I was afraid of saying the wrong thing."

"If that's the case, why did you speak now?" Fu Linye demanded.

Yinzhu wrung the corner of his robe and swallowed nervously. When he replied, it was in a small voice. "I was scared of the esteemed guards in the prison. Ever since I entered the jail, I've been hearing the sound of lashings every night. This servant's godfather was beaten half to death even after he told everything he knew, important or not. This servant is truly...very afraid..."

"You are in a solemn place of interrogation. How dare you ramble on?!" Fu Linye rebuked.

Yinzhu trembled in fright where he knelt on the ground. "Th-this servant...h-had no idea she would commit such a d-despicable act!"

"It's easy to beat a confession out of someone under harsh interrogation," Fu Linye said to Kong Qiu. "This person's words cannot be trusted. How can such a statement be submitted before the emperor?"

"All proceedings from the joint trial are here in writing. The authenticity of this statement may be determined by His Majesty himself," said Kong Qiu. "Once the statement has been transcribed, the secretariat elder will require a copy too."

At this point in the case, Fu Linye hadn't expected to be thrown a wild card. He could grind Xiao Er under his heel right now because he was certain Xiao Er could not retaliate. As long as Yuan Liu was dirty, Xiao Er could not be absolved. But now that Caiwei Palace was implicated, everyone was tainted. How could they bear to dig deeper?

He immediately grasped that Yinzhu's appearance was more than simple coincidence. This eunuch hadn't just held off until the joint trial before he was willing to speak up—someone had planted him here.

Fu Linye burned with anxiety. He was different from Wei Huaixing, who had the Wei Clan behind him: a great clan tied to seven others. If Wei Huaixing was dragged down, he would at most be investigated and penalized. But what of Fu Linye? He had no influential name to fall back on.

After watching Fu Linye's face move through several expressions, Kong Qiu said, "Caiwei Palace is part of the imperial harem.

Investigation by outside officials is inappropriate; we must discuss this matter before the throne. Go home and rest, Censor Fu. We shall meet again in court."

Fu Linye rose to his feet. Even through his anxiety, he managed to plaster a smile on his face as he respectfully bowed to Kong Qiu then retreated at speed.

Outside, the sky was still dark and the air bitterly cold. Fu Linye urged on his driver, who steered the horse carriage noisily over the snow as it rushed toward Ouhua Pavilion. Lifting the hem of his robe, he leapt out and hurried upstairs.

Xi Hongxuan, who was well-versed in opera tunes, sat with Shen Zechuan discussing his latest work. Shen Zechuan had tired of the garb of the Embroidered Uniform Guard and stepped out today in a loose, wide-sleeved robe. He leaned against the chair as he listened, opening and closing the fan in his hand.

Fu Linye was not expecting his presence.

Shen Zechuan closed his fan gently and turned, seemingly oblivious to Fu Linye's frazzled state. He did not rise but merely smiled and said, "The lord censor has come a little too late. You've missed the highlight of the evening."

Xi Hongxuan was less than pleased. He remained seated as well, waving away the madam who had hurried up after Fu Linye and bidding her close the door. Fu Linye was left to find his own seat. "Linye, what are you doing here? You should've sent someone ahead to announce you. It's just a few steps away; did you have to rush like this and disgrace yourself?"

Not only was Fu Linye Xi Hongxuan's senior in age, his rank was higher—yet Xi Hongxuan chastised him as if berating a child. His already grim mood darkened further; he loathed Xi Hongxuan's uppity attitude. Fu Linye spoke as though he didn't hear the rebuke.

"It's of utmost urgency." He smiled as he lifted his robe to take his seat. "I rushed here as soon as I left the Ministry of Justice, how's that for urgent?"

Only then did Xi Hongxuan ask, "Well, what's the matter?"

Fu Linye looked at Shen Zechuan. Grasping his closed fan, Shen Zechuan said, "Where are my manners."

He made as if to rise.

"Lanzhou, what's—just sit down," Xi Hongxuan hastened to say. "We're in the same boat, whatever the weather. What is there that you can't hear? Linye, go ahead and speak! Don't you recognize Shen Lanzhou? He's the great xiansheng of our Xi Clan!"

Fu Linye had initially classed Shen Zechuan as a dog who begged for scraps at the Xis' door. He had no idea Xi Hongxuan held him in such high regard.

The censor-in-chief had indeed come at the wrong time. Had he been a little earlier, or a little later, Xi Hongxuan might not have laid such thick flattery on Shen Zechuan. But it so happened that they'd just finalized their plans to keep the Yao Clan down, tying the two of them to the same rope. Xi Hongxuan had seized the moment to show Shen Zechuan some due respect, a step up from the buddy he'd been in the past.

Shen Zechuan smiled and looked at Fu Linye, who had little choice but to say tactfully, "Lord Judge, please remain seated."

Xi Hongxuan shifted his legs to step on the tiger skin rug. "Go on. What's so urgent then?"

"I was assisting with the trial at the Ministry of Justice earlier when some new information came to light: Fuling, the female attendant who talked Guisheng into the assassination, was involved somehow with Caiwei Palace. Second Young Master Xi, the mistress of Caiwei Palace is Imperial Concubine Mu. This matter will be presented to

His Majesty tomorrow morning. At that point, it will become more than just a matter of striking Xiao Er!"

There was a moment of silence. Xi Hongxuan placed a hand on his leg and turned to Shen Zechuan. "Perhaps I forgot to mention it to you earlier—Mu Ru is affiliated with us as well."

Xi Hongxuan had of course forgotten no such thing; he simply hadn't wanted to reveal it. His guardedness with Shen Zechuan extended to keeping this secret. Shen Zechuan knew this all too well, so he merely asked, "Wasn't Mu Ru originally given to Pan Rugui? I seem to remember her younger brother."

"That's right." Xi Hongxuan shared half the truth: "Pan Rugui died, right? So she had nowhere to go. After his manor was searched and seized, they wanted to take her from Pan Rugui's residence to become a courtesan for the high-ranking officials. His Majesty couldn't bear to see it, so he asked me for help. I leaned on that scrap of connection I had with Yanqing and had her swapped out, then hid both siblings in another manor. Later, His Majesty could endure it no longer and insisted on bringing her into the palace. Secretariat Elder Hai made quite the scene over it. You remember all that."

Shen Zechuan nodded indifferently, as if the matter held little interest for him. "I heard about it. This is bad news then. The case should be near to closing. How did new complications arise?"

His eyes never left Fu Linye as he said this. Although he smiled, it sounded like he was blaming Fu Linye for not keeping closer watch.

Xi Hongxuan frowned too. "You're the associate judge; you're meant to supervise. Can't you think of some way to suppress this? It will only stir up trouble if it's presented to the throne."

Fu Linye had a bellyful of complaints of his own. He could only say, "Second Young Master Xi, my words carry little weight. We're talking about Kong Qiu! He's stubborn and doesn't heed a word of advice. And he's Secretariat Elder Hai's man; why would he listen to me? Our top priority should be deciding what to do next. If Concubine Mu is implicated, who would dare continue the investigation? His Majesty would be the first to oppose it!"

Scowling, Xi Hongxuan thought for a moment. "Where is Yinzhu?"

Fu Linye frantically waved his hands. "We can't kill him! Second Young Master Xi, Secretariat Elder Hai is already on high alert. If we silence the eunuch now, it will confirm his suspicions!"

"It was going so well. How did Caiwei Palace come up out of the blue?!" Xi Hongxuan covered his teacup with the lid. "No. We can't allow this investigation to continue. During our audience before the throne tomorrow morning, we must think of a way to turn His Majesty off the notion."

Mu Ru could still be of great use. They couldn't let anyone take her off the board now.

"You're right." Fu Linye fidgeted anxiously. "Best to pin it all on Fuling! Wrap this case up as fast as possible, and everyone can breathe a sigh of relief. But I tell you, from the way Kong Qiu looked, nothing will stop him from getting to the bottom of this!"

"The key lies with Secretariat Elder Hai." Shen Zechuan pressed his fingertips to the teacup, soaking in its warmth. "Hai Liangyi reviewed Kong Qiu's exam papers during the imperial examination back in the day. Kong Qiu can be considered half his student; he has always held Hai Liangyi in the highest regard."

"And Hai Liangyi clearly wants to stick him in the Grand Secretariat," Xi Hongxuan said. "He handles all his cases beautifully, and he's the perfect age for it too. And then there's his common background in the Chijun Commandery—he hits all the right notes for Hai Liangyi. What fucking rotten luck! We set Xiao Er up to suffer, and all of them secretly enjoyed the show and waited to reap the benefits. Now that something's gone wrong, they all want to feign ignorance."

Shen Zechuan looked up. "How about this? Lord Fu, when the statement is presented before the emperor tomorrow morning, don't mention Caiwei Palace. Just say the Imperial Army's name has yet to be cleared. Yuan Liu hasn't pled guilty yet, right? This is an opportunity. As long as Yuan Liu is alive, then Xiao Er has accepted bribes. He won't be able to clear his name."

Fu Linye rubbed his leg nervously. "Even if *I* don't mention it, Kong Qiu will bring it up! We can't keep it under wraps."

"One sheep is lost, but we can still mend the fold." Shen Zechuan nudged his fan open bit by bit, then snapped it closed again. "As I recall, Your Excellency's speech before the emperor was a righteous one, all for the sake of the empire and state. If you suddenly sing a different tune because of a confession that hasn't been verified, I'm afraid even His Majesty will question your loyalty. Keep the focus on Xiao Er and you'll look like a man of integrity."

"That's right!" said Xi Hongxuan. "We can't lose our composure now. You've already made your stand; it would look ill to pull back now. Stay the course. As for the rest, leave it to me. It's almost dawn; you mustn't stay much longer. Go home for a bath and a change of clothes. Keep an eye on which way the wind is blowing when you're before the emperor and improvise if you must."

Fu Linye had arrived in a hurry; without taking a single sip of tea, he left in a hurry as well.

The instant he was gone, Xi Hongxuan spat at his back. "If he hadn't been so eager for accolades and reported the matter of the Quancheng silk to the top without so much as a word to me, Hai Liangyi might not have noticed what was going on." Xi Hongxuan's temper flared.

"These men from low places are the most short-sighted! For that scrap of glory, he dared keep us in the dark. See what's happened now? What a waste of the gift Yanqing left us! After this, Xiao Er will keep a close watch over the account books. It'll be difficult to get any leverage there in the future."

"Thirst for position and wealth are ailments of the rich," Shen Zechuan said. "Right now, we need to keep him under control. How's it going with the Eight Great Battalions?"

"Han Cheng's younger brother took over the post," replied Xi Hongxuan. "Xiao Er's already put his fingerprints all over the Eight Great Battalions. To think he managed to install his own people in all the important posts so quickly! It won't be easy to dismantle what he's built there."

"Even so, there are descendants of the Eight Great Clans among the soldiers he selected for appointment." Shen Zechuan smiled. "We will get our chance."

When Shen Zechuan emerged and stepped up into his carriage, he came face to face with a seven-stringed zither.

Qiao Tianya lifted the curtain and poked his face in, cloaked in his strongman disguise. "The qin is mine. My lord mustn't throw it away. It took me quite a lot of finagling to get it."

Shen Zechuan didn't touch it. "It looks valuable. Where did you get the money?"

Qiao Tianya laughed merrily. "Tips from the ladies."

This seven-stringed qin was obviously not something mere money could buy. Presumably it had something to do with his family—Qiao Tianya seemed to have little desire to speak of it, and Shen Zechuan did not pursue the matter.

The horse carriage delivered Shen Zechuan safely home to tidy up.

He stayed only long enough to change his robes before he turned his steps back to the palace.

Li Jianheng had dismissed morning court and bid the central officials to take a seat in Mingli Hall. After he read the statement from beginning to end, he was quiet for a long time.

Hai Liangyi had only recently recovered from his illness, and Li Jianheng had instructed someone to serve him a bowl of warm goat's milk. The elder took a few sips in the silence. No one in the hall said a word.

"What's this about Caiwei Palace?" Li Jianheng began. "Yuan Liu's involvement hasn't even been fully investigated."

"This matter concerns the imperial harem, so we await Your Majesty's ruling," Kong Qiu answered.

"What ruling?" Li Jianheng was growing anxious. "Even if this Fuling woman went to Caiwei Palace, it can't—it can't have anything to do with Concubine Mu. Who knows if what this eunuch says is true or false?"

"Naturally, it's false," Hai Liangyi said in a steady voice.

"Right, it's false!" With Hai Liangyi's support, Li Jianheng's voice grew louder and clearer. "Eunuchs are treacherous creatures. They'll fabricate every kind of lie to survive. This Yinzhu thought he could save his own life by dragging Concubine Mu into it. We will see his head roll!"

Xiao Jiming, who had not spoken a word regarding this case, raised his eyes. "Be that as it may, this involves the safety of the Son of Heaven. It cannot be dismissed out of hand."

In one utterance, he had gone right for the bullseye.

"Of course we are not dismissing it," Wei Huaixing began. "We haven't finished with Yuan Liu—"

"The presiding judge on this case is Kong Qiu, the Minister of Justice," Xiao Jiming cut in. "The Left and Right Censors-in-Chief of the Court of Judicial Review, as well as a representative of the Embroidered Uniform Guard, are associate judges. Yet Vice Minister Wei, who has no part in this trial, has repeatedly intervened. It's inappropriate."

He spoke with poise and courtesy, pausing to leave Wei Huaixing ample time to respond. But Wei Huaixing didn't dare say a thing, so Xiao Jiming continued. "This case concerns the Imperial Army and the emperor's own harem; it should never have become a public spectacle. It's not the reputation of anyone here that is at stake, but the dignity of His Majesty. More than ten days have passed since the assassination attempt, yet we have nothing conclusive on a little judicial administrator of the Imperial Army, nor verification of a single witness statement from the brothel that accused him. Everything has been delayed in the hands of Censor Fu, the investigating censor from the Chief Surveillance Bureau, who is distracted from the main case. From what I can see, neither the presiding judge nor the associate judges have executed their duties as they should. Putting aside the waste of time and energy, it seems we have a problem of ministers overstepping their authority."

Fu Linye thought of the warning Xi Hongxuan had given him last night. Facing Xiao Jiming now, he once again found himself in a difficult spot. But Li Jianheng hadn't said a word, and Hai Liangyi clearly had no intention of helping him out of this fix; he could do nothing but force himself to composure. "The heir is accustomed to how it's done in Libei; Qudu is not the frontier. Many matters are managed differently here based on the different concerns, so—"

Zhao Hui stepped out. "In the military, such behavior would be considered insubordination, and the offender executed under military law. The heir shouldn't be the one to speak on this matter, but in all this time, not one of you has thought to remind His Majesty. Even the lord censors-in-chief seem to have handled this case as if in a drunken stupor! It has been over ten days since the token of the supreme commander of the Imperial Army was suspended. The censor has thrice conducted a search. What has he turned up? We are owed an explanation."

"Did we not uncover the business of the Quancheng silk?" asked Fu Linye.

"You're being asked about the assassination case!" Li Jianheng flung down the confession statement with a clatter. "Why are you still bringing up these irrelevancies?"

"Xiao Chiye is at the root of all these problems," Fu Linye answered hastily. "Everything begins and ends with him. Your Majesty, the assassination must be investigated, but his bribery charge should not be overlooked!"

"What bribe did he take?!" Li Jianheng stood and pointed at Fu Linye. "Quancheng silk! You keep talking about Quancheng silk! You think we don't know of this? We were still hanging about with him on the streets back then! We know more about this silk than you do! The assassin came inches from our person, yet that doesn't concern you, and instead you fixate on insignificant trifles. It would appear that the safety of the Son of Heaven is of no importance to you!"

Mere days ago, Li Jianheng had been chewing his brush handle as he cursed Xiao Chiye. Fu Linye hadn't expected him to do an about-face and berate him now; he crashed to his knees and crawled forward in a panic. "Your Majesty! Your Majesty is this subject's sovereign. It would devastate me if so much as a strand of your hair was harmed. Your Majesty!"

"Let's be clear about our priorities," Xiao Jiming said. "For this assassination case, Minister Kong has worked through the nights, and Ce'an has handed over his authority token. To avoid a conflict of interest, he doesn't dare ask about the progress of the case and has been home reflecting on his faults every day. It would be best to clarify everything now—the facts of the case, the current progress of the investigation, and our future course of action. At least this way, my people can prepare for what's to come."

The Vice Minister of Rites, Jiang Xu, stepped forward. "The case is clear as day and involves the Imperial Army. It does not concern the Prince of Libei's manor. Who conducted a search there? This goes against all propriety. Should the news spread, everyone will think His Majesty aims to investigate the Prince of Libei, to the detriment of Qudu's relationship with the frontiers."

Li Jianheng had known about the search of the prince's manor, but now he had to feign ignorance. No matter how stupid he was, he understood that Xiao Jiming had observed everything over these past few days. There would be no end of trouble if they continued targeting Xiao Chiye.

Li Jianheng kicked Fu Linye a few times. "How dare you! Who allowed you to search the Prince of Libei's manor? My order was for you to investigate the Imperial Army's office compound!"

Shrinking in on himself, Fu Linye choked out, "It wa—wasn't th—this subject! Judge Shen was the one who went!"

Shen Zechuan seemed momentarily stunned. He said, perplexed, "I assisted Your Excellency in the investigation according to the imperial edict. It was Your Excellency who exhorted me, saying, 'The Imperial Army is as impenetrable as a metal bucket. I'm afraid they're keeping two sets of account books. When the time comes, I'll be relying on the lord judge to do a thorough search of the prince's residence,' and so I went. There were numerous servers and attendants in the hall at the time. Call any one of them for questioning and they will confirm it."

Fu Linye hissed through clenched teeth, "I only told you to do a thorough search. I did not mention the prince's manor!"

"I take orders from the Son of Heaven," Shen Zechuan said, his countenance severe. "I would never speak a word of falsehood before the emperor. If I went to the prince's manor on my own initiative, how could there have been a censor accompanying me?"

Fu Linye saw malice flash in Shen Zechuan's eyes and knew he had attacked the wrong person in his extremity. He looked around. "Vice Minister Wei, didn't you—"

"Shut up!" Wei Huaixing cut him off. "How dare you scramble to implicate others for what you've done before His Majesty?! Have you no shame? Protracting the case with irrelevant concerns is one thing, but eroding the goodwill between His Majesty and Libei has serious implications! Do you understand the gravity of what you've done!"

At this point, Fu Linye knew he had been shoved out as the scapegoat. He had to take the blame for Li Jianheng, for Wei Huaixing, for Xi Hongxuan, and everyone else in between. None of these were people he could afford to offend. The gods were fighting, and it was up to him to clean up the mess.

Fu Linye's head knocked against the floor. "This subject had a momentary lapse in judgment!"

"And yet you still dared to make excuses!" Li Jianheng admonished, jabbing a finger at him. "Ce'an's token may have been suspended, but before this case is concluded, he retains his position as supreme commander! Investigate him as you will, but how can you show such contempt for the Imperial Army? It appears to us that you aren't investigating the case at all, but trying to eliminate your enemies!"

Li Jianheng hadn't lost his temper since denouncing Xiao Chiye that day, but now he was attacking Fu Linye until he trembled from head to toe. Fu Linye was a sensible man; he knew to shed tears as he knelt, ensuring Xiao Jiming received every drop of dignity owed to him.

Xiao Jiming waited until Li Jianheng had finished berating Fu Linye before speaking. "His Excellency is simply eager to get to the bottom of this case. Since it has caused such a commotion, why not dismiss Ce'an from his post? All the memorials of indictment submitted by the Chief Surveillance Bureau recently seem to make reasonable sense. Ce'an cannot be excused for his negligence of supervision. He is indeed ill-suited to carry out his duties before the throne."

He smiled again. "All testimonies point to him. If he truly committed such a disgraceful, treacherous deed, the offense warrants execution of the whole clan. Everyone is present here today as witness: I, Xiao Jiming, should also be stripped of my Libei military token to avoid a conflict of interest. I've already dispatched a letter to Libei asking Father to remove his crown and robe, and to enter Qudu with my wife and son as commoners without rank to stand trial."

Xiao Jiming's words sank into the silence of the hall. Li Jianheng panicked. He didn't know whether to respond or remain silent, and looked helplessly toward Hai Liangyi.

Hai Liangyi held Xiao Jiming's gaze for a moment before breaking into laughter. "Heir Xiao jests. Isn't this case as good as closed? Why joke with this old subject?"

Kong Qiu composed himself and swiftly added, "That's right—the secretariat elder is right. Although Yuan Liu bought a house on credit from the Donglong broker, it was a private affair between himself and Fuling—no wonder he kept it quiet. The supreme commander oversees twenty thousand men; how could he possibly investigate every single matter personally? As for the bribery case, Yuan Liu has been denying that all along; we must not only listen to Xiangyun's one-sided statement. This subject has already found that Xiangyun most likely bears a hatred toward the supreme commander born of unrequited love. Her testimony cannot be trusted!"

Li Jianheng stepped forward. "The case is closed; there is no need to mention it again! Heir Xiao, please rise!"

He didn't want to pursue this any further either. The introduction of Caiwei Palace meant Mu Ru would inevitably become involved. Fu Linye was already a pawn to be disposed of at the earliest convenience; to these people, Mu Ru was an even lesser being. If she was really connected to these cases, then he would lose his beloved concubine; he would really be all alone in the world.

Li Jianheng watched these people talk and laugh as usual and felt they were not human at all. What stood behind them was something colossal that overshadowed even the throne, a force as unstoppable as floods and hurricanes. Being a sovereign did not mean he was free and unrestrained. Every move he made reverberated across the entire map. Those against whom he raged and those in whom he delighted equally became his fatal vulnerabilities. He could never be his own master. He was a prisoner chained to the dragon throne.

How terrifying.

Li Jianheng hugged himself, all alone, somewhere deep in his heart.

Walking beside these people was the same as skating on thin ice. If he were to accidentally fall through someday, he would end up like his imperial brother: trampled to a bloody pulp in the blink of an eye by the hooves of the players contending for power.

His life and death mattered not a bit. It only mattered that his surname happened to be Li.

What if there were someone else in this world surnamed Li? Li Jianheng trembled and broke out in a cold sweat at the very thought. *Impossible,* he muttered gloomily to himself.

There's no way.

HEAVY SNOW

OVER SEVERAL DAYS, the capital was blanketed in snow. With the assassination case hastily concluded, the sharp turbulence of the days before was swiftly buried under the snowstorm, turning Qudu into a soft expanse of white. It was then that Li Jianheng heard Xiao Chiye had taken ill.

He had reportedly caught a cold, yet still persevered in self-reflection until he eventually collapsed and became bedridden, too ill to even get up. Braving the snow, Li Jianheng set off in a carriage to the Prince of Libei's manor with his retinue and various ministers in tow, intending to become true friends with Xiao Chiye once again.

The emperor's entourage left them alone in the room. Xiao Chiye's complexion was pallid as Chen Yang helped him sit up to meet Li Jianheng.

"We feel very ashamed to have believed those lies and chastised you that day," said Li Jianheng.

"The ruler and his ministers depend on each other," Xiao Chiye said. "That's as it should be. Your Majesty needn't take it to heart."

Li Jianheng fell silent, as did Xiao Chiye. In the end, both had come to the point of addressing each other as ruler and subject, even in private.

Li Jianheng forced a laugh. "We used to think you were made of iron and would never fall sick. We didn't expect you to be laid up in bed like any common man."

"This subject has merely an ordinary body made of flesh and blood, one that bleeds if stabbed," Xiao Chiye said.

Li Jianheng recalled the night at the hunting grounds, when Xiao Chiye rode into the Embroidered Uniform Guard's siege on his own. He had risked his life, fighting tooth and nail, and ultimately lifted him onto the throne.

Humans were strange this way. When they abhorred someone, they only remembered their worst qualities. But once guilt came calling, they only remembered their goodness. It was as if all the words they had used to curse that person became arrows in their own heart, pricking them with shame.

There were plenty of things Li Jianheng had wanted to ask Xiao Chiye, but as he sat there now, he didn't feel like asking anymore. As Xiao Chiye said, a body of flesh and blood would bleed. Then, what about friends that had grown apart?

"Sitting in this position isn't a choice we...*I* willingly made," Li Jianheng said eventually. "Ce'an, you don't know what it's like—how it feels to be in such a precarious position, not knowing what tomorrow may bring. Everyone around me imagines sitting here would make them happy and carefree. I used to think so too. But that's not the case at all."

Xiao Chiye said nothing.

Li Jianheng's eyes suddenly grew hot. He didn't even know why he was sad. "I was always a hopeless case, you know? I'm only too aware of that. If my brothers had lived, this throne would never have fallen to me. What have I done wrong? My highest ambition was to be an idle prince. You all shoved me up here without asking...

I've done my best, Ce'an. I've really done my best. But I'm not capable enough to control all the powers of the world; I can only let them control *me*!"

He covered his face in agony, his voice thick with sobs. "Ce'an, it's too high up here. I can't see anything clearly!"

Xiao Chiye's eyes grew hot too. "We're brothers. Why would I blame you?"

Li Jianheng scrubbed at his tears. "Even so, I've marred our friendship."

"Why blame yourself for something you had no choice in?" asked Xiao Chiye. "I've been too brash in my conduct. I deserve to be put in my place."

"It's your nature," Li Jianheng said. "You can't be faulted for this. Besides, they're only egging me on for their own sakes. I've let you down, Ce'an."

They appeared to have made up and returned to being each other's closest confidants. But the lightheartedness of youth had vanished, leaving an awkward atmosphere—closer than deference, but never quite as close as before.

Li Jianheng couldn't stay long; he left when he was done saying his piece. Before he went, he showered Xiao Chiye with gifts and urged him to rest well.

As soon as everyone cleared out, Xiao Chiye tossed away the pillow supporting his back. Rising easily to his feet, he dressed and slipped into his shoes before heading to Xiao Jiming's study.

Xiao Jiming was there, listening to Zhao Hui's report on military affairs. When he saw Xiao Chiye enter, he waved him over and motioned for him to sit beside him.

Zhao Hui continued without pause. "The Ministry of Revenue has already reviewed the military expenditure from last year, while the

Grand Secretariat is still in discussion regarding the sum for this one. The snow has been heavy this last month. In Juexi, the people are happy—the favorable snow is an auspicious omen for a bountiful year, and they can look forward to a good harvest. But people are already starting to freeze to death in Zhongbo."

"In recent years," Xiao Jiming said, "the prefectural yamen in Zhongbo has been short of manpower. Now, with this heavy snow crushing roofs, there are few hands available to repair the collapsed houses." Sipping his hot tea, Xiao Jiming thought for a moment. "Tell the Ministry of Revenue to take forty thousand taels from Libei's military funds at the start of the year to be used as an infrastructure repair fund for Cizhou."

Cizhou was perched right next to the Northeast Provisions Trail. This favor from Xiao Jiming would render very timely assistance, like delivering coal in the middle of an ice storm.

Understanding his intent at once, Zhao Hui noted it down.

Xiao Chiye poured tea for Xiao Jiming. "The prefectural yamen of Zhongbo lacks manpower, and few officials from the capital are willing to fill the void. But leaving it empty isn't a long-term solution either."

"In the past, Hua Siqian was unwilling to tackle it. It's a hot potato; taking on the problem means having to fork over your own money." Xiao Jiming ran his fingers along the teacup's rim. "But Secretariat Elder Hai is in charge now. He will likely seek a suitable candidate for Zhongbo in this year's spring examination."

"Most of the newly minted officials are inexperienced and cannot command the necessary respect," said Xiao Chiye. "They could maybe make it as local, low-ranking officials, but as major provincial officials, they won't hold their own. Hai Liangyi will still need to pick a candidate out of the central administration."

"Capable talents who can assume responsibility and lead independently are exactly what we're short on right now," Xiao Jiming said. "Zhongbo is a frontier land, far from the capital and its oversight. Under governance of the Shen Clan, every kind of corruption thrived below the surface—plenty of things can't be accounted for. It was already a problem when Shen Wei was alive; then, five years ago, the whole region was thrown into disarray and became the chaotic mess it is today. Back then, the common folk fled their homes in the wake of the Biansha massacres, but the imperial court never produced any plan to resettle those people. Those who remain in Zhongbo are mostly the remnants of military households from the garrison troops, along with groups of roving bandits. As they say, inhospitable environments breed reprehensible people—the situation in Zhongbo is exactly that. If just any official is sent there, not only will he fail to get the situation under control, he'll probably be taught a hard lesson."

"If the imperial court is willing to send a general with an army to quash the bandits, they'd at least be able to work some real benefit." Zhao Hui closed the book neatly. "But considering how things stand in the empire, they probably wouldn't dare."

Of course they wouldn't dare. At present, Qudu had the Libei Armored Cavalry to the northeast and the Qidong Garrison Troops to the southeast, both massive military forces out in frontier lands. Holding them in check was already a strain. Taking the risk to send yet another army out would make the frontier even harder to deal with if the leader of those troops was conferred any title. But ignoring the plight of Zhongbo was no solution either. There had to be a compromise.

"That's a headache for the Grand Secretariat to deal with." Xiao Jiming set aside talk of military affairs and turned to Xiao Chiye. "How did it go on your end?"

Xiao Chiye had an elbow propped against the armrest of the chair. He had wanted to prop up his legs, too, but after several attempts, he couldn't find a comfortable position and gave up. "You gave His Majesty quite the scare. He's so frightened he insists on rekindling our friendship, no matter how displeased he might be."

"You were just drinking buddies to begin with." Xiao Jiming laughed. "Let your fair-weather friend be frightened. Better that than the opposite."

"Fu Linye has contributed quite a bit to this outcome," Xiao Chiye noted. "I'll have to find a chance to thank him."

"You would do better to thank the friend who's been helping you in secret," said Xiao Jiming. "Fu Linye's an experienced official; he shouldn't have been careless enough to fall for a trap. For this case to have concluded so smoothly, someone on the inside has put in quite a bit of effort on your behalf."

"Uh huh." Xiao Chiye laughed and changed the subject. "Where's Gu Jin? Call him in. I have orders for him."

Xiao Jiming turned and motioned to Zhao Hui. "Call them all in. I have orders too."

Zhao Hui stepped out, and Meng flew in through the open door. He landed on the clothing rack, where the snow he shook off dampened all the clothes that had been hung to dry.

The men appeared one at a time. Ding Tao barely took off his shoes before hopping in and rushing over to stand ramrod straight before Xiao Jiming. Chen Yang and Gu Jin entered more sedately.

"Shizi!" Ding Tao held Xiao Jiming in the highest esteem. Flashing a mouth full of white teeth, he said, "Go ahead and give your command, Shizi! I, Ding Tao, will not hesitate to brave fire and flood for you!"

"Huh." Xiao Chiye lifted his teacup. "Why have you never said that to Er-gongzi?"

"You're always throwing me out," Ding Tao said.

"What wrong have you done to make Er-gongzi throw you out?" Xiao Jiming asked lightly.

"I haven't done anything wrong," Ding Tao chirped. "It's just that Er-gongzi is always telling me to keep an eye on that—"

Xiao Chiye almost spat out his tea. He slammed the lid over the cup and shot a glance at Chen Yang, who promptly rapped Ding Tao on the head. Ding Tao, still oblivious, covered his head and didn't dare say another word.

Xiao Chiye had burned his tongue on the tea. "Drag him out and bury him on the spot! What are you squealing about? Let Gu Jin explain!"

Ding Tao protested, "I'm not—"

Chen Yang covered his mouth, dragged him out, and dutifully began burying him in the snow.

What should I say? Gu Jin thought to himself in a panic. *What the hell do I say?* At that instant, he saw Xiao Jiming was about to put down the teacup, so he dropped to one knee and respectfully took the cup from him before setting it on the table. "Careful, Shizi, it's hot!" he blurted clumsily.

Watching all this play out, Xiao Jiming seemed in no hurry to pursue the matter. His eyes roved over each of them until Xiao Chiye felt as if he was sitting on a pincushion.

"What's the matter?" Xiao Jiming asked. "Is Er-gongzi hiding someone in the manor?"

"Of course not!" Xiao Chiye denied it at once. "Dage, I'm not even betrothed. How could I tarnish a maiden's reputation."

Xiao Jiming gave him a long look. Xiao Chiye didn't know if his brother believed him, but at the very least Xiao Jiming dismissed the topic and gestured for him to continue.

Xiao Chiye at last found a comfortable position and settled in. "I'm thinking of asking Gu Jin to look into Xiangyun Villa."

Zhao Hui pondered. "Xiangyun Villa is on Donglong Street; it's frequented by all sorts of characters. It won't be easy to investigate without alerting anyone. Does Er-gongzi suspect Xiangyun?"

"There's definitely something we don't know about her," mused Xiao Chiye. "Wei Huaixing holds her testimony in his hands. Why would she offend me for no good reason?"

"Shizi, someone said it was a hatred born of unrequited love," Zhao Hui said to Xiao Jiming.

"If she's your old flame, you must have a new lover," Xiao Jiming said evenly. "I've been in the capital for quite a few days; why have I heard no mention of this?"

"I'm just bored of fooling around, that's all," Xiao Chiye replied. "Nothing else to it."

"Do you know you blink when you're talking?" Xiao Jiming said. "That means you're lying. What family is this maiden from? This has been much on the mind of your father and sister-in-law. If there's really someone you like, just tell me what's standing in your way; whatever it is, we'll handle it."

"There's no one." Xiao Chiye couldn't sit still any longer; he wanted to flee, but he didn't dare. "No one. Really. What would I get married for? Just to ruin some girl's future?"

"Once you're married, you'll mature a little." Xiao Jiming had a sudden urge to pat his head, but it wouldn't do to diminish Xiao Chiye's authority in front of his subordinates. He lowered his voice. "How long can your sister-in-law and I keep you company? There should be someone in the capital who can light a lamp for you and chat over a meal. No matter who's caught your eye, Father and I will do all we can. Even if she's from a noble clan, as long as you like her, we'll see it done."

Xiao Chiye had been planning to laugh off the topic, but on hearing this, a thought occurred to him. "Marshal Qi! You could do it even if it's someone like Marshal Qi?"

The expression in Xiao Jiming's eyes shifted; he wouldn't have expected Xiao Chiye to fall for someone like Qi Zhuyin. After a moment's pause, he managed, "Well. I won't object as long as she doesn't hack you to death first."

That night, as Xiao Chiye got into bed, he stepped on something. When he bent to pick it up from the woolen rug, he found it was a pearl used as a button.

Xiao Chiye looked from the pearl to the space under the bed. He opened the window and shouted. "Chen Yang!"

In moments, Chen Yang appeared. Xiao Chiye deliberated for a moment, then said, "Make a trip to the jeweler on Shenwu Street tomorrow morning."

Before Chen Yang could reply, Xiao Chiye tossed a small box at him.

"Tell them to make these into earrings. Make one each of every design available." Xiao Chiye thought long and hard before continuing. "Keep it simple. Nothing flashy."

Chen Yang looked at the box. "All of them?"

"All." Xiao Chiye closed the window. After a pause, he opened it again.

Chen Yang hadn't moved. Still holding the box, he called out in confusion, "Yes, my lord?"

"Put it on my account!" Xiao Chiye said.

ROMANTIC LIAISONS

YUAN LIU DIED a sudden death in prison. It was Chen Yang who went to collect his body for burial; per Xiao Chiye's orders, he also settled Yuan Liu's family in a new house in the city of Dancheng and hired a respectable teacher for Yuan Liu's son.

Xiao Chiye's illness persisted until the snow melted in Qudu. By the time he could step out to attend court sessions, Xi Hongxuan had been promoted to the Secretary of the Bureau of Evaluations in the Ministry of Personnel.

Shen Zechuan was the one who returned the Imperial Army's authority token to Xiao Chiye at the palace. Xiao Chiye seized the chance to look him up and down, practically stripping him with his eyes.

"Thanks," he said, plucking the authority token from Shen Zechuan's hand. "Judge Shen."

"Don't mention it." Shen Zechuan's fingers curled slightly, as if he couldn't bear to let it go.

Xiao Chiye flashed the authority token in front of him. "Have you grown so attached to it?"

Shen Zechuan grinned. "Yeah. I got used to how it feels in my hands."

Xiao Chiye saw that their attendants had all retreated to a respectful distance, so he said, "I didn't know you were so easily satisfied. You're content just feeling my token?"

Shen Zechuan clasped his hands behind his back. "Considering how recently you recovered from major illness, perhaps Er-gongzi should show a little more restraint when looking for his fun."

"I've been chaste of heart and free of desire for the better part of a month." Xiao Chiye was growing sleepy in the warm sunlight; he shifted his feet. "The heartless cad I've yearned for day and night never came to visit me once. Now that I'm up and about, how else can I mend my broken heart?"

A breeze swept over Shen Zechuan. "Bad eggs like that often ditch the old for the new and leave behind a string of jilted lovers. You'd do better to forget him before it's too late; he's not worth wasting the prime of your youth."

"Bad what?" Xiao Chiye asked.

"Er-gongzi," Shen Zechuan said.

Xiao Chiye had an urge to squeeze the back of his neck, but this wasn't the time or place. "Well put. Such eloquence. I ought to give you a round of applause."

"You're far too kind," Shen Zechuan said modestly. "Your sincerity is enough."

"It sounds like you've made a point of checking on some of those old flames," said Xiao Chiye. "Does it bother you?"

"I hardly went out of my way," Shen Zechuan answered. "One hears all sorts of things while simply drinking wine in Xiangyun Villa. For example, that Er-gongzi is a regular patron and an old hand at romantic liaisons."

"Impressed?"

"Indeed, indeed." Shen Zechuan looked him in the eye as he

remarked slowly, "But rumor cannot compare to experience. That man of legend doesn't seem to be the same one I encountered."

"To be fair, you haven't had many encounters." Xiao Chiye fastened the authority token to his belt. "You'll have a better understanding once you've played with me a few more times. It's not like we haven't tried the low-and-slow approach. How did that taste?"

Shen Zechuan pursed his lips tightly.

Xiao Chiye grinned. "Seems you still remember it. Then, do you also remember what you promised?"

"To pass Xiangyun a message on your behalf," Shen Zechuan said. "I'm to play matchmaker and earn myself a cup of wine at your wedding. Of course I remember."

"I knew you could be counted on," said Xiao Chiye. "If you manage to seal the deal, how should I thank you?"

"Treat it as a wedding gift," Shen Zechuan said absently. He looked away, across the courtyard.

Han Cheng was exiting the hall. He waved a hand at both of them as the junior eunuch beside him came running over.

"This way, my lords. His Majesty is waiting!"

Li Jianheng sat on the dragon throne as the ministers discussed official business. Spring was fast approaching, a time when the planting and cultivating of mulberry and hemp were important matters. Meanwhile, Cen Yu, the Left Censor-in-Chief of the Chief Surveillance Bureau, had submitted a memorial regarding the illegal appropriation of space from public ditches throughout various residential districts in Qudu. As the weather warmed, the snow was starting to melt; if the clogged ditches weren't cleared soon, the streets would be flooded once the rainy season hit.

This was so minor an issue, at least compared to the other topics being discussed, that it seemed an insignificant detour. Li Jianheng didn't hear him out before letting the matter drop. The loud voice of the Provincial Administration Commissioner from Zhongbo drew his attention away.

Cen Yu tried to speak up again several times to no avail. As he left the palace after the court dismissal, he heard someone calling him; when he looked back, it was Shen Zechuan.

Shen Zechuan bowed. "Forgive me the presumption of stopping Censor Cen. This humble official has a question."

"Judge Shen, please go ahead."

"The censor-in-chief submitted a memorial about the clogged public ditches," Shen Zechuan said. "Is Your Excellency referring to the recent upsurge of ditch water in the residential districts around Donglong Street?"

Cen Yu motioned for Shen Zechuan to walk with him. "That's right. The illegal appropriation of the public ditches around Donglong Street has been a problem since the reign of Xiande. The residential district has flooded every spring for the last several years. But since there have never been any real casualties, no one seems to think it important."

Shen Zechuan showed him a small, resigned smile. "Your Excellency, to tell you the truth, this humble official currently lives there."

Startled, Cen Yu asked, "Has it already flooded?"

"My humble abode is on elevated ground," Shen Zechuan said. "But in my neighbors' attempts to lay claim to the public ditch and expand their own courtyards, the eaves of their roofs have pressed against mine, and sewage water has begun to flow into my courtyard. Before this morning's court, this humble official took a walk through the surrounding neighborhood. The houses on lower ground have already flooded."

"Standing water brings a terrible risk of spreading disease," Cen Yu said worriedly. "Even without the flooding, everyone is fighting for those few inches of land—their houses are all built so close, with no brick or stones between; it's all wood planks. It's a disaster waiting to happen if there's a fire."

Shen Zechuan thought a moment, then said, "Worry not, Your Excellency. This humble official will speak to my own chief commander. Maybe he can report to His Majesty and send men to clear out the ditches before it's too late."

"All right. I'll also talk to the secretariat elder again." As Cen Yu made to leave, he turned back to Shen Zechuan with a smile. "I appreciate the judge's thoughtfulness. If we can resolve this matter soon, we'll have done a good deed."

Shen Zechuan cupped his hands in respect and saw him off.

The red plum blossoms in the courtyard had withered. When Shen Zechuan arrived, Xiao Chiye was standing in his study, looking at the last of the blooms.

"It's been awfully damp with all this melting snow." Xiao Chiye brushed his hand over a branch. "That house of yours is uninhabitable now, is it not?"

Shen Zechuan had indeed been troubled about this recently. He tugged at his collar as he took off his boots. "The courtyard is already flooded."

"Zhao Hui mentioned the public ditches when I passed through there five years ago." Xiao Chiye turned back. "All this time, and no one has fixed the problem."

"Those who get soaked in sewage are worthless lowlifes anyway.

Think of the time and effort it would take to address it properly," Shen Zechuan said with a wry twist of his mouth. "Who would be willing to do it?"

"Aren't you going to?" Xiao Chiye closed in on him. "This is the first year of Tianchen; there will be a merit and achievement review by the Chief Surveillance Bureau. If there's some merit to be gained, the entire imperial court of officials will be fighting to do it."

"I doubt it." Shen Zechuan was about to step onto the straw mat, one hand on the wall, when Xiao Chiye blocked his way. He glanced up. "Hm?"

Xiao Chiye knelt to pick up Shen Zechuan's boots, pressing the leather a few times. "Is the Embroidered Uniform Guard so stingy they can't bear to provide you a good pair of deerskin boots?"

Shen Zechuan's socks were damp, so Xiao Chiye asked the servants to light the charcoal brazier. His face was pale and drawn today; surely that was from the cold.

"Deerskin boots won't keep out the water either." Shen Zechuan moved his foot out of reach, refusing to let Xiao Chiye grab it. He looked down at Xiao Chiye. "The low-lying areas on Donglong Street are all dirt-poor brothels. They're soaking in filthy water now."

Xiao Chiye looked up from his squat. "Those brothels aren't picky with patrons; they let anyone with a few copper coins do as they please. They can't afford to pay taxes and are in arrears year after year. The lower levels of the Ministry of Revenue who pass their days doing nothing but counting their own copper coins are a worthless lot, leaving them in the lurch like that."

"The residential neighborhoods have been submerged as well."

"They're used to waiting; they think it'll be fine once spring is over." Xiao Chiye got up. "There are plenty of people willing to work, but those willing to do so for no credit are few and far between. I haven't eaten since the court dismissal. Let's have our meal together."

The maidservant came over with a pair of thick wooden clogs for Shen Zechuan. Even after putting them on, he was still shorter than Xiao Chiye. Looking at Shen Zechuan's slender and beautiful ankles in those socks, Xiao Chiye thought again of the harmful decoction he'd been taking.

"I don't see you putting on any weight in the new year." Xiao Chiye pushed the door open and led him outside.

"I'm so busy I only sleep four hours a day." Shen Zechuan stomped lightly on the ground with his clogs. "I thought the position of southern judge was an idle one. Who knew there'd be so much to learn about managing military craftsmen?"

"If Xi Hongxuan can't keep you well"—Xiao Chiye glanced over at him—"switch over to Er-gongzi's camp while you can."

"Then I imagine I won't get even four hours." Shen Zechuan followed him along the veranda. "The remaining men in the Embroidered Uniform Guard are mostly in grandfathered positions; they're following in their fathers' footsteps and rely on their ancestors to eat. The Imperial Army's benefits aren't worth much in our eyes."

The spring thaw had left the courtyard wet as well. Xiao Chiye strode over a puddle and turned back to look at Shen Zechuan.

Even in clogs, the hem of Shen Zechuan's moon-white robe would trail into the water unless he held it up. It was already dark; the pale and charming face of the moon hung high on the horizon, leaving their surroundings crystal-bright and turning Shen Zechuan's reflection translucent. So focused was he on the path underfoot, he didn't notice Xiao Chiye had stopped walking. He lifted his white robe and, like a child, skipped over the puddle and landed right in front of Xiao Chiye.

Without thinking, Xiao Chiye leaned down, looped an arm around his waist, and hoisted him over his shoulder. The wooden clogs slipped to the ground; Xiao Chiye scooped them up. Clogs in one hand and the other wrapped around Shen Zechuan, he strode toward the room where they had shared wine under the plum blossoms.

Chen Yang took a few steps back and dismissed everyone in the courtyard with a wave of his hand. On the rooftop, Ding Tao didn't dare make a peep, eyes wide as he watched the second young master carry Shen Zechuan inside. Qiao Tianya and Gu Jin each settled on the projecting corners of the eaves and took their sips of wine.

"You didn't look well this morning," said Xiao Chiye. "Your skin is hot. Are you ill?"

Lying over his shoulder, Shen Zechuan watched the moon skim across the puddles on the ground. "Perhaps."

"Grand ambitions can't be accomplished in a single stroke." Xiao Chiye ascended the steps and kicked open the door. "Life is the most precious thing of all."

"That wasn't what you said when you hated me." Shen Zechuan landed softly on his feet. He gazed up at Xiao Chiye. "It's just a cold. I can sleep it off."

Back to him, Xiao Chiye shed his own boots and outer robe as the maidservants filed in and began to set the table with dishes.

Shen Zechuan had finished washing his hands and was about to tug at his collar again when Xiao Chiye reached out and tugged it for him. Brushing the fabric aside, he glimpsed some red rashes.

"It's been too damp lately." Shen Zechuan nudged Xiao Chiye's fingers away with the back of his hand. "In their bid to stake their claims on the space, my neighbors' roofs have blocked out all the light."

"I see." Xiao Chiye let the matter drop.

The two men took their seats. Between bites, Xiao Chiye asked, "That house of yours no longer befits your status. Why haven't you moved?"

"It's close to the Temple of Guilt, which makes it convenient for me to see Shifu. It's also on Donglong Street. If Xi Hongxuan makes any move there, it's easier to look into it from close by."

Xiao Chiye watched him eat. "Ji Gang-shifu can't stay at the Temple of Guilt as a footman forever. It'd be more convenient for you to move somewhere where you can live together."

"I'll look for suitable residences."

As a matter of fact, he still had the deed to Grand Mentor Qi's residence, but it wouldn't do for him to live there; it would draw too much attention. Moving was simple in theory, but Xi Hongxuan's attentiveness made it difficult. He dared not put his master and teacher at risk.

By the time they finished the meal, it was late, and a chill clung to the air. As Shen Zechuan stood and prepared to take his leave, Xiao Chiye opened the window and whistled toward the rooftop.

Three guards and one Meng poked their heads out in unison.

Leaning against the window ledge, Xiao Chiye watched Shen Zechuan pick up his coat and said, "Close the doors. Judge Shen is staying tonight."

Shen Zechuan looked back at him.

Xiao Chiye wasn't smiling. His flippancy of the morning seemed to have been scattered by the night wind. Those eyes held dense woods and thick fog, hazy and impenetrable in the moonlight.

Perhaps he really is an old hand when it comes to romantic liaisons, Shen Zechuan thought. *Just the look in those eyes is enough.*

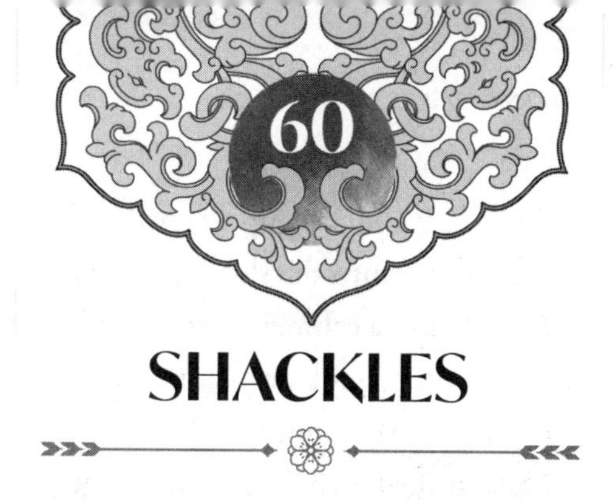

60

SHACKLES

"THERE'S A MOUNTAIN of trouble coming with the new year. We've yet to finalize our next steps; if you leave now, who knows when we can meet up again," Xiao Chiye said. "Why not rest here tonight?"

Shen Zechuan smiled. "Keep your hands to yourself."

The words curled around the tip of his tongue, lingering suggestively. His eyes stirred up waves of lust in Xiao Chiye; even the fingers he had released from the coat at Xiao Chiye's words plucked at the strings of desire.

Xiao Chiye fixed his gaze on Shen Zechuan, and the thought filled him:

This despicable man.

Surely Shen Zechuan was the real bad egg. He never ceased to push against Xiao Chiye's bottom line, testing his patience with cunning naivety, as if leaning into his ear and daring him, *Come touch me*. This fox had wrapped its tail around his legs, tickling him, until Xiao Chiye saw every glance from him as provocation.

"These are serious matters," Xiao Chiye said as he closed the windows. "We'll discuss them seriously."

"We can prepare a memorial regarding the public ditches for tomorrow morning; I'll bring it to His Majesty myself." Perched on a rattan chair, Xiao Chiye picked up Shen Zechuan's outer robe from the floor. He reached into the sleeve pockets and, one by one, set the items he found onto a cabinet shelf.

"You can't." Shen Zechuan sank deeper into the bath and thought a moment longer before continuing, "You're the supreme commander of the Imperial Army; you're not in charge of public works, nor answerable for the complaints of commoners. It doesn't concern you. Submitting a memorial out of the blue will draw suspicion."

"Then *you* bring it up. You live there, so it won't be odd for you to mention it. I'll make a request to tag along as the accompanying supervisor." Xiao Chiye fished an ivory folding fan from Shen Zechuan's sleeve pocket. "Why are you carrying an ivory one?"

The literati, at a certain level, kept items of elegance in their sleeves and were particular about portraying themselves as distinguished and sophisticated. Trinkets of ivory and ebony were considered kitsch and tasteless. Descendants of the noble clans, cultured or not, would never carry folding fans of sandalwood or ivory when they went out. Most favored fans of plain bamboo, adorned only with writings by renowned calligraphers.

"For fun," said Shen Zechuan. "An uncouth object like this suits me best."

He had been in the Temple of Guilt for five years, so he couldn't engage in the pursuit of elegance with the youth of the nobility; it was fitting for him to play a commoner feigning sophistication. Besides the ivory folding fan, he made sure the jade pendant hanging from his belt was in the most garish style he could find.

After feeling through Shen Zechuan's pockets, Xiao Chiye concluded they were truly polar opposites.

Xiao Chiye's likes and dislikes seemed distinct and readable at a glance, yet dig deeper, and one would find they were murky under the surface. Most of the activities he indulged in were forgotten as soon as he closed his eyes; there were none he truly held close to his heart. On the other hand, what appeared to be absent, meaningless hobbies to kill time were born of his sweat and blood. He wasn't partial to any dish or drink. Everyone agreed Er-gongzi loved to drink, but when asked, none could tell what wine the second young master preferred.

Shen Zechuan, on the contrary, looked as though he had no preferences and would go along with anything, but take the time to smooth his fur, and his preferences were perfectly clear. He didn't like strong or bitter tea; after one sip, he wouldn't touch it again. He liked fish; if the setting was right and no one was watching, he could debone a fish as cleanly and precisely as a cat.

Xiao Chiye found it fascinating.

Holding that robe, it was as if he was caressing Shen Zechuan's waist. If he slid his fingers upward, he could trace up Shen Zechuan's spine to the curve of his shoulder; he could recognize the shape of Shen Zechuan's shoulder blades even with his eyes closed.

He lowered his eyes, lost in thought.

All bark and no bite.

Shen Zechuan seemed intimidating at a glance. But after the embraces they'd shared, Xiao Chiye could sense the joy and anger beneath his gentle words and flattery. He was like the moon reflected in that puddle: a single provocation wouldn't stir up great waves. But in truth, he had already put a black mark against you in his book and would surely find the next opportunity to kick back at you.

Robe draped over his shoulders and hair damp, Shen Zechuan emerged. Turning, he saw Xiao Chiye seated in the chair, playing with his ivory fan. His clothes were hung up neatly nearby.

"We haven't finished our discussion." Xiao Chiye stood up. "Have some ginger soup, then we'll sit and chat."

Shen Zechuan reached out to raise the door curtain, but Xiao Chiye beat him to it, raising it with the fan. They stepped out to the inner chamber. Most of the lights had been extinguished, leaving only a single glazed lamp still lit.

After draining the bowl of ginger soup, the feverish warmth Shen Zechuan had felt in his cheeks seemed to recede. Although he had been fine most of the day, his head now felt heavy.

"Xi Hongxuan has been transferred to the Ministry of Personnel. The assessment for officials is around the corner, and he's in the Bureau of Evaluations," Xiao Chiye said. "He can interfere with the performance reviews. Was this your idea?"

Shen Zechuan shook his head with his mouth full of ginger soup. Swallowing, he replied, "It's probably Xue Xiuzhuo's idea."

"I have men in both the Ministry of Rites and the Ministry of War. If they're transferred out because of the review this year"—Xiao Chiye looked at him meaningfully—"our losses will far outweigh our gains."

Shen Zechuan nodded. "No need to worry overmuch about that. Other than the in-law connection between Zhao Hui and Jiang Xu, the Vice Minister of the Ministry of Rites, the others aren't conspicuous. I can't see how Xue Xiuzhuo would trace them back to you. Let everyone go about their business as usual. Besides, the assessments aren't carried out by just one person. Secretariat Elder Hai will send his people to evaluate the reviews too. Xi Hongxuan won't dare act too boldly."

"This year's review concerns Zhongbo. The snowstorm a while back was hard on the whole region; more than ten people died. Hai Liangyi likely plans to send someone this year to restore order."

"Zhongbo." Shen Zechuan looked pensive. "Zhongbo...is no easy task at the moment. If they send a civil official, there's no guarantee he'll be able to stand against the bandits, nor could he command the newly recruited garrison troops. This region needs a comprehensive plan; even Secretariat Elder Hai would fret over it."

"There's no suitable candidate in Qudu right now," Xiao Chiye said. "As long as the one assigned isn't from a noble clan, everything else can be dealt with. Cizhou is right next to the Northeast Provisions Trail. If it were to fall into noble hands, that's planting the seeds of trouble. We need to plan ahead for rainy...days." His voice softened as he looked at Shen Zechuan's weary face—he had fallen asleep at the table.

Since Shen Zechuan's promotion, he had been running nonstop between both sides. At night, he often stayed in Ouhua Pavilion with Xi Hongxuan, who had fair maidens in his arms and all the spare energy that came with an idle position. And since he was now tasked with writing tunes for Li Jianheng, he didn't even have to attend morning court; he had plenty of time to rest. But Shen Zechuan had to stand guard before the throne every day. He got no sleep at night and spent his days dealing with military craftsmen of all sorts. When he had additional assignments, he was even busier, to the point he scarcely had a moment to eat.

He had neither time nor attention to worry about his residence on Donglong Street, starved of light from the protruding edges of his neighbors' eaves. Only yesterday, he had realized his courtyard was flooded and the bedding in his house so damp it was impossible to stay there. While he could send Qiao Tianya to the temple to stay with his shifu and xiansheng, he himself couldn't risk it.

Never mind gaining weight after the new year; he looked thinner now than ever.

Xiao Chiye watched him for a long moment, then reached across the small table to stroke Shen Zechuan's cheek. His skin was alarmingly hot. Medicine had yet to be applied to the rashes on his neck, yet Xiao Chiye was hesitant to disturb him.

But his touch woke Shen Zechuan, who forced himself to focus. "...We do have to plan ahead for...for rainy days. As for the Heir of Libei—"

Xiao Chiye leaned down. His arms were strong and sturdy; lifting Shen Zechuan was no effort at all. The bowl on the table pitched over and tumbled to the ground. Xiao Chiye kicked it aside and said leisurely, "Er-gongzi will take you to the nuptial chamber."

Shen Zechuan wiped sweat from his brow and draped his arms around Xiao Chiye's shoulders. "Are we done discussing serious matters for tonight?"

"We're done." Xiao Chiye clasped him closer. "Now it's time to repay your debt." He bent to lay Shen Zechuan on the bed.

Shen Zechuan lifted a hand to shield his eyes from the lamp and said quietly, "No lights."

"I can see you better with a little light." Xiao Chiye undressed Shen Zechuan where he lay.

Even after Shen Zechuan's chest was exposed, he kept his eyes covered until he felt a cool touch on his neck. He peered at Xiao Chiye through the gaps between his fingers and saw him dipping his fingers into a jar of ointment and dabbing it on the rashes. The process was like greasing a piece of jade. The more he applied, the smoother it felt—so smooth Xiao Chiye's heart was pounding in his chest.

He really didn't have the makings of a gentleman.

"I'll have to tie you up so you don't roll all over the place. Otherwise, this'll have been a waste." Xiao Chiye closed the box of ointment and produced a handkerchief. Sitting by the bed, he methodically wiped his fingers and said, self-mocking, "In all my life, the only one Er-gongzi has ever served is you."

Shen Zechuan slipped under the covers, leaving a wide space on one side of the bed, and turned his head to the side to sleep.

Xiao Chiye sat for a while, watching him, then rose to blow out the lamp. The bed sank as Xiao Chiye hugged Shen Zechuan's waist from behind and pulled him closer to hold him captive in the curve of his arms.

"There, I've got you bound," Xiao Chiye said. "If you kick me, I'll throw you out straightaway."

Opening his eyes, Shen Zechuan looked up at the window where hazy moonlight streamed down. His icy hands reached for Xiao Chiye's strong wrists, shackled around his middle. "So hard."

"Yeah." After a moment of silence, Xiao Chiye said, "I'd advise you not to venture downward."

Shen Zechuan let the silence stretch before saying, "I can only hope that's your authority token."

"Is it the authority token?" Xiao Chiye tilted his head and pressed his nose to the shell of Shen Zechuan's ear. "What do you think?"

His words burned.

"You can't bear it when I whisper in your ear, and you start trembling from just one question," Xiao Chiye said. "How dare you laugh at me for being inexperienced when this is all you've got?"

Shen Zechuan took a moment to compose himself. "Then why don't we try switching positions?"

Xiao Chiye grabbed Shen Zechuan's waist and rolled over so Shen Zechuan was sitting on top of him. He loosened his grip and laughed. "Undress me; untie my belt," Xiao Chiye guided Shen Zechuan's hand down to his waist. "You can do as you please."

Shen Zechuan's breathing was unsteady; there was no way to tell if it was from illness or the searing heat between them. "Tonight—"

Xiao Chiye grabbed the back of his head and kissed him fiercely even as he took his hand and brought it lower. Shen Zechuan shrank back. Xiao Chiye laughed again, until Shen Zechuan, indignant, started to struggle.

Turning over, Xiao Chiye pinned him down again. The bed creaked, and the mattress sank beneath them. Shen Zechuan's palms were sweating, fever-hot.

The pleasure of their entangled bodies, their exchange of breath, urged them on as those intoxicating whispers lingered in their ears. Shen Zechuan loathed that numbing heat, yet even as he pushed Xiao Chiye away, he pulled him harder against him.

Xiao Chiye tore away their remaining clothes and slid his hand along Shen Zechuan's spine, just as he'd envisioned as he sat in the rattan chair. Shen Zechuan twined his arms around Xiao Chiye's neck and bit his lips. The tips of their noses brushed, a flicker of intimacy in this moment of madness and depravity.

Kissing him hard again, Xiao Chiye said, "You lunatic."

Gradually, the kisses that began like a raging storm settled into tenderness, the softness of lips and tongues melting away their defenses. It was in the silence between these moans and murmurs that the lunatic finally fell asleep.

Xiao Chiye caressed Shen Zechuan's cheek with a thumb and propped himself up in bed. Shen Zechuan slept soundly, a lock of Xiao Chiye's hair still caught in his fingers. Xiao Chiye leaned down and studied him, his thoughts racing.

Desire is a shackle.

Xiao Chiye had invited Zuo Qianqiu to Qudu to ask his shifu one question: *Can desire be conquered?*

But in the end, he never asked it aloud. He already knew it was a question Zuo Qianqiu couldn't answer. The only one who could answer it was Xiao Chiye himself. Everyone said he'd been born at the wrong time, but he was already here. Having desire wasn't his fault.

He was merely human.

His name was Xiao Chiye.

He seemed the polar opposite of Shen Zechuan, yet in truth, they were the same. In all the world, the only one who understood Xiao Chiye's suffering without any words was Shen Zechuan. This was something both had known with certainty since their first kiss.

Xiao Chiye dropped a kiss on Shen Zechuan's brow, then on the bridge of his nose.

It didn't matter what this feeling was called. They invaded and staked their claims on each other; as they struggled, they grew closer and closer still. The pit of desire was bottomless, the abyss of misery inescapable. This intimacy was a way to dull their pain, but the method was addictive; only by holding each other close could they find relief.

After that first night of stolen pleasure, they had tacitly begun to shed their shells and reveal their true selves. The chasm of the past had become a puddle; all it took was a single leap or a helping hand to reach the other side, where they could merge into one.

Xiao Chiye kissed Shen Zechuan again, and Shen Zechuan, in his slumber, tightened his grip on that lock of Xiao Chiye's hair.

A crisp breeze blew through the night. Ripples washed over the pale moon in the puddle, while the heartbreaker and the heartless flirt slept together in the dark, nestled under a blanket of moonlight.

COLLAPSE

RAIN BEGAN TO FALL just before dawn. Chen Yang, washing up in the resting hall, wiped his face and looked out at the drizzle of misty rain interspersed with flakes of snow.

Those who served in the courtyard were already bustling about. "Tell the kitchen to light the stove," Chen Yang instructed the attendants beside him. "Serve the medicine while it's hot, then prepare the ginger soup. Have Master's and the judge's officials' robes been steamed and perfumed with incense? Hurry and send them over. The ground is slippery from the rain and snow; step carefully, lest you fall and disgrace yourself."

Chen Yang held an umbrella overhead and made his way to the kitchen, where he checked on the preparations for breakfast. When the cook saw him, he immediately called the attendant to fetch the meal boxes.

"I heard last night that the judge had fallen ill, so I made fish soup and some light side dishes. There's porridge and steamed twisted rolls." The cook handed a stack of other boxes to Chen Yang. "Breakfast for you gentlemen. You were on guard all of last night. Drink something hot to dispel the chill."

Chen Yang put a hand on the containers and laughed. "All right. And you even prepared shaojiu wine for Gu Jin—I'll thank you on his behalf. Have them serve Master's breakfast without delay. I'm heading over to attend him now."

The cook saw him out; Chen Yang turned down any help from the kitchen assistant and hurried back into the courtyard under the safety of his umbrella.

No servant was allowed to touch the daily meals of the personal guards out of sight of the cook; the guards took turns to collect them personally. This was a strict rule established all the way back in Libei.

Chen Yang arrived at the courtyard and called down the others; they stood and ate together.

Mouth full of steamed bun, Ding Tao looked toward the house. "Master is up."

"Is the carriage ready?" Gu Jin asked. "It's a little late today."

Chen Yang nodded. "I didn't expect the weather today. Master will still get rained on later when he's registering his attendance and standing by at the palace. The lord judge's cold is bound to linger. Does he not plan on taking a leave of absence?"

Who is he asking?

Gu Jin and Ding Tao exchanged a glance, then turned as one to Qiao Tianya, who had shown up for the free meal.

Qiao Tianya gulped a huge mouthful of porridge and held up a finger. The other three said in unison, "Swallow first!"

He swallowed, then explained, "He won't risk even a single day off. My master is still a newly appointed official. How would he dare take leave when the senior officials above him are still hard at work? He can't be busier than the chief commander, can he?"

"You Embroidered Uniform Guard are terrible," said Ding Tao. "You have to talk about seniority even when falling ill!"

"There's nothing we can do," replied Qiao Tianya. "Everyone, above and below, is watching him."

As the four of them ate and chatted, the door to Xiao Chiye's chamber opened; maidservants began to move in and out with serving trays in hand. The masters were awake.

After a full night's sleep in Xiao Chiye's arms, Shen Zechuan's fever had broken—he was drenched in sweat—but the rash on his neck was still red.

Xiao Chiye had already dressed. Seeing Shen Zechuan stir lethargically, he laid a hand against his forehead and said, "There's medicine on the table. Drink it while it's hot."

Slipping into his boots, Shen Zechuan got out of bed to drink the medicine. They stood back-to-back, dressing before the mirrors, as the sound of cloth rustled around them.

Shen Zechuan fastened his belt and pushed the window open to peer up at the sky. "This rain came at a bad time."

"If anything happened last night, we would have heard about it. It's not too late to hurry and unclog the ditches today."

Xiao Chiye came closer, stepping out of reach of the maidservant behind him who was trying to fasten his crown. Shen Zechuan reached out to take it. Xiao Chiye propped his elbows on the window ledge, and Shen Zechuan put it on for him. Eyes met eyes.

"Smells bitter," Xiao Chiye said.

"If you come closer," Shen Zechuan said, "the bitterness will be even stronger."

The maidservants bowed low, not daring to make a sound.

Qiao Tianya was holding up an umbrella as they stepped out the door. Shen Zechuan descended the stairs but hadn't yet crossed the courtyard when he saw Tantai Hu hurrying over. Tantai Hu looked less than pleased to see Shen Zechuan, but still bowed a greeting before rushing up the stairs.

"Lao-Hu!" Chen Yang approached him. "What's the matter?"

Xiao Chiye had already stepped into the courtyard. Gu Jin draped his overcoat over his shoulders as Xiao Chiye looked at Tantai Hu without a word.

"Supreme Commander!" Tantai Hu dropped to one knee. "Urgent word from the Donglong Street patrol squad: Ouhua Pavilion has collapsed!"

Shen Zechuan halted his steps and waited for Tantai Hu to continue.

Tantai Hu wiped rainwater from his face. "It collapsed on the second young master of the Xi Clan—but more importantly, His Majesty was inside too!"

Xiao Chiye's gaze was piercing. Above, the rain and snow seemed to fall harder.

Shen Zechuan took long strides out of the office of the Embroidered Uniform Guard. Ge Qingqing was waiting at the bottom of the steps. As Shen Zechuan fastened his authority token, he was already saying, "Tell me what happened, in detail."

The Embroidered Uniform Guard followed him swiftly out of the courtyard. Ge Qingqing spoke low, his hand on his blade hilt. "His Majesty snuck out. No one knew about it when the building collapsed this morning. While the courtesans were being dug out, men from the Eight Great Battalions were still searching for Xi Hongxuan in the wreckage. It wasn't until morning court was about to commence and the eunuchs lifted the curtain that they realized His Majesty was gone! They went first to Caiwei Palace to check with Concubine Mu, but she was as clueless as they. As you can imagine, chaos erupted. They requested the presence of the empress dowager and Third Lady Hua, who interrogated the palace maids serving the emperor. That's when they found His Majesty had disguised himself as a eunuch and insisted on going to Ouhua Pavilion with Xi Hongxuan last night."

Shen Zechuan's brows were drawn low. "There are several layers of guards in the inner palace. Without help, he wouldn't even make it out of Mingli Hall."

"That's the odd thing." Ge Qingqing lowered his voice to a whisper. "During my investigation, I heard the guards say no one came in or out of his chambers all night."

Shen Zechuan watched, detached, as the Eight Great Battalions marched past in formation. His expression remained unchanged. He had hurried the entire way in the rain; no one dared even hold up their umbrellas at the moment, lest they look more concerned with their own health than the emperor's. Dark clouds shadowed the face of every official, as somber as if their own parents had died.

Hai Liangyi and Xiao Chiye stood before the rubble that had been Ouhua Pavilion. Its collapse had brought down half the street of closely clustered buildings with it. The sewage in the gutters had overflowed in the downpour, and all of Donglong Street reeked to high heaven. No one could pass without wading through the swill.

Pan Xiangjie, the Minister of Works, was the current head of the Pan Clan, one of the Eight Great Clans. Although he shared the same surname as Pan Rugui, that was where the similarities ended—a eunuch, no matter how powerful, was nowhere near a noble minister's league. Pan Xiangjie was the same age as Hai Liangyi. He had never dared commit any major blunder in his post. Knowing he would never climb to the heights of the Grand Secretariat, he had always been careful and prudent in hopes of a peaceful retirement, especially since his son was already Vice Minister of the Ministry of Revenue. Never had he expected to wake up that morning to the sky falling in.

He swayed on his feet, so overcome with anxiety his hands were trembling. It was all he could do to urge repeatedly, "Hurry...hurry up and dig. His Majesty is still inside!"

The rain seemed to have washed all expression from Hai Liangyi's face. He had never thought Li Jianheng's mind so addled—that he would go so far just to play! Several times, he wiped rainwater from his eyes as though wiping away tears. Turning to Xiao Chiye, he said, "Dig... Get His Majesty out first!"

Xiao Chiye unfastened his overcoat and waded through the muck to take a closer look. The current commander of the Eight Great Battalions was Han Cheng's younger brother, Han Jin, who had rolled up the legs of his trousers and lifted the hem of his robe to follow Xiao Chiye down.

"Supreme Commander!" Han Jin shouted through the rain. "The base of the building has been hollowed out. We can't dig down there!"

Not only had the foundation been hollowed out, it was filled with large copper vats. No one was bold enough to mention it. The vats had been smashed to shards when the building collapsed; if Li Jianheng was down there, he was surely a goner. He would be the first emperor in the history of the Zhou empire to be crushed to death while sneaking out to play. Which historian would dare record this? The very thought was crushingly depressing.

"His Majesty would've been resting in the upper levels last night." Shen Zechuan removed his blade and sloshed forward into the water. "And this place isn't deep."

"There's no guarantee it won't collapse further." Xiao Chiye straightened up. "Get the men from the Ministry of Works!"

Cen Yu, having rushed over, arrived at this moment. The instant Shen Zechuan saw him, he turned to Hai Liangyi. "Secretariat Elder, it is imperative that the public ditch be dredged today. If this rain doesn't let up, the whole city will flood."

"We're right up against the Kailing River at the back too!" Cen Yu said. "I just came from there. The buildings along the banks have already collapsed; their foundations are soaked through! How long has it been since the stone of the dam was last repaired? Once the water level rises, half of Qudu will flood! What has the Ministry of Works been doing all these years?! Pan Xiangjie, you addled fool! How many times have I told you about this?!"

Pan Xiangjie fell to his knees in the mud. "What could I have done?!" The man's hair was practically gray, yet he wailed like a child. "How can you blame me? The Ministry of Revenue lord their power over us. I mentioned this to them years and years ago. What can I do if they don't allocate the funds and manpower?! Cen Xunyi, what could I possibly do?!" He scooped up the filthy water in his hands, struggling to speak through his sobs. Banging his head against the ground as he kowtowed, he cried, "We're all going to pay for this with our lives!"

"You are a senior official of the imperial court!" Hai Liangyi bellowed. "Pull yourself together! His Majesty's fate hangs in the balance; we don't know if he's dead or alive. This is an emergency. If you want to shift the blame, at least wait until we get him out! Take eight hundred men from the Imperial Army's patrol to join the Ministry of Works's effort to unclog the public ditch immediately. Tear down the illegally built houses! As for the Ministry of Revenue, have them total the state treasury money and gather those whose houses have collapsed at the Temple of Guilt so we can centralize the distribution of aid. The Eight Great Battalions shall patrol the major city gates. Entry and exit into the city must be accompanied by official documentation. We are at a critical juncture; we will need everyone to work as one to stabilize the situation. Don't lose your heads now!"

Hai Liangyi turned to Shen Zechuan. "The Embroidered Uniform Guard guards the inner palace. We can't afford to let anyone take advantage of the situation to stir up trouble. Should anyone defy these directives, you have my order to execute them on the spot!"

The rain poured around them. Hai Liangyi's direct, merciless commands instantly buttressed the shaky morale of the crowd. He took a few steps forward and removed his black official's hat.

"His Majesty is the Son of Heaven." Water running down his face, Hai Liangyi said with finality, "Our Great Zhou has reigned for a century. This is not the day it will fall."

Li Jianheng lay face-down beneath the broken lumber. Icy water pouring on his neck jolted him awake; he found he could barely breathe. His chest was tightly wedged in the rubble, and his ribs ached terribly.

He coughed and rasped out, "H-help—"

The word was hoarse and weak, too soft to be heard over the downpour.

Li Jianheng shifted his gaze and saw that the courtesan beside him had gone cold. Her ghastly pale flesh was squashed between broken walls, the splayed strands of her hair tacky with blood. Li Jianheng began to tremble; he could no longer recognize this as the beautiful woman who had clapped and danced for him last night.

"Help," Li Jianheng struggled to say, his head hanging. "*Help.*"

Choking coughs rang out below him. Xi Hongxuan was half-submerged, his torso horrifically bent backward. He had crashed down right on top of the copper vats, and his back was bloody and mangled. Gasping for air, he said, "Your Majesty, stop calling. They can't hear you."

Li Jianheng was beside himself with horror as he elbowed at the broken pieces of lumber, all in vain. He'd lost one of his shoes, and he was so cold his face was bloodless. "No. Someone will definitely come to save me..."

"Of course." Xi Hongxuan chuckled quietly. "You're the Son of Heaven."

"What are you laughing at?" Li Jianheng demanded.

Xi Hongxuan spat sandy mud. "This thing called fate... Don't you find it strange how people seem to repeat the same life with each cycle of reincarnation?"

Li Jianheng widened his eyes but could see nothing. "No," he said darkly. "There's no cycle."

"Tell me." Xi Hongxuan shifted his body with some difficulty. "Your Majesty's birth mother, with the surname Yue. Didn't she drown to death too?"

Didn't she?

The foul water splashed from his neck down his spine. Under this incessant drip, Li Jianheng swallowed. With difficulty, he recalled those ephemeral childhood memories. He looked at the courtesan's bloated and pale flesh again; this time, he seemed to see his mother there beside him.

The woman's face was pressed into the swill bucket, her fingers having clawed at the ground until they were bloody stumps. As water splashed on his face, Li Jianheng saw her ghastly white neck, her pallid arms.

Didn't she?

Hot tears pricked at Li Jianheng's eyes. He frantically covered them with his hands and shouted, "Shut up! Shut up!"

Xi Hongxuan fell silent.

But Li Jianheng didn't want to be next to the corpse any longer. He cried and cursed, hurling abuse and profanities. "Don't mention her! We are the supreme ruler on the imperial throne! Our..." Panting heavily behind his fingers, Li Jianheng's face was harrowed. "Our mother is the empress dowager!"

FAMILY BACKGROUND

LI JIANHENG NEVER spoke of his birth mother to anyone—this subject was his nightmare. His mother had no formal title and was merely a lowly palace maid. The official records had her surname shoddily listed as *Yue*, and that was all there was.

Not long after Li Jianheng was born, the Xiande Emperor's birth mother, Lady Lu, brought the babe into her palace. However, the only care he received there was being fed and clothed. At the age he should have begun schooling, no one gave him a thought—thus he grew up ignorant and incompetent, and spent all his time playing with eunuchs.

He had no mother, only a wet nurse responsible for his daily care.

His nurse was the arranged partner of the Xiande Emperor's personal eunuch. She recognized power and little else, and as a result, mistreated Li Jianheng where she could get away with it. Every day, she dressed him up enough to appear presentable, yet he often woke up hungry in the night back in the privacy of his room. Once, Li Jianheng mentioned this to his older brother, and the Xiande Emperor threw a fit at his personal eunuch, who then went home and beat the nurse. From that day onward, the nurse gave Li Jianheng nothing but cold food and the cold shoulder. She never hit him, but had a tongue so sharp Li Jianheng never dared mention his treatment again; before he learned how to speak a whole sentence, he already knew a plethora of vulgar insults.

His nurse told him his birth mother was a cheap whore of the palace. Because of her illicit pregnancy, the lady she served kept her inside to "convalesce." In reality, she was kept indoors for years, constantly plagued by illness. Even then, she secretly wished to one day meet her son.

When Li Jianheng was five, the Guangcheng Emperor came to Lady Lu's palace to check the academic progress of Li Jianyun, who would become the Xiande Emperor. As they spoke, the Guangcheng Emperor spotted Li Jianheng playing with crickets and called him over. This was his first time meeting his father.

The Guangcheng Emperor asked him some questions.

Li Jianheng held a cricket tightly in his hands. He didn't dare look at the emperor; he spoke ineloquently, stuttering over every question.

The Guangcheng Emperor found this child stupid. Li Jianheng was already five, yet was unable to articulate himself, had not an ounce of decorum, and appeared meek; he possessed none of the aura of a royal scion.

For his part, Li Jianheng had very much wanted to talk to the Guangcheng Emperor but was terrified by this stranger who didn't feel like his father. During the lengthy questioning, he began to cry. The Guangcheng Emperor utterly disdained him. As a result, the first time he saw his father was also the last. Only after the Guangcheng Emperor left did Li Jianheng realize he'd unwittingly squashed the cricket to death in his small hands.

Back then, Li Jianyun was still in good health, the most favored son after the crown prince. He, too, thought Li Jianheng useless. But still he pitied him, so he petitioned the Guangcheng Emperor and started to bring Li Jianheng along to classes with him.

When Li Jianheng got to know the other princes, he found they were all living in the lap of luxury. He slowly came to realize that these boys weren't truly his brothers. They ridiculed him; they spoke of protocols and propriety; they made him bow and scrape before them. Li Jianheng didn't know he wasn't required to kneel and kowtow to his brothers upon seeing them—this was what they taught him, and not a single eunuch or palace maid ever stepped forward to pull him up.

It was only when the crown prince and Li Jianyun were around that everyone acted with brotherly affection. But Li Jianheng didn't know what to say and had no one to talk to. Gradually, he stopped coming to class on time. He started to lie to Li Jianyun, feigning illness and sleeping in, doing his best to avoid his lessons at every opportunity. Eventually, Li Jianyun felt Li Jianheng was a lost cause—he couldn't be taught or set straight—and gave up on the boy.

One day, Li Jianheng followed a eunuch through a doghole in the palace walls. Whenever he squeezed his way through, the eunuchs would cover their mouths and snicker, then give him castoff candies from the Imperial Bakery. The child was like a puppy coaxed into wagging his tail for a few scraps. Through that doghole, he obtained many foods he had never tasted before. It was also through that doghole that he first saw his mother.

Li Jianheng didn't recognize this woman with the surname Yue.

A eunuch egged Li Jianheng on, telling him to call her a *useless invalid*, so Li Jianheng spat on her and called her just that. The woman had leaned against the wall and cried as she gazed at him. Li Jianheng found her too odd; the way she looked at him frightened him, so much that he felt like crying too.

His nurse had scolded him again when he returned. But when Li Jianheng got up to pee in the middle of the night, he heard his nurse having a secret tryst with the same eunuch who had goaded him to curse the strange woman. He accidentally kicked over the chamber pot and was caught red-handed by the two of them. After that night, newly afraid Li Jianheng would rat them out, the nurse gave him plenty of candy and never scolded him again. Instead, she held him in her arms and coddled him all day long. There were many kinds of sweets, including one called silk-nested tiger's eye candy. There was only so much of it every day, and Li Jianheng couldn't bear to eat it; he tagged along behind Li Jianyun and offered it to his older brother.

That year, Li Jianyun's health started to deteriorate, until he was too sick to even attend his classes.

Lady Lu ordered an investigation of his food and drink but turned up nothing. Every night, she wept at Li Jianyun's side. The imperial physicians came and went, but Li Jianyun never improved.

At the same time, the nurse also stopped giving Li Jianheng sweets. Li Jianheng had cried and wailed, demanding them, but the nurse told him the useless invalid woman he had cursed in the Eastern Courtyard had told on him and forbade him from eating candy again. Li Jianheng couldn't shake that silk-nested tiger's eye from his mind. He hated that sickly woman; the nurse assured him that if Li Jianheng wanted that candy again, he merely had to tell Lady Lu that the sickly woman had given him the sweets to begin with.

Li Jianheng didn't dare tell Lady Lu, but he secretly told Li Jianyun. Li Jianyun had stared at him from where he lay on his sickbed. In that instant, Li Jianheng felt his elder brother looked just like his father.

A short time later, Li Jianheng was awakened in the middle of the night. The nurse led him out to the main hall, which was filled with splashing sounds. From where he stood behind the hanging curtain, he saw a blur of human figures. Li Jianyun, who was lying on his bed with an overcoat draped over his shoulders, beckoned to him.

Li Jianheng ran over.

That sickly woman was half-naked, her head pressed into the bucket of filthy water. Again and again, her face was shoved in. As she choked and coughed below the surface, water poured into her mouth and nose. Her fingernails, clawing against the ground, had become bloodied pulp.

Li Jianyun held onto Li Jianheng and said nothing. The sight frightened him to no end, and he glanced back many times at his brother. There was no smile on Li Jianyun's face, and so Li Jianheng didn't dare to smile either.

Every time the woman was shoved down, there came a gurgling sound. She raked her nails against the bucket in agony, her bony fingers clawing out wood shavings, turning her nails into a dirty, mangled mess. Li Jianheng had looked at her, but he couldn't remember her face clearly anymore. Only the sound of sloshing water stuck in his memory.

The nurse standing behind him was a tall, robust woman, which Li Jianheng didn't like. All the women he chose in the future were either petite or sickly.

Li Jianheng didn't like water either, after that; he found it filthy.

From that night on, the nurse treated him very well, and so did Li Jianyun. No one mentioned his studies anymore, and Li Jianyun no longer made him practice calligraphy; he even assigned eunuchs to entertain him. Li Jianheng was finally free to play from morning until he fell asleep at night. When he was in his teens and old enough to move into his own manor, Li Jianyun sent him a number of pretty women. Once Li Jianheng got a taste of the pleasures of the bedroom, he spiraled out of control.

It wasn't until many years later that Li Jianheng learned that sickly woman whom he had watched drown was surnamed Yue.

"Our mother is the empress dowager!"

Li Jianheng's fingers trembled. He seemed to be saying it to Xi Hongxuan and, at the same time, to himself. He muttered it over and over like a man gone mad.

Xi Hongxuan sniffled and listened to Li Jianheng rave. He couldn't help but grin. "Your Majesty, if you truly wish everyone to think this, then you must accord the empress dowager the honor befitting a mother. The empress dowager..." he hissed in pain, then continued, "lacks a son at the moment!"

Li Jianheng felt a stabbing pain in his chest as he gasped for breath; he hastily wiped his tears with wet fingers. "I—we know!"

"I doubt you know," Xi Hongxuan said.

"Who gave you the audacity to—to speak to us in such a manner?" Li Jianheng demanded.

"The words of a man on his deathbed always come from the heart." Blood oozed from the corners of Xi Hongxuan's mouth. He spat a few more times. "If you and I don't get out of here, there will be no sovereign and his minister; just two drowning rats in a pit. What kind of emperor are you? Back when Xiao Er lifted you onto the dragon throne, you ingratiated yourself with him and worshiped him like an ancestor! Have you forgotten? You have always been his master. He's *supposed* to risk his life for you! What logic is there in parents being grateful to their sons and grandchildren? The Xiao Clan enjoys prestige and power only because of the Libei Armored Cavalry. Grateful to Xiao Chiye? Such a ridiculous sentiment would be totally unheard of under the Guangcheng Emperor, only a few decades ago! I truly worry when I look at you! How does it feel being a waste of an emperor? You sit so high, yet you aren't even as happy as I was when I romped around the saltworks as an imperial merchant. If you continue to suffer such trifling indignities in your position, you may as well drown here with me today."

In pain after having spoken so much, he grimaced and spent a moment catching his breath. As he listened to Li Jianheng's sobs, he began to weep himself. "Your Majesty." Xi Hongxuan laid his heart bare. "My mother was a woman from Qinzhou, of low birth. She only won my father's favor because her ma and pa made some money with guidance from the late Madam Yao. I might be a lawful second son, but I lead a dog's life back at home. Why do you think I preferred to make my living on the Sea of Xuhai when I was eighteen, battered by wind and waves? It's because my parents wanted to hand the entire family fortune to my eldest brother! Later, I met with disaster at sea and was badly injured. My constitution was wrecked; I recuperated in Qinzhou for the better part of a year. See how obese I am now—it's all because of the tonifying herbs I consumed that brought me back from the brink of death. Ugly, right? Ha ha! But before I was injured, I was a handsome man. Before I set out to sea, I met a woman and fell in love. We were engaged to be married. But by the time I returned, she had married another—she had become my dearest sister-in-law. What a dedicated brother Xi Gu'an was. After hearing of my ill fate, he even took care of my woman for me. Is there any more wonderful sibling bond? I'll be thanking him all my life!"

Xi Hongxuan cried and laughed as he spoke into their damp and narrow prison. "All my life! Your Majesty, who in this world isn't pitiful? Out of pity for me, would you let me become the Grand Secretary who wields power over the whole imperial court? You pitied Xiao Er and truly made him your supreme commander, at one stroke the most sought-after man in Qudu. But who will pity you? If Xiao Er were sincere toward you, would he have let Xiao Jiming say what he did before the throne? Wasn't that just Libei throwing their weight around?!"

He took a breath to continue. "And then you have that eighth son of the Shen Clan, cursed with Shen Wei as his old man. What kind of place do you think the Imperial Prison is? He fell into Ji Lei's hands at fifteen and might as well have been skinned alive the way he spent those days in prison. He may be free now, but look at him—he's clearly more specter than man. Everyone in this world is pitiful. If you pity every life, how can you be emperor? As the saying goes, every man for himself, and the devil takes the hindmost.

"Your Majesty, don't listen to those blabbermouths who speak of your lowly birth mother. Your surname is Li; mine is Xi. For us, that's enough! From birth, our classes—both the low-born and the noble—define us! All those platitudes claiming no one is born to rule except through merit are empty words meant to comfort fools. Without order, there would be no countries and states. Your name is Li Jianheng—you are naturally superior to Xiao Chiye. So what if the Xiao Clan dares harbor ill intent; what are you afraid of? *You* are the one acknowledged by the people of this land. They can rattle their sabers; in the end, they will be nothing but traitors! If you raise your arms and call for aid, who in our Great Zhou would disobey? This is what it is to be the Son of Heaven!"

This is what it is to be the Son of Heaven!

The words thundered in Li Jianheng's ears and snapped him to his senses. In this wet and filthy pit, for the very first time, he came to truly understand who he was. Before he knew it, tears had covered his face. He reflected on all that had led up to this day and felt he had been living in vain.

Xi Hongxuan, unwilling to let this opportunity slip, strained to continue, "They laugh at you for being uneducated and cowardly. But who in this world doesn't fear death?! Let them talk; the blade isn't against *their* throats. When it is, nine out of ten will piss their pants! You're a sovereign, not a craftsman! When it comes to matters of learning, the scholars from the Imperial College will provide the answers. As for government affairs, isn't that what the Grand Secretariat is for? Does it not exist to advise you? You are an emperor. You are *the* emperor!"

"We are the emperor." Li Jianheng felt both hot and cold as he trembled and repeated, "You're right. We are the emperor."

Xi Hongxuan was listening closely; seeing that he'd more or less achieved his desired effect, he heaved a sigh of relief.

The fucking nerve of whoever had tampered with Ouhua Pavilion! With the building so damaged, any evidence of foul play would be washed away, and blame would fall squarely on Xi Hongxuan's head. If he couldn't win Li Jianheng over now, the storm of indictments from the Chief Surveillance Bureau alone would flay him alive. He could wave goodbye to his newly appointed position as the Secretary for the Bureau of Evaluations of the Ministry of Personnel; Hai Liangyi might well chop his head off. Marinating in this filthy water, Xi Hongxuan carefully sifted through his network of connections. He didn't want to die or be exiled. It had been no easy feat to take Xi Gu'an out of play and climb to his current position, not to mention the good fortune of meeting such a rare good master as Li Jianheng. No, he had to live. Lips blue from blood loss, Xi Hongxuan chanted silently to himself: *Hurry up.*

Xue Xiuzhuo, Hai Liangyi, Shen Zechuan, or even Xiao Chiye; whoever it was, hurry up and dig them out. Li Jianheng must not die here. If he died here, everything Xi Hongxuan had done would go down the drain.

Just as Xi Hongxuan was about to close his eyes, a loud rumble sounded just above them. Debris from the broken wall rattled down, followed by a surge of putrid water that brought with it distant voices and the sound of heavy rain.

Xi Hongxuan almost wept with joy. He could hear Li Jianheng being pulled to safety. Then, under the shouts of the Imperial Army as they counted off and heaved, the heavy structure pinning him down was lifted.

The water had already reached Xi Hongxuan's waist. He waved his arms feebly and yelled, "Help, help—"

Xiao Chiye looked down at Xi Hongxuan from above.

The unending rain washed down on him. Xi Hongxuan felt a chill up his spine. Even as the water swelled to Xi Hongxuan's chest, Xiao Chiye looked as if he had no intention to pull him up.

"Xiao Er," Xi Hongxuan spat, every syllable laced with hatred. The floodwater was breaking over his head. He choked on foul water and flailed, struggling for breath.

By the time Xiao Chiye reached in to drag Xi Hongxuan out, his mouth was filled with putrid water. Xi Hongxuan dug his fingers hard into Xiao Chiye's arms. Gasping for breath, he craned his neck pathetically and hissed, *"Fuck—your—mother!"*

Xiao Chiye shoved him down with a hand. Xi Hongxuan clawed at the mud as sludge filled his mouth and nose. He was suffocating; he scratched with all his might, but he couldn't budge Xiao Chiye's iron arm.

Xiao Chiye clearly had the intent to kill, but he couldn't actually hold Xi Hongxuan down until he died. There were people behind him, and Li Jianheng had been awake and lucid when he was brought out.

Xiao Chiye lifted Xi Hongxuan by the back of his collar and leaned down to say menacingly, “Why don’t you say that one more time.”

DREDGING THE DITCHES

XI HONGXUAN SHOOK as he puked up sewage, his face terrifyingly pale. Behind them, Han Jin saw that something wasn't right and hastily waded over. Xiao Chiye let go and watched as Xi Hongxuan was carried to safety. As the rain drummed down, the watching officials sobbed as they chased Li Jianheng's sedan and swarmed toward the palace gates.

Pan Xiangjie ran until his shoes fell off. The old man lifted the hem of his robe, panting and heaving yet not forgetting every few strides to cry out "Your Majesty!" The crowd around him was in a similar state. Only Hai Liangyi remained as dignified as ever as he kept pace with the sedan all the way back to the palace.

The waiting imperial physicians rushed over to meet them, and the chaotic procession continued into the inner palace, where Mu Ru, plainly dressed in white, ran out to receive them. When she saw Li Jianheng covered in blood, her tears flowed without cease.

The empress dowager, too, came out with Hua Xiangyi at her arm. She turned to Han Cheng, instantly hostile. "I understand you're anxious, but how could you allow the elder officials to run all this way? They're advanced in age, and now they've been soaked in the rain. It will make matters that much worse if anything happens to them!"

The Embroidered Uniform Guard knelt before her with a rustle of wet cloth. "This humble subject has erred!" Han Cheng said.

"Quick, prepare soup and distribute dry clothes." The empress dowager next addressed the ministers. "It touches me to see everyone's sincere loyalty. His Majesty is safely back in the palace; there's no need for any rush. It's so cold out. Everyone, please head to the adjoining hall to get out of the wind and have a bowl of hot soup. We cannot afford anyone to fall ill at this juncture."

The officials kowtowed in gratitude.

The empress dowager continued, "Grand Secretary Hai and everyone in the Grand Secretariat, as well as the excellencies of the various ministries—please step this way for a word."

Cen Yu wasn't among those summoned. He had remained on Donglong Street to help dredge the public sewers with Xiao Chiye. Yu Xiaozai, the lowly censor from the Chief Surveillance Bureau, followed carrying Cen Yu's straw cloak.

Xiao Chiye's hair and face were thoroughly drenched. Everyone on the street shivered in the chilly wind, yet he wasn't affected at all. When they were digging the two men out earlier, he had lifted a beam weighing nearly a hundred catties by himself. At present, he was wrapping a handkerchief around the web between his thumb and index finger with a grim expression.

"The low-lying districts are full of poor households. To even afford a house of shoddy lumber is a victory for them. When they heard the houses must be demolished, nine out of ten refused." With his bare feet still underwater, Cen Yu lifted the hem of his soaked official's robe and tucked it into his belt. "Today, Donglong Street was the only street flooded because it runs along the Kailing River. But if this rain doesn't stop, Supreme Commander, by tomorrow the other streets will be the same."

"If the imperial court is willing to offer a subsidy of five taels of silver to each household, they will be willing," Tantai Hu said, covered in mud to the waist. "They just want a roof over their heads. As long as we fork out the money, it won't be a problem. This humble subject feels that those protesting loudest are actually the large manors. Many of those residences violated regulations by expanding their property into the public ditches, and there're plenty of cases where they've come to blows over a few inches of space. Now that we're telling them to tear their walls down, there's no way five taels of silver will convince them to wreck their perfectly good homes. They won't even come to the door when we knock!"

"I'm afraid it won't be easy to come to an agreement regarding any subsidy." Cen Yu had served in the court for a long time; he was all too familiar with these ins and outs of politics. "It was only because of Grand Secretary Hai that the Ministry of Revenue was willing to shell out for aid relief to the flood victims here; that sum still has to be accounted for. They'll never agree to pay five taels to each household as well."

"Your Excellency, excuse an uncouth fellow like me for griping, but how can you still be thinking about money *now*?!" Tantai Hu's chest heaved. "Once the water rises and people start dying, the city will become a breeding ground for disease! At that point, even a hoard of silver would be useless!"

"Well now, don't get so worked up." Yu Xiaozai raised his hands placatingly. "You're not familiar with the treasury's constraints. The Ministry of Revenue has its own difficulties. It's not that they begrudge this amount of money. The annual review nears. Why wouldn't they want to resolve this business as neatly as possible? Averting potential disaster will make them look good too; they should be only too happy to sign off on it. So what's stopping them? They're embarrassingly short of cash! Let's say they take this sum of money out now to deal with the emergency. In the coming days, we will enter the spring plowing season. Several regions were struck by natural disasters last year; in those places, there was no harvest at all. After the local governments send in their reports, the Ministry of Revenue must deliberate over the allocation of money so the affected prefectural yamen or provincial administration commissioners can buy seed from neighboring provinces with good harvests. This is a major undertaking concerning the sustenance and survival of hundreds of thousands of people. How could they dare touch the remaining money in the state treasury?"

The censor continued, "Since these people expanded their properties illegally, by law they should be punished for illegal appropriation of the public ditches. Now instead of punishing them, you want the court to hand them money. If the Ministry of Revenue doesn't think this through, they'll be indicted by our Chief Surveillance Bureau in the future. Really, everyone is in a tight spot."

Yu Xiaozai had an uncanny ability to calm people. When those lightly accented syllables left his mouth, one felt even the most major issues could wait. Every word he spoke was the truth. He took no sides but laid out the problem precisely as he saw it.

The success of the spring planting season in the various regions determined the empire's course of action in this year. The army provisions of two major strategic frontier lands relied on the harvests of Juexi's thirteen cities and Hezhou's shipping routes. No one dared be careless; this matter took precedence over everything else.

But where did that leave them?

Going ahead with the demolition by force would rouse public wrath. Half the men in the Imperial Army hailed from military households in Qudu. There weren't many who lived on Donglong Street, but there were some. When Hai Liangyi entrusted this matter to the Imperial Army, he was effectively entrusting it to Xiao Chiye. Had it been handed to the Eight Great Battalions, there would be no consideration or compromise; Han Jin would level everything. No one could overlook the potential risk of such brash action.

Hai Liangyi had meant for Xiao Chiye to think of a solution.

Xiao Chiye pulled the handkerchief tighter around his hand. As he opened his mouth to speak, he saw a man walking toward them through the rain.

Shen Zechuan cupped his hands in greeting. "I guessed everyone would be here. Any progress on the public ditches?"

"It's a problem." Cen Yu sighed gustily. "We can't just tear the houses down."

"As I understand it, the difficulty for the Ministry of Revenue is that they can't predict the expenses for the upcoming spring planting." Although Shen Zechuan looked calm, his cheeks were flushed. He looked out into the rain. "This expenditure can be estimated. This humble one has seen the Embroidered Uniform Guard's archives, so I have some insights. Supreme Commander, if I may?"

Xiao Chiye pinned his gaze on him. "Please go ahead, Judge Shen."

Shen Zechuan took a moment to gather his thoughts. "Last year, when the new emperor ascended the throne, a general amnesty was granted across the empire. As part of this, Juexi got a three-tenths exemption on their taxes. They had a bumper crop last year. Other than Huaizhou and Dunzhou, which both reported impact from disasters, the rest of the regions brought in their harvest as usual. Supreme Commander, Dunzhou's granaries truly are hard-pressed this year. The prefectural yamen will need to buy seed from Cizhou, whose granaries are filled to the brim. But there were heavy storms at the start of the year, and the snow in Zhongbo crushed many houses. Did not the Heir of Libei set aside forty thousand taels from Libei's military budget this year to relieve Cizhou? Have Cizhou repay this favor now. Ask the heir to send a letter to Cizhou's prefectural prefect, Zhou Gui, telling him to discount the grains sold to Dunzhou by forty thousand taels. The Ministry of Revenue can allocate fewer funds to Cizhou and instead put that money toward house demolition subsidies."

Yu Xiaozai pondered it. "But at the end of the day, appropriating public ditches is still a crime. Can the Ministry of Revenue stand behind this decision?"

"The illegal appropriation of public ditches should indeed be punished under the law. But these are special circumstances. We can't apply the same rigid rules to a situation every time." Shen Zechuan paused. "The imperial court pities the disaster victims. This subsidy is a kindness, an act of imperial magnanimity. Censor Cen is the most appropriate person to step forward and raise this matter. The Ministry of Revenue isn't heartless. As long as it's justifiable, the accounting is clear, and the reserve is sufficient, they'll surely proceed without delay."

The annual review was just around the corner, and the evaluations that came of it were integral to the promotion of all positions within the various bureaus. Everyone would be more than happy to be graded as Outstanding. So long as it was reasonable, they would certainly be willing.

"Returning to Cizhou." Shen Zechuan looked to Xiao Chiye. "Zhongbo wants to rebuild the city this year. Although we still don't know who will be assigned to the role, it will require a great expense of manpower. The supreme commander will owe Cizhou a favor after this. When it comes time to rebuild the city, the manpower can come from those whose houses were demolished today; let them send people from their households to Cizhou to provide manual labor, escorted by the Imperial Army. It shouldn't take them more than a month. This can be considered their punishment for illegally appropriating the public ditches. These five taels of silver will not end up owed or overdue; the ones issuing them and the ones receiving them can do so with peace of mind."

What was more, Cizhou would cease to be indebted to Libei and instead enter a relationship of mutual assistance. As long as Zhou Gui wasn't a fool, he would understand it as an opportunity to make friends.

As Shen Zechuan finished, Yu Xiaozai shook open the straw cloak and draped it over Cen Yu, who didn't waste a moment. He strode forward and laid a heavy hand on Shen Zechuan's shoulder. "Judge Shen, time is pressing, so I'll be brief. Once this is over, I, Cen Xunyi, will prepare a simple meal in my abode and respectfully await your visit!"

He donned his bamboo hat and left with Yu Xiaozai.

"How's everything in the palace?" Xiao Chiye took hold of Shen Zechuan's wrist.

Tantai Hu looked as if he wanted to speak, but pressed his lips shut.

Shen Zechuan lifted the authority token hanging from Xiao Chiye's waist and looked at it for a moment. "The empress dowager has summoned the ministers of the various bureaus to take them to task. It's just as well you aren't among them. The public ditches must be dredged as soon as possible. Everyone was being courteous earlier, but you have to understand that if you don't unclog the ditches in the next few days, you'll be called to account."

The two of them stood there together. It was inappropriate for Xiao Chiye to touch Shen Zechuan more than this—but seeing the unhealthy color on Shen Zechuan's cheeks after standing in the rain, he couldn't help but say, "The secretariat elder told you to keep watch in the palace, so go. Sit in the office and drink a cup of hot tea. All you have to do is keep your eyes on the door."

"That's Han Cheng's job." Shen Zechuan looked down the street. "Shifu is still in the temple; it makes me worry. There's no time. Do what you need to do. I have to go with the men from the Ministry of Revenue and handle disaster relief for the victims."

Xiao Chiye wanted to say more, but Han Jin was calling him, shoes in hand. He could only let go. He backed up a few steps, then turned and left with Tantai Hu and Chen Yang close behind.

Shen Zechuan had a splitting headache, though the pouring rain had cleared his mind some. He turned around to call Ge Qingqing, and they took some men down to the districts on lower ground.

Clearing the public ditches was a monumental task. The work was dirty and exhausting. The men from the Ministry of Revenue had to change their shoes and lift their hems when they waded into the water, and anyone with a title was taking refuge under a tent, refusing to go near it. In any case, this was a task Hai Liangyi had given the Ministry of Works and the Imperial Army; they were here merely to assist.

When Shen Zechuan arrived, he saw there were just a handful of men working. Many of the old-timers in the Ministry of Revenue were used to putting in no more than a token effort. These men were cunning; unless they had something to gain, orders would fall on deaf ears.

"It's about to be dark soon," Ge Qingqing observed. "Why are there so few people here?"

An official bowed his way over to Shen Zechuan and, fawning, invited him to sit. "They didn't want to come. The Imperial Army hasn't finished digging out the ditches, have they? Let them finish up tonight, and we can recruit more people in the morning. Your Excellency, come sit down. Look how soaked you are! Have a cup of hot tea; at least warm up. You'll freeze out here!"

Shen Zechuan didn't budge. He peered into the makeshift tent and smiled. "Did you set this up yourself? Well done."

The official held out the tea and grinned from ear to ear. "I sure did! Everyone's been so busy; who'd have time to think about us? It was all we could do to build it ourselves..." His voice trailed off as the members of the Embroidered Uniform Guard standing solemnly behind Shen Zechuan watched him without a single smile.

Shen Zechuan himself showed little emotion. He accepted the tea and took a sip.

The official sidled closer. "This is fine tea from Hezhou, specially steeped for Your Excellency—"

With a flick of his wrist, Shen Zechuan splashed the tea over the official's face. The man yelped in shock and staggered back several steps. Shen Zechuan flipped the teacup over and tapped the bottom with his fingertips, emptying it of tea leaves. The smile on his face was even more bewitching amid the downpour.

"This tea," Shen Zechuan said pleasantly, "was a toast from me to you. Why didn't you drink it?"

The official, flustered, hastily wiped the tea off his face. "It was t-too quick—"

"When the King of Hell calls for you, it won't do for you to dawdle." Throwing the teacup aside, Shen Zechuan said, "The Grand Secretary gave strict orders to the Embroidered Uniform Guard to supervise disaster relief efforts. Perhaps the threat of immediate execution hanging around your neck isn't as tight as it should be. The tea is now on the ground, but it's still up to you to drink it. If you couldn't receive it while standing, why don't I send you on your way so you can finish it six feet under."

The official dropped to his knees in a panic. "Y-Your Excellency, how can you say these things?! This humble subordinate is a sixth-rank official of the imperial court. H-how could I be—"

"Think who you're speaking to; the Imperial Prison has no officers below the fourth rank!" Ge Qingqing lifted the hem of his robe to kick the official into the water. "If the judge orders you to drink, then drink you must. You're welcome to consider whether you'd like to drink it alive or dead."

The official tumbled into the sludge. As Shen Zechuan stared down at him with his hand on his blade, he cupped the water in his palms and scooped it into his mouth, crying out, "I'll drink it! I'll drink it!"

The men around them who had been lounging where they sat, jesting and lazing about together, all quietly stood and filed into orderly ranks.

Shen Zechuan swept a glance across them. "Can we begin clearing the ditches immediately?"

"We are at Judge Shen's disposal," they chanted as one.

"I'm a mere supervisor; what would I know of the details of this work?" Shen Zechuan fished out a blue handkerchief to wipe his hands and said with a smile, "I wouldn't dream of putting you at my disposal. The Embroidered Uniform Guard will follow your lead, gentlemen. Shall we?"

Who would dare remain behind?

The official kneeling in the muddy water trembled as he tried to climb up. When Shen Zechuan glanced at him, he bowed his head and stammered, "Y-Your Excellency..."

"There's an entire street of water here," Shen Zechuan said soothingly before leaving. "Make sure to finish before you join us."

Night had descended, but the rain showed no signs of stopping. No matter how imposing the Embroidered Uniform Guard might be, they still had to trudge through the water to do their work, soaking until they reeked all over. When Shen Zechuan next straightened up, the world spun around him. He braced his hand on a plank at the side of the ditch and steadied himself for a moment, unnoticed in the commotion.

Ge Qingqing whispered, "It's no use rushing now. Rest a moment!"

Shen Zechuan forced a smile as Ge Qingqing walked away. He felt he mustn't open his mouth; he could already taste the bile in his throat. Pushing himself up from the plank, he bent to feel around for his waterskin under the partially collapsed building.

Suddenly there was a weight on his back as something dropped over Shen Zechuan's head. The fabric covering him lifted to admit Xiao Chiye, who was panting as he burrowed his way in, shoving a still-warm food box into Shen Zechuan's hands. In the next moment, he burrowed his way out and made to leave.

Shen Zechuan pulled aside the overcoat draped over his head. Xiao Chiye, who had already taken a few steps away, turned back. Stepping over the collapsed debris, he crouched to cup Shen Zechuan's face in his palms and kiss him hard. He pulled back and rubbed Shen Zechuan's cheeks vigorously.

The rain crashed down around them. Xiao Chiye was breathing heavily. Wordlessly, he looked at Shen Zechuan in the darkness for a split second, then turned and ran off. He leaped over all the obstacles on the ground with a stunning agility as he put back on

the dirty, wet robe hanging over the crook of his arm and sped off into the alley.

If time weren't so tight...

Xiao Chiye tugged at his collar as he made his way across the wreckage. Stepping on filth as he hurried toward the Imperial Army, he cursed—

Damn it!

DOWNPOUR

THE OVERCOAT was too big; it slid down Shen Zechuan's shoulders. He tugged it back up. Warmth enveloped him as his nose was filled with Xiao Chiye's scent.

Shen Zechuan fished out the handkerchief to wipe his cheeks, damp from Xiao Chiye's hands. On this dark night, with the sound of rain falling all around, he couldn't help but sniff that handkerchief again. That, too, smelled like Xiao Chiye. Shen Zechuan lowered his eyes for a moment and nuzzled the tip of his nose against the handkerchief as the gloom on his brow dissipated.

The top layer of the meal box was filled with steamed twisted rolls, while the bottom contained hot medicinal soup. Steam rose the instant he lifted the lid. Getting one's hands on a hot meal on a night like this was no easy feat; even Xiao Chiye would have had to run like mad to make his way here before it got cold, only to go sprinting back again.

Ge Qingqing had thought to find a cup of tea for Shen Zechuan. When he climbed up from the ditch and saw him drinking the medicine, he first looked astonished, then glad. "Ah, it's been arranged. That's great. I was just thinking of sending someone to buy a bowl of medicine."

Shen Zechuan finished and wiped the corners of his lips with his fingers. "How much of this street has been torn down?"

"Just past Ouhua Pavilion. It's hard to clear out the areas where the collapse is severe." Ge Qingqing rolled up his sleeves. "There's something fishy about all this."

"Yet another inexplicable event." Shen Zechuan sat up and put his thoughts in order. "Only His Majesty himself knows who smuggled him out of the palace. If he refuses to speak, then this case is a dead end."

"If you ask me, that collapse was no coincidence. Donglong Street floods every year, yet only Ouhua Pavilion happened to collapse last night." Ge Qingqing gazed out into the rain, then looked back at Shen Zechuan. "Any ideas?"

Shen Zechuan had been thinking about it since morning. The collapse would have wiped away any traces in Ouhua Pavilion, but this was certainly no coincidence either. Xi Hongxuan was a man who treasured his life. He had just renovated Ouhua Pavilion, and those who knew the details of the hollowed-out stage's construction were few and far between.

Shen Zechuan watched the rain. He murmured, as if to himself, "No need to fret. Whoever's behind it is bound to make another move. We still don't know who the target was this time."

The imperial physician retreated from the emperor's bedchamber and bowed to the empress dowager and the assembled ministers. From behind the curtain, the empress dowager leaned forward to listen to the imperial physician's detailed report of Li Jianheng's condition. When she heard the bleeding had stopped, she breathed a sigh of relief.

"This matter is bizarre." The empress dowager straightened in her seat. "To think not a single person knew the Son of Heaven had left the palace. How can anyone sleep soundly if this is the state of our patrols in the heart of our capital?"

None of the old ministers uttered a word; all hung their heads in silence like clay sculptures.

"From my place in the imperial harem," the empress dowager continued, "I shouldn't be intervening in governmental affairs. But this, once again, concerns His Majesty's safety. A mother cannot help but worry—I watch this with my hair turning gray and tears running dry.[11] How can I take another scare like this? My ministers, I am owed an explanation!"

On hearing this, Pan Xiangjie's heart jumped in his chest.

After a moment of silence, Kong Qiu spoke. "The patrols in the inner palace might not necessarily have been able to stop His Majesty even if they wanted to. In this subject's opinion, Xi Hongxuan should be punished most severely! If he hadn't used those temptresses from foreign lands to lure His Majesty, then why would His Majesty have left the palace?"

"That's right." The Minister of Revenue, Wei Huaigu, was the lawful elder brother of the Wei Huaixing who had so recently targeted Xiao Chiye. Wei Huaigu was head of the Wei Clan; he wasn't usually in the habit of speaking out, but this time he lifted his head. "Xi Hongxuan deserves to be punished, but his crime does not deserve death. This subject feels that the fault lies with the Ministry of Works. Are they not the ones in charge of repairs to public works in Qudu? Minister Pan, how could you allow the public ditches to grow so clogged?"

When he saw Wei Huaigu was about to shift the blame, Pan Xiangjie fell to his knees and beseeched the empress dowager, "I ask that Your Majesties discern the truth of this matter and render fair judgment! The Ministry of Works notified the Ministry of Revenue of the blockage of the public ditches as far back as the reign of the Xiande Emperor and requested they allocate money for us to carry

---

11 *From the poem "Bidding Farewell to My Old Mother" by Huang Jingren.*

out repairs. But the Ministry of Revenue delayed the approval of these funds again and again. What could the Ministry of Works do? This is no minor repair!"

Wei Huaigu was unfazed; this man was a tougher nut to crack than his brother Wei Huaixing. "Any release of funds by the Ministry of Revenue must go through the Grand Secretariat. Without Secretariat Elder Hua's say-so, who would dare approve this spending? Besides, Qudu was cleaning up the mess that is the six prefectures of Zhongbo in those years; the treasury was nearly emptied. Of course we'd have liked to help, but we didn't have the means."

"Everyone has their difficulties," Pan Xiangjie fired back. "Why are you targeting only the Ministry of Works? The Left Censor-in-Chief, Cen Xunyi, wants to indict the Ministry of Works for negligence in irrigation works; he's saying we've failed to secure the embankment of the Kailing River. But did it collapse today? No! This is proof—the Ministry of Works has never cut corners in our projects; we work diligently! Had we the money, we would've cleared the public ditches long ago!"

Neither the Ministry of Revenue nor the Ministry of Works was willing to shoulder the blame. Wei Huaigu and Pan Xiangjie were both elders of the Eight Great Clans; neither would take a step back. They stood their ground and passed the buck back and forth.

Kong Qiu held back a sneer. He came from a humble background; Hai Liangyi himself had elevated him to his current position. He could work with these ministers from the noble clans, but he would never be of the same mind as them. Watching them kicking the blame around irked him to no end.

The Ministry of Works had reported the matter of the ditches before, this was true. But who had reported it? Some subordinate, a minor official who worked in back offices and had never set foot in court. If Pan Xiangjie had recognized the severity of the problem, he would have taken it up with the Ministry of Revenue himself. But he hadn't done so.

As for the Ministry of Revenue, they had clearly known of the issue. But what was the relationship between Wei Huaigu and Hua Siqian? These two clans were intermarried just like the rest of the Eight Great Clans. Though they hadn't seemed to be on close terms in recent years, old ties remained. Wei Huaigu was far more resourceful than Wei Huaixing; he was someone who could discuss political affairs with Hua Siqian on equal footing. But he had never brought this matter up. Everyone involved had muddled their way through—if they drowned in these political seas, then they deserved it; one could only blame their rotten luck!

Sitting behind the curtain, the empress dowager saw through every one of these men. Hua Xiangyi stood behind her, listening with rapt attention.

At last, Hai Liangyi coughed a few times. Covering his mouth with a handkerchief, he said, "There was indeed mention of this matter in the Grand Secretariat's reports. But it appeared only once, and no one followed up after that. Now that a building has collapsed, everyone remembers it, but is this the first time the water level has risen? Let's not bicker over what happened long ago—did the water level rise in the spring of last year and the year before? Did the Ministry of Works report it then?"

Pan Xiangjie turned away, voice filled with remorse. "When the Grand Secretary puts it that way...the Ministry of Works has indeed been negligent. But we really had no choice. What's important now is to dredge the ditches without delay."

"That's right, the situation is critical," Wei Huaigu said. "The Ministry of Revenue has allocated money to the disaster victims.

Appropriation of blame can wait until the public ditches have been cleared. Who's digging now—is it the Eight Great Battalions?"

It was the Minister of War, Chen Zhen, who replied. "The Imperial Army is doing it. Supreme Commander Xiao is soaking in the water as we speak."

Before the empress dowager could respond, a palace maid rushed out from the inner room and fell to her knees. "Your Majesty! His Majesty's back is covered in rashes!"

The empress dowager jolted to her feet. "What?!"

Hai Liangyi doubled over and began coughing violently. Hua Xiangyi took the empress dowager's arm to support her and promptly made a decision. "Summon the imperial physicians! And hold the secretariat elder steady, quickly!"

Xi Hongxuan, too, had broken out in a rash. A military medic of the Eight Great Battalions was first to discover it; he promptly grabbed the hem of his robe and raced out to report to Han Jin.

Han Jin wiped his face, dumbfounded. "Isn't it just a rash? Just get him warmed up and he'll be fine!"

"It's not." The medic was so anxious he stomped his foot. "How can that be just a rash? It's an infectious disease!" Han Jin froze; the surrounding men of the Eight Great Battalions, still up to their knees in the water, had all gone pale. Han Jin turned and saw the Imperial Army bustling about a short distance away. He sloshed through the flood to them and grabbed Chen Yang, yelling, "Where is the supreme commander? Call him over now—it's an emergency!"

Xiao Chiye pushed a broken plank aside and waded over. "What is it?"

Han Jin smeared his dirty, shaking hands on his clothes. "We have to stop the demolition, and we can't stand around in this water anymore! Supreme Commander, an epidemic has broken out!"

There was a cold glint in Xiao Chiye's eye. "Who caught it?"

"Xi Hongxuan." Han Jin's breathing was panicked. "Then, is—is His Majesty..."

"Gu Jin!" Xiao Chiye called out. "Run to the palace and report this matter to Secretariat Elder Hai! Immediately!"

Gu Jin climbed up the embankment and sped off. Within a few steps, he had somersaulted onto the rooftop and stepped across the ridge of the roof to leap his way to the palace gates.

"Take me to Xi Hongxuan," said Xiao Chiye steadily. "Now."

Xi Hongxuan was delirious with fever; the medicine that had just been applied to his crushed legs was already damp with sweat. He lay on the bed, incoherent.

The medic dabbed sweat from his own brow and explained, "Four hours ago, he looked as if he had caught a chill. I gave him medicine, and his fever subsided. But when I examined him just now, his fever had gotten much worse! When I changed the poultices on his legs, he was entirely covered in these rashes!"

Xiao Chiye looked at the red welts. "Are you sure it's contagious?"

"During the years of Yongyi, a pox like this broke out in the city of Dancheng," the medic explained. "It was reported to the Court of Imperial Physicians; they'll have records of it on file. Supreme Commander, once this rash spreads over the body, the patient will run a high fever. In another four hours, they'll fall unconscious and vomit continuously. I'm afraid some of the people displaced by the flood might already be sick. The Temple of Guilt must arrange for the decoction of the appropriate herbs before it spreads further!"

Now truly afraid, Han Jin asked, "What caused this? If we don't know how he got it, how can we continue draining this ditch?"

"We're arriving at the spring thaw," the medic said. "It's damp and cold, and the low-lying district has been gathering sewage and filth all year. Their houses are clustered together, so cramped most don't even have windows. Lack of sunlight will make people prone to illness."

"But if that's the case, how did Xi Hongxuan get infected?" Xiao Chiye furrowed his brow. "Ouhua Pavilion is on high ground, and servants clean the connected alleys behind it; there's no contact with any filth. Did he get infected just because he soaked in the swill water for a few hours during the collapse?"

The medic hesitated. He wiped his sweat again and mustered the courage to say, "I'll be honest with you, Supreme Commander. I suspect he didn't contract this illness after the cave-in, but from fooling around in the brothel before then. But if Second Young Master Xi is already burning up, then His Majesty—"

"Supreme Commander!" Meng Rui lifted the curtain and entered, face grave. "More than ten people have collapsed in the Temple of Guilt. Two men here from the Ministry of Revenue have also collapsed!"

Xiao Chiye was preparing to issue new commands when Chen Yang charged in next, bringing a gust of rainwater with him. "Master! Lao-Hu is down with a fever!"

The sound of the rain outside grew suddenly urgent. Like battle drums pounding on all sides, it poured down with a vengeance, determined to shatter this pitch-black night.

Xiao Chiye dashed out into the downpour. "It'll be too late if we wait for approval. Go—fetch herbs from all the apothecaries on Shenwu Street. Take anyone who's weak, anyone with a cold, fever, or vomiting, to the Temple of Guilt, and evacuate everyone who's healthy. Those on duty from the Ministry of Revenue must start decocting herbs immediately! Ding Tao!"

"Gongzi!" Ding Tao answered.

Xiao Chiye dragged Ding Tao over, chest heaving as he ordered in a hushed tone, "Tell Shen Lanzhou to get out of there now!"

POX

RAIN DRUMMED against the ground, throwing up muddy splashes.

People hurried in and out of the Temple of Guilt. Makeshift rain shelters had already been pitched, and the bitter aroma of herbal medicine choked the air. Even the men from the Embroidered Uniform Guard watching the stoves kept their noses and mouths covered with handkerchiefs.

Qi Huilian, wrapping a cloth around his head, joined Ji Gang to distribute the medicine. Seeing a feverish, unconscious man mumbling incoherently, he paused and scrutinized him.

Ji Gang was clearing away bowls in the courtyard with nimble fingers. When he saw the grand mentor stop, he asked, "What's wrong?"

"This is the Dancheng pox." Qi Huilian pulled open the patient's collar. "The rash will spread over his body. Don't get too close; it's contagious."

"Can it be treated?"

Qi Huilian's scalp itched; he scratched it a few times. "Yes, but not easily. The work on the public ditches must continue, but who knows if anyone infected spat or pissed in the water? If the men digging are infected without realizing and spread it to others, won't it be all over the city soon?"

"An awful shame." Ji Gang peered at the man beneath the rain shelter. "What should be done then?"

"What should be done..." Qi Huilian pulled up the cloth to cover more of his face as a fresh wave of people entered. He whispered, "It comes down to fate. But first, someone must reassure the public; there must not be unrest. Then, assemble all the big and small apothecaries in Qudu. Those infected must be strictly quarantined."

"We can't stay either." Ji Gang set down the bowl in his hands. "Someone else will take care of all this. I'll tell Chuan-er to leave."

"Lanzhou can't leave. *He's* the one taking care of it. Can you count on Han Cheng to step forward and handle this? Those men will be first to hide from what's coming."

"No!" Ji Gang paled. "Chuan-er's only a fifth-rank judge right now. He can't even attend court like those of the fourth rank and above. How can they let him handle it? This is a major crisis. There are plenty of people with more authority and power! Let them take over!"

"Whom are you trying to reason with?" Qi Huilian set down the bowls he held. "If Han Cheng keeps him here in the name of gaining experience, there's nothing you can do about it! Once the pox begins to spread, which high-ranking official would be willing to come here and take charge? Not even Hai Liangyi will come! Besides, Lanzhou can't go now. This is the opportunity of a lifetime. If he handles it well, it's another chance for promotion! A promo—"

Ji Gang shoved him. "What the hell are you saying?!"

Qi Huilian tumbled to the ground. He climbed back to his feet, temper flaring. "If he lets this chance pass, then what's the point of all he's done?! This is exactly the time when people trample one another to get ahead. He must seize this opportunity! Don't you understand?"

"I don't care to understand." Ji Gang flushed with rage. "I'm telling him to leave; I have to take him away!"

Ji Gang started toward the temple doors, but Qiao Tianya blocked his path. "Most of those in the Temple of Guilt are about to be evacuated. Only infected patients remain inside. Shifu shouldn't go in." He smiled. "Xiansheng's journals and notes have already been moved to the old residence. Master told me to rent a small house on Shenwu Street for the both of you. It's close to the palace gates, on high ground; there's no way it will flood."

"Step aside!" Ji Gang cried. "The infected are inside, so how can Chuan-er stay in there? I need to speak with him!"

Qiao Tianya was no longer smiling. He said solemnly, "Shifu, why put me on the spot? Master has given orders; there's no changing them. Everyone here is infected. Master will only worry if you remain. For the sake of his duty to you as a son, I'm asking you to come with me."

Listening to the sounds of coughing all around, Ji Gang grew only more anxious. He grabbed Qiao Tianya's arm and pushed it aside. Qiao Tianya had anticipated such a move; he readily accepted the attack. Half his arm had gone numb, but his legs were fast as ever as he moved to obstruct Ji Gang.

"Shifu!" said Qiao Tianya, voice low. "Calm down! For Master to make such an arrangement, he must have some countermeasure in mind. I need to return for him later. If we leave now, Master can go back earlier too, all right? There are eyes all around. Do you really think you can whisk him away? Where would you go?"

Qiao Tianya's final question was, at last, what calmed Ji Gang down. He looked into the interior of the temple for a long time, then flicked his sleeves and pointed a trembling finger at Qi Huilian. In the end, he said not another word.

Shen Zechuan sat on a bench behind the privacy of a curtain and closed his eyes to rest. His ears were ringing, and he'd begun to feel dizzy. Yet his face betrayed none of his discomfort. It was only when he heard someone calling him that he opened his eyes; the instant he did, every trace of weariness vanished from his features. It was an official from the Ministry of Revenue. "Lord Judge, the supply of herbs is insufficient. What will we do tomorrow?"

"This is a matter of grave importance; there will be no break in the supply of medicine." Shen Zechuan gathered the overcoat tighter around himself. "The man from the Court of Imperial Physicians ought to be here soon. He'll have an update on our current supplies. Tell them to continue decocting the medicine. Don't scrimp."

The official murmured his acknowledgment.

Taking in his panic-stricken expression, Shen Zechuan asked, "Which department of the Ministry of Revenue do you work for?"

"This humble subordinate is merely a clerk, a minor official in charge of the records of official documents."

"However minor one's post, we all work for the people." Shen Zechuan reached up and pinched the space between his brows, composing himself for a moment before continuing. "What's your name?"

"This humble subordinate is Liang Cuishan."

"You'll take over supervision of the distribution of herbs. Record everything in detail, no matter how small," Shen Zechuan said. "I'd hazard a guess that the Imperial Army has already gone to secure the medicine since time is so tight. We can't wait for the palace's orders; any supplies we use, starting today, must be clearly recorded." He paused. "Go and rest for now. Keep a close watch on your health and report it immediately if you feel any discomfort."

Liang Cuishan took his leave. The moment the curtain fell, Shen Zechuan put a palm to his forehead. It was scalding.

Ge Qingqing ducked inside. Shocked at the sight, he stepped forward and whispered, "Judge..."

“When did Xi Hongxuan get the rash?” Shen Zechuan asked evenly.

“Four hours after they applied the fever medicine,” Ge Qingqing answered. “It started spreading upward from his legs.”

“I got the rash first, before the fever,” said Shen Zechuan. His head was still clear. “The symptoms don’t match; mine’s probably not the pox. But as a precaution, I should drink that medicine too.”

Ge Qingqing sighed with relief. “Thank goodness you didn’t take leave this morning!”

The emperor himself was sick. Which imperial physician would dare say he caught it out fooling around in town? They would look for any other explanation. But who could possibly have infected the emperor? If not his personal eunuchs, it would have to be the guards who stood before the throne—including Shen Zechuan. Had he begged illness this morning, it would be leverage against him; if his rash was made out to be the pox, he would forever lose the right to stand before the throne. Shen Zechuan still carried the burden of Shen Wei’s crimes on his back. Once he fell, it would be nigh impossible for him to claw his way back up a second time.

Shrewd as he was, even he found it hard to breathe at this moment. Schemes and intrigues he could handle; only providence was a force that couldn’t be reckoned with. Had he been just a little less cautious, he would’ve fallen into someone else’s clutches. His life and death would now be at the mercy of any word against him.

Shen Zechuan closed his eyes.

Ge Qingqing withdrew. Shen Zechuan listened to the sound of the rain, his thoughts far away. Those murky old memories rose up with the wet pattering. He knit his brows, frustrated and bone-weary.

He didn’t like snowy days, or rain. Cold and damp reminded him of the Chashi Sinkhole, of Ji Mu, of all the days he had spent on his knees at the mercy of others. Cold and damp made him uneasy, gloomy; they turned him into nothing more than a body, empty of everything but frigid sufferance and irritability.

Wrapped in his thoughts, Shen Zechuan leaned against the wall, intending to close his eyes for a moment. But the longer he sat, the drowsier he became, until he genuinely fell asleep in that little corner.

It was deep in the night when Xiao Chiye entered the Temple of Guilt with the imperial physician who had hurried over. Behind him, Ding Tao looked miserable—he hadn't managed to find Shen Zechuan.

Xiao Chiye strode up to the Embroidered Uniform Guard decocting the medicine. "Where's the judge? I'm looking for him."

Half his face covered, the guard handed him a bowl of medicine. "It doesn't matter who you're looking for; you have to drink this first. Supreme Commander, your men in the Imperial Army still have to go down into the water. Please be careful!"

Xiao Chiye gulped down the decoction without a word.

The man rose and shouted into the rain shelter, "Qing-ge! Is Qing-ge there? Where's our judge? Supreme Commander Xiao is looking for him."

Ge Qingqing had been dozing on a bench. At this shout, he swiftly sat up and straightened his clothes before walking over. When he saw Xiao Chiye, he said, "The judge is resting inside. He hasn't slept all night. Please take a rest too, Supreme Commander. The Eight Great Battalions said they have to guard the city gates, so we'll be the ones digging the rest of that ditch tomorrow."

"Physical work naturally must be done by sturdy men," Xiao Chiye remarked as they walked. "Watch the door. Don't let anyone in."

He lifted the curtain and ducked inside. No lamp was lit. He glanced around; only when he took a few more steps into the dark did he see Shen Zechuan resting against the wall.

Xiao Chiye was covered in filth. He removed his outer robe, sat beside Shen Zechuan, and poured sewer water out of his boots. It was cold even indoors; he put his boots back on and went out to seek some embers from the temple's stove, then came back and started a fire in the copper basin.

Shen Zechuan opened his eyes. "Are you done digging out Donglong Street?"

"Yeah." Xiao Chiye stoked the fire. "Why aren't you sleeping on the bed?"

"I was just resting my eyes," Shen Zechuan said. "But once I sat down, I couldn't get up."

Xiao Chiye shifted the basin closer to the bed. "Come sleep here. I'll wake you up in a bit."

Shen Zechuan didn't have the energy to feign courtesy. He lay down, and Xiao Chiye gathered him into his arms from behind, pressing his face against Shen Zechuan's hot cheek. At first Shen Zechuan could hear Xiao Chiye whispering, but that, too, soon became hazy.

Only after Xiao Chiye heard Shen Zechuan's breathing grow even did he reach out to unfasten his collar and take a closer look at that red rash.

Not the same as Xi Hongxuan's.

Xiao Chiye refastened his clothes and drifted off with Shen Zechuan in his arms.

He was awakened by a scalding heat. Dazed, he opened his eyes a crack. Once he got a clear look at the man in his embrace, his mind cleared in an instant. Shen Zechuan seemed to be on fire, his temples damp with sweat. Xiao Chiye laid a hand on him and felt Shen Zechuan burning up all over. He swiftly sat up. "Lanzhou. *Lanzhou?*"

Shen Zechuan's clothes were soaked through. His brows were drawn tightly together, and his breath came in short pants. Roused by Xiao Chiye, he said groggily, "Qua...quarantine... You can get infected even if you aren't near the water..."

Xiao Chiye wrapped him in his overcoat and shouted, "Chen Yang, summon the imperial physician!"

Chen Yang, dozing against the wall outside, jerked awake. He leapt off the steps, made his way under the rain shelter, and dragged the imperial physician inside. The man lifted the overcoat to take a look, then said, urgent, "Supreme Commander, the judge has contracted the pox. Though it looks like he caught a cold first..."

Xiao Chiye grabbed the imperial physician's arm. Staring into his eyes, he asked in a voice cracking with frost, "The judge has *what*?"

Panicked, the imperial physician corrected himself. "H-he's... overworked and overstressed...of course that's the reason he fell ill..."

"That's right. The judge fell ill here today." Xiao Chiye tightened his grip. "He wasn't ill before this."

"Right, right, right," the imperial physician repeated.

"All the medicine in Qudu is here. I know Your Excellency has the miraculous hands of a healer." Xiao Chiye softened his tone. "You can heal him, right?"

Under the force of Xiao Chiye's gaze, the imperial physician's knees knocked together. He gripped the edge of the bed for support and nodded hastily. "I can, yes, of course I can..."

RAIN CEASED

NO ONE WAS ALLOWED in or out of the imperial palace, so the empress dowager arranged for Hai Liangyi and the other officials to rest in the Grand Secretariat's compound. Within the palace and without, the capital buzzed with anxiety.

The serving eunuchs and palace maids carried out the daily cleaning of Li Jianheng's bedchamber with extra caution, each handpicked by the empress dowager herself. Every time they exited his room, they washed their hands and changed their clothes, and they were confined to the emperor's outer chambers even during their breaks. Mu Ru kept watch at Li Jianheng's bedside, insisting on taking over his personal care. She taste-tested all his medicine and administered it herself. Even when she ate or slept, she never left Li Jianheng's bedchamber.

Li Jianheng drifted in and out of consciousness, keeping the Court of Imperial Physicians on tenterhooks. When they prescribed and decocted medicine, they were scrupulously careful—they knew their lives hung by a thread. An air of dread hung over all; each man looked as wretched as if he grieved his own parents. Meanwhile, the men of the Court of Imperial Physicians working outside the palace made arrangements for the supply of medicine in Qudu. All healthy disaster victims relocated from the low-lying district were required to take the medicine as a precaution. The Ministry of Revenue

and Embroidered Uniform Guard assisted with the distribution of aid; they set up a shack outside the Temple of Guilt, where they dispensed medicine and rice porridge each day at set times.

Han Jin had withdrawn the Eight Great Battalions from Donglong Street the night Xi Hongxuan fell ill. On pretext of patrolling the various city gates, the Eight Great Battalions threw all the responsibility of dredging the public ditches to the Imperial Army. However, half the Imperial Army had been awaiting orders on Mount Feng; now, they were trapped outside the city. Xiao Chiye didn't have that many elite soldiers with him. Fortunately, some men from the Ministry of Works remained down in the city. Together with the dozens of men from the Embroidered Uniform Guard, the group braved the rain to dig through the ditches of the four main streets.

By the fourth day, everyone was exhausted. Chen Yang, Ge Qingqing, Qiao Tianya, and Gu Jin returned from dredging and fell asleep sitting against the wall. Ding Tao and Xiao-Wu were the youngest; the older men took turns straightening their legs for the youngsters to use as pillows as they slept. Ding Tao couldn't even summon the energy to lick the ink out from his brush, so his note-taking came to a halt. It had been but a few days, yet every one of them looked as disheveled and unkempt as a streetside beggar.

Xiao Chiye scarcely slept. He led the men to dig the ditches before dawn, and there was not a moment to rest throughout the day. At night, when he returned to the Temple of Guilt, he watched over Shen Zechuan.

Before, Shen Zechuan had at least been able to remain awake and clearheaded, but now his fever wouldn't recede, and he couldn't stop vomiting. Without food in his stomach, he retched up bile. When he did manage to get down any medicine, he would bring it all back up in the middle of the night. Thus, when Xiao Chiye returned, he would take Shen Zechuan in his arms, face-to-face, and sit against the wall so Shen Zechuan could rest his head on Xiao Chiye's chest or shoulder. Each time Shen Zechuan felt nauseous, Xiao Chiye rubbed a soothing hand over his back.

In the dead of night, all was quiet. The Temple of Guilt was a deserted island beyond the reach of the everyday world. The rain had ceased, but the birds in the trees were silent as the thick blanket of night shrouded the city.

Shen Zechuan's breathing was labored. He coughed violently, his chest heaving with the effort. Xiao Chiye, dozing lightly beneath him, jerked awake. He placed a hand on Shen Zechuan's back and wearily moved his legs to gently rock the man in his arms.

"Lanzhou," Xiao Chiye coaxed him. "Where is Lanzhou?"

Shen Zechuan looked sickly and wan, moments away from vomiting. He opened his eyes a sliver and replied in a hoarse voice, "Here..."

"That's it; give it a sway, rock the illness away," Xiao Chiye said. "When you've recovered, Er-gongzi will take you horseback riding."

Shen Zechuan laid his head on Xiao Chiye's shoulder and hummed huskily in acknowledgment.

"This is actually how you hold a child." Xiao Chiye ran a palm down Shen Zechuan's back. In this close and quiet moment, he whispered, "When I had a rash as a boy, my mother held me this way. What are you going to call me when I'm holding you like this?"

Shen Zechuan nuzzled against Xiao Chiye's cheek and buried his face in his neck. After a long moment, he said in a muffled voice, "Call you Daddy."

Xiao Chiye's chest rumbled as he chuckled. "Are you touched?"

Shen Zechuan coughed. He didn't answer.

"When I tamed horses back in Libei, I ate and slept with them," Xiao Chiye said. "Once, when Snowcrest was a foal, we were stranded in heavy rain. We snuggled up just like this to stay warm. He's probably forgotten it."

Shen Zechuan listened, drowsy.

"Don't you forget," said Xiao Chiye said. "If you're touched, you have to remember and repay me in the future."

Shen Zechuan's lips parted, but he made no sound. Xiao Chiye extended a finger to brush damp hair from his forehead and lowered his eyes to look at Shen Zechuan's pale profile.

"Oh, Lanzhou."

He murmured to him in hushed tones; wrapped in these soft sounds, Shen Zechuan drifted off. He lay immersed in the agony of his illness, wallowing in torment. But from the bitter depth of his misery, he tasted sweetness.

Xiao Chiye was like the blazing sun, like the wind over the grasslands. He stood out from the masses. Under the gloomy pall of rain and snow, Shen Zechuan had slipped that handkerchief into his sleeve; it was like hiding a rousing and passionate dream. In his dream, he felt the wild galloping of horses over a thousand li of grasslands, and the spreading of wings that soared across ten thousand li of clear skies. They blurred and morphed into an indescribable sight—a vision he would be hard-pressed to recount in detail.

This man was a kind of temptation unto himself. Every *Oh, Lanzhou* was laced with an affection as deep as the sea. His casual frivolity and quiet steadfastness blended into a perfect contradiction. The words he whispered to Shen Zechuan were outrageous, yet the arms in which he cradled him were dependable beyond compare.

Shen Zechuan was powerless to resist. Those deep yet careless kisses had deceived him into dropping his guard, had turned him into a villain on intimate terms with Xiao Chiye. Now, made helpless by illness, he had grown muddleheaded enough to rely on him.

His vomiting subsided a short while later. Xiao Chiye fed him medicine, spoon by spoon. Each time Shen Zechuan showed signs of drifting off again, Xiao Chiye would murmur, "Where is Lanzhou?" The words seemed to have an inexplicable power: time and time again, Shen Zechuan came back.

At first, Xiao Chiye had slept himself as he held Shen Zechuan at night. But after several people in the Temple of Guilt died one after another in the days that followed the flood, he no longer dared sleep as he listened to Shen Zechuan gasp for breath.

On the ninth day, two more people died under the rain shelter. The Imperial Army and Embroidered Uniform Guard couldn't leave the bodies lying around, but neither could they bury them here. Xiao Chiye left it to Ge Qingqing to make arrangements.

When Ge Qingqing led the men to carry out the corpses, Qiao Tianya was squatting by the stove, fanning the fire. As he watched the medicine brewing, he turned something over in his mind.

Xiao-Wu approached them. "The supreme commander is waiting for the medicine—is it ready?"

"The public ditches have been cleared; there's no hurry today. Tell the supreme commander to wait." Qiao Tianya added some firewood and shifted the handkerchief covering his mouth and nose aside to say, "Keep an eye on the supreme commander. He's with my master every day. If he comes down with the pox too, we don't have extra medicine for him."

"There was a plague in Luoxia Pass during the reign of Yongyi. Apparently, His Lordship the prince led his men to handle it then, and he never caught it." Xiao-Wu squatted down to wait. "I heard the gege from Libei saying the Xiao Clan has a heaven-sent gift. Their physique is stronger than any common man."

"Tantai Hu is pretty sturdy too. Didn't he still fall ill just the same? It never hurts to be careful. Have you drunk this morning's medicine?"

"Yeah, I did," Xiao-Wu answered honestly.

Qiao Tianya shifted on his slightly numb legs. "How's Tantai Hu today?"

"He's been able to keep some food down since yesterday," Xiao-Wu reported. "Chen-ge said it's because he's strong, and we caught it in time. He's got enough medicine, and there's an imperial physician checking up on him too. He'll be fine!"

"Until he recovers completely, we can't be too careful." Qiao Tianya seemed preoccupied as he tossed the fan to Xiao-Wu. "Watch the fire for me. I need to talk to them."

He rose and headed toward the rain shelter. Qiao Tianya ducked under the curtain; it was dim inside, but not damp. The bedding, crucially, could stay dry, and an attendant from the Court of Imperial Physicians washed and changed the sheets daily. Xiao Chiye was already speaking to Tantai Hu, so Qiao Tianya waited.

Finally, Xiao Chiye turned. "What is it?"

Qiao Tianya lifted the hem of his robe and took a seat on a bench at the side. "I have something urgent to discuss with you."

Xiao Chiye caressed his thumb ring as he looked at Qiao Tianya with calm eyes, waiting for him to speak.

"The Court of Imperial Physicians and the Embroidered Uniform Guard have records of this disease on file. Have you seen them?" Qiao Tianya asked.

Xiao Chiye nodded.

"So you know the cause of the outbreak in the city of Dancheng. Xiao—Supreme Commander," Qiao Tianya corrected himself.

"Before my master fell ill, he checked the Embroidered Uniform Guard's archives and specifically told me to make note of certain points. I've been thinking about this pox for a few days now, but since he's still sick, I can only discuss this with you."

"What did Lanzhou say?"

"He said there's something queer about this disease." Qiao Tianya propped his elbows on his knees and whistled to summon Ding Tao. "Recite the details of the Dancheng pox to the supreme commander. You have an eidetic memory; you remember, right?"

Ding Tao thought a moment. "There was an outbreak in Dancheng in the summer during the reign of Yongyi. The Court of Imperial Physicians sent a delegate with the Embroidered Uniform Guard to learn what they could, and they discovered something strange about this disease. After tracing the course of the pox through the city, they found a burial mound behind the site of the first outbreak. It was ill-kept, with no one assigned to maintain it. The corpses buried there before the start of spring were sodden and rotting."

He paused. "There was a food stall in service nearby. The weather was hot that summer, and flies were everywhere. The stallkeeper was first to fall ill. No one paid it any mind; he himself suspected it to be a cold. He took some medicine and carried on with his business at the stall. And then—oh my. A score of people fell ill after buying his food. That was when the prefectural yamen of Dancheng realized something was wrong."

"A burial mound, huh?" The imperial physician was packing his case. "All kinds of people are thrown there. Perhaps one of them had some disease or was bitten by a wild animal. If the corpse was exposed and rotting, it would have been a feast for the flies. Anyone who gets too close would be at risk of infection." He fastened his case and said, "It wasn't easy for anyone back then. Dancheng was sealed off for half a year, and a great number of people died. We're lucky we caught it this time before it could spread, and we have experience with the disease now. Otherwise we couldn't have acted so quickly."

"That's true, but how did this outbreak happen in Qudu?" Qiao Tianya mused. "The low ground along Donglong Street was indeed submerged in sewage. Someone was bound to fall ill eventually. But there were no homicide cases on Donglong Street and no unburied corpses. I'll be honest. Supreme Commander, no offense, but venereal disease is the kind of infection one expects to find on Donglong Street. How did we end up with the Dancheng pox instead?"

The imperial physician tactfully found an excuse to head out.

"No one ever determined how the Dancheng pox spreads." Chen Yang thought for a moment, then continued, "The collapse happened in heavy rain, and everyone was stuck in the water, so perhaps..."

"There are plenty of infectious diseases," Qiao Tianya said. "For example, that outbreak of rat plague in Luoxia Pass—there's no way Hezhou would have an outbreak of the same plague. Different regions have different climates and conditions; what applies to one won't apply to all. This humble servant is a paranoid man; an honest person oughtn't make unfounded insinuations. Even so, I suspect this disease didn't start on Donglong Street at all, but—"

Qiao Tianya jerked his thumb toward the roof.

A silence fell over the rain shelter. Everyone had turned a little pale.

"Isn't it a coincidence?" Qiao Tianya chuckled. "The celestial being met with misfortune upon descent to the mortal world. It's virtually impossible to guard against something so unexpected—like dodging a pit only to fall into a well. The palace hasn't sent any word the past few days. Supreme Commander, the public ditch has been cleared and the water level has fallen. So why do I feel this matter is just beginning?"

"Those who live in the heavenly palace are immortals," Xiao Chiye said slowly. "And immortals value their lives. They wouldn't dare play with them this way. The possibility you speak of—only someone at the end of his rope, who had staked everything on one throw, would dare it."

"I don't know about that," Qiao Tianya said. "The Directorate of Ceremonial Affairs currently lacks a leader who can take charge and control the eunuchs of the Twenty-Four Yamen. Much of the inner palace is in a state of unsupervised chaos. If someone wanted to bring in some—let's say, *contamination*—he could easily bluff his way through any closed doors. The Embroidered Uniform Guard and Imperial Army guard the outside of the palace. There's nothing we can do about the inside. I feel we should take precautions."

Why did Li Jianheng leave the palace? Was it really just to have fun? He had survived an assassination attempt mere weeks ago. He wasn't a courageous man; how would he dare sneak out on the sly? He wouldn't—unless someone put him up to it.

Xi Hongxuan discussed all his pending plans with Shen Zechuan these days; he must have never expected to meet with misadventure on this outing. And now he was lying in his sickbed with his life hanging by a thread. So who convinced Li Jianheng to leave the safety of the palace and ensured Ouhua Pavilion collapsed at exactly the right moment?

Xiao Chiye contemplated the question in silence.

Intuition told him it wasn't the empress dowager. Li Jianheng had just begun showing signs of filial respect toward her; this was precisely the moment for her to stage a comeback. She couldn't bear to let Li Jianheng die.

Who else is there?

This time, the intent wasn't to intimidate Li Jianheng but to remove him from the board. But who would benefit from Li Jianheng's death?

The curtain lifted once more; the imperial physician poked his head in and said joyfully, "Supreme Commander, the lord judge is awake!"

Xiao Chiye jumped to his feet, left the shelter behind, and strode into the temple room. Shen Zechuan, who had drifted in and out of consciousness for days, sat with his eyes half-lidded. Xiao Chiye crouched quietly at the side of the bed and gazed at him.

Lifting a finger, Shen Zechuan weakly caressed Xiao Chiye's brows and eyes. Xiao Chiye grabbed his hand and pressed it to his cheek.

"Go ahead and touch." Xiao Chiye leaned closer and laughed roughly. "I'll let you touch."

SHARING A PILLOW

SHEN ZECHUAN was still slightly dazed; Xiao Chiye's stubble tickled his palm as he stroked his face. He gazed at Xiao Chiye. "...Prickly."

The two of them were several inches apart, yet it seemed as if there was no air between them at all. Xiao Chiye was dirty and unkempt; there had been no time to tidy up these last few days. Now, he leaned into Shen Zechuan, oblivious to his slovenly state as he let Shen Zechuan caress his cheek.

Chen Yang gripped the door curtain outside, reckoning it was time to start on the many important matters at hand; however, Xiao Chiye had yet to give his permission to let the others enter. He remained stuck at the entrance with a group of guards, all staring at the sky or the ground with carefully blank expressions.

"Is it not comfortable to touch?" Xiao Chiye asked.

"It's comfortable," Shen Zechuan replied.

"Have you gotten your fill?" Xiao Chiye couldn't help but laugh.

"Almost." Shen Zechuan pursed his lips and whispered into Xiao Chiye's ear, "So prickly, it's hurting me."

"Where does it hurt?" Xiao Chiye tilted his head and pressed their foreheads together.

Shen Zechuan gazed at him with eyes like mountain lakes misted with fog, twin pools of yearning he revealed only to Xiao Chiye.

Xiao Chiye gazed back, watching the corners of Shen Zechuan's eyes curve with the barest hint of emotion.

He suddenly covered Shen Zechuan's eyes. After a moment's pause, he said, "Now's not the time to tempt me, is it?"

"What bad thoughts were you thinking?" asked Shen Zechuan. "I'm just looking at you."

"Not letting you," Xiao Chiye said. "Do it when we get back."

Outside, Chen Yang coughed a few times and raised his voice. "Master."

Xiao Chiye lifted his palm from Shen Zechuan's eyes and stood up. "Come in."

Only then did Chen Yang raise the curtain; everyone filed inside.

Shen Zechuan leaned against a pillow, overcoat draped around his shoulders. As he drank his medicine, he listened to the account of what had transpired in recent days. When Qiao Tianya had spoken, Shen Zechuan considered for a moment. "You're right. There's something fishy about this, start to finish. I too suspect the collapse of Ouhua Pavilion was no coincidence, but deliberate sabotage using the public ditches as cover."

"It's only been half a year since His Majesty's ascension. So many matters are waiting to be settled; this is the time for those around him to make their mark." Xiao Chiye sat on the bench beside the bed. "Who would want him dead?"

This was also the thing Shen Zechuan couldn't figure out. He drained his medicine and handed the empty bowl to Qiao Tianya. "It's difficult for us to investigate within the palace. We need a suitable person on the inside."

Leaving the position of the Director of Writ at the Directorate of Ceremonial Affairs vacant so long was no good thing. But neither

Xiao Chiye nor Shen Zechuan could interfere in this; the palace was the empress dowager's territory. Her Majesty had final say over who would be appointed to the post. Anything was better than nothing—if they could plant an agent within the palace, it would be better than being completely blind.

"You wanted to investigate Xiangyun before," Shen Zechuan suddenly said. "Did you discover anything?"

"I was so busy I forgot," said Xiao Chiye. "Gu Jin."

Gu Jin stepped up. "I went to Xiangyun Villa, but I didn't find much of note. Xiangyun herself keeps only a handful of patrons. I investigated them one by one, but couldn't connect any of them with the perjury from the assassination case."

Shen Zechuan had the nagging feeling he'd missed something. In each of these incidents, an unseen hand had pulled the strings behind the scenes. There must be some tangible link between them. He lost himself in thought. Perhaps his mind was still fogged after his recovery—he couldn't fit the pieces together no matter how he tried.

"His Majesty remains unconscious, and his illness has yet to subside. We have a few days to spare; there's no need to rush." As Xiao Chiye spoke, he stretched his shoulders and arms. "The public ditches are dredged, so everyone should rest while they can. We'll get to the bottom of this one way or another. Right now, it's more important than ever to conserve our strength for what's to come."

The guards chorused their agreement and retreated. When they had left the room, Xiao Chiye sat at the edge of the bed and took off his boots.

"You've had your fill of sleep, but Er-gongzi is barely hanging on." Xiao Chiye stretched out beside Shen Zechuan. "Come closer. Be my blanket and cover me."

Shen Zechuan turned his head to look at him. "Use the overcoat."

Xiao Chiye closed his eyes. "You do it."

Shen Zechuan tucked the pillow under Xiao Chiye's head. Xiao Chiye made a blind grab for Shen Zechuan and gripped his wrist, pulling him into an embrace.

"Too thin." Xiao Chiye ran a hand over his ribs. "Your bones jab me when I hug you. Once autumn arrives, wild game from Libei will be here too. You'll get proper nourishment then; we'll have you fattened up by winter."

Xiao Chiye's breathing was heavy with drowsiness. He turned his head and pressed the tip of his nose to Shen Zechuan's temple, then forced a smile and said, "Sleep with your Er-gongzi a while."

He really was exhausted. He'd hardly closed his eyes these last few days, driven to stay awake day and night like a lone wolf pacing his den. No matter how strong he was, he'd reached a point where his strength and energy were spent. Now that Shen Zechuan was on top of him, Xiao Chiye found this weight perfect; he lay warm and content under the pressure of his body.

He had thought to sleep just a few hours, then wake up by nightfall and do a proper tally of the medicinal expenses incurred over the last few days. Who knew he would sleep until nearly dawn the next day? Head foggy, he rolled onto his side and buried himself in Shen Zechuan's arms.

Xiao Chiye floated in his daze a moment more before his mind cleared and he propped himself up. His head had slipped off the pillow at some point, and it seemed he had lain on Shen Zechuan's arm for the latter half of the night. Shen Zechuan was curled on his side with his head on the pillow, while his other hand had pulled the overcoat over Xiao Chiye like a protective embrace.

Dawn had yet to come. It was dark inside the room.

Xiao Chiye fell back onto the pillow and tugged Shen Zechuan closer, face-to-face. The overcoat just about covered both of them.

"Did your arm go numb?" he asked, voice scratchy from sleep.

Shen Zechuan, half-awake, hummed an affirmative "Mm-hmm."

Xiao Chiye rubbed Shen Zechuan's stiff arm. "You could've woken me."

"Xiao Er..."

"Hm?"

Shen Zechuan opened his eyes to look at him. "You were calling for Shen Lanzhou in your sleep."

Xiao Chiye smiled and murmured, "Just dreaming about what I think of in the daytime."

They were pressed tight together under the coat. Shen Zechuan's gaze stoked the fire in Xiao Chiye's heart; after finally getting some sleep, he was bursting with energy. He itched to tease Shen Zechuan, yet he couldn't quite bear to disturb his rest.

A nameless bird trilled outside, echoing through the silence before dawn.

"You asked about Xiangyun earlier; did you think of something?" Xiao Chiye said.

"Where is Mu Ru from? Was she the girl the emperor bought before?"

"She was a birthday gift presented to His Majesty from the villas in the countryside." Xiao Chiye wrapped his arms more firmly around Shen Zechuan. "She was kept in his villas outside the city at first. It took a lot of effort just to train her. I've seen her registered birthplace; she's a native of the city of Jincheng. You think she's the one?"

"After the assassination attempt, His Majesty came to detest eunuchs—besides Shuanglu, he never got close with another. The palace maids who wait on him are all carefully selected. The only one who could encourage him to sneak out of the palace is Mu Ru." Shen Zechuan sank into thought again. "If it's her, there must be a reason. She's borne no imperial heir; she survives only at the whim of His Majesty. If anything, she should be the one most concerned about His Majesty's safety."

"That's the thing," Xiao Chiye said. "Whoever pulled off a scheme like this must have thought it through carefully. There has to be a larger goal. The Xiande Emperor's sudden death and the Hua Clan's fall from power didn't just remove a few officials. It shifted the entire political climate of Great Zhou. In the past six months, Hai Liangyi has been locked in a stalemate with the noble clans and still hasn't truly stabilized the government. It would benefit no one for the current emperor to meet with misfortune now."

"When His Majesty wakes up, we may know more," said Shen Zechuan. "The Ministry of Works is on the hook this time. Pan Xiangjie will be hard-pressed to absolve himself of blame; he's certain to be censured and investigated. Have you seen the clerk from the Ministry of Revenue, Liang Cuishan?"

"Yup, I've seen him." Xiao Chiye thought for a moment. "He's diligent."

"I asked him to keep a detailed record of all the medicinal herbs coming and going since day one. Once we're done here, the Ministry of Revenue and the Chief Surveillance Bureau will come to check the ledgers. You only have to hand over his notes."

"Oh, well done." Xiao Chiye was unstinting with his praise. "When the epidemic broke out, there was no time to wait for orders from the palace; I had my men collect whatever we needed from the apothecaries. The Imperial Army has our own handwritten notes, but it's not as convincing as the testimony of one of the Ministry of

Revenue's own. If it's all in black and white, the Imperial Army and the Ministry of Revenue won't have to rip into each other over it."

Xiao Chiye hated dealing with the Ministry of Revenue. Reconciling the accounts with them every year was a hassle of the highest order. After this major incident with the public ditches, this ministry was sure to come under scrutiny; he wouldn't put it past those old foxes to drag the whole Imperial Army into the mire with them just to put the Grand Secretariat in a fix. After all, the law couldn't be enforced if everyone was an offender. Even without the current crisis, political affairs were always most complicated at the beginning of spring, when official documents piled into mountains and gave the Grand Secretariat a massive headache.

Shen Zechuan laughed. "You have no wish to see the Ministry of Revenue, but they're also afraid to see you. The incident with the Quancheng silk last time implicated Wang Xian. I saw he's already been transferred to the Ministry of Rites. Was that your handiwork?"

"I have no personal grudge against him. Collecting debts back then was simply official business. But because of me, he was slapped with a reputation for bribery. Shifting him over to the Ministry of Rites is merely a stopgap measure," Xiao Chiye said. "There's no way he'll come out ahead in the review this year. Even if he's appointed to a post outside the capital, it'll be somewhere remote and barren."

Wang Xian had been unlucky. During the time he served as Secretary of the Ministry of Revenue, Xiao Chiye had repeatedly given him a hard time. A few years ago, when the Imperial Army's equipment was in need of repairs, Xiao Chiye had personally hounded him for money each time the Imperial Army provided manual labor, yet he had no actual relationship with Xiao Chiye at all. Who would've expected a calamity to come flying out of the blue for Wang Xian? Xiao Chiye was denounced before the emperor, and by sheer coincidence, that Quancheng silk had passed through Wang Xian's hands; he had no way to explain himself. In the end, while Xiao Chiye and Li Jianheng maintained their brotherly bonds and sang the harmonious tune of ruler and subject, Wang Xian was stripped of his position as secretary and nearly imprisoned. He had no future as an official in Qudu; even if he were to be assigned somewhere outside the capital, his prospects were poor. He was sure to be given an assessment of *Negligence of Duty* for the annual review. Half a lifetime of prudence and caution—wasted. It was a grave injustice.

Something clicked for Shen Zechuan. "Don't tell me you're thinking of getting him assigned to Zhongbo?"

Xiao Chiye laughed. "To think you could guess even this."

He'd already extended Wang Xian a helping hand in having him moved to the Ministry of Rites. At the very least, Xiao Chiye had secured the man his livelihood. However much Wang Xian had disliked him in the past, he owed him a debt of gratitude now. Xiao Chiye indeed planned to transfer Wang Xian to Zhongbo if he was assigned outside the capital. At present, Zhongbo was full of rogues and bandits. Everyone wanted to send their own people to get a foothold there.

"The rest of the prefectures are out of our reach, but we must put someone in Cizhou." Xiao Chiye relaxed in Shen Zechuan's arms. "That was a good suggestion you gave regarding the demolition subsidy. Cizhou's prefectural prefect, Zhou Gui, will be on good terms with us now. If we can get Wang Xian under his command, he'll understand the implication. The Grand Secretariat is looking for people to handle supervision of the six prefectures of Zhongbo this year. But no matter whom the imperial court deploys, I need eyes in Cizhou."

Cizhou was close to the Northeast Provisions Trail. By installing his own people there, Xiao Chiye could keep tabs on the grain supply route for the Libei Armored Cavalry even from Qudu. He and Xiao Jiming exchanged hardly any correspondence, yet the two brothers understood each other perfectly.

"The Quancheng silk was a trap. If Fu Linye hadn't been so eager for quick returns and backed himself into a corner, this account would've become a blade buried deep in the Imperial Army's accounts." Shen Zechuan tilted his head and asked, "Was this transaction handled by Xue Xiuzhuo?"

"It was," said Xiao Chiye. "Xue Xiuzhuo, huh. What do you think of him?"

"I didn't pay him much mind at first. But I looked into his evaluations for the past few years—they were all outstanding. He joined the imperial court during the reign of Yongyi, in the last three years of the Guangcheng Emperor. It was only when the Xiande Emperor ascended that he assumed the post of Chief Supervising Secretary of the Office of Scrutiny for Revenue. He held this position for eight years until the attempted coup at the Nanlin Hunting Grounds last year. Then he was promoted to the Court of Judicial Review, where he became the Assistant Minister and went on to handle two major cases that concerned His Majesty's safety—the Hua and Pan treason case, and the Court Officials' Feast assassination case. He has a sterling reputation, extensive contacts in the Eight Great Clans, and good relationships with the officials from common backgrounds headed by Hai Liangyi." Shen Zechuan pondered all that for a moment. "But I know nothing of his background before he entered the imperial court."

"I know all about it," Xiao Chiye said. "Ask me."

Shen Zechuan raised his brows slightly. "Tell me."

"That doesn't sound like someone who wants a favor." Xiao Chiye gathered the overcoat around them and pressed his forehead to Shen Zechuan's. "Try coaxing me a little and I'll see what I can do."

His tone was coy, only meant to tease. He didn't expect Shen Zechuan to look into his eyes, part his lips, and murmur a soft, "Ah, Ce'an..."

That tiny puff of warm breath landed on Xiao Chiye's cheeks and slid over the straight ridge of his nose to his lips, where, almost imperceptibly, the two of them touched.

Xiao Chiye suddenly rolled over and propped himself on his elbows above Shen Zechuan, leaving a narrow space between them. He took hold of Shen Zechuan's chin to raise his face closer and said, "All talk and no action—Er-gongzi won't fall for it."

TORRENT OF PASSION

THE PINCH MADE Shen Zechuan squint a little, though it was hard to tell if it was from discomfort or pleasure. "What *will* you fall for?" he asked. The look on his face was alluring, fanning the flames higher.

Xiao Chiye stroked his thumb over the corner of Shen Zechuan's lips. "Why don't you feel for yourself."

"I'm afraid some men say one thing and mean another." As Shen Zechuan spoke, the tip of his tongue appeared like a shadow—a moment of moist warmth on Xiao Chiye's thumb, yet just out of reach.

"Who're you calling a hypocrite?" Xiao Chiye leaned closer and pressed down on him. "Er-gongzi is an honest man."

"One part of him at least." Shen Zechuan sighed. "You're so hard."

"I'm well rested." Xiao Chiye was feeling him up now. "I've abstained for so long. Give me a little reward?"

Shen Zechuan pressed a gentle kiss to his lips. "I just recovered; let's save it for another time. I really...don't have the energy."

"Who could bear to let you exert yourself in bed in your fragile state?" Xiao Chiye asked. "Could I?"

"You could." Shen Zechuan gazed at him and said softly, "Every word you say now is only to cajole and trick me. Once we get into bed, it all counts for nothing."

Xiao Chiye chuckled. "Is that so? And what did I say when I cajoled you?"

Shen Zechuan lifted a finger to block Xiao Chiye's lips as he moved to kiss him. "If you want to hear it, first tell me about Xue Xiuzhuo."

Xiao Chiye tightened his arms around him. "What do you want to hear? His background is nothing impressive. Xue Xiuzhuo is a son of common birth, born to a concubine in the Xue Clan. He was not a favored child in his early years. Look at his age—he's a few years older than Xi Hongxuan and Yao Wenyu. In the normal course of things, he shouldn't have attended school at the same time as them, so how did they become fellow students? It's because he was neglected at home, and the carelessness of his family delayed the start of his education."

"He has a refined air," observed Shen Zechuan, "and a certain deftness in the way he conducts himself. Compared to Xi Hongxuan, he seems more like a son of lawful birth from the noble clans."

"He was already eleven when he enrolled in the academy," Xiao Chiye continued. "He's talented and intelligent, and he's willing to work hard, so it didn't take him long to stand out from the middling noble clan descendants. But his time in the sun didn't last. A few years later, Yao Wenyu enrolled in the academy."

Xiao Chiye went on, "Everyone wants to associate with 'Unpolished Jade Yuanzhuo' and show they're also genuine talents. But at the time, their teacher was Chang Zong, who was renowned for being harsh and exacting. Once Yao Wenyu joined them, criticism and punishments increased for the others—no one could outshine Yao Wenyu when it came to strategy and literary essays. The moment his writings surfaced, no one else's work could catch Chang Zong's eye. Xue Xiuzhuo's luster was stolen in just a few years. After that, he never displayed his talents again.

"Later on, Yao Wenyu became Hai Liangyi's student. You know what Hai Liangyi's like, so you can guess how talented Yao Wenyu must be for Hai Liangyi to accept him. But what most people don't know is that the one who sent a visitation card to Hai Liangyi first wasn't Yao Wenyu, but Xue Xiuzhuo. He kowtowed thrice to Hai Liangyi, but in the end, Hai Liangyi didn't accept him. Had it happened to anyone else, even if they didn't fall out with Hai Liangyi, they would still resent him. But that's what's so impressive about Xue Xiuzhuo. He was there the day Yao Wenyu underwent the rites to formally become Hai Liangyi's student. He even held his hair crown. Hai Liangyi disliked him, yet Xue Xiuzhuo never once uttered an aggrieved word. The secretariat elder's residence was bestowed by the Guangcheng Emperor. He's particular about his peace and quiet; he doesn't receive officials as private guests, and he doesn't keep excessive attendants to run errands. One year, his pavilion collapsed. When Xue Xiuzhuo heard, he didn't even take his meal—instead, he went to replace the stones for Hai Liangyi personally."

"He certainly holds Secretariat Elder Hai in high esteem," Shen Zechuan said. "Now that you mention it, when I looked up his past evaluations, I also saw his essays on contemporary politics from his early years in public service. They were all discourses on increasing income and reducing expenditure, as well as straightening out the local farm and field registers—the very issues Hai Liangyi confronted when he first entered the Grand Secretariat."

"He really is more like Hai Liangyi's student than Yao Wenyu is," Xiao Chiye agreed. "Hai Liangyi served in the Ministry of Revenue for over ten years; he's only too aware of all the dirty tricks used in provincial account books. To get to the bottom of the mess back then, he assigned Xue Xiuzhuo, who took on the post of the Ministry of Revenue's Chief Supervising Secretary with the specific purpose of inspecting and auditing the various accounts." Xiao Chiye lay back down on the bed with Shen Zechuan in his arms. "His current social connections were all established back then. He remained Chief Supervising Secretary for eight years, and his reviews were all outstanding. He should have been promoted long ago, but he never was. Why? I think Hai Liangyi intentionally held him back."

"Perhaps Secretariat Elder Hai was moved by his sincerity. To think he was willing to spend the time to polish Xue Xiuzhuo. Even if they aren't teacher and pupil in name, the relationship between them surpasses that." Shen Zechuan furrowed his brow. "As the Chief Supervising Secretary of the Office of Scrutiny for Revenue, he could travel outside the capital. He had subordinates handling the accounts under his supervision, and also held the special privilege of directly petitioning the emperor. He could befriend anyone he wanted."

"Exactly. The Provincial Administration Commissioner of Juexi is Jiang Qingshan. He's not a man to be underestimated. When Xue Xiuzhuo blew the whistle on Hua Siqian, Jiang Qingshan was the man he investigated the problematic accounts with. Jiang Qingshan's achievements are remarkable. Back when Qudu failed to provide relief funds to Juexi, he bore the costs and kept the thirteen cities from succumbing to starvation. He's bold and decisive, with the courage to act first and report later—a man with an iron will. But he has a bad temper and doesn't often socialize with officials from the capital. Even when the Hua and Pan factions were at the height of their power, he never paid Pan Rugui ice respect. He's dauntless, and he has the capability to go with it. That's why even though Hua Siqian loathed him, he never could get him demoted. But a man like that, who wouldn't even give Yao Wenyu the time of day, is still on familiar enough terms with Xue Xiuzhuo to address him as a brother. You can imagine how good Xue Xiuzhuo is at making friends."

Xiao Chiye paused. "It's entirely because of Xue Xiuzhuo's own merit that Secretariat Elder Hai has promoted him now. Last time, you spoke of luring the noble clans into a trap. I think you've hit the nail on the head. Xue Xiuzhuo may very well make it into the Grand Secretariat."

"I had noticed he's very contradictory," Shen Zechuan said. "His essays on contemporary politics in his early years were all about the commoners' welfare and livelihood. He went to the regions outside Qudu and enacted practical change. Yet today he's inseparable from members of the noble clans' younger generation like Xi Hongxuan. The Quancheng silk is a critical point. I think he's shrewd; he's not acting at random but planning far ahead."

"Didn't you suspect there was a man at the helm hiding in Qudu?" Xiao Chiye's brows drew slightly together. "He's a good candidate."

"His official rank was low six years ago when Zhongbo fell; he was very young. How could he have manipulated those old foxes from the noble clans? Just one Wei Clan would be a pain to deal with. If such a person really exists, I'd guess he'd be around the same age as Hai Liangyi. Otherwise, with such modest credentials, it would be hard to convince any others."

"Still, there's too much we don't know. We'll need to tread carefully around him in the future." Xiao Chiye rubbed Shen Zechuan's wrist. "The collapse of Ouhua Pavilion is not without its silver lining. Xi Hongxuan is frightened out of his wits. Even if he wants to drink with you in the future, he has nowhere to go."

"Wine can be drunk anywhere. His Ouhua Pavilion has collapsed, but he has other establishments. It's Xiangyun who's really gone for good." Shen Zechuan looked at him sidelong. "Er-gongzi has suffered a loss."

"If Xiangyun's gone, I can always find someone else." Xiao Chiye looked back at him. "There are beauties aplenty; isn't there one right here?"

Shen Zechuan's fingertips made slow circles on Xiao Chiye's palm. "If you don't have five hundred taels, I won't drink with you."

"I'm dirt-poor." Xiao Chiye caught his teasing fingertips. "I have no money, so I'll have to give you something else."

"What rare item could possibly move my heart?"

Xiao Chiye guided Shen Zechuan's hand down to his waist. "Er-gongzi is a fine specimen of a man. So, what do you think?"

"I, Shen Lanzhou, am also quite dashing," Shen Zechuan said lightly. "I can admire myself in the mirror; I don't need another person."

"You don't know how to have fun," said Xiao Chiye. "How can admiring yourself compare to being admired by me? We both have to be reflected in the mirror to create a captivating sight."

Eyes shining with desire, Shen Zechuan asked, "What would you consider a captivating sight?"

"Seeing is believing." Xiao Chiye tested Shen Zechuan's temperature with his wandering hand. "Try it with me one of these days, and you'll find out."

Shen Zechuan gasped softly under his caresses. It had been a long time since either of them had been satisfied, and they'd just survived an epidemic. All the energy they had recovered with rest pooled in their bellies, weighing them down. And now, their sensuous touches had ignited both their bodies.

"Shen Zechuan, a man with a pure heart and few desires." Xiao Chiye sighed with deep feeling. "Which is it?"

"That's Shen Zechuan; you were calling for Shen Lanzhou." Shen Zechuan asked, "Whom do you want?"

"I want them both." Xiao Chiye scooped Shen Zechuan up, turned him on his side, and pressed against him from behind. "Are you giving them to me?"

Face half-buried in the bedding, Shen Zechuan panted wordlessly. Xiao Chiye leaned down to his ear and bit him. Shen Zechuan's ears were sensitive; his breath hitched under Xiao Chiye's licks and bites, and the corners of his eyes blushed scarlet.

"Chen Yang boiled some water. You can wash up before dawn." Xiao Chiye lowered his head and whined, "Lanzhou."

The bed was a makeshift cot meant for emergencies. It was small and narrow, and squeezing onto it was a strain on both of them. Xiao Chiye didn't dare be too rough. He took his time, entering slowly. The Embroidered Uniform Guard outside all had keen hearing; Shen Zechuan didn't make a sound. His fingers clenched the overcoat amid those deep thrusts and shallow withdrawals, overcome with the sensation of melting in Xiao Chiye's embrace.

Their breaths came ragged—both were afraid the other would cry out, so they kissed, neck against neck. The bed swayed. Xiao Chiye burned hot with repressed desire, but he couldn't rock too hard into Shen Zechuan. He ground against him with increasing urgency. Between kisses, he whispered, "Cry out for me again."

Shen Lanzhou managed, "Ce... *Mhn*..."

Xiao Chiye laughed. He quickened his pace and said, "What does 'Ce, mhn,' mean?"

Shen Zechuan was at the limit of what he could bear; he didn't dare reply. Xiao Chiye pressed his fingers into Shen Zechuan's mouth as he tightened his arms around him from behind, driving deep until Shen Zechuan almost moaned out loud.

Outside, dawn was breaking. Shen Zechuan had just woken, and this wasn't the time or place; Xiao Chiye stopped after one round. Even after they rushed to the conclusion, Shen Zechuan remained flushed for a long while. Though their lovemaking had left them both drenched in sweat, he lifted not a finger to clean up.

Liang Cuishan looked at the sky and saw it was near dawn. He sorted his ledgers from the past days in preparation for making his report to Shen Zechuan.

When he stepped into the courtyard, he saw Ge Qingqing drinking tea under the rain shelter. He greeted him and asked, "Is His Excellency feeling better today? This humble subordinate has tidied up the records; I've come to report the details."

Ge Qingqing didn't speak. Chen Yang happened to approach at that moment; it was he who replied, "His Excellency has just recovered, and the epidemic has only just passed us by. He's still concerned about infecting others, so he won't be receiving guests today. If you'd like, I can pass these to him on Your Excellency's behalf later."

Shen Zechuan had given Liang Cuishan direct orders to accurately record the herbs supplied and used at the Temple of Guilt. He didn't dare to be sloppy in any particular, so naturally, he couldn't hand the accounts over to Chen Yang or anyone else. "I'm glad His Excellency is on the mend. If it's not convenient today, this humble subordinate will request an audience again tomorrow."

Chen Yang nodded, and Liang Cuishan took his leave. As he went, he noticed the area around the room had been cleared of people, and there were personal guards standing watch. The Embroidered Uniform Guard was on duty, and Shen Zechuan was personally appointed by the emperor, so Liang Cuishan reckoned there was some other work to be done. Without daring another look or question, he hurried away.

Xiao Chiye lifted the curtain and stepped out. He had changed into a clean robe, and had a pair of worn boots on his feet and Shen Zechuan's ivory fan in his hand. "Was he here to report on the medicine ledgers?"

"I told him to come back tomorrow," Chen Yang said.

Xiao Chiye descended the steps. Now refreshed, the hostility that had haunted his expression over these last days had dissipated. He asked, "Has Lao-Hu's fever subsided?"

"Yes. He's feeling more spirited, too, and his appetite seemed to have returned this morning. He wanted to pay his respects to Master, but I told him to come again tomorrow too."

"I'll go see him." Xiao Chiye weighed the fan in his hands. "The water in the streets has receded, and the sky is clear. News from the palace should be coming soon; we'll likely be here another two days at most. How about Xi Hongxuan?"

"He's awake. But men from the Eight Great Battalions are keeping a tight watch. No one's allowed to see him."

"There's no hurry," Xiao Chiye said with the hint of a smile. "His Majesty has surely woken by now as well. Xi Hongxuan can't escape this. The Chief Surveillance Bureau is waiting to impeach him."

The public ditches had been dredged, and the epidemic was contained. The crisis had been beautifully handled. Those at the top were saved from public outrage, all due to the work of those who had crawled through the muck at the bottom. It was time to settle the score. Xiao Ce'an had slept his fill and eaten to his heart's content. He had all the spirit and energy he needed to dally with the noble officials.

Xiao Chiye suddenly turned to Chen Yang at his side and asked, "Are they done with the earrings I sent you for the last time? When we return to the manor in a few days, I'll go collect them."

"I told them to make them as quickly as possible," Chen Yang said. "They should be done by now. But why would the master go himself? I'll collect the package on your behalf."

"I have to collect this one personally." Xiao Chiye tossed the ivory fan to Chen Yang and took the lead with long strides. "Let's go. We need to pay Tantai Hu a visit."

RECOUNTING MERITS

LI JIANHENG HAD BEEN insensible for days, delirious with nightmares and mumbling incoherently. Mu Ru stayed by his side, personally administering his medicine and wiping down his sweat-soaked body.

The empress dowager didn't call for her royal sedan that morning. Instead, she took advantage of the good weather and took a leisurely stroll with Third Lady Hua.

"Lady Mu is still watching over him?"

Holding out a supporting arm for the empress dowager, Aunt Liuxiang replied, "She hasn't left his side for a minute."

"After everything she's done, the emperor's affection toward her will have doubled," the empress dowager commented to Hua Xiangyi, who followed a step behind. "In sickness and in health, as they say—their relationship will be stronger than before."

"Lady Mu seems delicate and petite," Hua Xiangyi answered, "but she's got guts."

"Just so," the empress dowager said. "Yesterday, the imperial physician mentioned His Majesty is much better and should wake soon. When he does, it'll be Lady Mu's time to shine. The girl was lambasted by the imperial censors, but even Hai Liangyi must sigh and commend her as a good woman today. If she were timid, would she have dared to risk illness like this?"

Hua Xiangyi smiled as she took the blue-and-white porcelain bowl of fish food from Liuxiang's hands and tossed bits of bait into the freshly melted lake. "How can she be His Majesty's favorite without a little gall? She knew the way to advance and retreat even when she was with Pan Rugui."

The empress dowager looked down at the brocade carp vying for food. "The appearance of this epidemic is suspicious. Lady Mu we could've dealt with by having her sent away for bewitching the emperor and leading him astray. But she's smart—she knows His Majesty's affection is a token of immunity. Look how she's exhausted herself taking care of him; when the dust settles, Xi Hongxuan will be the only one in for a rough time. In the previous sally against Xiao Chiye, the noble clans lost Wei Huaixing. Fu Linye, too, has been denounced and demoted. In the end, no one benefited. And now that the Imperial Army has stepped up in this emergency and dredged the public ditches, Xiao Chiye can expect a reward."

"Xi Hongxuan deserves to be punished," Hua Xiangyi said. "He who thinks not of challenges in the future is sure to be beset by calamity in the present. Auntie, I think his transfer to the Bureau of Evaluations in the Ministry of Personnel has blinded him with success. It's no coincidence misfortune has befallen him. If he'd been more prudent, how could anyone have outmaneuvered him like this?"

She went on, "Now someone has served him up as a stepping stone for Xiao Er to tread upon; it's only fitting that he's penalized. What's more, while I was inquiring about some matters in Qidong, I heard the Heir of Libei provided Zhongbo's Cizhou forty thousand taels in aid during the great snow before the new year. It's also partly thanks to these forty thousand taels that Xiao Er was able to persuade the Ministry of Revenue to distribute aid during this crisis. Now Cizhou and Libei have become friends who have weathered adversity together. When the imperial court sends a Provincial Administration Commissioner to manage the six prefectures in the future, they'll have to consider Libei's interests too."

The empress dowager rubbed the bait into crumbs between her fingers and sprinkled them into the lake. "Yes, the one who benefits most this time is Xiao Chiye. I'd almost believe he released the contagion himself, given the outcome." The empress dowager paused. "Lady Mu is in good health, so why is there no news of an imperial heir? If we can't rid ourselves of her, we must keep her within our grasp. Once she bears a child, I can stop worrying about the future."

In truth, the Li Clan had at one time had quite a number of descendants. But during the Guangcheng Emperor's reign, the crown prince had slit his own throat, and the princes below him in rank either died or were deposed, leaving only the Xiande Emperor and Li Jianheng. The Xiande Emperor reigned for a mere eight years, and because his health was poor, only Imperial Concubine Wei had ever gotten with child. But during those few days of national mourning, someone had drowned the woman in a well without so much as a squeak. Only Li Jianheng was left. Since he had ascended the throne, there had been no news of a pregnancy from the imperial concubines in the palace.

The empress dowager despised Mu Ru, who had spent years in a eunuch's compound. She'd originally intended to pick an astute girl from the Hua Clan in Dicheng and appoint her imperial consort. Li Jianheng wasn't a passionate or devoted man; once he had a new lover, he would brush off his old flame. But who would've expected Mu Ru to be clever and courageous enough to sway the emperor with pillow talk *and* to speak up numerous times for the empress dowager? If the empress dowager wanted to raise the future crown prince at her knee, she had to keep an eye on Mu Ru's belly.

"Lady Mu has also profited from this misfortune." Hua Xiangyi genteelly wiped fish bait off her hands. "She has a younger brother. Does Auntie remember?"

"Fengquan," Aunt Liuxiang quietly reminded the empress dowager.

"I vaguely remember such a person," the empress dowager said. "Did he not take Pan Rugui as his grand-godfather? When Pan Rugui was executed, I'm guessing His Majesty secretly retained him for Lady Mu's sake."

"Fengquan received a recommendation from Auntie once for promotion. I'm sure he remembers your kindness." Hua Xiangyi moved to support the empress dowager herself. "Auntie, this pair of siblings are without anyone to rely on. Help them a little, and to them you'll be like Guanyin, the Goddess of Mercy."

The empress dowager took a few steps forward. "Fengquan is a eunuch. Call him back to the palace. There are plenty of vacancies in the Twenty-Four Yamen. Liuxiang; arrange a good post for him. Consider it a fulfillment of those siblings' wish."

Liuxiang murmured her acknowledgment.

The empress dowager turned to her niece. "Has Qidong replied? How can we have the wedding in autumn? Autumn winds in the Cangjun Commandery are strong. I can't bear to marry you out in those conditions."

Hua Xiangyi merely smiled; Aunt Liuxiang was the one who answered. "The old commander replied. He said he'll leave it up to Your Majesty to decide, as long as it falls on an auspicious hour and day. The messenger even specially brought a few chests of Hezhou silk and satin for the third lady. The head ornaments they brought were also crafted with care and attention—he has put his heart into this."

"And why shouldn't he?" The empress dowager's smile faded. "He has received such momentous imperial favor."

Liuxiang lowered herself at once in obeisance. "He should, of course. To show the third lady due respect, the men Qidong has chosen for the bridal escort are all celebrated generals, and the one leading the procession is none other than Marshal Qi herself."

The empress dowager's expression darkened, though she didn't fly into a rage. "I wrote to the Bianjun Commandery specifically asking that the Earl of Biansha, Lu Pingyan, travel to fetch the bride, yet he's come up with all sorts of excuses to decline. It's obvious he doesn't dare accept because of the Prince of Libei. The Lu Clan are a bunch of blockheads! We'll see how much Libei can help them in the future. As for Qi Zhuyin heading the procession...as a daughter, her seniority is forever a notch below. The nerve of Qi Shiyu to suggest it!"

The empress dowager was still seething when a eunuch trotted over and knelt before them. "Greetings to Your Majesty. Someone from His Majesty's chambers has come with a message—His Majesty has woken up!"

Liuxiang was first to react. "Prepare Her Majesty's sedan!"

Tantai Hu, a coat draped over his shoulders, was carving a crude cricket from wood to give to Ding Tao and Xiao-Wu. The moment Chen Yang lifted the curtain, the three stood to pay their respects.

"You've only just recovered; sit." Xiao Chiye motioned for them to rise from their bows and found a chair himself. "How are you feeling?"

"Thanks to the supreme commander for your concern." Tantai Hu brushed the wood shavings off his hands. "My fever is gone, and I've eaten. I can return to duty today."

"There's no rush." Xiao Chiye was wearing a worn robe today. After sitting a moment, he asked, "You fell ill so suddenly. You're usually in good health, so what happened? What did the military medic say?"

"The medic couldn't explain it either," said Tantai Hu. "I've been wondering—why me? Even when I trained bare-chested in the rain with our Imperial Army, I never caught so much as a cold. I saw the list the supreme commander had Chen Yang compile of those who fell ill. There are some elderly men and women and a handful of youngsters, but too many of the young and strong."

"The outbreak of this pox was bizarre," Chen Yang piped up in agreement. "His Excellency the lord judge may be right. This is no natural disaster, but a man-made one."

Xiao Chiye leaned back in thought. "Regardless of which it is, while we've been working to contain it, time has passed. Any clues have most likely been disposed of by now."

"It could have been worse. At least I'm the one who fell ill." Tantai Hu was still anxious. "If the supreme commander had been laid low instead, the patrols in Qudu would be in chaos!"

Startled, Xiao Chiye's hand, which had been stroking his thumb ring, stilled. He said nothing, and the others didn't dare interrupt his contemplation.

"This never crossed my mind." After a long moment, Xiao Chiye bared his teeth in a fearless smile. "Never mind. It's a bad debt, no? Thankfully we had a plan; it's not all that worrisome. Rest up today. Who's looking after those children in your home right now?"

Tantai Hu hadn't expected Xiao Chiye to remember the children; his eyes stung. "When I fell ill, I entrusted them to Chen Yang. They're in the Imperial Army's office compound. With the brothers there watching out for them, they'll be fed at the very least. They're all right."

"Most of the men in the Imperial Army were originally from local households in Qudu. Those of you recruited from outside to fill the posts have no houses and no wives; it isn't easy to raise any children. And you fell ill while digging ditches in a disaster; consider that a meritorious service. Chen Yang will report it to the Ministry of War and see that you get a promotion at the start of spring. In addition to your monthly salary, the internal administrative division of the Imperial Army will allocate some child support funds from my personal account."

An allocation from Xiao Chiye's personal account meant the money was withdrawn from the commander's salary—it could be considered money Xiao Chiye gave him with his own hands.

Tantai Hu dropped to one knee when he heard this. "That's far too much! I'm already more than grateful the supreme commander didn't boot me out and continues to let me serve!"

"Credit where credit is due; you deserve it. I'm giving it to you, so take it." Xiao Chiye rose and said to Chen Yang, "Get a record of the soldiers who dug out the ditches and make sure they get a bonus on their salaries. Epidemics are no laughing matter; everyone here is risking their lives, so is a little silver not deserved? Let it be known that promotions and assignments will be assessed according to one's merits and demerits if something like this happens again. For people like Lao-Hu, I, Xiao Ce'an, will take care of the whole family."

Whatever grudge Tantai Hu still held toward his commander now utterly vanished. After receiving such kindness, it wouldn't do for him to harp on Shen Zechuan again.

Xiao Chiye meant every word of it; he paid a call to the others from the Imperial Army who had fallen ill and similarly rewarded them for their risk. Even the young ones like Ding Tao received a hefty bonus.

Shen Zechuan drank his medicine as he watched the bustling scene outside the window.

Qiao Tianya had set up the fire basin and was occupied roasting a few potatoes. As he poked the fire, he said, "Look how everyone's gotten a promotion and a windfall. Master, what about me?"

"I'll keep it in mind for the future." Shen Zechuan set the bowl aside.

Qiao Tianya was watching the potatoes crisp with undivided focus. "Xiao Er knows how to manage his subordinates. To think he could consolidate the Imperial Army and turn it into his very own impenetrable fortress in the span of just a few years—he certainly has put the work in."

"It's not surprising he'd put work into something that concerns his own safety," Shen Zechuan said. "The Imperial Army is his newly sharpened blade. The more smoothly he can wield it, the better. Tantai Hu is a high-ranking military officer he recruited from outside Qudu. If he isn't properly managed, the people under him will become the roots of trouble."

"He's made the most of his opportunities, but he's also won their hearts. The supreme commander has those men in the palm of his hand. By first punishing then rewarding them, he's made them obedient. Even the roots of trouble have become a stabilizing force. Given Tantai Hu's disposition, a bribe of a thousand gold wouldn't shake his loyalty." Qiao Tianya peeled the cooked potatoes and sighed. "Now that I compare... Master, you're really too coldhearted."

"The Embroidered Uniform Guard is not the same as the Imperial Army. The men in the Embroidered Uniform Guard all came out of distinguished clans. Every last one is ambitious and arrogant. Being coldhearted is perfect. Until we face life-or-death tribulations, there's no way for true camaraderie to form; everyone keeps a scale in their heart. Since Han Cheng assumed the post of chief commander, he has already doled out quite a number of 'rewards' to those below him. But how many genuinely think well of him?" Shen Zechuan paused. "Now that you've eaten the potatoes, leave the meat later. You must have put on seven or eight catties since you started following me."

"Would Master like to hear a tune?" Qiao Tianya asked. "I can play and even sing. I can do without the money, but at the least you could reward me with two pieces of meat, right?"

"Get out," said Shen Zechuan mercilessly.

Xiao Chiye was just returning as Qiao Tianya walked out. Qiao Tianya moved aside to make way, and Xiao Chiye strode through the door, hooked a chair over with his leg, and sat beside the bed.

"Did you sleep well?"

"So-so," Shen Zechuan replied.

"That residence of yours has been torn down," Xiao Chiye said. "Where do you plan to live after you get out of here in a few days?"

Shen Zechuan sighed. "On the streets, I guess."

Elbows propped on his knees, Xiao Chiye whistled lowly. "I have a small courtyard behind Plum Blossom Manor. Do you want it?"

"If we're too close, people will become suspicious." Shen Zechuan gathered his clothes around him, offering a brief glimpse of the marks on the nape of his neck.

"If we're too far, it'll be hard for us to meet even once every few days." Xiao Chiye reached out to smooth Shen Zechuan's back collar. His eyes lingered on those teeth marks.

He was the one who had left those marks, kissing that spot like Shen Zechuan was prey in his mouth.

Shen Zechuan raised his eyes to look at him. "I suppose I'll see you in the imperial court, hm?"

Xiao Chiye averted his gaze. "That makes us sound like strangers."

"Well, what's to be done?" Shen Zechuan looked at him. "Where's my fan?"

Chen Yang happened to be lifting the curtain at that moment, tray in hand. Without thinking, Xiao Chiye said, "Gone. Chen Yang lost it."

Shen Zechuan looked toward Chen Yang who, despite his shock, nodded solemnly and said with deep grief, "Your Excellency, this humble subordinate..."

"It's just a fan. Er-gongzi will compensate you on his behalf," Xiao Chiye said leisurely. "That ivory fan is so gaudy. Let me gift you one."

"Even if it's crude, it came from Xi Hongxuan," said Shen Zechuan. "How can I put on the persona of a tasteless rascal if I meet him later without it?"

"I'll give you something even more tasteless, inlaid with gold and jade. Er-gongzi has deep pockets."

"The military drill ground on Mount Feng will need renovations at the start of spring." Shen Zechuan spread his palms. "Er-gongzi, how much have you tightened your belt? You'll soon be so poor you'll have to go vegetarian. Where on earth would you find the money for gold and jade?"

Chen Yang set the tray down and backed out of the room.

"What? Are you checking my secret stash?" Xiao Chiye said.

"Hmm, you have a secret stash?"

"A big one."

Shen Zechuan smiled. "Then that's really..."

Chen Yang, who had just exited, called from outside the curtain, "Master! An imperial edict has arrived from the palace."

Both schooled their faces to seriousness. Xiao Chiye immediately rose; a moment later, he held out his hand and brought Shen Zechuan up as well.

REOPENING

THE TEMPLE OF GUILT had received the imperial edict unexpectedly; neither Xiao Chiye nor Shen Zechuan were wearing their official robes. Everyone gathered in the courtyard and knelt to receive the words of the emperor. The eunuch who had come to deliver it looked unfamiliar; not daring to put on airs, he began to read out the edict the moment he saw the intended recipient.

When he had finished, he bowed slightly and said to Xiao Chiye, "Supreme Commander, please rise!"

Xiao Chiye took the imperial edict from the eunuch's hands while Chen Yang called for someone to serve tea.

"The Temple of Guilt stinks of illness," Xiao Chiye said, "so I won't invite Gonggong inside for a seat today."

"The supreme commander has been hard at work for days, tending to your duties without rest. If anyone should sit, it's the supreme commander." The eunuch merrily took a few sips of the tea, then furrowed his brow and sighed. "How is this tea fit for distinguished men? Supreme Commander, now that His Majesty is awake, the secretariat elder says you and the judge may take a rest."

"There are people under the rain shelters who are sick. I'm still on duty, no? I wouldn't dare be careless." Xiao Chiye let his features fall into easy amiability as he acquainted himself with the eunuch over this exchange of pleasantries. Both stood in the courtyard, drinking tea as they chatted and laughed. Xiao Chiye asked, "Did His Majesty wake up today?"

"That's right," the eunuch, Fuman, replied. "Just this morning. The imperial concubines are all weeping tears of joy. The empress dowager personally instructed the Court of Imperial Physicians to see to his every need."

The contents of this imperial edict were mere formality. It commended the Imperial Army, the Embroidered Uniform Guard, and the Ministry of Revenue for their timely action. Any mention of rewards was vague and brief.

Fuman had only recently assumed office, and he usually served in the Grand Secretariat compound. The officials of the Grand Secretariat held eunuchs in contempt; Hai Liangyi in particular loathed them. Whenever Fuman had been on duty thus far, he hadn't been permitted to look Hai Liangyi in the eye; he had to retreat to the side and kneel down to reply. Whatever Hai Liangyi asked, he would answer. He didn't dare smile, much less crack a joke. Here, he had not only received a cup of hot tea; he also saw that Supreme Commander Xiao was a naturally carefree man who didn't fuss over trifles. He gradually relaxed as they conversed, intending to use the opportunity to get in Xiao Chiye's good graces.

Fuman shuffled two steps over and murmured, "This humble servant has been going around the Grand Secretariat these days serving the secretariat elder tea. I've come to hear some rumors about the supreme commander."

With no change in his expression, Xiao Chiye lifted a hand to motion for the others to step away. He draped an arm around Fuman's shoulders and said, "Then you must be the secretariat elder's new favorite. I also have to keep a weather eye on the skies before I act and watch for an impending storm. Perhaps Gonggong can give me a pointer or two?"

"I wouldn't presume to give any pointers," Fuman hurried to say. "For the sake of the sovereign and his people, the supreme commander conscientiously carries out his duties; the secretariat elder knows this too. The Grand Secretariat deliberated for several days over the conferment of an award. The supreme commander only has to wait—it'll come!"

Xiao Chiye smiled. "I wouldn't dare take all the credit this time. This crisis wasn't something I could resolve alone. I'd feel uneasy with too great a reward."

"Oh my. Supreme Commander!" Fuman slapped his leg. "You're far too humble. Is Shen Zechuan the officer from the Embroidered Uniform Guard who oversaw this mission?"

"That's right," Xiao Chiye said. "A frosty fellow."

Fuman, who had only heard that the two of them were on bad terms, promptly laughed. "Who would have guessed the supreme commander would find himself working together with *him*? Since this business has been successfully handled, he's bound to receive a reward too. But he serves in the Embroidered Uniform Guard, which falls under the authority of the emperor himself; the Grand Secretariat can't overstep their bounds. His reward will depend on His Majesty."

"An exception was made for him when he was promoted to southern judge before the new year. It's too soon for him to be promoted again," Xiao Chiye replied. "The Grand Secretariat didn't object?"

Fuman carefully set the teacup aside. "He's a thorn in the supreme commander's side, so it's natural you would take special note of his actions. But the gentlemen of the Grand Secretariat are all busy with other matters. If His Majesty really does promote Shen Zechuan, no one would dare deny him such a small thing. His Majesty has met with one misfortune after another. Even Secretariat Elder Hai would acquiesce to any of his whims right now. But I'll tell the supreme commander something in strict confidence—there is a danger to his speedy promotions. The officials who hold positions of the fifth rank and above in the Embroidered Uniform Guard are all lads from established families. That Shen Zechuan... His background speaks for itself. Head to the streets now and yell Shen Wei's name at the top of your lungs, and you'll be spat on by everyone in sight. Any promotion will only encourage these noble sons to humiliate him, covertly or overtly. With merits and rewards will come resentment and jealousy. The Embroidered Uniform Guard has always been a massive beast as ferocious as any wolf or tiger. Whether or not he can hold onto his prize will depend on his capabilities."

Xiao Chiye exchanged a few more words with Fuman before summoning Chen Yang. As Chen Yang saw the eunuch out, he gave him a hand up onto his horse. It was only when Fuman was halfway back that he noticed a heaviness in his sleeve. He fished it out for a look and beamed with delight.

"The supreme commander is generous indeed." Fuman stuffed the money back into his sleeve. "A man worth befriending."

When Liang Cuishan arrived, he gave Shen Zechuan a clear tally of the herbs and medicines. Shen Zechuan asked him a few questions, and he answered each one readily and thoroughly. It was really a shame for this man to stay a minor, unranked clerk.

"These last few days have been chaotic," said Shen Zechuan. "There are countless apothecaries in Qudu, big and small, and the supply and distribution of medicinal herbs has been a complicated mess. I can see the great effort you've made to record everything so clearly."

"That is what this humble subordinate does in his official capacity. I've only performed my duty." Liang Cuishan added with sincere concern, "Your Excellency looks much better today."

"A little medicine was all it took. I'm fine now," Shen Zechuan said. "Make copies of this ledger and give one to the Ministry of Revenue; you have to report back to your superiors. Give the Imperial Army a copy too so they know what to expect."

At the height of the epidemic, everyone had been on pins and needles; they had set aside old grudges and hatred. But now the rain had stopped, and it was time to weigh the merits and rewards of each man. Between the three parties involved in this matter—the Imperial Army, the Embroidered Uniform Guard, and the Ministry of Revenue—it was hard to imagine there would be no blaming or backstabbing.

As a minor official, Liang Cuishan had seen it all. He understood Shen Zechuan had bad blood with the Imperial Army and had expected to find them at each other's throats. But unexpectedly, Shen Zechuan didn't step forward to claim his accomplishment or speak up about his own efforts; even with the job completed, he didn't hog the credit for himself.

Liang Cuishan hesitated. "It was Your Excellency who instructed this humble subordinate to keep these ledgers. For me to hand them over like this..."

"I was sick in bed. You did most of the work on your own." Shen Zechuan closed the book. "I can see you're organized and methodical in your work, and you've served in the Ministry of Revenue for so many years. Why are you still just a clerk?"

"This humble subordinate has served in the Ministry of Revenue since the second year of Xiande," Liang Cuishan said in a pained voice. "At that time, the one in charge was a member of the Hua Clan...

This humble subordinate is embarrassingly short of money. I don't have the funds to make connections, so all I can do is run errands. The higher-ups only let me attend to the official duties for my original post, and my reviews for the past few years have been in the lower-middle range, with neither merits nor demerits."

After a moment of silence, Shen Zechuan said, "His Majesty is encouraging new opportunities to show one's skills, and the Six Ministries lack talents. There's no need for you to feel disheartened; the chance will present itself in due time."

Liang Cuishan had guessed by now that Shen Zechuan meant to recommend him for promotion. He swiftly bowed. "Your Excellency's recognition and appreciation of this humble subordinate is a kindness I will never forget!"

Shen Zechuan rose to leave. He said nothing further as he lifted the curtain and stepped out. Liang Cuishan looked at the floor blankly; it took him several seconds to realize tears were streaming down his cheeks.

What he hadn't told Shen Zechuan was that he was from Juexi, and his first few decades were spent studying day and night. He passed the imperial examinations at an age several years later than most. He was supposed to assume a post at the Ministry of Personnel, but someone had bribed their way into taking his place. From there he was transferred to the Ministry of Works, where he received outstanding reviews for the few years he worked there. As he was good with numbers, he was transferred to the Ministry of Revenue, where he initially thought he could showcase his talent. But once there, he found himself under the thumb of a distant descendant of the Hua Clan—a disgrace who'd muddled his way to officialdom. Liang Cuishan did the job, but it was this person's name on the reports submitted to the top. He had tried several times to transfer elsewhere, but his superiors, eager to exploit his labor, refused to relinquish him. He was held back again and again until he eventually became a clerk in a position so minor he couldn't even be considered a legitimate official.

He had given up dreams of glory in this life, disillusioned with worldly affairs. Who could've expected his misfortune would turn out to be a blessing in disguise? Every cloud indeed had a silver lining.

Two days later, as Xiao Chiye had predicted, the order forbidding access to the palace was lifted. The operations of the Six Ministries returned to normal, and the men of the Embroidered Uniform Guard and Imperial Army were withdrawn from the Temple of Guilt. Any who had yet to recover were left under the care of the Court of Imperial Physicians.

Shen Zechuan was once again neatly turned out as he stood before the door to the Temple of Guilt, dressed in his embroidered python robe and phoenix-tail belt, authority token hanging from his waist and sword at his side. Xiao Chiye had tidied up as well, and appeared attired in a scarlet court robe with an embroidered lion mandarin square, tall and long-legged.

They put on a great show of bidding each other farewell.

"I'm heading this way." Xiao Chiye whistled for Snowcrest and patted his horse's neck. "Is Your Excellency entering the palace with me?"

"Please go on ahead, Supreme Commander," Shen Zechuan said politely. "This humble subordinate must report to the chief commander."

"Being a subordinate sucks." Xiao Chiye swung up astride. "Don't you want a turn at the top?"

"I'm afraid of heights." Shen Zechuan looked up at him. "You'd do better to worry about yourself up there."

"Things are only going to get more complicated from here. Whether I stay on top depends on whether you're willing to show mercy." Xiao Chiye tapped at his own chest with the horsewhip. "Be gentle."

They parted ways before the Temple of Guilt. Instead of going to look for Han Cheng immediately, Shen Zechuan directed Qiao Tianya to take the carriage to the house where he had settled Ji Gang and Qi Huilian.

The little building was surrounded by a courtyard, with a half-dead pear tree jutting over the top of the wall. Shen Zechuan passed through the courtyard and ascended the steps, only to find the doors to the main hall tightly shut. There was no sign of Ji Gang or Qi Huilian.

The back of Qiao Tianya's neck prickled in the odd atmosphere. He could see from the messy footprints on the ground that there had been people here. Palm on the hilt of his blade, he strode forward with a smile. "No one here? If that's so, this humble servant will draw his blade—"

A sudden gust set the withered branches of the pear tree swaying as the weeds in the courtyard battered the hem of his robe. Qiao Tianya surveyed his surrounds with keen eyes; he had already sensed that both the interior and exterior of the courtyard were teeming with people.

"Draw a blade? What for? We're all friends here." A weak voice echoed feebly from inside the house. "Lanzhou, why aren't you saying a word?"

Shen Zechuan's eyes had already sharpened ruthlessly, yet he forced a laugh. "Second Young Master, have you recovered?"

"Would I dare come see you if I hadn't? My good brother, why didn't you tell me you were hiding such a bigwig here?"

Shen Zechuan laughed out loud and motioned for Qiao Tianya to step back. He shoved the door open, stirring up the dust inside. An entire room of guards turned to look at him, their drawn blades glinting with snowy-white light.

Xi Hongxuan sat in the middle of it all, wrapped in fox fur with a teacup in hand. He had lost quite a bit of weight and didn't look well at all.

Showing no signs of fear, Shen Zechuan strode in. "One is a fool and the other a lunatic. What kind of bigwig could he be? If you wanted them, why didn't you just tell me?"

Xi Hongxuan couldn't bring himself to laugh. He said gloomily, "If Qi Huilian is no bigwig, then Hai Liangyi is common as dirt! Lanzhou, oh, Lanzhou, you've hidden this all too well! To think the Grand Mentor of Yongyi taught you personally. Ha! Is he banking on you becoming emperor?"

"He's already crazy." Shen Zechuan pulled out his handkerchief, fastidiously wiping dust from his hands. He cast a glance at Xi Hongxuan. "You're afraid of a madman?"

"I am!" Xi Hongxuan flung the teacup down. "A madman taught a rabid dog whose bites caught me off guard and turned me into a bloody pulp!"

Blades pressed in swiftly from all sides.

Shen Zechuan smiled. "You're not speaking sense. If you wish to kill me, at least let me die knowing why."

"Did you..." Xi Hongxuan said, voice dripping with hostility, "... team up with Xiao Er to screw me over?"

The room seemed to hold its breath. Shadows fell along Shen Zechuan's face. After a moment of silence, he flashed a smile and leaned against the edge of the table. "That's right." Shen Zechuan scrutinized Xi Hongxuan with a wicked darkness in his eyes as he continued contemptuously, "If I dared to say that, would you dare believe it?"

TRAP

IT WAS SO QUIET one could hear a pin drop.

Hands braced on the chair's armrests, Xi Hongxuan's next words cracked through the heart-stopping tension. "Obscuring truth with falsehood. You're setting traps again! Shen Lanzhou, do you think I won't kill you?"

"The blade is already at my neck." Shen Zechuan turned to look askance at one of the blades in question. "You can give the command to take my head at any time."

Xi Hongxuan didn't dare relax even a little. In this confrontation, he wasn't willing to miss the subtlest shift in Shen Zechuan's expression. Although he was sitting steady in the chair, deep down, he was more anxious than Shen Zechuan. Yet the more he warned himself against being influenced by him, the more he was taken in by the man's careful expression and tone.

"For whatever it's worth, we were brothers," Xi Hongxuan said with an insincere smile. "Lanzhou, tell me the truth and I'll leave you in one piece."

"All talk. Kill me then." Shen Zechuan goaded him. "Come on."

Xi Hongxuan's fingers dug tightly into the armrests as he stared down Shen Zechuan, who was far too calm and composed. "Aren't you worried about Qi Huilian? Once you're dead, I'll skin that old dog and sell him to the empress dowager as a bid for leniency."

"If you'd handed her Qi Huilian twenty years ago, she might have pardoned your negligence," said Shen Zechuan. "Today he's worth nothing alive and even less dead. You're a veteran merchant; would you really accept a losing deal like this? I think you've lost your mind too; that fever must've addled your brain."

"Qi Huilian is feigning insanity," Xi Hongxuan said. "You think I can't tell? He's at death's door, yet he's tucking his tail between his legs and struggling on. To survive, he's put on quite the convincing act!"

Shen Zechuan sneered. "Oh, please. What do you expect me to say? He's just a lunatic."

"If he's a lunatic, whom are you studying under?" The tendons in Xi Hongxuan's neck strained as he leaned forward. "The Temple of Guilt transformed you into a new man. How did the last remnant of the Shen Clan who resembled a lapdog six years ago become so fearless and resourceful, huh? Lanzhou, you tell me!"

"Man proposes, heaven disposes." Shen Zechuan's expression was grim. "You know what it's like being a lapdog at the beck and call of others, to be kicked around. If I don't shed my skin, how can I break free of my past and make it out there? I'd rather rely on myself than others. Look at us; you and I are both fleeing perilous circumstances, yet now even we are at odds. Xi Hongxuan, you're so eager to rid yourself of someone as soon as he's outlived his usefulness, like killing the donkey the moment it leaves the millstone."

"If you hadn't leaked my secrets, why did Ouhua Pavilion collapse? We called ourselves brothers inside those walls, but the moment you step out, you stab me in the back. Of the two of us, who's more ruthless?" Xi Hongxuan asked in a chilling voice. "But as fate would have it, I didn't die. You want to play both sides, but there's no such thing as having your cake and eating it too."

"What can Xiao Er give me that's worth this level of suspicion?" Shen Zechuan asked sarcastically. "He's not Xiao Jiming; he can neither become the Prince of Libei nor command their Armored Cavalry. He's a trapped beast in Qudu! What's the difference between him and me? Whatever it is he has, I don't lack it."

"He has a good life that you don't," said Xi Hongxuan. "He's the second son of the Prince of Libei, a legitimate and lawful heir, born to the same mother who birthed Xiao Jiming. Even if he can't inherit his father's title, he has tens of thousands of willing troops at his disposal. Aren't soldiers precisely what you lack?"

Indifferent, Shen Zechuan answered, "I hold a post in the Embroidered Uniform Guard; what do I need an army for? I can only survive within Qudu. There's nowhere else I can put my abilities to use. I'm the eighth common son of Shen Wei, while you are the second lawful son of the Xi Clan. Yet have either of us had a life of ease? There's no difference between lawful and common sons. When it comes to humans, even heaven can't reach a verdict until the end."

"Such treacherous words. You regard the social order of this world as nothing." Xi Hongxuan pointed to his feet. "But you have to admit—some people are born to be masters. The succession, generation after generation, of the noble clans sustains that. This is fate! If there's no difference between those of common and lawful birth, how can a bloodline maintain its legitimacy? A Li is fundamentally a cut above a Shen!"

Shen Zechuan stared at Xi Hongxuan and broke into laughter. Insanity stirred in those expressive eyes as he said, "That's right. That's right."

For a split second, Qiao Tianya saw Shen Zechuan's murderous intent; he thought Shen Zechuan would draw his blade. He didn't expect him to continue in a genial tone, "Well, if that's the case, then what future could I have following Xiao Er? You believed the rumors and laid a trap to kill me today, but you will surely regret it in the future."

Xi Hongxuan faltered, besieged by doubts, but his expression remained stony. He merely lowered his eyes. "Even when faced with imminent death, you're a consummate actor. You came straight here from the Temple of Guilt. Isn't that proof enough that this place is important to you?"

"Of course." Shen Zechuan's emotions seemed to have sunk into deep waters; not even a ripple could be seen. "This is Qi Huilian we're talking about. He's crazy now, but he's still the Qi Huilian who was the top scholar in all three levels of the imperial examinations, a man personally sought out by the crown prince of the Eastern Palace. Now that he's fallen into my hands, I won't hand him over to anyone else while he lives."

Shen Zechuan was right—Xi Hongxuan was bluffing. He had no idea if Qi Huilian was genuinely insane or simply putting on an act; he merely wanted to catch Shen Zechuan off guard. Perhaps Xi Hongxuan wasn't as capable as Xue Xiuzhuo, but he possessed one unsurpassed ability, and that was eloquence. He could incite the Imperial College to rise in rebellion with a single teahouse meeting, all thanks to his silver tongue. Yet this also happened to be his fatal flaw.

If he were certain beyond a shadow of a doubt that Shen Zechuan and Xiao Chiye were setting him up for a fall, he wouldn't have given Shen Zechuan the chance to open his mouth. He'd dragged his sickly body all the way here because he couldn't be sure. Xi Hongxuan had to put his skills to use in a battle of words, hoping to trick Shen Zechuan into telling the truth.

"What do you want Qi Huilian for?" Xi Hongxuan asked warily.

Shen Zechuan was suddenly struck with an idea; he bent over and said to Xi Hongxuan, "Qi Huilian was the crown prince's teacher. After the incident at the Eastern Palace, I heard there remained an imperial grandson, still an infant. Ji Lei didn't reveal the child's whereabouts to me before his death. I thought Qi Huilian might know, so I've kept close watch on him."

A change came over Xi Hongxuan's countenance in spite of himself. "The empress dowager would never leave survivors. It's common practice to stamp out trouble at its source. What are you daydreaming about?"

"If there's no imperial heir in the wings, who would conspire to murder His Majesty?" Shen Zechuan said. "If he dies, there's nobody else surnamed Li in all the Zhou empire. You didn't do it, and neither did I. Instead of falling out with me, why not lay down your sword and discuss countermeasures?"

Xi Hongxuan didn't move. "How do I know it wasn't you? Save for myself, no one is more familiar with the structure of Ouhua Pavilion. If anyone could tamper with it, it's you. Look how I encounter calamities one after another, yet you get promoted again and again. The list of your meritorious deeds is growing by the day!"

"I've only just attracted His Majesty's favor. Now is the time for me to accumulate merits and climb my way up. Why on earth would I want him dead? Not to mention, you and I have been conspiring together for quite some time; what makes you think Xiao Er would trust me based on some empty promises?" Shen Zechuan's lips curved in a smile. "If I were to kill you, it would be at a time when there's much more in it for me."

He spoke half in jest, but at these words, the blood of those listening ran cold. Xi Hongxuan covered his mouth and coughed, using the motion to evade Shen Zechuan's gaze.

They had conspired to kill many people by this point, yet Xi Hongxuan still didn't have the courage to face Shen Zechuan head-on. This wasn't a momentary fear, but one accumulated over the course of their acquaintance. He could never forget the way Ji Lei looked, flayed alive. It was this same fear that spurred him to act quickly once his suspicions were roused.

Xi Hongxuan thought, *This man cannot live.*

When the time came, he had to kill him, no matter what. Such a man would certainly not let himself be used for Xi Hongxuan's own purposes. His talk of there being no difference between lawful and common birth already revealed his lack of proper reverence for the Eight Great Clans. Both of them were attempting the dangerous feat of bargaining with a tiger for its hide. It was only a matter of who would act faster in the days to come.

Xi Hongxuan had made up his mind. He smiled back. "I'm scaring you only because *I* was so scared after being crushed in that pit. Lanzhou, you'd understand if you had been the one lying there. What are you all waiting for? Sheath your blades. Don't hurt the judge."

The surrounding blades returned to their sheaths, one by one. Xi Hongxuan didn't tell his men to retreat from the room. Pulling his fox fur closer, he said, "Everything happened too quickly these last few days. We've had no communication; it's inevitable we would come to suspect one another. Everything is back in order now that we've cleared the air. Come, Lanzhou. Take a seat, and we'll talk."

"A naked blade can't distinguish friend from foe," replied Shen Zechuan. "Second Young Master, next time, give me some warning so I'll be better prepared to receive you."

"You're remarkably composed in the face of danger." Xi Hongxuan lifted the teapot to brew the tea. "As you know, what we're doing could cost us our heads. I really was forced into a corner this time; otherwise, how could I have treated you so? I had no choice, I tell you! I got too anxious thinking how Xiao Er will be happily riding the crest of success after this. Come, come—sit. Don't tell me you hold it against me?"

"I, a man with the surname Shen, am unworthy of such courtesy." Shen Zechuan's eyes swept over the room. "How would I dare to sit by your side?"

Xi Hongxuan guffawed. "That was all bullshit! Words spoken to disparage others. How can you be the same as them? Take a seat."

Only then did Shen Zechuan sit down.

Xi Hongxuan held out the tea and said with an apologetic smile, "If you ask me, that surname Shen is really holding you back. Don't you think so? Had you been born in the Han Clan or Fei Clan, there wouldn't be this animosity between us. Lanzhou, don't be upset! Now tell me seriously. What are you keeping Qi Huilian for?"

Shen Zechuan touched his sleeve pocket before he remembered his ivory fan was lost. "The old loon was scared stiff when the crown prince slit his throat. When I was in the Temple of Guilt, I ran into him all the time and heard his ravings. I thought I'd keep him, in case of future need."

"You should have asked me about the imperial grandson." Xi Hongxuan brushed aside tea foam in his cup. "Forget about it. It's impossible."

"No chance at all?" Shen Zechuan turned the teacup gently in his hands. He didn't drink.

Xi Hongxuan drank the tea and grunted twice. "Ji Lei and Shen Wei carried out that task; they were ruthless. Even the fair and beautiful crown princess was strangled to death, and you've pinned your hopes on them having shown an imperial grandson mercy?

After killing his father, they would've become sworn enemies of the child. You think they'd willingly sow seeds of future disaster for themselves?"

"Is that what Xue Xiuzhuo said?"

Xi Hongxuan cast him a glance. "Why are you bringing up Yanqing now?"

"An old friend, is he not?" Shen Zechuan's gaze never faltered. "It appears you know each other well. Weren't you promoted to the Bureau of Evaluations this time precisely because you listened to his advice?"

"Both of you are master strategists. I listen to whoever makes more sense," Xi Hongxuan replied. "They say scholars hold one another in low regard. Why are you smart people always belittling each other?"

"That's not it," said Shen Zechuan. "You were transferred into the Bureau of Evaluations, and subsequently, this sought-after review assignment fell to you. That would make anyone's eyes green with envy. It's hard to say this wasn't the reason you were set up. Xue Xiuzhuo has been an official for some years, yet he never thought of this possibility? Why did he persuade *you* to go?"

Xi Hongxuan lowered his cup. "Even if that's the reason, who would've expected someone to strike out at me because of it? Yanqing's not at fault."

"He rendered meritorious service by protecting the emperor at the Nanlin Hunting Grounds, yet he knew to conceal his abilities and bide his time. Instead of angling for a top position back then, he went to the Court of Judicial Review to gain experience." Shen Zechuan smiled at Xi Hongxuan and let the matter drop. "I just find it strange."

"Oh my!" Xi Hongxuan smiled and said as if he hadn't heard him, "This interruption almost made me forget. Lanzhou, now that

I've recovered and His Majesty has awoken, the Chief Surveillance Bureau will certainly impeach me. Help me think of a way out of it. I can't be transferred away from Qudu."

"The fault lies with His Majesty, but no one will blame him. Both the Ministry of Works and Ministry of Revenue are already shirking responsibility. You've happened to land right in the middle, so you're a natural target." Shen Zechuan set his teacup aside. "This will be tough to wiggle out of."

"Pan Xiangjie and Wei Huaigu, ha! At the end of the day, what they really want is money. A formal rebuke isn't a big deal—they're only targeting me because they want to take advantage of the situation to make me cough up the funds to cover the hole this will leave in the budget myself. How many died this time? As long as His Majesty is unharmed, everything else can be bought."

"Without tens of thousands of taels, I'm afraid it'll be hard to settle this," Shen Zechuan replied with a smile.

"I have the money," Xi Hongxuan set his teacup down too. "But I'm not willing to give it to them. I'm at fault for accompanying His Majesty to the brothel, but the public ditches are no business of mine. If they plan on using me as a scapegoat and slapping unreasonable demands on me, I won't be so obliging."

"An official even one rank higher can oppress an official beneath him." Shen Zechuan spoke calmly. "You aren't in the wrong, but it will still become your fault. You can't reason with them, and you can't shift the blame. It's certainly a dilemma."

"It's not. I'm telling you, the emperor's heart is with me," Xi Hongxuan said. "Even if they want to punish me severely, they still have to wait for the emperor's word. We mustn't lose our heads before Xiao Er is dealt with. Trust me—when His Majesty wakes up, he'll be a changed man."

NOBLE TITLE

HE SPOKE WITH such certainty that Shen Zechuan cast him a sidelong glance. But Xi Hongxuan didn't elaborate. "You don't have a proper residence now, so it'll be inconvenient to keep Qi Huilian around. Why not leave him with me?"

"It's hardly appropriate to leave a raving lunatic at your place either," Shen Zechuan said evenly. "What do you want him for?"

"If you ask me," said Xi Hongxuan, holding his hand flat like a blade, "it'd be best to finish him off. You don't want to get yourself involved in all those old affairs. The more you know, the worse off you'll be." Xi Hongxuan brandished his hand and looked at Shen Zechuan. "Or are you unwilling?"

"Of course I'm unwilling," Shen Zechuan said. "He's an old minister from the reign of Yongyi. He knew Shen Wei well. I have use for him alive."

Had Shen Zechuan readily agreed, Xi Hongxuan wouldn't have believed him. He spoke with seven parts truth and three parts falsehood to throw Xi Hongxuan off.

As expected, Xi Hongxuan made no further mention of killing him. "Are you still thinking of investigating Shen Wei's case? You should have said so earlier. Lanzhou, do you have to go so far as to hide such a small matter from me?"

"When did I hide it?" Shen Zechuan smiled as he lifted the teapot and poured for Xi Hongxuan. "Isn't it obvious? As long as Shen Wei is guilty, I'll never be able to hold my head high."

"The evidence against him is conclusive, and his infamy has spread far and wide. Even if some extenuating evidence comes to light, it won't be enough to change the minds of the masses," Xi Hongxuan said. "A treasonous act like betraying your country for personal glory can never be scrubbed clean, even over several lifetimes. Besides, relying on an imperial pardon is pointless. Rumors take on a life of their own; Shen Wei has already been crucified under an ocean of spittle. I pity you, of course I do—but I can only advise you to forget about this matter. There's nothing you can do to clear Shen Wei's name."

Shen Zechuan set down the teapot in silence.

Sensing the heaviness of the atmosphere, Xi Hongxuan continued, "You're already an Embroidered Uniform Guard of the fifth rank, and you still take that slander to heart? No—you must look ahead. You've acquitted yourself well this time, so you can look forward to a promotion, yes?"

"Nothing is confirmed," Shen Zechuan said. "I've barely settled in my post as southern judge. Charging to the top isn't necessarily a good thing."

"Right, we must act carefully. We're gambling with our lives here." Xi Hongxuan tucked his fox fur about him. "Our first priority should be investigating this incident with Ouhua Pavilion. Our enemy is hiding in the dark, while we are exposed in the open. If we can't get to the bottom of this, it will be hard to guard against them in the future. This time I'm the one who got crushed, but what about next time? You should watch your back. I can't stay much longer today. Lanzhou, I'll see you at my residence in a few days."

He rose to his feet and surveyed his surroundings again. "This courtyard seems decent enough. If you need money, just ask. Don't take what happened today to heart, all right?"

Xi Hongxuan smiled. Shen Zechuan smiled, too, as if there was no ill will between them. As if what happened earlier was merely a harmless joke, and now the pair of them were reconciled.

Qiao Tianya saw Xi Hongxuan off. When he returned to the courtyard, he spied Shen Zechuan standing with his back to him, facing the main hall. He was wiping his hands with a handkerchief.

The setting sun reached into the courtyard to cast its scarlet hue over Shen Zechuan's embroidered python robe. His bowed neck was fair as jade. He wiped those slender, flawless fingers; they were quite clearly clean, yet he seemed to detest them to bits.

Shen Zechuan turned his head slightly. "Is he gone?"

"I saw him get into the carriage." Qiao Tianya stopped a short distance from Shen Zechuan. He didn't move forward but bent to pick a trampled leaf off the ground and scrutinized it. "The men he hired are martial masters from all over the empire, yet there's no sign that a fight broke out. Ji Gang-shifu must have been on his guard, and the grand mentor didn't resist."

"Shifu burned his face to conceal his identity and live in hiding. He's too wise to start a fight at a moment like this." Shen Zechuan folded that blue handkerchief neatly. "Xiansheng cannot remain in Xi Hongxuan's hands too long. We need to think of something."

Qiao Tianya crushed the leaf as Shen Zechuan contemplated. When Shen Zechuan suddenly turned, he was dazzled by the sunset's glow. He neither flinched nor hid from it, looking toward the towering imperial palace in the distance.

"Legitimate bloodline..." Shen Zechuan murmured. He asked Qiao Tianya, "Who lives there?"

Qiao Tianya followed the line of his gaze. "The Li Clan."

"Wrong." Shen Zechuan's eyes were cold and indifferent as he said with a mocking smile, "It's a deer—a prize for the taking. If Zhou were to lose its deer, all the heroes of the world might pursue it. Today, you say it's the Li Clan. Tomorrow, I can say it's a cabbage seller on the street. Whoever manages to sit atop the dragon throne is the rightful ruler."

Qiao Tianya prided himself on being a rebellious nonconformist, but not even he expected Shen Zechuan had the audacity to voice such a sentiment. Astonished, he took a few steps back and looked out again at the palace, musing, "Seditious words like these are tantamount to treason."

"Do you know? There are countless gentlemen in this world, good men who are steadfast and loyal." Shen Zechuan slipped the handkerchief back into his sleeve. "The Earl of Biansha, Lu Pingyan, is known as the Vicious Beast of the Border Town. He has spent his entire family fortune to defend the Bianjun Commandery. Although conferred a noble title by the emperor, all he eats are pickled vegetables and taro. As for Lu Guangbai, because he isn't on good terms with the Eight Great Clans, he's hard-pressed to fill his soldiers' bellies when war breaks out, and he's never been bestowed a noble title despite all those illustrious military achievements. So tell me, is it satisfying to be such a loyal official and honorable gentleman?"

"Before we talk about satisfaction, ask your conscience," Qiao Tianya replied. "To be an outspoken and candid minister, you must sacrifice the self and give up your personal desires for the greater good. Look at Feng Yisheng of Suotian Pass—his entire family died martyrs in battle, loyal heroes all. That is what we call the epitome of righteousness."

The madness Shen Zechuan had suppressed earlier swept over him again. He burst into laughter. "Qiao Tianya, you're not at all the free spirit you make yourself out to be. You're a prisoner to the norms. It's men like you who can truly become gentlemen."

"Master—"

The last glimmer of sun on the horizon disappeared, and darkness shrouded the courtyard. The pear tree bared its withered branches, casting long shadows over Shen Zechuan's upturned face.

"In this world, someone has to be the traitor. I don't believe fate is determined by the heavens. If the blade's against my throat, I'd show no mercy even if it was Li Jianheng holding it, let alone Xi Hongxuan. The bloodline legitimacy Xi Hongxuan speaks of is the baseless ravings of a fool. Anyone will die when a sword slashes their neck; whether one is a lawful son born to the legitimate wife or a common son born to a concubine, there's no exception."

In the cold and dreary dusk, a lone crow screeched mournfully. Shen Zechuan looked back at Qiao Tianya. "My ambition is not to be a gentleman, nor a good person. Since vindictiveness has become the tenet I live by, then a kindness given is kindness given, and a wrong done is a wrong done. Xi Hongxuan will pay with his life for what happened today."

The wind scuttled the clouds away above them, scraping the last remaining leaves off the tips of the branches.

The impeachments from the Chief Surveillance Bureau came down in a deluge. Xi Hongxuan, Pan Xiangjie, Wei Huaixing—

even Hai Liangyi—were censured one after the other. Cen Yu took charge as principal commentator as the various parties mauled one another on the floor of the imperial court.

Li Jianheng, who had just left his sickbed, hardly spoke and simply let them argue among themselves as he held court in Mingli Hall.

Hai Liangyi had been ill before this latest crisis, and lately looked to be in increasingly poor health. He'd had not a moment to rest, and now, he couldn't help but let a few sharp coughs escape as he listened to the Ministry of Works and the Ministry of Revenue arguing again.

"Secretariat Elder," Li Jianheng hurried to say, "there's no need to rise. If you have something to add, you may say it while seated."

Hai Liangyi bowed his thanks and covered his mouth with a handkerchief. When his coughing eased, he said, "The Grand Secretariat has already laid our recommendations for rewards and punishments on His Majesty's desk yesterday. If Your Majesty finds any part inappropriate after reviewing it, you may reject it and the Grand Secretariat will discuss again."

Li Jianheng had never been diligent in these things; Hai Liangyi assumed he would hem and haw. He didn't expect him to say after a moment's pause, "We've seen it. There are indeed some parts we would like to ask the secretariat elder to further clarify."

The entire hall of officials stood dumbfounded as these words left his mouth.

Li Jianheng opened the memorial. "The Imperial Army has done well in dredging the public ditches. Xiao Chiye is already a second-rank supreme commander of the Imperial Army. A reward of gold and jade is simply too meager."

"The military drill grounds on Mount Feng are undergoing expansion this year, and the money for it will be arranged by the

Ministry of Revenue," Hai Liangyi answered. "They've essentially waived his biggest expenditure this year. This humble subject feels the reward should not be overly excessive; this is sufficient."

"But managing the distribution of medicinal herbs, the quarantine of patients, and the dredging of the public ditches is no small matter," said Li Jianheng. "He has handled all of them admirably."

Hai Liangyi pondered it. "It's true he has rendered meritorious service. But these deeds were not something the Imperial Army achieved on its own. If he's shown too much special favor—"

"We would like to advance his noble rank." Li Jianheng closed the memorial and looked at Hai Liangyi. "He's the second son of lawful birth to the Prince of Libei. Had he gone into battle and slain our enemies, he would hold a noble rank and title by now."

Hai Liangyi didn't answer immediately.

"We were thinking about this in the days we were confined to our sickbed," Li Jianheng said. "We wish to confer the title of Marquis of Dingdu—'stabilizing the capital'—upon Xiao Chiye. What does the secretariat elder think?"

"You mustn't, Your Majesty," Hai Liangyi said. "Without military achievements, one cannot be conferred a noble title. Xiao Chiye has made great contributions this time, certainly, but not to the point that he can be made a marquis. The Lu Clan of Qidong's Bianjun Commandery has numerous military achievements to their name, yet only old General Lu Pingyan currently holds a title as the Earl of Biansha—one rank lower than a marquis. Xiao Chiye has not stabilized the borders, and he has not driven out any enemies. I fear it will be difficult to justify to the public why Your Majesty has made him a marquis out of the blue."

"To begin with, he rendered meritorious service protecting us at the Nanlin Hunting Grounds, and now he has, yet again, shown no fear in the face of danger. Containing the pox is a public good. This matter concerns the peace and stability of Qudu; is that not considered a merit? Meanwhile, the Earl of Biansha, Lu Pingyan, has deployed the garrison troops of Bianjun Commandery without permission on numerous occasions. His noble rank hasn't advanced because his merits and demerits offset each other." Li Jianheng's eyes reddened as he spoke. He covered his face, voice thick with emotion. "Are you saying our life is worth nothing? Our intent in bestowing the title of marquis on Xiao Chiye is to commend him. There will be no increase in the number of soldiers in the Imperial Army, nor any establishment of private rights. It's merely a title. Is this not acceptable either?"

Wei Huaigu had initially planned to impeach Xiao Chiye for distributing medicine without authorization, but seeing which way the wind was blowing, he changed tack. "Your Majesty's proposal is reasonable. Xiao Chiye's decisive and fearless action in times of danger is to be commended. But the secretariat elder makes a compelling point too. If this humble subject may make a suggestion, why not honor Xiao Chiye with the title of earl first?"

"No." Hai Liangyi wouldn't budge. "The idea is nonsensical. Your Majesty, if you grant Xiao Chiye a title today, then you'll greatly disappoint the old general at the frontier. This is an established rule of the imperial court—a noble title cannot be conferred without military achievements."

"Why not first elevate Lu Pingyan to marquis, then confer the title of earl upon Xiao Chiye?" Li Jianheng said. "Does the secretariat elder still object?"

He spoke of conferment as if titles were a child's toys, to be swapped at will.

Hai Liangyi's coughing intensified. He wanted to say more, but Pan Xiangjie beat him to it, speaking in a rush, "This humble subject thinks it's a good idea. This would be Your Majesty's first conferment since your ascension. It's a special honor. Secretariat Elder, one mustn't be a stickler for convention on every particular. Xiao Chiye has made a contribution; what's wrong with making an exception?"

Upon seeing the noble clans begin to band together in urging Li Jianheng, Kong Qiu sank down in a kowtow. "This humble subject thinks the secretariat elder has the right of it. Your Majesty, Lu Pingyan has spared no effort to defend the Bianjun Commandery. Even if he is conferred a new title, it shouldn't be decided in such a hasty and sloppy—"

"Hasty? We've painstakingly asked the opinions of everyone in attendance, yet you say we're being hasty!" Flinging his sleeves, Li Jianheng rose to his feet and pointed at Kong Qiu. "We can see you're never out of step with the secretariat elder. The sovereign and his ministers—exactly who is your sovereign, and whose minister are you?!"

The entire court of ministers knelt and chorused, "Your Majesty, please be appeased!"

Kong Qiu immediately said, "Your Majesty is this humble subject's sovereign, and this humble subject does his Majesty's bidding! Nevertheless, it is inappropriate to bypass convention and press ahead with this conferment!"

"We *will* confer the title upon him!" Li Jianheng wept. "Time and time again we've met with calamity, and it's only with Ce'an's help that we averted disaster and escape unscathed. And now that we want to bestow a title upon him, you people obstruct us at every turn! If the secretariat elder has final say over all matters of this imperial court, perhaps the secretariat elder should sit on the throne instead!"

These words struck Hai Liangyi like a knife to the heart. Unsteady on his knees, Hai Liangyi covered his mouth and coughed violently.

This man never met with officials outside the court and capital, and never held any private feasts. He worked tirelessly day and night, just to avoid being drawn into any faction or clique. And he taught and guided Li Jianheng with utmost care, all so no one could find fault with his conduct even behind his back. He was the most trustworthy minister, the right-hand man of the emperor, not some tyrannical official lusting for power!

Watching Hai Liangyi cough, doubled over where he knelt, Li Jianheng didn't dare create more of a scene. He called someone to help Hai Liangyi up. Yet he still said, "No matter what, Xiao Chiye shall be conferred a title!"

The imperial edict was issued a few days after the commotion in Mingli Hall. Almost instantly, a wave of memorials flooded in from all over.

Lu Guangbai brought his father out to receive the imperial edict at the Bianjun Commandery. Lu Pingyan was promoted to the rank of marquis. Even he was at a loss as to how to react as he held the edict in his hands.

The Lu Clan had buried generations of its people in their yellow sand. In his heyday, Lu Pingyan had been known as the Vicious Beast of the Border Town. He was renowned for his military exploits, his name spoken alongside those of Xiao Fangxu and Qi Shiyu. Now, injured and growing frail—though before he retired from active duty to take up an advisory post—he finally received his reward. Yet this honor was granted merely to pave the way for a junior of the younger generation.

Xiao Chiye was asleep in his residence when he got word of the arrival of the imperial edict. He dressed at once and came out to kneel.

After reading the emperor's words aloud, Fuman beamed and moved to help him up to receive it, only to find a pale-faced Xiao Chiye who looked as if he had no intention of doing any such thing.

This title mustn't be accepted!

What Hai Liangyi had said was true, and Xiao Chiye knew it. Though he had rendered meritorious service protecting the emperor at the Nanlin Hunting Grounds and played a critical role in the latest crisis with the ditches, his contributions were nothing compared to the hard-won military merits earned from battling with sharpened steel at the frontiers.

And who was Lu Pingyan? None other than the general his old man, Xiao Fangxu, regarded as his own brother!

Now that they had humiliated Lu Pingyan to confer a title on Xiao Chiye, how could Xiao Chiye hold his head up among the various garrison troops at the frontiers? How could he command any respect among his men? And most crucially, what would the Lu Clan think? How could Xiao and Lu still be brothers?

Dingdu... Dingdu, *stabilizing the capital.* He would be more than *stable*—this title was clearly meant to nail him down here in Qudu. Did Li Jianheng's bout of illness fucking scramble his brain?!

Rage bubbled up in Xiao Chiye, worsened by his interrupted sleep. He tugged at the official's robe he'd hastily thrown on and squashed down his fury to say expressionlessly, "Go and report back to His Majesty that Xiao Ce'an is unworthy of this title. He doesn't dare accept this overwhelming favor from His Majesty, nor this heaven-sent noble rank."

CONFERMENT

XIAO CHIYE DIDN'T dare accept the imperial edict, and Fuman didn't dare persuade him further. He hurried back to the palace to make his report.

After hearing the whole story, Li Jianheng leapt to his feet. "Are the orders of the Son of Heaven something he can reject as he pleases? When we reward him, he should kneel and accept it! Go back!"

Cursing his fate, Fuman climbed onto the horse again and returned to Xiao Chiye's residence. Finding Xiao Chiye still kneeling, he held out the imperial edict again and bowed. "Supreme Commander, Supreme Commander! Why do this? Isn't this what we crawled through the ditches for?"

"I don't want this noble rank," Xiao Chiye said with a hint of displeasure. "Don't waste your breath on me."

Fuman stamped his foot in anxiety. But he couldn't accept the edict on behalf of Xiao Chiye. All he could do was play for time.

When word of Xiao Chiye's reply was brought back to the palace, Li Jianheng flew into a rage. "Let him kneel, then! In order to reward him, we rebuffed even the secretariat elder, and he still puts on airs? Let him kneel we say!"

Thus the sovereign and his minister—one within the palace walls and the other without—remained in a deadlock.

The ground was icy in the first three months of the year. Xiao Chiye knelt with a straight back, determined to see Li Jianheng revoke his order. Perhaps he could've accepted the edict, then handled the matter in a more diplomatic fashion. But he wasn't willing.

The Lu Clan of Qidong was held in check by the Qi Clan at the top and invaded by Biansha at the bottom. They weren't in the same league as the Qi and Xiao Clans; in slighting Lu Pingyan, Li Jianheng had picked the easy target. The food and clothing expenditures of those twenty thousand troops of the Bianjun Commandery were all in the imperial court's control; they had no military fields. If they had, the Lu Clan wouldn't be forced to stoop so low demanding payment every year, or be so poor that they sold their family lands and heirlooms. When Lu Guangbai entered the capital to make his annual reports, had he ever been taken seriously? Yet which mid-ranked official in the capital would normally dare dismiss a general of the empire? They all took their cues from above. In the Xiande Emperor's day, it was rare for Lu Guangbai to successfully seek an audience with the emperor. This was more than a simple matter of being liked or disliked; it was about the balance of military power in the empire.

The Xiao and Qi were both great generals stationed at the frontiers. Yet why did the Hua Clan guard against the Prince of Libei so rigorously and go to such lengths to trap Xiao Chiye in Qudu? The Xiao Clan was the dominant force in the Libei Great Commandery—there was no leash in the entire territory that could bring them to heel, and thus Qudu could only turn Xiao Chiye into the collar that restrained the Libei Armored Cavalry. Qidong, on the other hand, had two equally celebrated generals: Qi Shiyu and Lu Pingyan. So why was Qi Shiyu eventually the one conferred the title of grand marshal of Qidong's five commanderies? Because Lu Pingyan and

Xiao Fangxu were on close terms, and on top of that, were connected through the marriage of their children.

The Lu Clan was the chess piece that served to balance the power between the three parties. Their position in the Bianjun Commandery was crucial, a heavy responsibility entrusted to them by the imperial court. Even so, the court was in no hurry to bestow titles and ranks upon them. With both the Qi Clan and the imperial court keeping them in check, the Lu Clan could only ever be a weapon used to fight foreign enemies. So long as they never became high-ranking military officials of the frontier, they would never become a second Prince of Libei.

As it stood, although Lu Guangbai was the commanding general in charge of the Bianjun Commandery's defenses, he could make no move on his own. He had to consult Qi Zhuyin for any mobilization of troops and consult the Ministry of War and Ministry of Revenue in Qudu for any disbursement of money. If Qi Zhuyin hadn't been generous in granting him the prerogative to deploy troops on his orders in times of peril, he would be in an even greater predicament than he currently was.

Now Li Jianheng had elevated Lu Pingyan's noble rank, yet it was a promotion in name only, with no accompanying rewards or authority. The Lu Clan would remain starving cattle working to their deaths at the Bianjun Commandery. Their reputation had gone up a notch on the surface, but it was an insult at the root. Half the Lu Clan's current difficulties were related to the Xiao Clan. Xiao Chiye could not—must not—accept the edict without protest.

If the imperial edict had been issued, then the Grand Secretariat had given the nod. In that case, there was no reason for the Son of Heaven to revoke his order. Yet Xiao Chiye could not meet it with great delight. Whether he had to kowtow, lash out, or even throw a tantrum, he had to show the Lu Clan his personal stance.

It was by virtue of power and might that Li Jianheng could trample the Lu Clan into the mud; the imperial court had the Lu Clan in their grasp. In contrast, it was by virtue of friendship that the Xiao Clan didn't dare do the same; both families had always regarded the other as a brother. If this friendship foundered, the Xiao Clan would lose their assistive force in the southeast.

Xiao Chiye knelt until dark. Fuman didn't dare sit; he stood at the side with the imperial edict in his hands. Eventually, they heard the sound of hurried footsteps from the entrance. A eunuch called urgently, "Supreme Commander, you may stop kneeling! Please get up! His Majesty summons you for an audience!"

Xiao Chiye lifted the hem of his robe and rose without demur, then swung astride his horse to make for the palace. Fuman scrambled onto his horse to follow. Xiao Chiye showed no signs of exhaustion, so he didn't dare complain either.

When they arrived, Mingli Hall was brightly lit. Li Jianheng sat on the dragon throne as someone announced Xiao Chiye's arrival. But he didn't summon him in; he remained seated, tracing characters at his desk.

Without a summons, Xiao Chiye could not enter. He knelt in the dark outside Mingli Hall. It was late, and the cold water that remained on the freshly scrubbed floor dampened his robe. The entire courtyard of eunuchs moved in silence, none daring to make a sound.

Li Jianheng stared blankly at the glazed lamp on his desk, sunk in thought in this silent night. By the time he returned to his senses, it was past midnight. He blinked for a moment, then suddenly rose to his feet and walked out.

The palace maids withdrew, and the eunuchs knelt where they were. Treading over their shadows, Li Jianheng crossed the floor. Xiao Chiye didn't lift his head.

Li Jianheng looked down. In the past, he had always looked up at Xiao Chiye. When they had run about on the streets together, he had considered Xiao Chiye a big brother. Xiao Chiye, too, had called him brother—they had been thick as thieves and together made every kind of mischief. Li Jianheng thought he had treated Xiao Chiye with utmost sincerity.

How had they come to this?

Li Jianheng was dressed in the emperor's vibrant yellow, a round-necked robe with narrow sleeves. He dug his thumbs into the amber belt at his waist as he moved to Xiao Chiye's side and looked up at the luminous moon hanging over the upswept palace eaves. He weighed his words for moment, then said, "There's no one else here. Let's talk."

The cold moonlight cast its pale light over them, adding to the chill of the wind.

"Aren't you usually bold and carefree?" asked Li Jianheng. "To think giving you a noble rank could scare you witless."

"It's incompatible with reason and intolerable under the law," Xiao Chiye said.

Li Jianheng paced atop the steps under the eaves. "Don't give me that. Since when are you one to speak of reason? Before the Nanlin Hunting Grounds, we were good brothers who would risk our lives for each other. After that incident, we became sovereign and minister, separated by an impassable rift. Ce'an, isn't it a good thing for me to be the emperor and you to be the supreme commander? Why do you have to put up a front with me? Just accept the rewards you're given. Cowering like this is unlike you, Xiao Ce'an."

Xiao Chiye understood what he meant. "If Your Majesty wants to reward me with gold and jewels, I'll promptly kowtow and give my thanks. But I won't do it for a noble rank. After serving as an official for six years, I have no notable achievements. I feel uneasy receiving Your Majesty's kindness and becoming a marquis with a snap of the fingers."

"What's there to be uneasy about?" Li Jianheng scoffed. "Given our relationship, you should have been conferred a title long ago. The Grand Secretariat interferes with my every move, picking at everything I do. I never had a chance before. But this time, you've earned it. When Lu Pingyan was conferred a title all those years ago, it was because he effectively resisted and repelled the Biansha Horsemen at the border. You protected the emperor in Qudu, and in doing so, ensured the safety of our empire and people. I see no difference."

"If the Grand Secretariat has qualms, there's no rush," said Xiao Chiye. "We can't hurt the old officials' feelings."

"Those old men are always thickheaded and obstinate," Li Jianheng said. "How can they be so inflexible? Even brothel girls know when to be flexible and read the room, changing their games according to time and season, yet these major ministers are still clinging to their rigid rules. How dull. After this scare, I've been thinking about many things. Whether I wished it or not, I've become the emperor. It's not productive to keep crying and whining. We all have to find some way to live on, right? I'm not an unreasonable man. If you have something to say, say it; it's not like I'll go execute anyone. I wanted to confer a title upon you, but the secretariat elder didn't agree. He led the others to oppose me, saying I was hasty and sloppy in my decisions. I spent nights tossing and turning over this, and they still say I'm too hasty!"

Li Jianheng turned as he spoke, and the golden dragon on his crown flashed in the moonlight, lending him an imposing air of elegance and nobility. He didn't tell Xiao Chiye to rise. After a long pause, he continued. "I'm the emperor; I can't renege on my word. Since the edict has been issued, you'll have to accept it. You've rebuffed me once, but we are brothers, so I won't hold it against you. But if you continue to dig your heels in, then it becomes a problem that can't be settled between brothers. Neither of us will look good then. Deal?"

Xiao Chiye was silent a moment. "Your Majesty, that won't do. The annual review is around the corner. It's a good thing to elevate old General Lu's noble rank; he deserves it. But not me. It's for the sake of Your Majesty's own reputation that I haven't accepted. I'm someone Your Majesty single-handedly promoted. If my honors don't match my deeds, how can I tend to official duties for Your Majesty in the future? Those who lead troops are concerned with their reputation and dignity. If you show old General Lu due respect, I will benefit by association too."

"Are these excuses for my sake, or are they for the sake of the Xiao Clan? Do you really think I don't understand just because you didn't say it?" Li Jianheng stared at him. "We're brothers who should treat each other with sincerity, yet you treat me like a fool. I rewarded you because of our friendship, but you turn it down out of self-interest! I told you to be candid with me, and you're still beating around the bush! Xiao Chiye," Li Jianheng bellowed, "where's your conscience?!"

The question reverberated through the cold, dreary night.

"You're afraid of offending Lu Pingyan. Why is that?!" Li Jianheng flung his sleeves. "You dare say you're loyal to us? You're doing all this for yourself! If you don't dare to say it, we'll say it for you. You're afraid of offending Lu Pingyan and ruining the friendship between your clans, which would make it hard to look out for each other in the future. But let us ask you this: The Xiao and Lu each have their respective military forces at the borders. What are you looking out for?"

Xiao Chiye clenched his fists, his thumb ring jammed in the web between thumb and forefinger.

"All of you are wolves and tigers." Li Jianheng pointed an accusing finger at Xiao Chiye. "All with your minds set on Qudu! We were merely sounding you out, and you showed your true colors! Military powers collude with one another, and the Xiao Clan makes common cause with the Lu Clan. What comes next? Tell us, what are you going to do?!"

Xiao Chiye abruptly rose onto one knee. He had an imposing physique, and kneeling like this, he resembled a panther ready to spring. Li Jianheng stumbled a few steps back and looked at him, badly shaken.

"Naturally it's to do those Biansha baldies in!" Xiao Chiye's expression was fierce as he looked at Li Jianheng. "Six years ago, when the Zhongbo troops were routed, my brother rode through the night to come to the emperor's rescue. He risked his life in that battle at Cizhou! Lu Guangbai held a spear in his hands and a dagger in his mouth and fought for three nights before he broke through the siege. He raced to Qudu without stopping to rest. Everything Your Majesty has said is an affront to the Xiao and Lu Clans' loyalty. You're right—the reason I haven't accepted the conferment is Lu Pingyan, but even more so, it's the unwavering loyalty of the generals who guard our frontiers. It's all thanks to Your Majesty's kindness that I, Xiao Ce'an, a good-for-nothing loafer, can live in Qudu without fearing for my life or worrying about heading off to war. If I can become a high-and-mighty marquis just like that, what will

Marshal Qi and General Lu, both of whom are still enduring hardships on the frontier, think?"

"More excuses. You're only doing this for your own untainted reputation!"

"My life is worthless, but Your Majesty is the ruler of our prosperous lands." Xiao Chiye's words were resolute. "If you reward me for this minor contribution and end up diminishing the generals' loyalty to Your Majesty, who would be at a greater disadvantage? Your Majesty, or me?"

Li Jianheng looked hesitant.

Xiao Chiye pressed ahead. "If this is merely a show I've put on to pander to the Lu Clan, why did Secretariat Elder Hai try so hard to dissuade Your Majesty? Your Majesty, you may not trust me, but don't you trust Hai Liangyi, whom the late emperor appointed and who has come to the emperor's rescue thrice? Your Majesty has repeatedly met with danger and misfortune, and immediately after, you dish out disproportionate rewards. Whoever it is that's instigating Your Majesty ought to have his head struck from his shoulders!"

Li Jianheng seemed to jolt to his senses. He retreated under the eaves, clutching the vermilion pillar for support. "The imperial edict has already been issued..."

"Your Majesty is the sovereign of a new reign. It was inappropriate to bestow rewards during the earlier period of state mourning. But now that the two great imperial affairs of the spring plowing and annual review are in full swing, why not seize the chance to proclaim a general amnesty and reward the generals at the frontiers according to the merit evaluation from the Ministry of War? Don't stop at advancing Lu Pingyan to the rank of Marquis of Biansha. The Lu Clan consistently exterminates the most enemies at the Bianjun Commandery, so it would be wise to reward them with an increase in military provisions. Juexi had a bumper harvest last year, and their granaries are filled to the brim. By awarding them grain, the state treasury can save on monetary rewards while relieving the Bianjun Commandery's most pressing needs. Old Commander Qi's wedding is fast approaching. Your Majesty, if you raise Third Lady Hua's status to commandery princess, you'd be raising Qidong's prestige as well."

Xiao Chiye's words were earnest, his gaze frank. "You are the sovereign of a great empire and the common ruler of our vast land. Who could still be discontent when you've bestowed such grace and favor on all?"

When the Xiande Emperor had ascended the throne, the empress dowager decided everything for him. He had thus missed his opportunity to make such a splash during his reign. Li Jianheng's dearest wish right now was to prove himself. He was suspicious and susceptible to other's provocation only because he was afraid of being declared unworthy of his position. Xiao Chiye's words pushed all the right buttons.

"All right..." Now aglow with delight, Li Jianheng came down from the steps to move toward Xiao Chiye. "All right! Ce'an, get up quickly. The ground is cold!"

Fuman, who had been kneeling below the steps all this while, listened with astonishment. Who would have thought that in just a few hours, Xiao Chiye could seize the opportunity to deal a counterattack and avert personal disaster? Xiao Chiye had a firm grasp on Li Jianheng's character—if he hadn't, he'd never have been able to hit the bullseye with a single shot.

The more Fuman thought, the more elated he grew.

There's a future for me in following the second young master!

TOAST EXCHANGE

THE SECOND MONTH of the year was a crucial time for the planting of mulberry and hemp. The various provinces hurried to submit their reports so the Ministry of Revenue might allocate funds. Mountains of trivial affairs piled up, and the ministers of the various departments grew so busy they were wan from exhaustion. Li Jianheng dispensed the planned rewards and conferments, and only then was Xiao Chiye bestowed the title of Marquis of Dingdu. Meanwhile, Shen Zechuan skipped another rank to receive a promotion to third-rank vice commander. He concurrently took up the duties of the northern judge and began to take charge of the Imperial Prison.

The Grand Secretariat initially opposed the promotion, but Cen Yu submitted a memorial with a strong recommendation of his own. After the outbreak of the pox, Hai Liangyi, too, had come to see Shen Zechuan in a new light, and thus it was decided.

Xiao Chiye carried the earring case on him, but never found an opportunity to run into Shen Zechuan. He was too busy with the Imperial Prison; as part of taking up his post, he had to go through all the cases that had accumulated before the new year one at a time. Despite being so busy he forwent meals and sleep, he still sent Qiao Tianya to keep a constant watch on Xi Hongxuan until he could find a way to rescue Qi Huilian and Ji Gang.

Young swallows clamored on roof beams, while weeping willows sprouted new shoots. The vermilion walls and green-glazed tiles of Qudu gradually appeared under the snow as the sky remained clear and sunny for several days. On a day when spring rain fell uninterrupted, Cen Yu hosted a feast and invited a few friends from the public ditches incident. Although Hai Liangyi received an invitation, he wasn't one to attend private banquets to begin with and had yet to recover from his illness. He declined.

By the time Shen Zechuan arrived, the feast had begun; he was led straight to the main hall. When he lifted the curtain, he saw a group of familiar faces.

Han Cheng, Kong Qiu, and Cen Yu shared a table. Xiao Chiye was already on his third cup of wine, listening with his elbows on the table to Yu Xiaozai—whose seat was at the bottom—telling jokes to an entire hall of important ministers.

The instant Shen Zechuan entered, Yu Xiaozai hurriedly made his obeisance. "Your Excellency is late. Please come have a seat up here."

Shen Zechuan removed his cloak with a smile. "There's much to do in the Imperial Prison; please forgive my tardiness. I'll sit lower down."

Cen Yu rose and beckoned to him. "That kind of stuffy etiquette won't do at private banquets. Once you're here, we're all friends, regardless of age. Why stand on ceremony? Lao-Han, you tell him!"

"It's just as he says," Han Cheng said. "Lanzhou, come sit up here. We useless old-timers also have the honor of being in the company of the young marquis today. Your Lordship, you have lowered yourself for us!"

"Chief Commander, how can you say so?" Xiao Chiye seemed a little drunk. He didn't look at Shen Zechuan and merely smiled. "Who here isn't a respected elder? I'll be looking to all of you for advice in the future."

Shen Zechuan had taken a seat across the wide table from Xiao Chiye; only if he stretched his legs would he be able to reach him. They exchanged no word or glance. Kong Qiu looked left and right at them and remarked with a smile, "I've long heard of the quarrel between the two of you. You won't even greet each other when you meet? You seemed to work quite well together during the flooding. Why cling to past grudges?"

"The way I see it," Cen Yu added, "both of you are promising young men, and neither deflects responsibility onto the other in your work. Why not take the chance to bury the hatchet with a smile today?" He raised his hands as he spoke. "The Embroidered Uniform Guard and the Imperial Army should look out for each other. There'll be plenty of opportunities to work together in days to come. Your Lordship, what say you?"

Xiao Chiye cast a lazy glance at Shen Zechuan, his expression indecipherable. "Why not? What wouldn't I do for a smile from Judge Shen? I should give my proper thanks to His Excellency this time too."

"Was there ever a time I didn't greet Your Lordship with a smile?" Shen Zechuan touched his wine cup. "All that's in the past. There's just been no opportunity before now, isn't that right?"

Han Cheng had shared the most drinks with Xiao Chiye. On seeing this, he took up his chopsticks again and said as he picked at the food, "Well, let's have a drink. Your Lordship, if you'll do the honors!"

Yu Xiaozai, who'd been standing all this while, promptly filled both their cups to the brim. Xiao Chiye held his in both hands and said without getting up, "Then, let's toast."

He remained seated, as befit his official rank. Shen Zechuan stood, revealing the bones of his wrist as he lifted his cup.

"Since this wine is to settle old grudges," Xiao Chiye suddenly said, "it can't be drunk in the common way. Judge, how about a nuptial exchange of wine?"

Han Cheng burst into raucous laughter. He pointed a finger at Xiao Chiye, shaking his head as he sighed, "Your Lordship, you're taking advantage. How can you put Lanzhou in such a spot?"

"How is this putting him in a spot?" Xiao Chiye said, "I can scarcely put into words how I love and respect him. Is this not meant to be an expression of our sincerity?"

Knowing Xiao Chiye's temper, Cen Yu suspected he still held a grudge over Zhongbo and meant to make things difficult for Shen Zechuan. Just as he steeled himself to speak up and dissuade Xiao Chiye, Shen Zechuan laughed.

"Sure," Shen Zechuan said. "We'll do as His Lordship says."

He held up the cup and leaned across the table, giving Xiao Chiye the faintest glimpse of his collarbone. Their arms intertwined. Shen Zechuan's throat bobbed as he swallowed; he could feel Xiao Chiye watching him. His gaze seemed to follow the wine down into that robe.

Xiao Chiye drank slowly. He held the wine in his mouth, his eyes never leaving Shen Zechuan. Shen Zechuan could feel his sturdiness where their arms were linked. When he finished, Xiao Chiye seemed to laugh, yet no one heard it; only Shen Zechuan lowered his eyes to look at him. His gaze was naked, brimming with dangerous desire.

Shen Zechuan withdrew his arm and sat back down, his back clammy with sweat. Xiao Chiye seemed unfazed. He leaned his elbows on the table again and tilted his head to listen to the conversation.

Cen Yu was speaking. "After the spring planting, it'll be the spring examinations. The Imperial College hopes to recruit new students

this year. The upkeep of so many students—looks like the Ministry of Revenue is in for another headache."

Kong Qiu snorted a laugh. "What does Wei Huaigu have to complain about? He's the money-keeper! It's his job to budget for it. To begin with, all of this should've been arranged much earlier. For him to wait till now to do it is already dereliction of duty."

"He's the money-keeper, and you're the living King of Hell!" Han Cheng set down his chopsticks, satiated with wine and food. "Zhongbo is a right mess, and the cases submitted to the Ministry of Justice from the six prefectures are as many as the hairs on an ox. They can't delay sending someone over to take charge there, can they?"

"The secretariat elder is still mulling over whom to send." Cen Yu lamented. "If Lanzhou formally joins the central administration as a court official, then he might have a chance at it."

Whether because of the heat or the wine, Shen Zechuan's face was slightly flushed. "I can't," he said. "I'm not yet qualified to be assigned out of the capital. I couldn't put down the unrest."

"Gain a little more experience and you'd do fine." Han Cheng's interest was piqued. "It's said officials from the capital are wily. But how can the capital officials be as slippery and sly as the provincial ones? Some years ago, I went to the outer regions with the Chief Surveillance Bureau to audit the accounts, and I tell you those 'local lords' and 'old masters' are a cunning bunch! They held two versions of all the account books in their residences. Cen Xunyi, even if you went yourself, you couldn't distinguish the real from the fake."

He continued, warming to his subject, "Every year when the imperial envoy heads down, there's a great flurry of activity. They get the news well in advance and drive away all the disaster victims and refugees in their territories before your arrival. You'll never see them—

this is the so-called *No hunger concern in the territory* you see in the evaluations. Once you arrive, they'll hold a banquet and think of all kinds of reasons to ply you with wine. You'll drink until daybreak, then sleep until nightfall. You'll be so drunk you can't even walk out of the prefectural yamen on your own feet. What energy would you have to check the accounts? Once the time is up and the silver is pocketed, the evaluation will be marked *Outstanding* and it's off to the next place to drink. That's considered the end of the audit."

"But there are still those who do their jobs," Cen Yu pointed out. "You can't tar them all with the same brush." He sighed. "When Xue Xiuzhuo went out a few years ago, he was a formidable force. All the accounts of the thirteen cities of Juexi were sorted out in perfect order without a single error. I really thought he would be assigned to the Ministry of Revenue. Who would've expected the secretariat elder to transfer him to the Court of Judicial Review instead?"

"Can he get anywhere as Wei Huaigu's subordinate?" Kong Qiu leaned back in his chair. He never had social dealings with Wei Huaigu and Pan Xiangjie. Everyone knew he was friendly with them in public but held them in little regard in private, so he wasn't afraid to speak out in Han Cheng's presence. "The current Vice Minister of the Ministry of Revenue might as well not exist. Wei Huaigu alone calls the shots; it's his final say in the overall management of finances. Wouldn't Xue Xiuzhuo be rendered useless there? The secretariat elder means to polish him; he intends him to achieve great things in the future."

Han Cheng laughed out loud. "Don't discuss state affairs at a private feast! How can you forget this? Lao-Kong, you ought to be punished!"

Seeing they were nearly done with their meal, Cen Yu said, "When Youjing here returned a few days ago, he told me about a game.

The night is young; why don't we give it a try? Youjing, take out those cards of yours."

Yu Xiaozai readily produced a wooden box, which he opened to reveal a small stack of carved wooden cards. "This humble subordinate learned this game when I went to the Port of Yongyi for inspection—you compose paired couplets to match the cards. My lords, would you like to give it a go?"

Han Cheng turned to Xiao Chiye. "I'm no good at literary games like this. Your Lordship, how about giving me some tips?"

Xiao Chiye sipped his wine. "Does the chief commander think so highly of Xiao Ce'an? Do I look like a man who reads?"

"It's all in good fun. Why not give it a try? Youjing, deal the cards!"

Yu Xiaozai dealt to Han Cheng, Xiao Chiye, and Cen Yu. Xiao Chiye fiddled with his wine cup; he had just given the cards a glance when something brushed his calf under the table. He paused and fixed his gaze on Han Cheng's hand.

Han Cheng frowned down at his cards. "What am I supposed to do with these flowers and plants! Your Lordship, do you recognize this?"

"Throw them a line based on foxtail grass," said Xiao Chiye. "I guarantee—"

A socked foot tapped Xiao Chiye's knee, its sole stepping on his kneecap as if testing its position.

"Guarantee they'll be stumped!" Han Cheng tossed a card out and said with a smile, "*The swallow teases the foxtail, spring arrives.* There, I composed the first line of a couplet. Go ahead, Xunyi, pair it up!"

Han Cheng wasn't a learned man, but he didn't let that hold him back; on hearing his bold attempt, Kong Qiu and Cen Yu laughed. As the three men chatted, Xiao Chiye shot a glance at Shen Zechuan.

Shen Zechuan was grasping his fan, a little bamboo one Xiao Chiye had sent him. He tapped it intermittently on the table as he listened to the conversation. As if sensing Xiao Chiye's gaze on him, the corners of his eyes curved in a tiny smile.

Beneath the table, that foot had slid between Xiao Chiye's legs, nudging the inside of his thigh as though seeking something. Xiao Chiye held the wine cup with his thumb pressed hard against the rim; otherwise he remained motionless.

After a while, Xiao Chiye laughed. "Isn't that a fox?" He picked out an ink-traced fox from among Han Cheng's cards and tossed it onto the table. "*A leaky roof meets a rainy night; a vixen whispers in my dream. Where to seek the tide of spring? In that drip-drop lies the hint.* Sorry, I made it dirty."

Han Cheng exchanged a toast with Xiao Chiye, then laughed again. "We're being serious here, yet you've gone and turned the fox into a vixen!" The foot slid slowly down Xiao Chiye's calf, brushing a few times along the curve of muscle.

"Well, men like me..." Xiao Chiye drank his wine and looked at Shen Zechuan. "...simply attract foxes."

"How is any respectable person supposed to follow that? Vixens and spring tides—it's too crude." Kong Qiu laughed, then sighed. "Xiao Ce'an, you don't even latch the door when you sleep. How can you blame someone when they come looking for action? You're obviously looking for it yourself."

Xiao Chiye didn't immediately reply. But when that foot stepped gently down on him, he laughed. The upper half of Shen Zechuan's body was so steady nothing seemed amiss. He left off tapping the fan and rubbed his fingertips together. In the stuffy room, Xiao Chiye could almost see the flush creeping into the corners of those eyes.

Just then, Cen Yu dropped his card on the ground. Yu Xiaozai immediately stopped what he was doing and made to lean over and pick it up.

Shen Zechuan prepared to retract his foot, but unexpectedly, Xiao Chiye reached down and grabbed hold of his ankle. His sole was stepping on Xiao Chiye's heated arousal through the fabric. Xiao Chiye slipped two fingers into his white sock and stroked his ankle.

Fan brushing the table, Shen Zechuan's hand dropped to the wooden surface. Yu Xiaozai had hiked up the hem of his robe and was bending down. "My lords, please lift your feet. Let this humble subordinate see where it has fallen."

Xiao Chiye was unruffled as he gripped Shen Zechuan's ankle. He exerted gentle force with his thumb, caressing the skin in his grasp until Shen Zechuan felt a tingle up his spine. He tightened his grip on the fan.

NIGHT RIDE

YU XIAOZAI was already squatting down when Xiao Chiye dropped his wine cup. Han Cheng, being nearest, suffered a stained robe. The cards were abandoned as Yu Xiaozai sprang up to fetch a handkerchief for Han Cheng to clean himself. Cen Yu had still been squinting at his cards when the wine splashed him. He hastily tried to dodge, prompting a loud laugh from Kong Qiu.

Han Cheng tugged at his sodden robe. "Your Lordship, you've had too much to drink; your hands are unsteady!"

Xiao Chiye raised his hands in apology. "Forgive me, forgive me. I'll have someone send you a replacement tomorrow as compensation."

"Forget it, it's only a set of robes." How could Han Cheng let Xiao Chiye compensate him? He bent his mouth into a smile. "We'll treat this cup as a toast from Your Lordship."

Shen Zechuan had withdrawn his foot. He leaned over and picked up the card from the floor. As he placed it on the table, he heard Xiao Chiye laughing. The lingering warmth on his ankle seemed to grow hotter amid that sound.

Now quite drunk, Kong Qiu struck a porcelain cup with his chopsticks and sang out incomprehensible lyrics, adding to the chaotic atmosphere. He was the polar opposite of his habitual demeanor in court.

Cen Yu, seeing Kong Qiu making such a spectacle of himself, tugged on his sleeve. "Boran! Stop singing. Go home and sleep! You still need to preside over Xi Hongxuan's trial the day after tomorrow!"

Kong Qiu lifted his cup higher and struck it with increasing glee. "I didn't forget. I'm investigating him!"

"Thankfully I was the one who invited you to this feast," Cen Yu said, struggling to keep hold of him. "Or else you would surely be impeached for behaving in such an uncouth manner."

"Let them impeach!" cried Kong Qiu. "Let them impeach! Imperial censors ought to have the courage to speak."

"Right, well said!" Han Cheng laughed. "We've all been saddled with such a massive pile of work we can scarcely breathe. How often can we enjoy ourselves to the fullest? Let the man sing!"

"It's time to wind down," said Xiao Chiye. "If we're carousing too late at night, the secretariat elder'll have our hides." He got to his feet and called to Chen Yang, "Send Lord Kong back in my horse carriage!"

The attendants swarmed in, and Chen Yang helped Kong Qiu out the door. Cen Yu wiped sweat from his brow and told the remaining men, "You don't know this, but Boran was also once an unconventional and uninhibited person. The secretariat elder is rigid about self-restraint and propriety; he had him whipped into shape. See what happens when you drink too much of this wine. Everyone, wait a moment while I tell the cook to put on some soup to sober you up. Drink it before you leave!"

"I was just thinking about your residence's dough drop soup!"

Han Cheng didn't stand on formality. "I'll take lots of vinegar in mine and drink it before leaving."

Shen Zechuan bowed. "The Imperial Prison still has urgent cases to be processed tomorrow morning, so I'm afraid I can't stay. Everyone, please enjoy your meal. If time permits in the future, I'll invite everyone for another round."

Han Cheng knew Shen Zechuan was indeed busy of late. "When you held the post of southern judge, you kept a close eye on the military craftsmen. Now that you've transferred to the office of the northern judge, there's no need for you to burn the candle at both ends. The men will remember your kind treatment; they won't make things too difficult for you."

Shen Zechuan murmured his acknowledgment.

Cen Yu insisted on sending him off. Shen Zechuan had no way to politely decline, so they walked out the doors together. The rain had grown heavier, and the city was covered in a thick layer of fog. The gust of cool air dispelled their wine-induced heat, leaving both refreshed.

Cen Yu led Shen Zechuan down the steps. "You must have pushed back a great deal of work to make time for our feast tonight."

"It wasn't too bad. The most urgent cases were finalized before today," Shen Zechuan replied with a smile.

Cen Yu nodded. "That's good. Assignments cannot be delayed."

He accompanied Shen Zechuan all the way to the gates, where he ordered someone to hold an umbrella and lantern for him. Cen Yu had a true appreciation for Shen Zechuan's talents—it was a pity this man served in the Embroidered Uniform Guard.

He couldn't help giving him some advice. "All the cases in the Imperial Prison are major affairs; not even the Three Judicial Offices can interfere," Cen Yu said. "In coming into this position, you've enjoyed what some would call a meteoric rise. You must speak with caution and act with prudence. They say standing close to the sovereign is as perilous as lying with a tiger—those who work well in the presence of the emperor are all born intelligent and quick-witted. But you needn't worry overmuch about your qualifications. You're already remarkably successful, given your youth. You have a long way ahead of you; just remember there's no need to be anxious about anything other than your assignments."

He paused. "The Marquis of Dingdu isn't a narrow-minded man either. You two are bound to work together in the future. Tonight you've buried the hatchet with a toast. Perhaps you'll never be soulmates, but it's still better to be friends who can look out for each other than enemies who clash each time you meet. Lanzhou, you're a talented young man. I hope to see you work hard and achieve success in your career!"

Cen Yu spoke with such sincerity Shen Zechuan was moved in spite of himself. He bowed low; Cen Yu helped him up, saying, "The road is slippery on rainy nights. Be careful on your way. Off you go."

At last Shen Zechuan pulled on the pristinely white fur coat Li Jianheng had bestowed on him and bade farewell to Cen Yu. He didn't step into the sedan but let Qiao Tianya hold up the umbrella for him as master and servant walked into the rain.

The two hadn't been walking long when the thunder of hoofbeats rose behind them. Qiao Tianya shook rainwater off the umbrella as he stepped aside; as expected, he saw Xiao Chiye on horseback, galloping toward them at full speed.

"Good timing. I—"

Qiao Tianya's voice was drowned out as Xiao Chiye bent to scoop Shen Zechuan up onto his horse and galloped off with him.

The water droplets kicked up by Snowcrest's hooves soaked Qiao Tianya. He spread his arms open and slowly finished, "—want to drink some shaojiu."

Xiao Chiye was strong and well-built. Even holding Shen Zechuan in his arms didn't slow him down. He hugged Shen Zechuan tightly to his chest, firm as an iron wall.

Snowcrest galloped through the rain like a bolt of lightning through the stormy dark. Its hooves sped over countless puddles, throwing up a spray of water as it charged for the city gates.

The guard at the top of the wall raised his lantern. "Who goes there?! Who's riding so late at night?!"

Xiao Chiye pulled his cloak up to fold Shen Zechuan under it before raising his authority token. "Open the gates."

"Supreme...Marquis!" The platoon commander atop the wall immediately made obeisance, then waved his hands and ordered, "Quick, open the gates!"

The gates opened with a deafening rumble, and Snowcrest shot through like an arrow. Night wind whipped against their cheeks. Snowcrest galloped faster and faster, while a circling gyrfalcon burst out from the rain and followed closely behind.

Shen Zechuan held onto Snowcrest's neck. "We can't go far. Tomorrow morning—"

Xiao Chiye grabbed Shen Zechuan's chin and lifted it to kiss him. Shen Zechuan was no practiced rider; other than Xiao Chiye, he had nothing to hold on to as they raced like the wind. With one hand pressed against the galloping horse and the other clutching Xiao Chiye for support, there was no way to look at the road in front of them. The driving rain stung his eyes as they kissed.

They hadn't seen each other for seven or eight days.

Xiao Chiye embraced Shen Zechuan tightly with one hand, pressing him to his chest as he kissed down along his cheek to the side of his neck.

Shen Zechuan's clothes were in disarray, the official's robe beneath his white fur coat tugged open. When he lifted his eyes, all he could see was the jet-black expanse of rain. Water droplets trickled along the curve of his collar, drenching his clothes and chilling his skin. He crushed Xiao Chiye's robe in his hand and gasped for breath.

The rain poured harder and louder as Snowcrest ran blindly into the black. The path before them was hidden in the long, dark night, the horse like a lone boat carrying a pair of lovers on their secret rendezvous. Shen Zechuan shivered. He closed his eyes as he took Xiao Chiye in, bathed in sweat and rainwater. Xiao Chiye said nothing as the horse's hooves trod through the mud. The path was uneven; each bump and jolt drew a gasp from Shen Zechuan's lips.

Xiao Chiye too was sweating lightly with exertion. Spurred by the potent wine, he clung to Shen Zechuan in this wild moment of pleasure, making every rise and fall strike just the right spot. He was in high spirits after this evening, and he used his strength skillfully, leaving Shen Zechuan incapable of resistance and unable to escape.

"Are you satisfied now?" Seeing that Shen Zechuan wanted to lean away, Xiao Chiye clasped his hand and pulled him back to enclose him in his arms.

Pressed tight against him, Shen Zechuan said, "Mmm..."

"Next time, make sure you get the right spot."

Xiao Chiye's hand came up to stroke Shen Zechuan's earlobe, fastening an object there. He pushed aside those drenched locks and kissed it.

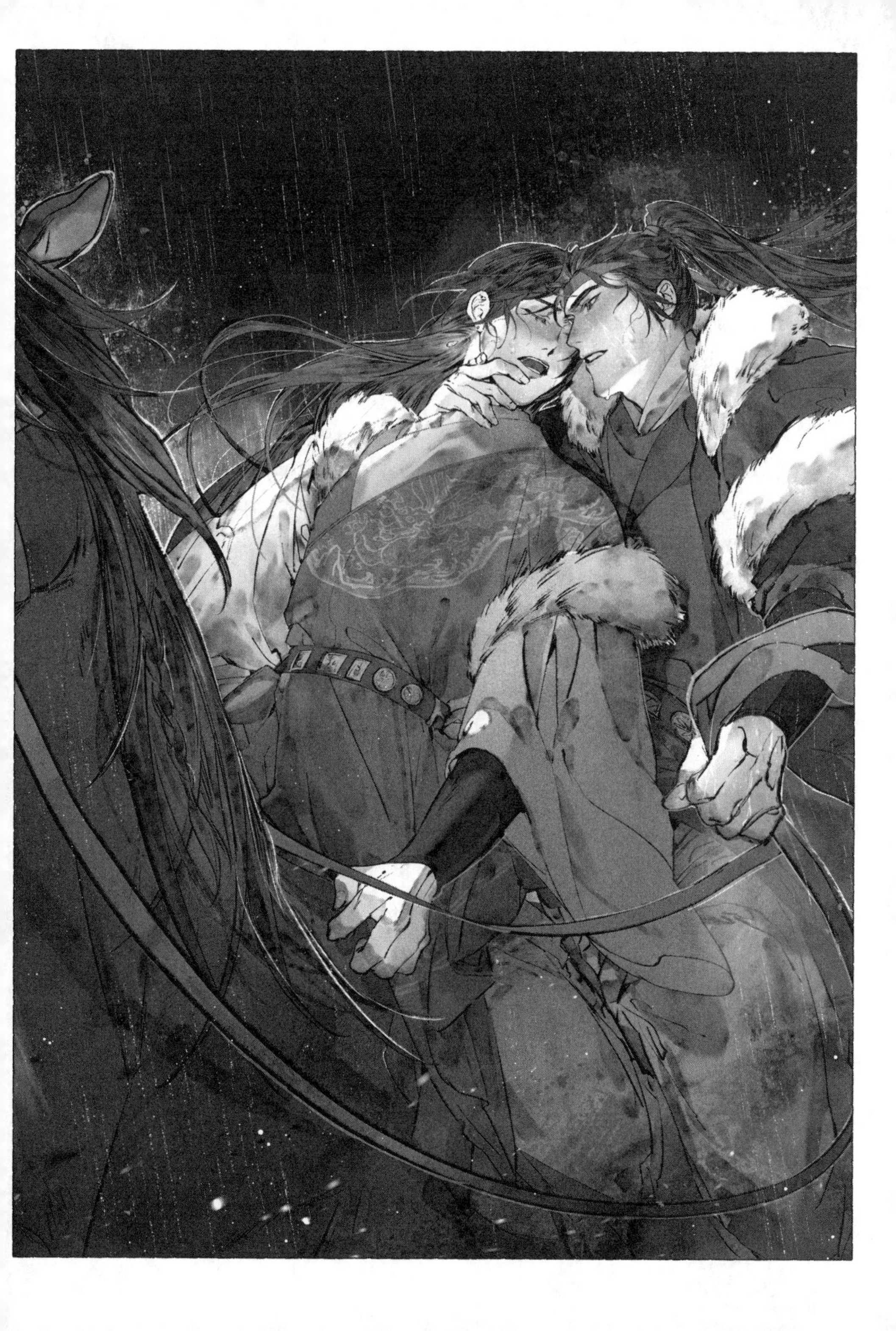

Shen Zechuan raised his head, and the jade earring swayed with his movement. He touched the pendant in a daze. Several times, he opened his mouth to speak but was disrupted by a jarring step and his gasps for breath. Riding the waves of euphoria, he gazed at Xiao Chiye with a conflicting blend of understanding and incomprehension.

Xiao Chiye killed off his last remaining inhibitions. He was done holding back.

A warm spring day was bad news indeed—this was the season for fun. Scoundrels all liked to have fun. As long as they were together, they could stir up a wave from calm waters; every time their eyes met, it was with impure motives. The shiver up each of their spines when they seduced each other was so strong it could shake apart their masks of decency. No one understood the ardent desire burning beneath their officials' robes.

As long as they were alone, they would bare their true colors.

THE STORY CONTINUES IN

Ballad of Sword and Wine

VOLUME 3

CHARACTER & NAME GUIDE

CHARACTERS

MAIN CHARACTERS

Shen Zechuan

沈泽川 SURNAME SHEN; GIVEN NAME ZECHUAN, "TO NOURISH THE RIVERS"

COURTESY NAME: Lanzhou (兰舟 / orchid; boat)

TITLE: Member of the Embroidered Uniform Guard

WEAPON: Avalanche (仰山雪 / Yang Shan Xue)

The eighth son of common birth to Shen Wei, the Prince of Jianxing. Due to his father's alleged collusion with the enemy during the invasion of Zhongbo that led to the slaughter of thirty thousand soldiers in the Chashi Sinkhole, he was sentenced to imprisonment and was obligated to pay his father's debt as the last surviving member of the Shen Clan.

Xiao Chiye

萧驰野 SURNAME XIAO; GIVEN NAME CHIYE, "TO RIDE ACROSS THE WILD"

COURTESY NAME: Ce'an (策安 / spur; peace)

TITLE: Supreme Commander of the Imperial Army

WEAPON: Wolfsfang (狼戾 / Langli): A single-edged executioner's blade forged by the best craftsman in Qidong.

The second and youngest son of lawful birth to Xiao Fangxu, the Prince of Libei. Sometimes called Xiao Er, or Second Young Master Xiao.

QUDU

CEN YU 岑愈: Courtesy name Xunyi. The Left Censor-in-Chief of the Chief Surveillance Bureau.

CHEN YANG 晨阳 ("MORNING SUN"): Leader of Xiao Chiye's guards.

DING TAO 丁桃: Young guard to Xiao Chiye. He carries a little notebook everywhere he goes.

FENGQUAN 风泉: A junior eunuch, Pan Rugui's "grand-godson" and Mu Ru's younger brother.

FU LINYE 傅林叶: The Right Censor-in-Chief of the Chief Surveillance Bureau.

GE QINGQING 葛青青: Judge of the Embroidered Uniform Guard who served under Ji Gang when the latter was still the vice commander.

GU JIN 骨津: Guard to Xiao Chiye. He has excellent hearing.

HAI LIANGYI 海良宜 ("VIRTUOUS AND PROPER"): Courtesy name Renshi. Deputy Grand Secretary of the Grand Secretariat and teacher to Yao Wenyu.

HAN CHENG 韩丞: Chief Commander of the Embroidered Uniform Guard after Ji Lei's death.

HAN JIN 韩靳: Military Commissioner of the Eight Great Battalions after Xiao Chiye's suspension.

HUA HEWEI 花鹤娓: The empress dowager, widow of the Guangcheng Emperor.

HUA XIANGYI 花香漪 ("RIPPLES OF FRAGRANCE"): The third lady of the Hua Clan, adored niece of the empress dowager. Betrothed to Qi Shiyu.

JI GANG 纪纲: Shen Zechuan's shifu. Once the vice commander of the Embroidered Uniform Guard, he is one of the three adopted sons of Ji Wufan, the former chief commander of the Embroidered Uniform Guard.

JIANG QINGSHAN 江青山: Provincial Administration Commissioner of Juexi.

KONG QIU 孔湫: Courtesy name Boran. Minister of Justice.

LI JIANHENG 李建恒: The Tianchen Emperor. As the final survivor of the Li Clan, he ascended the throne after the death of the Xiande Emperor.

LI JIANYUN 李建云: The Xiande Emperor. Son of the Guangcheng Emperor and elder brother to Li Jianheng.

LIANG CUISHAN 梁漼山: A clerk in the Ministry of Revenue.

MU RU 慕如: Imperial Concubine Mu. The daughter of a common family and sister to Fengquan. Adored by Li Jianheng, she was officially appointed as an imperial concubine after his ascension.

PAN XIANGJIE 潘祥杰: Minister of Works. Head of the Pan Clan of the Eight Great Clans.

QI HUILIAN 齐惠连: Grand mentor to the deceased Crown Prince of Yongyi, and later, Shen Zechuan's teacher.

QIAO TIANYA 乔天涯: Previously named Qiao Songyue. The former judge of the Embroidered Uniform Guard, he now takes Shen Zechuan as his master.

TANTAI HU 澹台虎 ("TIGER"): Member of the Imperial Army.

WEI HUAIGU 魏怀古: Minister of Revenue.

WEI HUAIXING 魏怀兴: Vice Minister of the Court of Judicial Review.

XI HONGXUAN 奚鸿轩: Secretary of the Bureau of Evaluations in the Ministry of Personnel. Xi Gu'an's brother and the second son of lawful birth in the Xi Clan.

XUE XIUZHUO 薛修卓: Courtesy name Yanqing. Assistant Minister in the Court of Judicial Review. A capable young official and son of common birth in the Xue Clan.

YAO WENYU 姚温玉 ("GENTLE JADE"): Courtesy name Yuanzhuo. Hai Liangyi's only acknowledged pupil, said to be an extraordinary talent.

YU XIAOZAI 余小再: Courtesy name Youjing. Investigating Censor in the Chief Surveillance Bureau.

LIBEI

XIAO FANGXU 萧方旭 ("RISING SUN"): Prince of Libei. Father to Xiao Chiye and Xiao Jiming, and one of the past Four Great Generals of the empire of Zhou.

XIAO JIMING 萧既明 ("APPROACHING BRIGHTNESS"): Heir of Libei and commander of the Libei Armored Cavalry. Xiao Chiye's elder brother; he is married to Lu Yizhi, Lu Guangbai's sister. One of the current Four Great Generals, he's known as "Iron Horse on River Ice."

LU YIZHI 陆亦栀: Heir Consort of Libei. Xiao Jiming's wife and Lu Guangbai's sister.

ZHAO HUI 朝晖 ("MORNING SUN"): Xiao Jiming's dependable deputy general.

ZUO QIANQIU 左千秋: Xiao Chiye's shifu and one of the current Four Great Generals, he's known as "Thunder on Jade Terraces."

QIDONG

QI ZHUYIN 戚竹音 ("SOUND OF BAMBOO"): Grand Marshal of the Qidong Garrison Troops. One of the current Four Great Generals, Qi Zhuyin is known as "Windstorm through the Scorching Plains" and commands all five garrisons in the commanderies of Qidong.

QI SHIYU 戚时雨 ("TIMELY RAIN"): Qi Zhuyin's father and one of the past Four Great Generals of the empire of Zhou.

LU GUANGBAI 陆广白 ("EMPTY EXPANSE"): Commanding general of the Bianjun Commandery in Qidong. Brother to Lu Yizhi and one of the current Four Great Generals, known as "Beacon-Smoke and Rising Sand."

LU PINGYAN 陆平烟 ("PACIFY BEACON SMOKE"): Lu Guangbai's father and one of the past Four Great Generals of the Zhou empire.

PAST

SHEN WEI 沈卫 ("DEFENSE"): Prince of Jianxing and Shen Zechuan's father. Found guilty of colluding with the Biansha Horsemen to invade Zhongbo, he allegedly self-immolated to evade justice.

JI MU 纪暮: The only son of Ji Gang and Hua Pingting, and Shen Zechuan's adoptive elder brother.

HUA PINGTING 花娉婷: Wife of Ji Gang and mother of Ji Mu; Shen Zechuan's shiniang. She was born in the Hua Clan.

INSTITUTIONS

The Embroidered Uniform Guard 锦衣卫

The Embroidered Uniform Guard, sometimes referred to as the Scarlet Cavalry, are the elite bodyguards who report directly to the emperor. They are a non-military secret police and investigative force. The Embroidered Uniform Guard is organized into the Twelve Offices, which include the Carriage Office, Umbrella Office, Elephant-Training Office, and Horse-Training Office, among others. The Xiuchun saber, a single-edged blade, is their signature weapon.

The Imperial Army 禁军

The Imperial Army of Qudu was once the Imperial Guard of the eight cities and the impregnable fortress of the imperial palace in Qudu. However, with the rise to power of the Eight Great Battalions, their duties were reduced significantly, and the Imperial Army became a dumping ground for sons from old military households. They are one of the two major military powers in Qudu.

The Eight Great Battalions 八大营

Led by a member of the Eight Great Clans, the Eight Great Battalions are one of the two major military powers in Qudu, tasked with patrolling and defending Qudu against external forces. Responsible for defending Qudu, the capital city and heart of the Zhou empire, the Eight Great Battalions hold the empire's life in their hands.

The Eight Great Clans 八大家

The Eight Great Clans originated from the Eight Cities of Qudu. One clan holds sway in each city—the Xue Clan of Quancheng, Pan Clan of Dancheng, Xi Clan of Chuncheng, Fei Clan of Chuancheng, Hua Clan of Dicheng, Yao Clan of Jincheng, Han Clan of Wucheng, and Wei Clan of Cuocheng.

The Grand Secretariat 内阁

The most distinguished and influential body in the central government, it is staffed with Grand Secretaries who are responsible for handling the emperor's paperwork, recommending decisions in response to memorials received from the officials, and drafting and issuing imperial pronouncements.

The Six Ministries 六部

The Six Ministries comprise the primary administrative structure of the Zhou empire's central government and include the Ministry of Works, Ministry of Justice, Ministry of Personnel, Ministry of Rites, Ministry of Revenue, and Ministry of War. Coordinated by the Grand Secretary of the Grand Secretariat, the heads of these ministries report directly to the emperor.

The Six Offices of Scrutiny is an independent agency set up to inspect and supervise the Six Ministries. It includes the Office of Scrutiny for Revenue.

Chief Surveillance Bureau 都察院

Also known as the Censorate. One of the major agencies of the central government, responsible for maintaining disciplinary surveillance, auditing fiscal accounts, checking judicial records, carrying out inspections, impeaching officials for misconduct, recommending new policies and changes in old policies, and other duties involved in regulating government actions.

The Court of Judicial Review 大理寺

An important central government agency responsible for reviewing reports of judicial proceedings, making recommendations for retrials, and participating in important judicial proceedings at court alongside the Chief Surveillance Bureau and the Ministry of Justice, which are collectively known as the Three Judicial Offices.

The Libei Armored Cavalry 离北铁骑

The Libei Armored Cavalry is a heavy cavalry established by Xiao Fangxu to counter external foes at the northern front during the

Yongyi era, when the Biansha Horsemen repeatedly assaulted Luoxia Pass. Currently commanded by Xiao Jiming, the Heir of Libei.

The Qidong Garrison Troops 启东守备军

Under the command of Qi Zhuyin, the Qidong Commandery Garrison Troops are stationed across five commanderies. They watch over the Qidong territories in the southern regions of the Zhou empire, which are led by the Qi Clan.

The Biansha Horsemen 边沙骑兵

The Biansha Horsemen are the aggressor forces against the empire of Zhou. The story begins with the aftermath of the war, where the Biansha Horsemen ravaged the six prefectures of Zhongbo and left them piled high with bodies. Also referred to in derogatory form as the "Biansha baldies."

The Twenty-Four Yamen 二十四衙门

Collectively refers to the Twelve Directorates, Four Offices, and Eight Services under which eunuchs serve.

NAMES GUIDE

NAMES, HONORIFICS, AND TITLES

Courtesy Names vs Given Names

Usually made up of two characters, a courtesy name is given to an individual when they come of age. Traditionally, this was at the age of twenty during one's crowning ceremony, but it can also be presented when an elder or teacher deems the recipient worthy. Though generally a male-only tradition, there is historical precedent for women adopting a courtesy name after marriage. Courtesy names were a tradition reserved for the upper class.

It was considered disrespectful for one's peers of the same generation to address someone by their given name, especially in formal or written communication. Use of one's given name was reserved only for elders, close friends, and spouses.

This practice is no longer used in modern China but is commonly seen in historically inspired media. As such, many characters have more than one name. Its implementation in novels is irregular and is often treated malleably for the sake of storytelling.

Diminutives, nicknames, and name tags

A-: Friendly diminutive. Always a prefix. Usually for monosyllabic names, or one syllable out of a two-syllable name.

XIAO-: A diminutive prefix meaning "little."

-ER: An affectionate diminutive suffix added to names, literally "son" or "child." Not to be confused with Xiao Chiye's nickname, Xiao Er, in which "er" (二) means "second."

LAO-: A diminutive prefix meaning "old."

-ZI: Affectionate suffix meaning "son" or "child."

-XIONG: A word meaning elder brother. It can be attached as a suffix to address an older male peer.

Family

DI/DIDI: Younger brother or a younger male friend.

GE/GEGE/DAGE: Older brother or an older male friend.

JIE/JIEJIE: Older sister or an older female friend.

-SHU: A suffix meaning "uncle." Can be used to address unrelated older men.

Martial Arts and Tutelage

SHIFU: Teacher or master, usually used when referring to the martial arts.

SHIXIONG: Older martial brother, used for older disciples or classmates.

SHIDI: Younger martial brother, used for younger disciples or classmates.

SHISHU: Martial uncle, used to address someone who studied under the same master (or shifu) as one's own master.

SHINIANG: The wife of one's shifu.

XIANSHENG: Teacher of academics.

Other

GONGZI: Young man from an affluent household.

-NIANGNIANG: Term of address for the empress or an imperial concubine, can be standalone or attached to a name as a suffix.

-GONGGONG: Term of address for a eunuch.

SHIZI: Title for the heir apparent of a feudal prince.

LAO-ZUZONG: Literally "old ancestor," an intimate and respectful term of address from a junior eunuch to a more senior eunuch.

GLOSSARY

GLOSSARY

CONCUBINES AND THE IMPERIAL HAREM: In ancient China, it was common practice for a wealthy man to take women as concubines in addition to his wife. They were expected to live with him and bear him children. Generally speaking, a greater number of concubines correlated to higher social status; hence a wealthy merchant might have two or three concubines, while an emperor might have tens or even a hundred.

The imperial harem had its own ranking system. The exact details vary over the course of history, but can generally be divided into three overarching ranks: the empress, consorts, and concubines. The status of a prince or princess's mother is an important factor in their status in the imperial family, in addition to birth order and their own personal merits. Given the patrilineal rules of succession, the birth of a son could also elevate the mother's status.

CUT-SLEEVE: A slang term for a gay man, which comes from a tale about Emperor Ai's love for, and relationship with, a male court official in the Han dynasty. The emperor was called to the morning assembly, but his lover was asleep on his robe. Rather than wake him, the emperor cut off his own sleeve.

IMPERIAL EXAMINATION SYSTEM: The system of examinations in ancient China that qualified someone for official service. It was intended to be a meritocratic system that allowed common civilians to rise up in society as a countering force to the nobility, but the extent to which this was true varied across time.

The imperial examination system was split into various levels. In the Ming and Qing dynasties, these were the provincial exam, metropolitan exam, and the palace exam. The top scholars at each examination level were known as the Jieyuan, Huiyuan, and Zhuangyuan respectively, and a scholar who emerged top at all three levels was known as the Sanyuan, or Triple Yuan, scholar.

KOWTOW: The kowtow (叩头 / "knock head") is an act of prostration where one kneels and bows low enough that their forehead touches the ground. A show of deep respect and reverence that can also be used to beg, plead, or show sincerity; in severe circumstances, it's common for the supplicant's forehead to end up bloody and bruised.

LAWFUL AND COMMON BIRTH HIERARCHY: Upper-class men in ancient China often took multiple wives. Only one would be the official wife, and her lawful sons would take precedence over the common sons of the concubines. Sons of lawful birth were prioritized in matters of inheritance. They also had higher social status and often received better treatment compared to the other common sons born to concubines or mistresses.

MANDARIN SQUARES: Large embroidered badges worn by civil officials of the imperial court. Depending on their pattern, which might incorporate real or mythical animals, flowers, and other symbols, these badges could indicate either the rank of the wearer, the season, or the occasion on which the badge was worn. For example, a mandarin square with a double gourd was worn between the twenty-third day of the twelfth month and the New Year.

Similarly, an emblem of tiger, mugwort, and five poisons (centipede, scorpion, toad, lizard, snake) was worn in celebration of the Duanwu Festival and Summer Solstice.

NEW YEAR AND SPRING FESTIVAL: The Lunar New Year, or Spring Festival, occurs on the first day of the first month of the lunar calendar. For the common people, this is an annual opportunity to gather with loved ones, indulge in meat that is normally too expensive for their tables, and put on new clothes. Yuanchun, also known as Yuandan, is Lunar New Year's Day.

NUPTIAL TOAST: Literally cross-cupped wine (交杯酒 / jiaobeijiu), refers to a formal exchange of cups of wine between bride and groom in a traditional wedding ceremony. It is a toast in which the bride and groom loop their arms together to drink from their own cup of wine. Wine from China is typically made of rice or grain.

OFFICIALS: Civil and military officials were classified in nine hierarchic grades, with grade one being the highest rank. Their salaries ranged according to their rank. The imperial examination was one path to becoming a court official, the other being referral by someone in a position of power, such as a noble, a eunuch, or another official.

QINGGONG: Literally "lightness technique," qinggong (轻功) refers to the martial arts skill of moving swiftly and lightly from one point to another, often so nimbly it looks like one is flying through the air. In wuxia and xianxia settings, characters use qinggong to leap great distances and heights.

TITLES OF NOBILITY: Titles of nobility were an important feature of the traditional social structure of Imperial China. While the conferral and organization of specific titles evolved over time, in *Ballad of Sword and Wine*, such titles can be either inherited or conferred by the emperor.

Significantly, conferred titles differ from imperial-born status. For example, an imperial prince like Li Jianheng is a bona fide royal prince with the surname Li (the surname of the founding Zhou emperor), whereas conferred princes like the Prince of Jianxing and Prince of Libei are titled and salaried officials of the imperial bureaucracy. Typically, these titles and lands conferred by the emperor can be inherited by their descendants—traditionally the eldest son of lawful birth—but do not place them in the line of succession for the throne.

WEIQI: Also known by its Japanese name, *go*, weiqi is the oldest known board game in human history. The board consists of a nineteen-by-nineteen grid upon which opponents play unmarked black and white stones as game pieces to claim territory.

YAMEN: An administrative office or department, or residence of a government official. For example, that of a local district magistrate or prefectural prefect. This is not the same as the Twenty-Four Yamen run by the eunuchs.

YELLOW REGISTER: In the Ming and Qing dynasties, households were classified and recorded into the Huangce (黃冊) or yellow registers according to their occupations, which remained unchanged from one generation to the next. These records provided information for taxation, as well as corvée and military conscription. Households were mainly divided into three categories: civilian, military, and trades, of which civilians were further divided into scholars, farmers, builders, and merchants, in order of respectability. Apart from the "good civilians" (良民 / liangmin), there also existed a permanent underclass of slaves (贱籍 / jianji) who were born into this class or relegated there as punishment for crime.

Tang Jiu Qing is an internationally renowned author who writes for the novel serialization website JJWXC. She started the web serialization of *Ballad of Sword and Wine: Qiang Jin Jiu*, in 2018. Her published works include *Nan Chan* and *Time Limited Hunt*, among others.